The Woman Who Drew Buildings

WENDY ROBERTSON

headline

First published in 2009 by
HEADLINE PUBLISHING GROUP

First published in paperback in 2010 by
HEADLINE PUBLISHING GROUP

1

Cataloguing in Publication Data is available from the British Library

ISBN 978 0 7553 3381 3

Typeset in Bembo by Avon DataSet Ltd,
Bidford on Avon, Warwickshire

Printed and bound in Great Britain by
Clays Ltd, St Ives plc

Headline's policy is to use papers that are natural, renewable and
recyclable products and made from wood grown in sustainable forests.
The logging and manufacturing processes are expected to conform
to the environmental regulations of the country of origin.

HEADLINE PUBLISHING GROUP
An Hachette UK Company
338 Euston Road
London NW1 3BH

www.headline.co.uk
www.hachette.co.uk

For the exceptional and inspirational Mary Davies
– writer, artist and healer

Acknowledgements

With thanks to Mary Davies, who shared with me her perceptions of, and insights into, 1980s Poland. Thank you to Fiona Wilson who entered the spirit of *The Woman Who Drew Buildings* and offered me her exquisite drawings to use in any way I wished for this novel. Thank you to Celine Kelly of Headline for taking such good care of my manuscript, to Maura Brickell and Gillian McKay, also of Headline, for getting it out there to my readers. But an especial thanks here to Harriet Evans, just departed director of fiction at Headline, for ensuring that this novel looks, feels and reads the way we wanted it to — the best yet.

Players

In England:
Adam Mathéve: ex-student
Marie Mathéve: Adam's mother; architectural historian
Sam Rogers: Adam's friend
Rachel Miriam Wiener: friend to Sam and Adam
Sharina Osgood: Marie's neighbour
Jack Longland: Marie's partner
Jessica Stanley: Marie's doctor

In Poland:
David Zielinski: Marie's host
Jacinta Zielinska: David's wife
Piotr Zielinski: their infant son
Alon Piotr: David's father
Felix Wosniak: David's friend
Agnieska Wosniak: Felix's wife
Theresa: Jacinta's friend

Part One

Adam 2007

Only Connect

He could have been any young man in this age of universal style, trudging down into this cathedral city with its university, its public school, its colleges and its prison. Under the crisp new baseball cap his blond hair was caught up in an elastic band before it snaked down his back. His parka jacket with its false military credentials drooped over his jeans, which in turn drooped over his brand-new boots. His compact rucksack was tightly packed. His pale, sculptured face had a tinge of gold, as if he'd recently been in the sun. The striped scarf looped into itself in the modern way around his neck seemed to signify his place up the style scale rather than down.

A gust of sharp autumn air made the young man hunch his shoulders and thrust his hands deep into his parka pockets. The day was bright, but still cold. In the blue sky clouds left trails, like unravelling white wool.

As he walked along the gleaming pavement he was

careful where he placed his feet – snug in their shiny new boots – as he skirted puddles still scummy from the residue of early-morning ice. He was feeling good, relishing this exposure to the elements. In these last two years he'd only felt sun on his head, fresh wind or rain in his face when he was being escorted between tall square buildings. But at that time, whatever the weather outside, he'd felt perpetually cold, huddling in on himself for both warmth and protection. Even the late-summer heat of Cornwall – where he'd recently been to warm up, to scrub off the last of the prison pallor – had made little difference to this habit of folding in on himself.

Now he sniffed the air and closed his eyes, revelling in the faint layers of scent that under-clothed the city: scent laid down by generations of miners, students and perfumed tourists, undercut by the smell of food: fish and chips, academic dinners, pizza and pasta, potatoes, beef, bread and beer consumed by generations of intellectuals and workers giving public and private service in this county town. The line of people went right back through a thousand years to hard-handed stonemasons and carpenters clambering wooden scaffolding, constructing gracious, glorious buildings they could never really inhabit. It came to the young man, whose name was Adam Mathéve, that the shelters of those workmen would have smelled something like the back corridors of prison: gamy and ripe and infused with unfulfilled desires.

He hesitated at the bottom of the station bank. His first

instinct was to turn to his right, along the road edging the back gardens of the Georgian houses of Western Hill, and on between the great edifice of St Cuthbert's Church and the sixties gargoyle of County Hall. Then on, on he might go, until he reached the sprawling Three Hills estate that had been his childhood home.

But that could not be his destination today. He'd had to memorise quite a different route with quite a different destination. He'd marked this route on his map with his ink pen: straight across the road, past the grey rise of the hospital, left under the rearing viaduct to the traffic lights, then right again, through more lights. One more right turn and he'd be there. This was where *she* lived now: this was his destination.

He took a deep breath and stepped out into the road, forcing a van to screech to a halt. He leapt back and it just missed him by inches. A burly man leaned out of the window, his face bulging with a potent mixture of anger and fear. 'Got a death wish, have you? What ya think yer freakin' doin', idiot?'

Adam opened his hands palms up and half smiled, 'Sorry, mate.'

The driver stared into the young man's fair face, his bright, watchful eyes. Then he shrugged, and put the van back into gear. 'You need to watch your step, son. Your lucky day today. Just had me brakes fixed. Last week these brakes were crap and I'd've run you down and we'd've both been in the shit.' He glanced in his rear mirror at the traffic, which was backing up. 'Like I say, you watch it, son, or you're dead.'

It had started to drizzle now. Adam crossed the road, pulled his hood up over his baseball cap and set off again at speed. At the second set of traffic lights he stopped. One part of him was shrieking to turn, to go back the way he'd come, up through the town, back to the station, on to a train to anywhere. Any place but here. The wind rose and the breeze started to drive the raindrops against his cheeks. A convulsive shiver rippled through his body from his heels to the nape of his neck: someone treading on his grave.

A double-decker passed in front of him, its brilliant surface urging him to go to the Christmas pantomime at the Sunderland Empire. He relaxed and smiled at that. At least – now – he could go to pantomimes, if he really wanted to. He eased the rucksack more comfortably on his shoulders, took a deep breath and turned the corner.

The building rose before him: red brick, three storeys high, gridded with windows. In its proportions it was not unlike some of the institutions he'd lived in during these last two years. But this building, with its artfully leaded windows, was different. His mother lived here. This was the place where – without any reference to him – she'd chosen to live now. This was certainly not *his* home. Home to him was Three Hills, a seventies experiment in private and public housing on the edge of the city: an aspiring, child-friendly place with open green spaces and trees grown large in the forty years of its existence. Growing up there had been good enough, in the web of the friends and families who had been his safety net when he had to fend for himself when his mother was away.

Adam had always known his mother was unusual, going about this business of buildings when other mothers stayed home and baked cakes. Her being away so much forced him to be self-sufficient. Despite this he had never felt abandoned. She'd always made sure he was safe and well fed. Her last words, before she stepped into her battered Mitsubishi Mirage, were always some variation of the following: *The list is on the fridge, Adam. A meal for each night, just to heat through. And money for each day in the envelopes in the desk drawer. Clean under-stuff and shorts on the bed in the spare room. Don't forget. Bath at night, wash in the morning. I'll ring you at eight o'clock every night.* And she did. But, as she always said, trusting him.

Adam had taken care of himself like this since he was twelve. Before that his stepfather Jack had taken very good care of him. Oh, Jack. A ripple of grief raced through him. Jack! He wanted Jack here with him now.

But he wasn't. And these days his mother didn't live on the Three Hills estate. These days she lived here, at this new place, Merrick Court, in this new block that had risen like a phoenix from land liberated by the demolition of a garage. He remembered the garage.

He looked up at the red-brick wall and wondered how she, who loved buildings to the exclusion of people, could bear to live in such a place. The building was neat enough, discreetly designed to meet the rigid planning constraints in this historic city. With its ersatz Victorian windows and ersatz narrow Georgian doors, it reeked of gentility, obviously latching on to the unique market here for posh downsizers and transient academics who wanted to live small but did not want to live scruffy.

Adam hated the place on sight. At least Three Hills had been honest, unapologetically modern; a cheerful seventies optimism, when people were surging forward, not casting nostalgic glances behind them.

He checked the address on his phone. *15a Merrick Court.* An arrow under the name plaque directed him through a Norman-style archway into an inward-facing courtyard with landings leading off two ornate concrete staircases that serviced four floors. Each landing had four neatly numbered Georgian doors. He noted all this in the split second before he caught sight of the crumpled figure of a woman in a long green coat at the bottom of one of the staircases. He recognised his mother only by her distinctive mane of grey hair: the mask of blood on her face made her look like a stranger.

A perverse streak of anger rose through him like bile. Then he darted forward to kneel beside her. He put his hand on her narrow shoulder and saw the seepage of red blood behind her head. It was glossy, like the icy step on which she lay.

He felt for his phone and rang the emergency number. 'Yes, she's fallen down some outside steps. Slipped on the ice, I think. Yes . . . unconscious . . . No, I don't know how long she's been here. I just got here. No, her face isn't cold . . . Her hands are . . . Yes . . . What? Yes, she's my mother . . . 15a Merrick Court . . . Yes. Warm.' He thrust the phone into the front of his rucksack, took off his parka and spread it over her. Then he scrabbled in the rucksack and found two sweaters to heap on top of the parka.

His mother seemed very small, lying there. Looking down he saw that the flesh of her foot, turned awkwardly, had puffed up like a ball and was spilling over her neat brown shoe.

He knelt again beside her. 'Christ, Marie, what have you done? What are you doing? Spoiling things again. I wanted to talk to you. I really wanted to talk to you. It was time to talk.'

But now there could be no talk, no new connection. He'd scripted this meeting in his head dozens of times in the last two years. But the conversation always took place in the house on the Three Hills. It might take place in various locations – on the doorstep, in the garden, in the little sun room out the back where she liked to sit with her notebooks and papers. He used to lie there in his prison pad and let the scene roll before him like a YouTube clip. She would fly into his arms and say how wonderful it was to see him again. That it had been too long. That they could start again now. Now, she would say, it would be like it had been before.

No, that wouldn't do, would it? That was when his

prison daydream would stop and he would have to rewind it. Marie couldn't say that, could she? He wanted her to say it would be *better* than before: after all, *before* had not been so good, even when Jack was still there. *Before* she was always away, and even when she was home she'd be preoccupied – immaculate, he remembered, in narrow linen trousers and a sweater topped off with a silk scarf – peering at her unique photo archive of European buildings; making notes, writing reports, glancing absently at him over her half-spectacles.

Part of him was proud that his mother did all this, this important stuff. He was proud of himself because he was independent and could manage without her. But there were crucial times when he wished she were there, just doing the ordinary things with him.

She'd been away the day he went off to university for the first time. He'd packed his own bag, cleared his own room, and called his own taxi to the station. She'd left a folder with all his financial arrangements neatly in place: fees paid, monthly allowance fixed up, contract phone agreement; everything taken care of with quiet Marie-esque efficiency.

She'd rung him from Brussels on his first night in college. 'Well then, what's it like, Adam? The hall?'

'All right, I suppose.'

'All mod cons?'

'Just about.'

'Good.'

His turn. 'How is the conference?'

'Good. All the usual people.'

There seemed to be nothing else to say. 'I'll have to go,' he said. 'Someone's knocking on my door.'

'Well, enjoy it all, Adam. A great opportunity. Lots of love.' This was said casually, but he always treasured the words.

'I will. But I've gotta go. Lots of love.'

In fact no one had been knocking on his door, but Adam's lie inspired him to go and knock on the room next door. That was when he met Sam Rogers, his liberation and eventually, he now saw, his nemesis.

That call from Brussels set the pattern of all telephone calls during the time he was in college: brief, stilted, without much emotional content except for the final message of love. He knew his mother was like that, stiff on the phone; always had been, even when he was younger and home alone. While he was at college their paths only occasionally crossed. Even during vacations, Marie would often be away. And the times she was at home, Adam himself was would be away on his travels to Cyprus and Ireland with Sam and their friend Rachel. His mother would happily buy him travel gear, fund his trips and give him lists of buildings to look out for. He could decode her actions as some kind of love, but she never once said she would miss him.

For Adam this was normal life. It did not make him unhappy. In prison he had time to think it through. Her actions did show her affection. He knew it wasn't that she *dis*liked him. She didn't dislike him at all. She was just preoccupied with more important things. And she wanted him to be as self-sufficient as she herself had always been.

But other mothers weren't like that. Sam's mother was not like that. Sometimes Adam thought she was like this because she'd been nearly forty when he was born and was a generation ahead of the mothers of his friends. But in the end he concluded it was not Marie's age, it was her character. She was always so close, so contained, whereas he – he finally realised – had always been looking for some openness, some declaration from her, some gush of affection that was never forthcoming. Even that thought embarrassed him.

He knew, by the time of the court case, that the notion of reaching out to Marie in this particular dilemma was unthinkable. So, although he could have done so, he decided not to telephone her from prison. How could he risk her talking to him in her usual abbreviated way, covering her shame and embarrassment? Things were bad enough in there without that.

Of course she was better at letters. She'd always been good at letters, written to him from all round the world in her round artist's hand, decorated with fragmentary drawings of the buildings she was visiting. He had loved and cherished her letters. This couldn't happen with the letters she sent him in prison. He only read the first one. The rest he returned unopened.

And in the twenty-six months he was inside, he did not allow Marie to visit him once, although she applied many times. He recognised the perversity of deliberately losing touch with her. All around him in prison were men who had been intensely anxious to keep in touch, eager still to be nurtured by their mothers, wives and lovers, even while locked away and out of physical contact. He knew some men who had even persuaded strangers to love and nurture them in letters, hooking up with unusual or lonely women who were touched, or turned on, by the thought of a man in confinement. Others were adept at appealing to the mothering instincts of prison visitors – not necessarily for privilege or advantage, but possibly (Adam thought) for the glimpse of maternal affection in the eyes of older women.

Adam told himself that in order to survive he'd chosen to take the opposite road; he did not want his mother tainted by that life. Even so, he still carried Marie's first letter in his pocket. The letter was creased and battered now, but he kept it in his wallet like a perverse talisman:

Dearest Adam

I hope you are coping as well as possible in that place. I am so very concerned that this experience will have hit you very hard. I was sorry I could not catch your eye in court. I was a little hurt to see you turn your face away. I wanted you to see my concern. I must tell you that what you would have seen in my face was understanding and not gratuitous blame. I cannot for the life of me see why they remanded you in custody. I know the poor boy died, but as yet it is not proved that you are really at fault. I talked to the policeman and he said that it was because your passport showed that you were already widely travelled and so they suspected that you would think nothing of leaving. It does not seem likely to me that an open, adventurous mind would show deviance. If that were the case, I myself would have been behind bars many years ago.

I will keep in touch with your solicitor and the police and will write to you again.

Lots of love always
Marie

That letter had sent him back to his cell in tears. For days, even the touch of the envelope would make his face tight with unshed tears. That was when he told the perplexed wing officer that he wanted his mother's letters returned unopened.

'Why's that, son? Everyone in here likes the comfort of letters.' The officer paused. 'Did she do you harm, like?'

Adam shook his head. 'Nah,' he said. 'She never did me no harm. That was the best thing about her.'

'Draws buildings, doesn't she? I read about her in the paper.'

'Yeah,' Adam had said. 'That's what she does. Draws buildings. She's very good at it. That's another good thing about her.'

★

And now at last he had come to find her, to tell her all that, to tell her all about everything, to tell her how much he loved all those things about her. And here she was, oblivious to his voice, getting colder by the second. No wonder he was angry.

The Tenderness
of Strangers

The shriek of a siren pierced the distant throb of the crossroads traffic, then faded as a massive motorbike rolled through the Norman archway of Merrick Court. The rider, weird and otherworldly in helmet and leathers, dismounted. He took off his helmet and became human, middle-aged and grizzle-haired. According to his name tag he was called John Armitage. 'What've we got here?' He unclipped his case from his pillion.

Adam stood up. 'It's my mother. She must have fallen. I've just got here.'

The paramedic nodded. 'Right. If you'd just excuse me, sir . . .'

Adam stood back and watched as the man squatted beside Marie and peered under the parka and jumpers. He felt her neck, touched her face quite tenderly, muttering to himself. Then he took out a phone and spoke into it. His face sober, he looked up at Adam. 'We need the ambulance boys here.' He paused. 'Were you here when it happened, sir?'

Adam shook his head. 'No. I just arrived. Turned the corner and there she was, lying there.'

'And *she* is . . . ?'

'Her name is Marie Mathéve. She's my mother. I'm Adam Mathéve. She lives here at number 15a.' He looked up at the landing.

'Marie. How old is she?'

'She's sixty-three, just.'

John Armitage took a thin silver wrap from his case and arranged it over the parka and jumpers. Then he touched Marie's face again. 'She's not so cold. Good that you kept her warm, son.'

Another motorbike rolled through the gateway and a younger paramedic alighted. He squatted by his colleague.

Adam gazed down at his mother, now looking even smaller beneath her silver blanket. He felt a surge of love for her. 'Her leg . . . the ankle's puffed up.'

The new man lifted the hem of the blanket. 'You're gunna have a sore head and a sore leg, poor lass.' The thread of tenderness in his voice made Adam's cheeks burn and tears well into his eyes. He sniffed to hold them at bay.

The second paramedic stood up. 'Mike . . .' He flicked his name tag and shook Adam's hand. Then he took out a small notebook. He checked on the spelling of Marie's name and wrote down Adam's name too. He looked at his watch and noted the time. 'And is your mam on any medication, Adam? Would you say she was fit?'

Adam shook his head. 'I couldn't say about any medication. I've been away for nearly two years. She's changed her whole life since then.' He paused. 'She's always been pretty fit. Very fit, in fact. Walked. Did the Great North Run a few years ago.' She hadn't told Adam about that. He'd found a report in a stack of old newspapers when he came home one summer.

Mike picked up Marie's handbag, extracted a bunch of keys and handed them to Adam. 'We can check on medication in her bathroom. You lead the way, son. John here can keep an eye on your mam.'

Adam started up the steps. He turned the wrong way on the landing and had to turn back, bumping into Mike. He flushed. 'This is all new to me. My mother moved while I was away.' He was relieved that the key he inserted in the narrow Georgian-style door actually turned. At least he'd got that right.

They let themselves straight into the living room. Mike looked around with a sure eye. 'En suite bathrooms in these small places. All right if I go through the bedroom?'

Adam nodded, his eyes straying round the room. He would have recognised his mother's space anywhere: matt white woodwork, pale yellow walls, books and CDs behind glass doors in alphabetical order. Etches and sketches of buildings in foreign places, all displaying her own neat touch. Bare polished floor dotted with thin woven rugs from Turkey. Two familiar round bevelled mirrors. On the desk under the window was a pile of notebooks, a small drawing slope and pens and pencils in separate pots. The only untidy touch was an orange-striped mug labelled *Love in a Cold Climate*, still half full of cold coffee. His mother had always loved her coffee.

He could imagine her here now, surrounded by her things: drinking her coffee, reading her book.

He followed the medic through to the bedroom. Here the only untidy thing was a messy pile of boxes on top of the wardrobe. He was just reaching up to take one down when Mike came in from the bathroom. He shook his head. 'Nothing much in there. Aspirins, lemon and honey cough syrup. Nothing that would create a problem for your mother. Seems a fit enough woman.'

Adam winced at the blast of a siren in the road outside. The medic grinned. 'Here come the cavalry! We can hand her over to the van boys. Don't worry, son. Your mam'll be in the best of hands.' He stared hard at Adam. 'Coming, then?' He turned away.

Adam took one last look at the boxes on top of the wardrobe and followed him. When they got down into the courtyard, John was talking to the ambulance medics, a man and a woman, who were trundling an empty stretcher on a gurney through the archway. The ambulance was parked outside.

John pulled on his gloves. 'Would you like to go in the ambulance with your mam, son?'

'Yes. Will that be OK? I've no wheels of my own, so it's either that or the bus.' Adam could hear his own voice, too keen and too young, as though it belonged to someone else.

'Leave you to it, then.' John and Mike roared away on their motorbikes and the other two took over. Adam watched as the woman medic carefully adjusted a brace around his mother's neck, murmuring, 'Stay with us, Marie, pet. Not long now.' Then with infinite care the two of them lifted her on to the gurney.

The woman asked Adam the same questions as Mike and John had, and he answered automatically, his eyes glued to his mother's pale face. He felt another wave of affection for Marie and clenched his eyes shut to stop tears forming. Now she was on the stretcher and being wheeled out of the courtyard into the ambulance. The female paramedic handed Adam his parka and his jumpers. 'You coming with us, Mr Mathéve?' she said.

He nodded and stumbled after them, pulling on his parka and stuffing the sweaters back into his rucksack. In the archway he turned back to look around the courtyard. Up on the landing stood an old man in braces and a collar and tie; at the other side was a young woman with a baby on her hip. Her face was white and worried. The baby started to cry and the girl held it up high and shook it, laughing into its face until the crying broke down to a gurgle. Adam was about to call up to them when there was a brief blast of the siren and he hurried away through the archway to the ambulance that was carrying his mother to hospital.

In the ambulance he sat beside the paramedic who was attending to his mother, murmuring all the while, as if her voice would bring Marie back into the here and now, from wherever she'd gone since she tumbled down the stairs. As the siren screamed and the ambulance bumped along, Adam closed his eyes, thinking suddenly of the beach in Cornwall where he'd gone for his first two weeks of freedom, to get rid of his prison pallor and to loosen up his spirit, ready to rejoin the land of the living. From his small hotel he'd become used at last to being in charge of his own body, his own movements and his own appetites. He surfed and swam; he lay on the sand soaking up the sun and resisting approaches from men and women who were made uncomfortable by someone so clearly on his own in such a beautiful place. But Adam was happy to be on his own. This self-sufficiency had saved his sanity inside, and it was a habit he was not about to break. In that, he realised now, he was like Marie. Even when the two of them were together, they were each in their own space.

His mind drifted back to a time in Almeria, the year he was fourteen: this was a rare occasion when he joined Marie on her travels. She had gone off with her sketchbook to check out Alcazaba, an Arab fortress built by the Caliph of Cordoba. He wandered off to look at a market and returned an hour later. She'd told him to find her by the cathedral in the old quarter. He'd walked through it but he couldn't see her there. Then, out on the road, he'd caught sight of a woman leaning backwards to take in the height of the fortress, her hand shading her eyes from the strong sun. She was slender and pale-faced; her mane of blond hair was swept back into a ponytail, her bare, bony feet pushed into sandals. She had a certain elegance. Adam guessed she must be French.

Then he blinked and realised this woman was Marie, his mother. He went and touched her on the shoulder and she swung round, her wonder at the building, at its age and history still clouding her eyes. Then she blinked and recognised him. 'Adam!' she said, her smile lighting up her face. 'I was looking for you. I thought you'd run away.' She touched his bare forearm and the fourteen-year-old Adam felt good. He knew he was all right. He knew they were all right. The two of them.

Now, in the ambulance, he touched his arm in the same place and he knew he was *not* all right. *They* were not all right. His mother was there but she was not there. The siren died as the ambulance turned into the hospital complex and parked under a long canopy.

'Now, Marie!' said the medic brightly, her face close to that of the unconscious woman. 'Let's get you to where it counts, shall we?'

Adam stood helplessly under the canopy as the medics wheeled his mother quickly through the entrance spraying details – *head trauma . . . sprained . . . pulse* – in the direction of a doctor who walked forward quickly to take over. The doctor was a heavily built redhead of some authority who reminded the dazed Adam of his third girlfriend at college. His first and second girlfriends – both blondes – in the end reminded him too much of his mother and he had dropped them like hot potatoes. His well-built redhead was a safe haven for a while after that.

And this doctor certainly knew what she was doing. Hypnotised by her intensity and authority Adam followed her, lamb-like, all the way to the cubicles, before she instructed a nurse to shepherd the boy back out into the corridor. 'Sit him down where he can do no harm. Poor boy's in shock.'

She had a beautiful voice, like threaded silver, quite at odds with her bulky, practical appearance. As the nurse led him away, Adam strained to hear that voice as she began to talk to another nurse about his mother. Around him the emergency department whirred and buzzed like a ticking clock on the verge of striking. A beefy man passed him, pushing a child in a wheelchair.

The nurse left him at the edge of the waiting room and went back to do more important things. He found a space and sat down, hugging his rucksack close to his chest. He closed his eyes. Wait. That was all he could do. Wait.

Up on the Mountain

Some hours later when the nurse came for him Adam was still sitting there, his rucksack clutched on his lap. The dry hospital heat, so like that of the prison, had made him discard his cap and his parka. It had made him loosen the band on his hair to cool down his head. His mouth was parched but he'd stayed in his seat. He'd not even gone for a drink, wanting to be there when they called him.

The nurse led him down a corridor and up in a lift. He'd never been in a hospital before, but much of this was very familiar – being led along echoing corridors into unknown spaces by a uniformed person in whose bureaucratic day you were a mere detail.

She left him in a reception area where the ward sister registered his identity as next of kin and took down his contact details. Then the sister led him to a side room, ushered him in and left him. His mother lay very still on the narrow bed, her head and her foot bandaged, her white hair

24

in tangles on the pillow. He stood two clear feet away from the bed, staring at Marie: at her narrow face, the fine blue veins on her paper-thin lids, her left hand palm up, open as a starfish on the bed, her right – the hand with which she drew and wrote – clutching the counterpane.

'You can touch her. It won't hurt to touch her, you know.'

He swung round to see the broad face of the red-haired doctor. He felt himself colour. 'I . . . I . . .'

Her slight smile sharpened. 'A shock, isn't it? Seeing someone you love like this?' She moved towards him and he backed off until he found himself standing close – too close – to his mother. He scowled at the doctor; he was mad at her, mad at himself.

She shook his hand. 'You're Mrs Mathéve's son? My name's Jessica Stanley. I admitted your mother. She's had an awful bash on the head.'

Adam spoke through lips that felt as if they had been coated in rubber. 'It was the stone steps. She fell down the steps outside her flat. What . . . How much . . .?'

'Well, Mr Mathéve, your mother is deeply unconscious. Her head is cut and badly bruised. There is a good deal of interior swelling so the scan's not telling us much at the moment. We'll do further scans as the swelling goes down. Just now it's a waiting game.' She moved back towards the door, a gliding, graceful movement. 'Oh! And her ankle is badly bruised but there is no break.'

'But she'll be all right, won't she? When all the swelling goes down?'

The woman looked at him for a long moment. 'We need to wait, Mr Mathéve. Be patient. We need to wait until she wakes up.'

He remembered his manners. 'Thank you, Doctor Stanley . . .'

She smiled slightly. '*Miss* Stanley is the form. Or even Jessica.'

When she was gone, he drew up a chair and sat close to the bed. He looked at his mother's veined hand where it clutched the counterpane: slender fingers, larger knuckles. He had an image of one of her hands holding a notebook steady while the other moved swiftly across the page, making a building come into sympathetic life. There was always something magical about her when she did this, as though her pencil was a wand that transferred the buildings to the page in a way that could only be hers.

'Marie,' he whispered.

That was when panic rose inside him like a sticky tide from his heels to his solar plexus. He tried to breathe long and slowly, just as he'd learned to do in prison when things seemed just too bad. You breathed very deeply and very slowly until the world slowed on its axis and everything fell back into some sort of place.

He'd learned this skill from the first friend he made in prison, a chiropractor called Tom who was on remand for allegedly killing a patient. Tom had soft, feminine ways and the pair of them had to take some knocks about their friendship in their four months' acquaintance. Then Tom had been found not guilty and Adam was left on his own again, embarrassed at the vague resentment hc fclt for his friend's good fortune.

Part of Tom's technique was that you breathed very slowly in and out. As you breathed in you took a look at what you were anxious about and imagined it – or him, or her – high on a mountain on the other side of a broad ocean. Then as you breathed out slowly you saw it as tiny, ineffectual and unimportant to the here-and-now you. After four or five breaths the image would vanish, and you could breathe deeper and deeper and let the world move again slowly and calmly on its axis. Adam thought now of the many times he'd placed Marie – and Sam, and Rachel – on that mountain so he could get a better night's sleep in his cell.

But all that mountain stuff was no use here. He could not put his unconscious mother on a mountain, over an ocean. She was very much here beside him under the tight hospital covers. She was breathing the same overheated air as he was. She was in this space with him.

He thought how angry he'd been – so angry – when he saw her lying there today at the bottom of the steps. Today of all days, when he'd expected her to be there for him, she wasn't. Now, after all his efforts to find her, she'd hidden herself away again, inside her own head. Even confined to her hospital bed she was still not there for him.

He'd come out of prison with the firm intention of speaking to her, of healing the rift. He'd actually telephoned to tell her that first morning after his release. A cross woman had answered the phone and said that no, Mrs Mathéve did not live here any more. Her new address was 15a Merrick Court, on the other side of the city.

On that first day, after the abortive phone call, he'd checked his bank account to find that his mother had been depositing money for him every month for the whole of the two years he'd been inside. That was when he decided to go to Cornwall. He was pasty and sluggish. He couldn't meet Marie like this. He'd buy a mobile phone and make contact with her when he got back.

And look at today, when he'd finally got to Merrick Court! Instead of the half-expressed, stumbling reconciliation he'd planned, there she was, sprawled at the bottom of the steps, still unavailable to him. And that anger had flowed sharp as acid through him even while he was ringing for help. But now, as he stared at her still, closed face, he knew his anger had gone: it was stupid to be angry with someone who did not even know your anger, was not even conscious of it. How stupid was that?

He touched the back of her drawing hand with a tentative finger. Her skin was warm and soft to the touch. He extended his palm so that the whole of his hand was over hers: not quite holding, but touching. He started to breathe very deeply and let the world slow down and expand just as Tom had taught him. Now he was able to put his anger with her on that far mountain. The acrid feeling finally drained away from him like water trickling down a mountain gully.

★

Whoosh! Like a cork forcing itself out of a bottle I am up here, my nose to the ceiling. What's happening down there? Roll over, Marie! Like swimming. No — more like treading water. Now I can see down there. Square room. Murmuring voices. Click of feet on tiles. A dream. Only a dream. Crikey. That's me down there on the bed! That wooden doll. That bandage! My hair. What a mess. Someone get a brush, a comb, will you? Nurse!

Adam. Adam's there. He has long hair too, right down his back. He must have grown it in that place. I imagined he would have his head shaved in that place. Is that not what happens? Short back and sides? Or have I seen too many films? Adam! What happened just now? The touch of your hand on mine made me leap, jump out of my skin. Literally! Right up here on to the ceiling. I can see you far below. I can see through the wall, see the length of the ward, the other patients behind their curtain partitions. This is just mad.

What's Adam doing here? What am I doing here, hovering on the ceiling like a moth? I must get back down there on the bed. Whoosh! Back into my wooden doll body.

Now I'm back on the bed. And I can't see Adam, because the eyes of this wooden doll body are sealed tight. I can't open them no matter how I try. Adam is talking to me but I can't flex my tongue to speak to him. He seemed angry at first. I felt his anger. I could tell that from the tone, although I couldn't quite hear the words. He was always such an angry, contained little boy. That always puzzled me, I must say. Hard to know why he should be so angry.

Me, I've never been angry enough. That's one of my problems. They say these things of mood and temper can be hereditary, but I don't think his father was like this. Quiet flashes of anger balanced by fireworks of passion, yes.

I feel leaden and woozy and somewhere I really hurt. The woman on the bed — me, I suppose — had bandages on her head. So it must be my head that hurts. I must have given myself quite a bash. A car? Not again. Not a car. I couldn't take that. I can feel Adam here, his hand on mine. I can see him behind my eyes: at five years old, with hair too long, eyes blue and questioning; at eleven, hair short-cropped for his first day at the big school. Who took that photograph for me? Jack, I think. In Turkey: I was in Turkey the day I got that photograph. Jack was so good with Adam. Then there is this other photo of him with his hair combed forward so you can't see his eyes. On his uni ID card. I was in Brussels the day he went to university. But he sent me a copy of that picture, nearly as small as a postage stamp. I always have it in my purse.

Do you still sing like you used to, dear Adam? Did they let you sing in that place? You would always sing. Even when you were angry.

I'm so very tired. Now I can feel the ache in my head. Like knives. I'm losing you, Adam.

Adam looked down at the slender figure of his mother on the bed, defenceless, with tubes attached to her arm and her body and a monitor ticking above her head. Her eyes were moving beneath the fragile tissue-paper lids. What was it Sam used to say? That we live a whole other life in our sleep. *Like living on another planet.* Of course Adam had objected to this, but as usual Sam won the argument because he went at an idea like a dog at a bone when he wanted to make a point. In the end Adam got bored and gave in.

He thought now about the dreams he used to have during those long nights in his cell: dreams of picnics on a high hill that he once climbed with Marie and his stepfather Jack. They had scrambled ever upwards on scree and over boulders, carrying rucksacks laden with sandwiches, flasks and foil cloaks in case of emergencies. Adam's legs were small and it was quite hard climbing up and up, always following on Jack's heels. Jack was always ahead and his mother was always behind him, watching his back. In the dream, he and Jack would finally reach the summit and would stand there and survey the range of mountains rolling away before them like thrown silk. But then he would turn around to find that his mother was not there at his heels. She was merely a tiny figure at the bottom of the crag, shouting, shouting. He thought she might be shouting his name but he couldn't quite hear.

'Mr Mathéve?'

Matthew jumped as the ward sister touched his shoulder. He didn't know how long he'd been sitting there, his hand over his mother's – just touching, not holding. 'What is it?'

'There's someone here who wants to talk to you. A policeman. He needs to ask you about the accident.'

'Why?'

'It's standard procedure, Mr Mathéve. Accident reports. You know.' She paused. 'Then you could go. Your mother's stable now, and you look dead beat. Go home. Come back tomorrow.'

The man standing just inside the door of the ward was short, muscular, curly-haired and not much older than Adam himself. He smiled genially and held out a hand. 'DC Box, Mr Mathéve. Sorry to drag you away but we do need a few details.'

They sat outside the ward in the bustling corridor and Adam related the events of the morning to the policeman. 'When I got there she was there at the bottom of the steps. I rang for the ambulance. The paramedics came. Then the ambulance. They say she has concussion. Deep concussion.'

DC Box checked back in his notes. Adam realised he must have talked to them all – the paramedics, the red-haired consultant – before he got to him.

'Right,' said DC Box. 'So, you were on a visit? When did you last see your mother? Whoops!' He smiled slightly, his eyes sparkling. 'Isn't that the big question? *When did you last see your father?* D'y'ever see that print? My grandma had it on her wall. I sometimes think that's what made me want to join the police.' He calmed down. 'No, seriously. When d'you last see her?'

'Well, I've just come back from holiday, but before that I'd not seen her for a couple of years.'

Box had his pencil poised. 'And why would that be, not seeing your mother for a couple of years?'

Adam hesitated. 'Well, I've been away at college. And when I had time off from that, she was away. You see, my mother travelled a lot. Buildings. She's very interested in buildings.'

Box was scribbling away. 'Takes all sorts. I see my own mam every week that God sends. Sunday dinner's her speciality. Fourteen sitting down, Sunday after Sunday. I have to get a note from the doctor to get out of it! But it does take all sorts, doesn't it?'

The policeman sat silent then, waiting. Finally Adam broke the silence. 'Why all this intense interest? In an accident?'

'Well . . .' Box flipped back to his earlier notes. 'As far as I can tell so far, there were no witnesses. People at the flats only came out when they heard the siren. I talked to the medics here. Could be the nature of the injuries may not really point to a straight accident. They're very cagey, this lot.'

Adam stiffened. 'You're saying it wasn't an accident?'

'I'm not saying that. It pays to be suspicious, though, in my game. See?'

'Are you saying you suspect me?' Adam felt a dangerous prickle at the back of his neck. 'Are you saying that? That I might—'

Box flicked his pencil in the air. 'Take it easy, Mr Mathéve. This is just procedure. You concentrate on getting your ma better.' He stood up, pencil still poised. 'So, where can I get hold of you?'

Adam hesitated, then said, 'I'll stay at my mother's. 15a—'

'I have that address. I could do with your phone number as well.'

Adam recited his mobile number and Box wrote it down. 'Right, Adam – can I call you Adam? – we'll keep in touch,' he said. 'One or two things to check out. But I'll get back to you.'

The old Adam would have objected to this combative style, but two years of dealing with people who reacted like adders to any slightly superior correction made him hold his tongue.

He watched Box march away through the tide of visitors streaming through the main door. Then he made his way back to the side room and stood there looking down at his mother, discomfort at Box's insinuations still zinging in his veins. 'That man out there thinks someone hurt you, Marie. He might even think it was me.' He pulled on his parka and his scarf and picked up his rucksack. 'They say I should go now. I'm going to doss down in your new place. If that's OK?'

Whoosh. Back up here. Ridiculous, clutching my gown behind me as though they can see my nether regions. And I know they can't. Poor Adam. Seeing . . . well, you know! How inappropriate . . .

I can hear the tone, your polite talk with the nurse, Adam, but not the words. I can hear the anxiety in your voice. I can only see the back of your head but I would know it anywhere. That double crown that makes the hair stand up. Couldn't keep it down any way, could we? Lucky sign, so they say. And there I am, laid out like a fish, tubes in and out, counter ticking. I would have liked to open my eyes to you, Adam, to look you in the eye, to see your face. But that thing there is like an empty bottle: right shape but nothing inside. Me. I'm here. But I'm still stuck here, up in the ceiling. Oh-oh. You're getting up to go. I have to get back. Back.

Marie's face stayed close and still. Adam shrugged and went to the desk to tell the sister he was leaving and would be back later. She shook her head. 'You look worn out, son. Go somewhere and get your head down. You can ring me any time to see how she is. We'll get you here if there's any change.' She looked at her computer. 'Seems like you're only five minutes from here. Have a rest, come back in the morning and we can all start afresh.'

Grateful for her kindness, he trudged out of the hospital. Once outside he checked his street map and realised that it was possible to reach Merrick Court by back roads inaccessible to the ambulance. The sister was right. The walk would take him no more than five minutes. Running, he could do it in less.

He started to run.

Marie's Kingdom

Adam closed the door behind him and looked around. It seemed a year since he'd stood there with the paramedic called Mike. Marie's orange-striped mug was still on the desk. He picked it up and took it through to the kitchen, rinsed it under the tap and left it to drain. He opened the fridge. So predictable: organic milk, cheese, Greek yoghurt, tomatoes, fresh pasta in a packet, two bags of ready-made salad and a bowl of cold boiled potatoes with their skin on. In the fridge door were two flat, round bottles of Portuguese rosé wine: always her favourite even before it became trendy again. He opened the freezer compartment to find just a packet of peas and three Sainsbury's ready meals: beef and dumplings, sweet and sour pork, and lasagne

Suddenly very hungry, he pulled out the beef and dumplings and a bottle of the wine. While the food whirled in the microwave he walked through to the bedroom. The scented quiet of the room seeped into him. He looked at his mother's bed with its familiar carved headboard, its woven cover and heap of cushions. There was no way he could sleep there. No way could he disturb all that. He would sleep on the floor. The little spare room was piled with things. The bed quite obscured. Maybe he should sleep on that couch in the living room. Yes.

His eye moved to the wardrobe and the pile of boxes on top of it. Now *this* he could disturb. He climbed onto a chair and started to pull down the boxes. He worked swiftly, and as he worked his spirits lifted and he started dropping the boxes so their contents spilled on the polished floor – books, notebooks, papers, brochures, bundles of clothes, bright scarves, packets of photos, sheaves of drawings in a disorganised pile.

The microwave pinged so he went and collected his meal and took it and the bottle of wine back into the bedroom. He sat on the floor by the window, downed almost half the bottle and surveyed his booty: every single thing a marker for his mysterious mother.

He scoffed the food quickly, took another long swig from the squat bottle and stared at the mess of books and papers and packages, wondering why Marie hadn't kept them in the sitting room on the shelves with all the other art and reference books, or in her antique filing cabinets with the rest of her papers.

He took his empty plate through to the kitchen, rinsed it and left it to dry: old habits died hard. This might be a new place but it was still Marie's kingdom, and her rules counted. Then he took the second bottle of wine from the fridge and a new notebook from the pile in her bottom left-hand desk drawer, and began to make a careful list of the things that had spilled out of the boxes. His face was burning with wine drunk too fast, his brain was racing, his hand was shaking, but one by one he listed the items.

- Article in Esperantist magazine by Marie Mathéve, recounting her 'Study in Poland'.
- Newspaper article about Marie Mathéve's visit to Poland on a Soroptimists grant to consider buildings.
- Photo of Marie and a younger (very pretty) woman leaning towards each other, making a triangle. On the back Marie has written *Jacinta Zielinska and me in the Chorzow flat.*
- Small published book of drawings of Krakow marked *Ex Libris David Adama Zielinski.* Paperback with a brown paper cover to protect it.
- Photographic slides, small and hard to see, with viewer.
- *Poland's Progress*, edited by Michael Murray, first published 1944, this the third edition, 1945.
- *Krakow* by Edward Hartig, 1964. Coffee-table book.
- *Poland* by Irena and Jerzy Kostrowicki.
- Official 1981 guide to Krakow.
- Official guide to Katowice.
- Two small red Sylvine notebooks still with their 30p price tag on. Marked *Poland Diary* 1981.

- One Winfield exercise book marked *Paris Diary* 1985.
- Daler sketchbook full of Marie's drawings, e.g. *Chorzow from my bedroom; steelworks; estate with tabac in foreground; old steelworks; coal mine looking towards Katowice.* Done in coloured markers, making them brighter and bolder than usual, but style is unmistakable.
- Spiral-bound Daler sketchbook with more subtle drawings from Paris: *Luxembourg Gardens; view from my window, eighth floor Rue de Rennes; Louvre*, 1985.

Adam surveyed his list. Marie always documented her journeys. Her journals, the articles, the artefacts had always been kept, listed and cross-referenced, in box files on specially built shelves in their old house. When she was away he had sometimes got them down and leafed through them, admiring her scholarly approach, her crisp writing style. Those boxes must be in storage somewhere. Here in the flat there were no shelves, no lines of box files, no cross-reference filing boxes, just this higgledy-piggledy pile of stuff that had been dumped in boxes and never even entered into the Marie Mathéve system. This material was either too important or too unimportant for that. Adam had never heard of any trip to Poland. This journey was unknown to him.

'Marie, how could you?' he whispered. He looked from the piles to the list in his hand and back again and his eyes burned as though they had been invaded by smoke. Tears spilled down his cheeks. 'What's all this about, Marie? What?'

He was crying again. The prison shrink once told him that all the crying was down to post-traumatic stress disorder. That even the toughest men inside sometimes cried. They harmed themselves and even killed themselves as a consequence of this condition.

A long buzz on the doorbell broke into his morbid thoughts. He scrubbed his hands across his wet cheeks, ran his fingers through his long hair and went to the door.

Standing in the doorway was a young woman – very young – with a round, large-headed baby on her arm. The girl had glossy blue-black wavy hair with a bright magenta streak falling down one cheek. Her skin was a glowing brown and her eyes were bright and opaque at the same time, like black treacle. Her smile was open and confident.

He frowned at her.

'I'm Sharina,' she said. 'Sharina Mary Osgood. And this is Arian. We live along the landing. We came to ask about Marie, didn't we, Arian? We were worried about her.'

'Yes,' Adam mumbled, only now realising how drunk he was. Hence the morbid thoughts. 'I remember now. I saw you. On the landing.'

'Poor Marie, lying there,' she said. 'Nice woman, that Marie. Always has time for you. Me, I liked her from the first. We got on, like, from the first day. I didn't have Arian then. There was just me.' Her voice was surprisingly deep for such a slight person, and her accent was local.

He still stood there. 'We . . . ell,' he said. He couldn't think of anything else to say.

She peered up at him, scowling. 'Been drowning our sorrows, have we?'

He stood up straighter. 'D'you want something? What do you want?' he said stiffly, now very careful to speak clearly.

She ignored that. 'What are you to Marie, then?'

'She's my mother.'

'Mother? She never mentioned no son. There was this photo, like. But she never said.'

'She wouldn't. But she's my mother. I'm Adam.'

She stared at him, her dark eyes like flint. 'Well, how is she? Me and Arian have been worrying about her all day. We saw her lying there.'

'She's very poorly. Deeply unconscious. Can't hear or see anything.' He paused. 'Just lies there.'

'Jesus. In a coma. I saw a film about that once.'

'Well, I . . .' He started to close the door but she took a step forward so he couldn't. Her booted foot was in the gap. 'Can I go and see her?' she said.

'I told you. She's unconscious. She wouldn't know.'

The girl nuzzled the neck of the baby. 'But me and Arian would know, wouldn't we, Arian?'

Adam frowned at the butterball child with the old-man eyes.

'Our Arian loves Marie. She minds you sometimes, doesn't she, pet?'

Adam's fuddled brain tried to deal with the image of his mother babysitting, and failed. 'Minds?' he said, thinking of his mother's immaculate sitting room. 'She minds him?'

'She has this nice blanket and a bag of toys. Keeps them behind her desk specially, doesn't she, Arian?'

'Well . . .' Adam said.

'I still want to see her.' Sharina stared at him defiantly. 'Which ward is she in?'

He shook his head.

'You can't stop me going to see her!'

'I don't know the name or the number of the ward. Never thought to ask.' He paused. 'It's special care. If you go to reception, I'm sure they'll tell you.'

Sharina stepped back. 'Right then. I'll go tomorrow.' She turned away, then turned back towards him. 'You want to get some black coffee down you, love. Marie wouldn't like to see you like that.'

Arian put his thumb in his mouth and nodded in agreement. Adam shut the door on them and leaned against it to stop his head spinning. Then he walked unsteadily through the sitting room, past the piles of papers and images, into Marie's pristine bedroom and threw himself on her bed. He was asleep in minutes. He woke up an hour later, drank a jug of water, went to sleep again and dreamed of climbing the mountain. But this time, instead of the rucksack on his back, he had the child Arian, balancing his fat feet in Adam's anorak pockets and lisping 'Golden Slumbers' into his ear.

Strangers Meeting

Adam dreamt he was lying in his cell in darkness, listening to the threatening night noises and imagining the mountain haloed by a rainbow, a poster that he'd stuck on his board. He woke up to discover that he wasn't in his cell. He was in Marie's bed, charged with an awkward surge of adrenaline and power. He screwed up his eyes to peer at her bedside clock. Three o'clock in the morning. He leapt out of the bed he'd sworn he wouldn't sleep in, straightened the bedclothes and walked through the flat turning on all the lights. He made some coffee, then, clutching the beaker to his bare chest, prowled through the flat again. After two circuits he sat on the floor in front of the pile of notebooks and papers.

He picked up a news clipping. Under the heading 'Off to study Poland's historic buildings' was a photograph of Marie, sitting at a desk, pen in hand. Her fair hair was looped back from her face and she was wearing swept-up glasses.

Soroptimists International have granted a bursary to Miss Marie Mathéve, an investigator for the Department of the Environment, to visit Poland to study the conservation of historical buildings. Miss Mathéve says, 'It is to foster international friendship I suppose. The bursary covers travel and I am hoping to get hospitality in the homes of Polish people. I want to see the smaller places, to see what they are doing to preserve their historic architecture.' Miss Mathéve is a Fellow of the Society of Antiquaries. Her work has included the listing of historical buildings.

He discarded the clipping and picked up one of the notebooks. On the front page Marie had inscribed: *Poland Diary 1981*. Below that was an elegant drawing of a church. He began to read.

10 October 1981, WARSAW

There is thick cloud over Germany but with a blue sky above. Foggy in Poland – had to circle the airport twice before we landed. I peered out of the window to see little farms and long narrow strip fields. Slow queues at the passport, money exchange. I arrived in Warsaw at 12.10. It was a good flight, without any ear-piercing pain. I couldn't see my Warsaw hosts among the waiting crowds. I am to stay here for a day and go on to Krakow to meet my other hosts there, and then on with them to Chorzow, some miles out from Krakow. All of these people – in Warsaw and Chorzow – are strangers to me. On the flight I read the Chorzow letter and looked at the images a dozen times. *We will meet you at Krakow station and take you on the further journey. The Zielinskis are very willing and overwhelmed that you will visit them in Chorzow. And to your very kind suggestion about supplies, they declare any margarine, cooking fat, cheese or sausage would be very welcome. Your cordial acquaintance Felix Wosniak.*

The letter is in English. Mr Wosniak has been corresponding with me in Esperanto (our common international language) but he speaks English too.

In the photograph the three of them are huddled together: the woman Jacinta between the two men. Felix is tall and willowy with receding dark hair. The Zielinskis are shorter, more sturdy and much fairer. Jacinta is round and pretty. She has a heart-shaped, eastern face but David, her husband, is tall and ghostly at the edge of the photograph: hard to make out.

The procedure through the Warsaw passport control is very slow. The officials seem obliged to read every word on every page of my passport and then kind of meditate. It gives me time to think again that, despite loving travel as I do, perhaps it's a mistake to venture behind the Iron Curtain like this. Of course at thirty-seven years old I'm quite beyond risk of white slavery, but I've read my fill of spy stories, where ordinary people get swept up into all sorts of skulduggery once they cross into Soviet territory. I have to keep reminding myself that although it may still be in the Soviet grip, Poland is *not* Russia. And it's only because the surviving buildings here have been hidden for a generation that I got my bursary. I'm not known for looking a gift horse in the mouth and am enchanted at the thought of those untouched medieval buildings.

However, once through the gate, the wait for the luggage is short and fortunately the customs woman does not open my case. For a few seconds, though, the thought of being thrown into jail for carrying sausage seems quite rational.

Met by my Warsaw hosts Pavel and Christine, who gives me a single rose wrapped in cellophane. They drive me to their flat, where Pavel gives me another flower wrapped in tissue. This small flat is in a big block at the crossroads opposite the power station. Flowers seem to be a luxury here – but even then only one at a time.

The flats are well insulated from the neighbours but there are no flower beds or window boxes. The living room is ten foot by ten lined with portraits of ancestors and Pavel's books. (He is a veteran

Esperantist and translator.) There is a hatch to the tiny kitchen, one small bedroom, a minute bathroom (note – general shortage of toilet paper). Our meal consists of hors d'oeuvres, soup with rice, hot meat, pastries.

Afterwards they take me through the mist and rain to visit Warsaw old town. Got a good impression of its extent and nature. (See notes and drawings below.)

We called at a large church to see monument to Chopin – church packed to the doors and standing in the aisles for evening mass – most impressive. (Religion is enjoying a comeback under these new more liberal protocols. Many of the members of this rebellious Solidarity union are, I'm told, Catholic.) Back to the flat, early to bed on a very hard bed settee in sitting room but slept pretty well. (Letter waiting here from David Zielinski about Krakow and Chorzow arrangements.)

Note for article: the old town of Warsaw was medieval but only became the capital city around 1600 when the royal residence was transferred from Krakow. The old city now an oasis of narrow traffic-free streets full of charm and visible history. Immediately outside is the so-called new town, which was destroyed and recently rebuilt in the style of the late eighteenth century. (NB See photos and notes of Lazienki Water Palace – orangery, temples, etc., Jewish Quarter.)

Midday meal beetroot soup with bits of meat floating in it – delicious . . .

I have been offered a car ride to Krakow from Pavel's cousin and have accepted with alacrity as did not fancy the train.

I talked with Pavel's mother (who lives with his brother in an equally small flat nearby) in a mixture of German and English. She is very kind and eager. She is small, shrivelled, but vitally alive and intelligent. She talked about the war, the environment and the long tormented history of Poland. She showed me her arm where she was tattooed with a number at Auschwitz and I had to fight back the tears of shame that we couldn't stop all that happening in this historic, civilised continent . . .

Adam closed his eyes and could hear his mother's quiet, measured voice coming to him from the page. It had her distinctive, precise tones but was at the same time the voice of a stranger: a young woman, full of curiosity. In his mind's eye he could see Marie more than twenty-five years ago, with her swept-up hair and her earnest scholarly ways, setting out on a lone journey into unknown territory. The innocent abroad! Marie would be thirty seven, relatively young then. It was weird to think of her doing all this before he was even born. And what about this Esperanto thing? What was that about?

He went across to the desk, opened Marie's laptop and Googled *Esperantist*. 'The word *esperanto* means "one who hopes". The goal of its inventor, L.L. Zamenhof, was to create an easy and flexible language that would serve as a universal second language to foster peace and international understanding.' Further on he read: 'Esperantists were executed during the Holocaust, with Zamenhof's family in particular singled out.'

Adam wondered now whether Pavel's mother had been condemned to Auschwitz because of her race or because she was a speaker of this lost language of peace. There was no way of knowing this from Marie's diary.

Suddenly very tired, he went back into the bedroom, stripped off and crawled back between the covers. The thought crossed his mind that his mother spoke Esperanto, a language he'd never even heard of. That was ironic. Then he fell asleep. He did not wake until ten thirty. He showered, threw his laundry into Marie's washing machine, got dressed in crumpled clothes from his rucksack and went straight to the hospital. On his way out he noticed the notebooks scattered across the floor. One was open at a page dense with writing.

He left them there on the carpet. They would keep.

Today we had breakfast of cold ham, liver paste,
coffee – powdered, instant, bitter – while I waited
for Pavel's cousin and his wife and their car to make
a visit to Wilanow Palace. Still waiting at lunchtime

(herb soup with half a boiled egg, then lettuce, rice and onions with a nice bit of veal!). At last they came to take me to Wilanow, a magnificent sixteenth-century palace newly restored with inlaid floors, stucco, frescos, French tapestries, Venetian mirrors and English grandfather clocks. Renaissance garden, nice little fountain in grounds . . . I did many drawings . . .

I anticipated the kindness of these people, but the energy, their sheer dogged recoverability against all odds is what strikes me most now . . .

And now (next day) Pavel's cousin is on time for our longer journey to Krakow. Our companions will be two Esperanto actors who are going to Krakow to join some celebration of Esperantist history. I am in a strange world.

As the car leaves Warsaw, my eye is drawn across this far-reaching land, very flat: open fields; small farms; no hedges; few tractors but still horses everywhere – ploughing, pulling, hauling everything, including low long carts of logs; women with buckets at a well. The houses are very small, mostly square and squat, the villages are grey and uninspiring, although here and there you see tall cement blocks of flats growing on the outskirts of these places. The future, I suppose.

In the middle of our journey the land becomes more undulating as the road passes through dense forests. We keep passing shrines to partisans killed in the war. Pavel's cousin tells me that many thousands of partisans hid in the forests during the war. We drive past an old church built of upright logs. As we draw at last towards Krakow the land is less wooded, with farmhouses. Now the houses are clustered in villages . . .

Pavel's cousin has made a phone call to my Chorzow hosts and they will be there to meet us at the main rail station at Krakow. And so they are: the small, pretty woman built something like a river hen, and the two men. One is tall and dark with slicked-back hair like a wartime film star. The other is heavier, more classically handsome, with fair hair and the well-modelled, sharp features that I noticed a lot in the streets of Warsaw. This must be David.

I take a deep breath and greet them in Esperanto. The dark man takes charge, introduces himself as Felix Wosniak, and his companions as David and Jacinta Zielinski. I am instantly pleased that they, not the dark man, are to be my hosts. They are younger than me, slightly nervous. But Jacinta has a lovely smile and David has a firm handshake and a very direct, intelligent look in his eyes. He smiles. 'Welcome to Krakow,' he says in stiff English. 'And we are to welcome you to our home in Chorzow, Jacinta and I. We have a journey to take in train.'

I smile up at David Zielinski and take another deep breath, pleased that the most important, the most exciting, part of my visit is beginning.

Learning Curve

It seemed to Adam, when he got to the hospital, that Marie had not moved a muscle. The monitor still ticked steadily; the drip stand stood sentinel. The sister said she'd had a comfortable night and all they could do now was wait. 'But she could do with a bit of company. Just talk to her, son.'

So Adam sat with his hand over hers and told her about his night in her flat. He admitted to getting quite drunk on her rosé and also that he had been reading her Polish journals. 'Tell you what, Marie! I was wondering why these weren't in the file boxes like all your other notes and sketches, wherever they may be. And the stuff in the boxes was such a mess too! Just thrown in there. Not like you at all. I was wondering something else too. I never knew you'd been to Poland. I knew about all the other places, but never Poland.'

But his mother lay there stubbornly, her eyes closed. Ward noises drifted through the open door. Nurses clipped in and out. They turned Marie, talking into her ear as though sharing secrets. They checked her stitches and adjusted the bandage round her head. Physiotherapists lifted the cover over her bandaged foot and talked to each other in low voices. A young auxiliary came and combed and plaited her hair so it lay like a silver-white snake beside her on the pillow. (This young woman fluttered her eyelashes at Adam but he didn't notice.) Early in the day there had been talk of cutting Marie's hair, but the doctor, Jessica Stanley, said no, the patient hadn't given her assent. Technically, she said, that was assault.

Up here again. Thank God they've done my hair. It was such a mess. Look at you, Adam. I'd not realised you'd grown into such a lanky thing. Perhaps that happens in prison, like plants growing spindly in the dark. But then you were long as a baby. They measured every baby, you know. You were the longest on the ward that month. In that clinic the nurses there called me Miss Mathéve, not by my Christian name like the younger mothers. Their politeness masked implicit disapproval. I was only thirty-eight but I was officially designated an elderly mother, do you know that? Some justice perhaps. There were mothers visiting their daughters and grandbabies in that ward who were younger than me. You had such long fingers and toes, Adam – a musician in the making, I thought. And you had this almost invisible cap of white fur. When they'd washed off the white birth grease and towelled you down, your hair glinted silver. For me you were a miracle, a pure miracle, an unlooked-for gift. An exquisite stranger.

I feel now I should have told you these things, shouldn't I? We should have sat together side by side while I told you the story of your own birth. But the time never seemed right for the telling. I should have told you at least how you made such a difference to my life. At the very least I had to stop giving in to my gypsy instincts and take any commission to fund our lives together.

But you were so good, so quiet and watchful. The perfect child. I felt myself lucky.

Back down into the husk body now. My head hurts. I can't move, not even my little finger. I can't see you, Adam. Not even the back of your head. My brain is screaming: I am here! I am here! And my head hurts even more. I am a bystander. A ghost in my own life. But it was ever thus, wasn't it, Adam?

Marie's face twisted for a second as though she were in pain and Adam thought of calling a nurse, but then her face composed itself again into sculptured, deadly stillness and he desisted. He struck the tight counterpane with the flat of his hand. 'Come on, Marie! Come on!'

Irritation flared through his body, and he was consumed with the desire for a cigarette. He got up and strode down the ward and out of the hospital to take refuge with the other addicts in a smoking shelter fifty yards from the main entrance. Smokers, he thought, are the new lepers. Funny thing was, he himself had never smoked until he went inside prison: he'd drunk all sorts – beer, vodka at parties – but he'd never smoked anything, not even a joint. He'd argued with

Sam (who smoked everything, legal and illegal) that smoking was ridiculous, like babies sucking on dummies. Sam had hooted with laughter at this, saying that Adam was in denial, afraid, a mummy's boy, too wimpy to take the plunge, and anyway, how could he dismiss something he hadn't tried?

But prison had succeeded where Sam with all his cocky charm had failed. Inside prison, smoking tobacco was the least worst thing you could do to numb the pain, to while away the time. Adam's chiropractor friend, Tom – an expert in exactly what tobacco did to your insides – failed to discourage him. He tried earnestly to warn him off, but eventually gave up, saying, 'I suppose it's least worst, old boy. Least worst in here at any rate.'

Of course prison had been a shock, terrifying. But in the end it was not as hard as Adam had first anticipated. The worst thing was being warehoused and moved around like an object, with no sovereignty over your body, your possessions or your daily routines. The fear inside those places was not about what happened but about what *might* happen: that something bad might happen even when in the end it didn't. Dark tales and myths flew about the place like black moths. Being suspended in such uncertainty could twang the steadiest of nerves, and in the end he learned that a smoke could steady him.

In his first week inside, Adam made another acquaint- ance besides Tom the chiropractor. This man, Henry Masterson, looked on Adam with some congeniality. With his china-white face and a thatch of iron-grey hair, Henry was impossible to miss. He made his way slowly round the prison on a Zimmer frame, nodding to left and right and stopping for a chat here and there; there was something feudal about his demeanour. The other prisoners gave him space and he was on good terms with the officers, to whom he always showed unctuous respect.

On Adam's first day off the wing, Henry sat beside him in the dining hall. He called him by his name and told him he reminded him of his nephew: 'He had this thatch of white hair just like yours. Practically albino he was, only he had proper eyes. Dead now, silly sod.'

The impact of Henry's friendship was to neutralise the threat that lurked in the corridors and the public places of the prison. Over breakfast each morning Henry would give Adam the gen about prison routines and the arcane rules, written and unwritten, that kept things in balance. He was a great yarner, and loved telling of his exploits as a young boxer and his work in the service of some of the most successful villains in his home city of Manchester: the clever ones, with mansions in Cheshire, who'd never seen the inside of a cell. And although he himself didn't indulge, he also knew everything there was to know about drugs – here inside as well as out there in the world. 'Mug's game, kiddo, though. I always say that to the lads in here. Rots your muscles as well as your head. And then what you left with?'

This was disingenuous. It was the observant Tom who told Adam the truth about Henry. 'He likes to play the good old boy, with his Zimmer frame and his oily winning ways, but don't be deceived. I got my partner on the outside to Google his case. It's all there. Chap has power in here and power outside. That frail old man still deals drugs, big time. Has great influence outside, even now. And, you'll see, it's the same inside too. What some guys here want, even more than tormenting some other chap for fun, is access to decent gear. And in here, oddly enough, that means good old Henry.'

Despite this warning, Adam got to enjoy his breakfast conversations with Henry. Before he arrived in prison he'd made up his mind to stick to his own company, his own cell. But things were not as straightforward as that. After a week he found himself hungry for talk, the sight of faces, the sound of voices, even angry voices: it was natural to crave the sounds of life. To experience life he had to fit in, to change himself. When his accent was mocked, he assumed the accent of his former schoolmates, and he lowered his tone to sound less girlish. He learned to bite his lip on his instinctive sarcastic comments that – far from going over people's heads – could light a fuse that took a long time to burn out.

He copied Henry, who would defuse situations with a grunt, smile, a shrug or a heavy fluttering hand. He earned credit for writing letters for the other men: to mothers, to fathers, to girlfriends, and in one case to a boyfriend in another prison. Sometimes these letters – which he wrote verbatim – were couched in a code that even clever Adam could not fathom. He wrote letters to judges, lawyers, solicitors. Adam's willingness to offer this skill, together with Henry's patronage, earned him his place in the complex economy of give and take that made up prison life. The pay-off in this economy was personal survival. And he had survived.

This morning, standing in the hospital smoking shelter with the other 'lepers', Adam's mind returned again to his twenty-six months inside. He realised that – as the cliché went – prison had changed him, but not necessarily for the worst. He was heavier now: all those carbohydrates! And his voice was different. It had gone through the grinder of cigarettes and prison-speak. And paradoxically, he was steadier now than he had ever been: the feeling of displacement that had dogged him all his life had somehow dissipated. He knew now that if you could find and make your place in jail, you would not be out of place anywhere. He could imagine Sam's argument against that, but he knew it was an argument he would win. Though now of course he would never be able to argue the point with Sam.

In prison he'd had a short, sharp, shocking lesson in masculinity, a quality that, despite the presence of his stepfather, Jack, had been absent as he grew up, even in his ambiguous years at university. At home there had been no rough edges against which he could file his sense of being a man.

As the only child of a single mother, life had been

unforced, negotiated, unspoken. Voices were never raised, disapproval would be a long, wearying talk about the sensible way to do things. Later in life it had dawned on him that this was not necessarily a good thing. He grew weary of Marie's soft looks, her distracted ways, the sad shadow in her eyes when he'd done something notionally wrong. Now he realised that even in her absence she'd controlled him. Her touch was delicate as a drover's whip, pulling him this way and that, always on the path called straight.

Marie's training in the subtle side of things, combined with his natural cleverness, had led to all kinds of achievement at school. Despite this, he'd been known there as a bit soft, called a mummy's boy by boys who saw a lot more of their mother than he did. That had lessened a bit when he joined the band, where he played the penny whistle, a skill that Jack had taught him when he was small. The band was made up of boys who celebrated the feminine side of themselves, were comically camp even while – all but one – being fully functioning heterosexuals. Adam felt at home with them.

But prison was another thing. The more he gave himself up to the surreal barter of life in there, the less he wanted to think about his mother. He'd endured her presence at his trial, knowing that her earnest eyes never left his face, but had never once glanced in her direction. He did not want her soft looks, her puzzled, delicate despair. He avoided her glance as he listened to the careful comments of the judge. And he welcomed his sentence. He thought it could have been much worse. His bluff solicitor said quietly in his ear, 'Keep your head down, your nose clean, and it'll be down to two years, son. Lucky in your judge today.'

That moment in court he had looked at Mr and Mrs Rogers, Sam's parents, who were sitting clutching each other like drowning souls. He had slept on their floor. He had eaten Mrs Rogers' full English breakfast. He had even laughed at Mr Rogers' jokes. He knew then that four years – or two with a clean nose – was not enough. Nothing would be enough.

Whoosh. That's better. But he's gone. Where has he gone? Stumped off again. But he is not so angry now. I can feel that, his anger getting less. Now there is just me, or the husk of me on the bed down there. No, I decided it was a glass bottle, didn't I? Empty inside because I'm up here. Thank God they've plaited my hair. And all the blood is off my face. I look less like a scarecrow now. Vanity, vanity! Here I am on my way out of this world and I'm worrying about my looks. I wouldn't have said I was a vain woman. What a time to discover that!

The boy keeps coming in and out and I'm whooshing up and down like a yo-yo. I've no sense of time passing. None at all. Has it been a day, a week, a month? What a lot of fuss goes on all around the bed. The machines tick. I can hear the nurses' voices but not the words they say. I would really like to see their faces. I try to haul myself down in front of the screen so I can see them but I keep bouncing up again like a helium balloon.

★

In the husk again, and now I'm back behind my closed eyes, seeing nothing. Everything is fainter, the murmur of voices more distant, and now no matter how hard I try I can't hear or see anything. Oh dear. My head hurts.

Sharina

'Well hello, Adam Mathéve!'

Adam, on to his second cigarette in the lepers' hut, looked across to see the girl called Sharina clicking on the brake of a scruffy buggy with the child Arian inside, all eyes under his furry Scooby-Doo helmet.

'Really!' The only other smoker in the shelter, a well-dressed woman with deep lines on her white face, frowned at the young girl in coloured scarves and pixie boots, and then stared across at the chubby baby in the ridiculous hat. This woman really did not want a child in her hut.

Her attitude made Adam smile at Sharina. 'Hi! So you came to see Marie, did you?'

Sharina blinked. 'Changed your tune, aincha?' She nodded at a seat ten yards away. 'Me and Arian're gunna sit there.' She surveyed the smoking shelter and the woman, who still was glaring at her. 'Not healthy here for me.

Never mind him.' She took off the buggy brake and marched away down the path.

Adam threw his half-smoked cigarette in the bin provided and followed her. She sat on the concrete bench and Adam sat down beside her, tucking his chin deeper in his parka. 'So you came?' he repeated.

'I told you, me and Arian wanted to see Marie. He's missing her, aren't you, love? We have tea and biscuits with her every day, you know.'

She leaned forward to loosen the neck of the baby's green anorak. Her curly black hair fell forward, masking her face, so Adam focused on her hands. Her nails were bitten rather than trimmed and her fingers were short and stubby. He felt such a rush of tenderness towards this strange girl that he could have wept. He sniffed. 'So you're going in to see her?'

'Yep! But you'll have to watch Arian while I do. They'll not let me take him in, will they? I'll see her and tell her Arian would have come if he could, and I'll tell him all about her when I get out again. He'll have to be satisfied with that.' She pinched one fat cheek. 'Won't you, sweetheart?'

So Adam was left on the bench outside the hospital with a stranger-baby wearing a furry hat. Arian looked up at him with his black-treacle eyes and put his thumb in his mouth. Adam placed his face on a level with the child. 'It's all right for you, Arian,' he said glumly. 'Your mother speaks to you. Do you know, my mother even didn't speak to me that much when she was awake. And it's a lost cause now, because she's asleep and doesn't seem to want to wake, even for me.' Without even thinking what he was doing, he blew a very wet and noisy raspberry at the baby, who took his thumb from his mouth and grinned broadly. Then, frowning with the effort, the little boy flapped his lips and tongue and tried his own wet version of a raspberry. Adam laughed out loud at this and blew back. They were on their fourth return volley when a silvery voice above him said, 'Is he yours?'

He straightened up to face the consultant Jessica Stanley, in a belted raincoat and brown boots, carrying a brown leather briefcase. She smelled of something clean – melon and cucumber maybe. He blushed at the excessive thought. 'No. No, Miss Stanley . . . Jessica. His mother is my mother's neighbour. She's gone in to see her.'

Jessica stared down at Arian. 'Now that's a funky hat!' she said.

Arian lodged his thumb back in his mouth.

'At least it proves his mother has a sense of humour.' Adam felt he had to defend Sharina.

Jessica smiled broadly. 'No criticism intended. This town's full of girls with designer buggies complete with blank-faced, designer-clad, overmatched skinny offspring. A cherub in a Scooby-Doo hat is a ray of hope, in my view.' She paused. 'How did you find your mother this morning?'

'Just the same. I've gotta say, it's really frustrating, sitting there, wanting her to listen, wanting her to speak.'

'It will be frustrating. But keep at it. Believe that under that veil she can hear, that she knows you are there. Bring in some music, read something to her.' She squatted down and chucked Arian under his chubby chin. 'Aren't you lovely? Aren't you?' At that moment she looked nothing like a senior consultant who held lives in her hands. She looked like any woman, which was a kind of comfort.

Adam hesitated. Then, 'I've found these journals of hers. Written in 1981, before I was born. About a journey she took in Poland. And drawings. She was . . . is a very fine draughtsman.'

'A draughtswoman?' Jessica stood up. 'Bring them in, Adam. Read them to her, if you can bear it. Talk about the drawings. We never know what can trigger the wakening. But it can happen, believe me.'

She reached into an outer pocket of her briefcase. 'Here's my card and my numbers. Anything you want to check out, just call. And talk to your mother – talk, read to her. Don't imagine she can't hear. There are those who believe people in your mother's state hear everything that's going on around them.'

Her tone was soft, and this was all so cosy, so confidential, that Adam had the savage desire to break it, to spoil it. 'Problem is, talking's the hard thing for me. I haven't seen Marie for two years now.' He paused. 'It's like this. I'm just out of prison. I was on my way to see her for the first time in a long while when I found her there at the bottom of the stairs.'

Jessica Stanley stood straighter, her body still. He wondered now if she regretted giving him her numbers. There were patches of red on her cheeks. 'Prison? Why? I'm sorry, it's none of my—'

'Well, now you know. I'm just out,' he said.

Arian started to cry then, and Adam bent down, unstrapped him and lifted him out of his buggy. He held him high and shook him gently and he stopped crying.

Jessica stared at him. 'As I say, it's nothing to do with me. But you have to find things to talk to her about. That's your job now, wherever you've been.' She turned and strode into the hospital, passing Sharina in the doorway. Beside her solid figure Sharina looked like a tiny scarecrow hung about with colour.

Sharina took Arian from him. 'No need to take him out of the buggy, Adam. He likes it in there. Gives him his independence.'

'He was crying. I took him out to make him stop.'

She frowned. 'He doesn't cry usually.'

'He's very sensitive,' said Adam. 'I was having a bad moment. And he started to cry in sympathy.'

'Ah yes.' She grinned and strapped Arian back in the buggy. 'That's my Arian. Real sensitive. Knows what you're thinkin' half the time, I'm telling you.' She looked up at him. 'Marie's in a bad way, isn't she, with all those tubes and things? Away with the gypsies. Not with us at all.' She stood up. 'You goin' back in to see her?'

He looked at his watch. 'No. I'll go back to the flat now,

then I have to go and sign up with . . . To sign up.'

She frowned at him. 'Oh! Sign on? I suppose you do.'

He let her think he meant sign on the dole. No point his telling her that he was signing on, as arranged, with the probation service in the city. 'Then I'll come back to the hospital again later this afternoon.' He realised he didn't want to go back to the flat just now. 'Do you fancy a pizza or something?'

She grinned, white teeth gleaming. 'You paying?'

'I asked you, so . . .'

'Right. There's this really good Pizza Hut by the bridge. Arian loves their pasta carbonara, don't you, sweetheart? So I have to love it too because we have to share. Pasta or pizza, we're in heaven, the pair of us. And they put what's left in a box for you to take home. Not bad, that!' She turned the buggy round so it was facing downhill. 'Let's away! Come on, Adam, me and Arian'll race you to the bridge!'

Eating Together

The town was buzzing as usual, as town and gown mingled with a heavy sprinkling of hardy tourists braving the punitive English autumn, for the pleasure of walking the winding Georgian streets of this city and the sight of its unique medieval cathedral.

Sharina parked the buggy in the vestibule of the crowded café, while Adam found the last vacant table. She collared a waiter, asked him to bring a high chair and settled Arian with a spout cup in one hand and a biscuit in the other. Then she sat back, stretched her pixie-booted feet in front of her and breathed in. 'I love the smell of Italians,' she purred.

Adam's eyebrows shot up. 'Italians?'

She laughed. He noticed her two front teeth were slightly crooked. 'Not people, divvy! I like the cafés, don' I?' She breathed in deeply once more. 'All those tomatoes and olive oil and garlic bread! The very breath of life.'

Adam, still confused, stared at her. He didn't know this girl at all. She was full of surprises.

The waiter, a short, plump boy, came to stand by the table. His presence did not make Sharina hurry; if anything she slowed down. She made a drama of peering down the menu and commenting on its contents before she chose a pizza *quattro stagioni* for herself. 'And you gotta choose pasta carbonara, Adam, so Arian can have a bit of that, and I can give you a slice of my pizza.' She sighed. 'I'm a bit sick of pasta carbonara to be honest. I always have to share with him.'

'I've got to say, you're very managerial,' Adam said, unable to stop grinning.

Sharina sat back in her seat and flicked the magenta streak out of her eyes. She sniffed. 'You! You don't realise how good it can be not to have to eat carbonara. But my Arian insists, don't you, sweetheart?' She pulled at the baby's sandalled foot and he offered her his biscuit. She took a bite.

Adam gave the order to the waiter. 'One *quattro stagioni*, one carbonara.'

'And a Diet Coke,' she said.

'Two Diet Cokes,' Adam said. He sat back and tried to think of something to say. 'Do you know, I'm sitting here and I know not a blind thing about you.'

She grinned. 'Blind date, then!'

He frowned. 'Hardly.'

She tossed her head and the magenta-streaked hair

dropped over her eye again. 'Blind no-date, then,' she said glumly.

'I was just . . .' His voice tailed off. He was still confused.

'Anyway,' she said. 'At least you know where I live, don't you?'

'Well, to be honest, I was wondering about that.'

'Oh were you?' She scowled. 'What you're really saying is how does a lass like me end up in a posh block of flats next to your mother?'

He blushed. 'No, that's not it,' he protested. 'Not at all. I didn't mean that. Don't put words in my mouth!' He paused. 'What I do know about you is that you're funny, you're very good with Arian and he's a very contented kid. Anyone can tell that. And that tells me something about you.'

'Well that's sommat,' she conceded.

'Anyway, you know nothing about me either,' he said.

She frowned across at him. 'I can tell lots about you,' she said.

'What?'

'Well, your voice is all mixed up, like you've gone through some kind of mangle. It doesn't match itself. That'd make anyone suspicious. But Marie's your mam, and that means sommat, me knowing Marie. You're posh and I guess you're clever, letters after your name and all that. Marie's son. That counts.'

He laughed. 'I might be her son, Sharina, but I'm not very clever. I've been known to act very stupid.'

'You would say that!'

'Well believe it! And I've gotta tell you, Marie'd be upset if she knew you called either of us posh!'

Sharina leaned over to chuck Arian on his fat cheek. 'Well, Arian, we wouldn't want to upset our friend Marie, would we?'

They stopped talking while the chubby waiter brought their meal. Sharina asked for a separate small plate for Arian and he sped off to bring one, telling her that she had a beautiful *bambino*. Adam wondered whether these boys got a bonus for putting on the Italian stuff – maybe they really came from Coxhoe or Consett or somewhere else equally local.

Sharina spooned some of Adam's pasta on to Arian's plate, telling him how lucky he was that Adam had offered to share his dinner with him. 'But mamma will give Adam a slice of her pizza, so there's no worry about him starving, don't you worry, Arian! Fair exchange.'

Adam said. 'That's a good name, Arian. Where d'you get that?'

She cut a small square from the centre of her pizza, put it in her mouth and spoke with her mouth full. 'Why should I get it anywhere?'

He flushed. 'Because all names come from somewhere.'

'They don't,' she said. 'You can make them up.' She paused. 'Why does my baby have to be called a name somebody else has?'

Adam scrabbled in his mind for a tolerable answer.

'Well . . . people . . . I'd have thought . . . well, unusual names . . .' His voice tailed off.

They munched in silence for a while and Sharina popped another spoonful of pasta into Arian's mouth.

Adam's mind raced. Two years in the company of more or less hard men and a week in a glass surf bubble in Cornwall had been a poor preparation for this conversation. Apart from the haunting memories of his mother and guilty memories of quixotic Rachel, he'd forgotten how strange and perverse women could really be.

At last, to his relief, Sharina relented and the silence was broken. 'Well, if you really want to know, he's called after a man in a book.'

Adam choked on his pasta. 'A book?' he spluttered, grinning.

'There! Don't believe me, do you? Books too good for me and my baby? Far too intelligent.' She looked round the café. 'I'll tell you one thing. I bet I've read more books than anybody here.' She was clearly angry.

Adam stared down at his pasta, defeated. He opened his mouth, but suddenly Sharina was standing up, hauling Arian from the high chair, slamming him into his buggy, charging out of the café before he could say anything.

The waiter came across. 'Ah, the ladies,' he said, with a sympathetic shrug that Italians must learn at their father's knee. 'So passionate!' He looked at the plates. 'Do you want all this in a box?'

There and then Adam abandoned his suspicion about

the man coming from Coxhoe or Consett. He paid the bill and left him a decent tip.

Outside in the street there was no sign of Sharina or Arian or the buggy. Adam looked at his watch. He should go back to the hospital. Marie might have woken up. The food in the boxes would keep. He would knock on Sharina's door when he got back, to see if she'd got her good humour and her appetite back. In the meantime he'd try to work out why he'd given such offence without meaning it. He had a lot to learn.

Sam used to say that sometimes Adam was a real dumb cluck. 'Got a blank spot where your empathy muscle should be, mate. We're all a mystery to you, aren't we?'

As he walked back up to the hospital, it suddenly struck Adam that Sharina was like Sam: the same life energy, the same certainty about things. The same accent, when he came to think of it. Sam was from round here too.

Jessica Stanley was standing by his mother's bed when he arrived. She shook her head when she saw him. 'Nothing just yet. But she seems comfortable and is breathing well.' Her eyes dropped to his canvas shoulder sack. 'You've got something to read to her in there?'

He held up the sack. 'Well, there's the remains of a meal I had in Pizza Hut. But in here . . .' he fished in the side pocket, 'I have one of her diaries.' He found himself telling her about Marie and her life on the fringes of architecture, and her journey in the eighties to Poland. 'That's the diary

74

I'm gonna to read to her,' he added glumly. 'Can't see it'll make any difference.'

Jessica leaned across and touched Marie's shoulder. 'Surprising in here. People come in covered in blood and then you just see them in their gowns. All distinguishing marks obliterated. It's only when they talk that we get to know them, or like you, when their dear ones tell us their tales.'

Whoosh! That red-haired one is more than a nurse, stethoscope round her neck. Adam's listening hard to what she is saying, leaning towards her. I wonder if he likes her. Lord knows I'm no expert in these things. Look at my life. How would I know about girls in Adam's? I was aware of the formidable Sam, and that scarecrow of a girl they called Rachel Miriam. But he was a boy and I could see she wouldn't count as what the films call 'love interest'. No breasts to speak of. I wish this doctor would go now, so I can get back down there into my body and Adam can talk to me again. He talked to me yesterday. Or was it last week? It's only down there that I can hear his voice properly. Up here I can only see things. All the voices just murmur, like extras in a film rhubarbing away. But down there, in that half-dead body, I can hear Adam reading my own words, making my poor battered brain hook up again to those days in Chorzow. Now I am remembering other things . . . Of course, it's not all down there in the notebook, is it? You disguise things a little when you write them down, don't you?

Reading Time

Adam sat back in the hospital chair, cleared his throat and
started to read out loud.

13 October 1981

At the Krakow station Felix and the Zielinskis
cluster round me, the men clicking their heels and
bowing over my hand, Mrs Z blushing and nodding
and smiling all at once, chattering words of
welcome in Polish.

Felix says 'Pleased to meet you' in Esperanto. I
feel really shy as we shake hands. Letters make you
think you know someone, but he seems today like a
stranger in a strange land.

I guess my smile is a bit uneasy. But David
Zielinski picks up my heavy case and strides ahead
with it, leading the way to the restaurant where

we're to have our lunch. I would love to get straight
on with the journey but Felix tells me they all set
out from Chorzow very early and are extremely
hungry. In any case our train to Katowice – where
we will go before catching the tram to Chorzow
(all these long distances!) – is not due for some
time.

The others nod their agreement. Felix is very
much in charge. There are people on the pavements
but few cars on the streets. Krakow is not as busy –
or as urban – as Warsaw. It is cluttered and quaint,
only a breath away from its medieval self. The
sound of a trumpet cuts the air and makes me
jump. David Zielinski puts a hand on my arm. 'Is
the trumpeter in the tower,' he says. 'On the hour
he blows his trumpet. Is old custom.'

For lunch (which I insist on paying for and they
don't complain) we have chicken, boiled potatoes,
carrots and coffee but the service is slow and it
takes over two hours. The three other people who
share our table smoke ten cigarettes between them
during the meal. Most people in here are smoking
and certainly don't look very healthy. Children look
pale. And at every turn here there are men in
uniform – khaki and blue – mostly baby-faced
youths. I am surprised that nobody seems bothered
by them, or afraid of them.

At the station, large knots of men stand in front

of the six televisions on the main concourse, watching a football match. There is another television in the waiting room. I have to wonder if it is a case of circuses instead of bread.

At last we proceed. The journey in the train (electrical and super-express) is comfortable and very fast – 316 kms in four hours. We pass the time by sleeping, eating apples, pears and cheese from my case. Jacinta in particular enjoys these. At nine o'clock we arrive at Katowice and catch our tram (no. 11) for Chorzow. A few of the men on the tram have obviously drunk a lot of alcohol so it's not too pleasant. David scowls at them, but Felix tells me they are harmless. 'The English saying is drowning their sorrows, is it not? We have much sorrows to drown.' Jacinta slips her arm through mine and hugs it to her side, a kind gesture of protection, I think.

Chorzow is a strange place. Like a kind of Soviet Middlesbrough. Tall, grey dusty buildings – lines of steelworks and mines rise inside a pall of grey air. In the middle of all this are these modern housing projects – battery pods to file away the burgeoning population of this crowded region – sheering up like cliffs from the worn pavements and the roads marked out with old tramlines. But the design shows that someone has made an effort. There are green spaces with trees between these

constructions, rows of shops and funny little
tobacco kiosks. David tells me there is even a
people's park here, with its own lake. But this city is
defined by grey, not green.

The Zielinskis live in one of these Soviet-style
blocks of flats, which look like tall grey cakes, the
windows and balconies laid on like icing. In the
dusky evening light the windows are like guttering
candles, flickering on and off. As we make our way
between the blocks a woman, pale, with upswept
dark hair, is leaning on the railing of her balcony,
smoking. She waves at Jacinta and greets her in
Polish. Jacinta calls back. I can feel my hostess
relaxing at my side, now she is on her own safe
territory. The woman on the balcony nods then
bows towards me in greeting.

Jacinta turns to me and speaks. In my other ear
David translates. 'Jacinta says that is our good friend
Theresa. You are invited to take coffee with her
tomorrow.'

Felix says in Esperanto, 'You will find, Marie, that
our people are very hospitable.'

My head is buzzing with all the strange words,
the smells of petrol and concrete and the distant
worry that this visit of mine might just be a big
mistake.

Felix takes his leave at the doorway of the block.
I can smell his hair oil as he kisses first my hand,

then Jacinta's. He shakes hands heartily with David, talking away in Polish. I try not to feel shut out.

Smiling and nodding, David takes my arm and ushers me into the narrow steel lift and presses the button for the eighth floor. I have seen lifts like this in high-rise blocks from Edinburgh to London. But at home such lifts are decorated with the boasting threat of graffiti, and are infused with the smell of vomit and beer that has passed through someone's gut. Here the walls are a clean dull brown and the lifts are pristine and smell of camomile and cleaning fluid.

The Zielinskis usher me into their flat. A narrow vestibule leads into a square room with a polished wooden floor. The large metal-framed window looks out over other blocks of flats interspersed with brave stretches of green grass studded with young trees. Just below us is a small circular building like a carousel: one of those tobacco kiosks.

The walls of the Zielinskis' sitting room are decorated with real paintings, stiffly executed: two of them depict soldiers on horseback and one is of a city, which I recognise from my books as medieval Krakow. On the narrow wall by the window is an image of the Virgin Mary with a perpetual red light shining below it. The room is furnished with a long couch, easily recognisable as a bed settee, an easy

chair, a bureau tumbling with papers and a narrow
dining table. The man sitting at that table with a
newspaper spread before him stands up to greet me.

Jacinta says, 'Here is father-in-law. Alon Piotr.'

The man clicks his heels and bows over my
hand. He must have been handsome in his youth.
Even now he is distinguished, although his face is
dry and creased: the stigmata of a lifelong smoker.

I look around. 'Your little boy?' I say to Jacinta.
In his letter Felix mentioned that the Zielinskis
have a boy aged five.

'Piotr is asleep,' says David. He nods at one of
the doors that leads from the room. 'And Casia also.'

'Casia?' I say.

He laughs. Then he shakes his head and leafs
through a battered dictionary. 'Ah. *Nanny*. Casia is
nanny for Piotr. Is very, very old.' He smiles, looking
suddenly very young. 'Very severe. My nanny also.
And my father's. Tonight Piotr sleeps with Casia, so
he does not disturb you.'

I wonder about this nanny. In a flat as big as a
shoebox?

Jacinta shows me the kitchen, a slip of a room
with a cooker, a fridge, a marble shelf for
preparation. A washing machine, jammed under the
window, takes up a quarter of the space. I get my
case and we make quite a business of unloading the
sausage, cheese, lard and bacon into the fridge, and

Jacinta claps her hands as though my gifts were rubies and diamonds.

Celebrations over, she leads me to a crowded bedroom with a high bed piled with woven covers and a boxy modern wardrobe. Under the window is an empty narrow cot with a teddy bear tucked under the covers.

Then she leads me to the door of another bedroom, tiny, more like a cupboard. It is neat as a pin, like a soldier's billet. There is a map of eastern Europe on the wall and shelves at shoulder height groaning with books. Clearly this is the old man's room.

Of course I am wondering now where on earth I will sleep. She looks at David and says something. He says to me, 'You will sleep in the bedroom. Jacinta and I sleep here in the sitting room. Tomorrow night and afterwards Piotr will sleep in his bed in your room, but he is a good boy. He will not disturb you. He is a good boy.'

Adam put down the notebook and rubbed his eyes. He could hear Marie's voice as he read her words, so full of wonder at the things she had seen and heard. He could sense the mounting excitement at the strangeness of it all. And he thought how brave she'd been, as she said, there among strangers in a strange land. He looked down at the still figure on the bed, his brain tumbling with what he'd just read about his mother in a very different place at a very different time. He was confused.

Oh Adam, you're breaking my heart, your voice in my ear. As you stumble over the strange words I can hear the echo of his voice in yours. I can smell the crowded atmosphere of that flat. But believe me, Adam, there's so much more to those times than the words I wrote in those pages. Was I cruel to keep them from you, those times before you arrived? I pushed them right out of our lives. And now you've taken my mind back there; you've sucked me back to that time, that place. Yaaargh! Where am I? It is there, then? It is here, now? My head hurts. Thumping. Thumping. What's that noise? Your voice?

Part Two

The Zielinskis 1981

With the Zielinskis in Chorzow

Marie fingered her face to see if it was still there. Her cheek was cold as ice. She rubbed it hard to unfreeze it, then tucked her hand back under the bedclothes to warm it up again. She was warm enough from the neck down: the heap of woven blankets saw to that. She lifted her head slightly to see through the gap in the meagre curtains. At home when it was this cold, the glass would be etched with butterflies, steeples and mountains of frost. This had always seemed like magic to her, making up for the cold, which she hated. But here the glass was quite clear. They must have double or even triple glazing perhaps. Despite their grim aspect, these were modern buildings, though as far as she could tell at this moment, entirely without heat.

From the next room Marie could hear the clatter of dishes, murmuring voices, the piping call of a child, the soothing tone of a mother, then the sound of harpsichord music, which was changed abruptly to military music, interspersed with urgent words that she could not understand. She lay back, closed her eyes and considered her dilemma. What on earth was she doing here up on the eighth floor, taking up almost half the available space in a freezing flat that was barely big enough for two but which housed five, now six with herself?

Such proximity! She was not used to being this close to anyone. Her house on the new estate – hers since her mother died – was sprawling compared with this. She loved her house. Everything there – the glass-fronted book-shelves, the huge work table in the dining room – was dedicated to her love for, her obsession with, architecture. She'd always counted herself lucky to live alone, so that she could concentrate on writing her reports on the precious buildings, streets and bridges that were in danger. It was worth taking care with the reports. She sometimes felt ashamed of her vanity, but she knew her work made a difference: buildings and streets still survived because of her intervention.

Occasionally she emerged from her selfish hermitage to dine with someone, or go to see a film or a play. Her relationships were limited to that. Apart from her mother, she'd never had anyone special in her life. Her friends, men and women, remained close acquaintances. Even then, the attraction of new acquaintances was nothing compared to her own passionate learning cycle, which she knew would take her the whole of her life to complete. She was content to be on her own. Privacy was her shield.

Now, in the flat in Chorzow, she looked towards the door. Perhaps the protocols of privacy were different in these crowded places. Jacinta or David could come through that door any time. This thought galvanised her into leaping out of bed, putting a chair under the door handle and getting dressed in double-quick time – knickers, bra, vest, tights, slacks, Viyella blouse, woollen jumper, double-tied scarf for her neck. She needed to be warm. Then she took the chair from under the handle, sat before a mirror on the wall and brushed out her hair, tangled by a chilly night of tossing and turning in the high bed.

Someone knocked on the door and she called, 'Come in.' Jacinta entered carrying a small carved tray with a china cup of watery coffee and a matching plate with a slice of greyish bread covered with some kind of marmalade. 'Good morning,' she said, the emphasis all on the consonants. 'I have here breakfast.' She smiled and touched her own dark curls. 'Lovely. Hair. You!' she said.

'*Bonan matenon!*' Marie tried some Esperanto.

Jacinta shook her head. 'No Esperanto,' she said. 'Only David Esperanto.' She laughed. 'Only David English also! He writes for you.' She took a piece of paper from her apron pocket. '*David at work,*' she read carefully. '*Jacinta not at work this morning to look after you. Father gone for walk to café for coffee and bread rolls, if available. Doctor says he must walk. Jacinta take you at ten o'clock for cakes with friend Theresa. D.*'

Marie found herself smiling and nodding vigorously,

encouraging Jacinta in her efforts. She picked up her coffee and sipped it, swallowing a grimace at its weak, bitter flavour. 'Thank you, Jacinta,' she said slowly.

'Thank you, Marie,' Jacinta echoed. She opened the door wider. 'Come! See Piotr!'

Marie picked up the tray and followed her into the sitting room. Jacinta turned off the blaring radio that was filling the space with military music. At the narrow table an old woman was cutting bread into tiny pieces and popping them into the mouth of the child beside her as though he were a small bird. Marie's heart turned over when she saw the child, pale-faced like a plant that has not seen enough sun, golden-haired and blue-eyed. He had the natural, unbidden beauty of a star in the night sky. Marie's body zinged with intense feeling. Until that moment she'd never regretted being single, never regretted not making love to the various men who had come close, never regretted her childless state. Now, in a second, she regretted all of that.

'Piotr! Here Miss Mathéve!' said Jacinta.

'He must say *Marie*,' she found herself saying. 'Say he must call me Marie.'

'Here *Marie*!' said Jacinta. 'Shake hand.'

The child jumped off his chair and ran across, bending his blond head over her hand just like his father. 'Marie,' he said. He was, Marie realised, far too old to be fed like a bird by the old nanny.

'And here Casia!' said Jacinta.

The boy jumped back up to the table. The old woman looked up then, straight at Marie. Buried in the deep wrinkles of her ancient face, her eyes were black and lively. And full of malice. Without saying a word, she turned back and continued feeding Piotr. Marie looked at Jacinta, who shrugged apologetically. 'Casia very old. Nurse David, also Alon Piotr.' She did the numbers with her fingers. Eight fingers, then nine.

'Eighty-nine?'

Jacinta nodded. 'Very old.' She shook her head. 'She is law.'

Marie smiled. '*A law unto herself*, we say. My mother was like that.'

Jacinta shrugged and smiled, not quite understanding. 'I go . . .' She mimed getting ready and putting on lip-stick.

Marie nodded to show she understood and watched Jacinta vanish into her bedroom – the room Marie had just slept in – to get ready. Marie followed her and sat on the bed to pin her hair up in its usual French pleat. Then she scrabbled in her suitcase for a small leather monkey she had brought specially for Piotr, thinking that a child of five might like such a thing.

She went back to the living room and placed it by him on the table. 'Monkey,' she said. 'This is a *monkey*, Piotr!'

His small face beamed, his teeth gleaming like small pearls. '*Monkey*, Piotr!' he mimicked.

His delight ignited such pleasure in her that she felt

warm for the first time since she had arrived in Poland. Then something happened that chilled her to the bone. The old woman reached out, wrested the monkey from Piotr's chubby hand and threw it violently into the corner of the room. Piotr opened his mouth and bawled, tears falling like outsize peas down his round cheeks.

Jacinta rushed into the room and grabbed him in her arms making shushing noises, talking away to Casia, who answered her, spitting the words out like daggers. Jacinta put Piotr back in his seat and spoke to him, her voice angry. She turned to Marie. 'I sorry.' She scrabbled in David's battered dictionary. 'He *naughty*,' she said at last.

Marie shook her head. 'No! No!' she said. 'Not naughty . . .'

Her voice faded. She could see that Jacinta thought her guest was being polite in defending Piotr, and when she turned in annoyance to Casia, the old woman was smiling and shaking her head. '*Naughty*!' she said in English, her old voice squeaking with malevolence.

The only thing Marie could do then was retrieve the monkey and put it back into Piotr's hands, saying, 'You are *not* naughty, Piotr. I know it and you know it!' He started to smile through the tears and she stayed there beside him, making the monkey dance, while Jacinta cleaned the flat with a carpet sweeper and a dustpan and brush, and Casia gnawed at some grey bread and slurped coffee.

When she'd finished cleaning, Jacinta whipped off her

apron and smiled at Marie. 'Now go Theresa for cakes,' she said.

Marie took a deep breath. 'Can we take Piotr with us?' she asked Jacinta innocently.

Jacinta spoke to Casia, who shook her head vigorously. She turned back to Marie. 'Casia say too cold,' she said. 'Too cold for Piotr.'

Marie looked hard at the old woman, who shrugged her thin shoulders, her dark eyes sparkling. Then she shivered dramatically and shook her head again.

As they came down in the lift, Marie wanted to ask Jacinta about Casia. The woman was not even the child's grandmother yet she definitely ruled the Zielinski roost. And she clearly saw Marie as an intruder with whom she was prepared to do battle. And win at all costs.

But it was no good asking Jacinta, even with the help of a dictionary. She'd have to speak to David. Between their shared Esperanto and his dictionary he might help her to understand. And she would let him know how uncomfortable, even threatened, the old woman had made her feel. But then she asked herself, would that be polite, to let him know that?

As they walked in brittle autumn sunshine along the paved footpaths to Theresa's building, Marie decided that criticising Casia to David might not be such a good idea. After all, the woman had been David's nanny, and his father's too. David would take Casia's word against that of a stranger. Wouldn't he?

She realised that during her stay here she'd have to be all the wise monkeys – seeing, hearing and speaking no evil. It was the only way to go on in such a tight space. She was learning.

A Woman of Experience

Theresa's flat smelled like Christmas – a warm cinnamony smell that reminded Marie of those times when her mother and uncles would sit around the fire after the Queen's Speech on Christmas Day, eating fruit cake and drinking brandy.

Theresa – taller, more slender and more fashionable than Jacinta – welcomed them with open arms and ushered them into the flat from the chilly landing. She was dressed for the cold in an emerald-green long-sleeved woollen dress, high-heeled boots and a long, fringed, embroidered shawl round her shoulders.

Her flat was an exact facsimile of the Zielinskis but, being less cluttered with things and people, it seemed more spacious. (That was when Marie first thought that one might live quite elegantly on one's own in a flat like this.) Under the window was a round carved table covered with a lace cloth set with china for three people. At its centre was a pretty iced cake on a cut-glass plate. 'Ah, cake!' said Marie, for want of anything else to say.

Theresa pulled out chairs for them to sit down. '*Czarlotka!*' she said. 'Lemon, apples, flaxseeds, almond, cinnamon,' she chanted. 'Is tradition.'

Jacinta said something in Polish and Marie looked at Theresa, who grinned. 'Jacinta say I spin silk out of rags,' she said. 'Means the shops are empty. These things hard to get. All things hard to get. The bloody Russians steal our harvests.'

'You speak English?' said Marie, relieved.

'A little bit. David, he speak more. Jacinta . . .' she smiled at her friend, 'she speak less.' She cut a piece of cake and put it on Marie's plate. 'David tell me you speak this special language of peace invented by one of our countrymen.'

Marie nodded. 'Esperanto.'

Theresa was shaking her head vigorously. 'I say David no! Everyone just speak English. Then everyone talk peace together.'

Marie decided that this was not the place to argue about the built-in bias in any language. She moved on. 'You speak very good English, Theresa.'

Theresa served cake to Jacinta, who was sitting back now, allowing her friend to take the burden of entertaining this demanding guest. 'I learn. Very good teacher at school, although he was predatory, like a fox with chickens,' she said. 'Then husband number one. He speak English.' She rolled her eyes in Jacinta's direction. 'He love bloody Russia too. He a spy and made me talk all time in English. Practice, practice, practice! No babies – just English. Not so, Jacinta?'

Jacinta was enjoying her cake. 'Theresa, three husbands,' she spluttered, laughing and eating at the same time. She was proud of her friend.

'Me, I divorce that bloody spy. Say to priest I get no sex, just English. Priest say OK. And fix it with Pope. That husband go America, so that's OK.'

'To spy?'

Theresa shrugged. 'Who knows? Maybe become good little American.'

'And husband number two?'

'Very handsome, very bad. Two wives. One in Warsaw and one in Chorzow. One in Chorzow is me.'

'We call them *bigamists*, if they have two wives at once.'

'Bi-ga-mist. Bigamist!' Theresa rolled the word round her mouth. 'I like this word. *Bigamist!*'

'And husband number three?'

All laughter fled the room. Marie could see Jacinta still as a statue, suddenly holding her breath.

Theresa put down her cup. 'Bolester? My Bolek an angel from heaven and to heaven he returned. I pray him every night.' She nodded to a shelf by the table, at a photograph of a slender man in a suit, holding a trilby. His hair had a slight wave and his eyes were smiling.

Jacinta said quietly, 'Bolek very ill.' She patted her chest. 'He die.'

'Doctor say is the smoke and the bad air from the steelworks and the mines. Chorzow no healthy city,' said Theresa sadly, frowning.

'I'm sorry, so sorry,' said Marie desperately, wondering how they'd got to this from a conversation about cake.

Theresa's brow cleared and she smiled. 'Bolek mad if we sad. He would meet you and make you smile and fall in love with him. And so with us. We should make you smile.'

'He looks like a very fine man,' said Marie.

There was a silence while Theresa busied herself cutting each of them another slice of cake. 'So, Marie! Why you here in Chorzow?'

'I will look at buildings in Krakow, in Katowice, in Chorzow. And write a report.'

'Ah! Reports. Husband number one write reports.' Theresa wrinkled her nose. 'Buildings all ugly in Chorzow. Concrete of bloody Russia. But fine history buildings in Krakow. Katowice also.' She went to a wall cupboard, produced a large book and placed it on the table beside the remains of the cake. She began to turn the pages, leaning over it eagerly like a child. The pictures of Krakow, all in black and white, had a dingy, wartime feel, even though the book had been published in the sixties. But as Theresa continued to turn the pages, Marie felt herself finding colour in the fine streets and the secret, shadowy places, in the heroic medieval statues and the massive staircases with heraldic finials.

The old views of the city were interlaced with modern

images, of people walking down broad pathways through a park in the rain, of an industrial-style university with a great learning-hall filled with ranks of students toiling over desks. There was an odd picture of a great crowd in the rain, many of them carrying umbrellas. Most of the men were wearing light-coloured double-breasted raincoats and the women were wearing headscarves. Marie thought of Theresa's first husband, the spy. The men in this crowd looked like spies from an American film. That couldn't be the case, of course. The picture was about a time and a place. One man's spy was another man's normal citizen.

Theresa closed the book with a snap. 'There! Many good buildings in Krakow for you go look, Marie.'

They munched cake and drank tea in silence for a moment. Then Marie said, 'So how are you and Jacinta friends, Theresa?'

Theresa laughed and translated for Jacinta, who also laughed and nodded.

'Me, I was Jacinta's secret agent,' said Theresa. 'I friend of Jacinta. Our mothers friends. Jacinta and David fall in love in university. But David's grandmother . . .' She shook her head. 'Too . . .' She frowned. 'Think high up, think too good . . .'

'Snobbish?'

Theresa beamed. 'Too *snobbish*! She too snobbish for Jacinta. Jacinta father a coal-mining man in Chorzow. David grandfather a maker of instruments. Wonderful old violins. Mandolins. And *his* father, and *his* father. Old family.' She frowned. 'Bloody Germans took them to camps. Most of them. But David father, Alon Piotr, he fly planes from England to kill Hitler so bloody Germans not get him. He get *them* with his bombs. Then war end. Bloody Germans out. Bloody Russians in. Kill all the partisans now. Family of Casia hide Alon Piotr's mama in war. So she walk straight back into same grand apartment from before war. Casia too. So now Piotr, great Polish hero, is home. Is married to nice woman but big snob Mama – Grandmama – is boss.' Theresa glanced at Jacinta. 'Alon Piotr lose this wife to big Communist, so David – beloved grandson – grows up in grand apartment but falls in love and makes baby with my friend Jacinta. Grandmama hates Jacinta – not good enough for the *snobbish* woman. Or for Casia. So David and Jacinta run away here to Chorzow. Get married here. Then Grandmama dies and now bloody Communists take Krakow apartment so all come here. Casia, old Alon Piotr and baby. Everyone! Stay with me.' She took a deep breath and then put a hand on her forehead. 'O-oh. All English to speak. Very hard.'

Marie looked around and imagined four more adults and a baby living here.

Theresa winked. 'Yes, not so much space. Casia needs big space! No?'

'But still, they got their own flat?'

Theresa nodded. 'Bloody Communists good at two things. Schools and flats. Then David work in office in the coalmine and Jacinta is bookkeeper at the steelworks. So they have flat for four. Which has five with baby Piotr.' She grinned at Jacinta. 'But still Casia think Jacinta not as good. Is *snobbish* like the grandmama!'

Marie nodded, smiling. 'Casia's also snobbish about me.'

Jacinta spoke at length to Theresa.

Theresa said, 'Jacinta say to tell you before the first war the family had big house in Krakow. Very rich silver merchants and makers of instruments. Jews, of course. Casia nurse there to old Piotr. Casia not Jew, so helps Piotr's mother stay safe from bloody Germans. Only her. Then Casia nurse to David. So Casia very honoured in David's house. Even if old hen makes herself boss.'

Marie smiled and nodded to Jacinta. 'I understand.'

'Casia is boss!' said Jacinta suddenly.

Theresa clapped her hands. 'Bravo, Jacinta. You speak English!'

Jacinta stood up and embraced her friend. 'Now we go shopping to make dinner,' she said. 'Casia and baby eating.'

Theresa turned to Marie and hugged her too. 'Come again. Come for cake,' she said.

'I will,' said Marie. 'I will.' The warmth of Theresa's welcome and her stories had dissolved the cold of the morning and the unlooked-for humiliations of the crowded Zielinski flat. Now she no longer wanted to run back to Warsaw and catch the first plane home. She'd learned a lot this morning. Casia or no Casia, she'd stay here and find out more about Poland, about the Zielinskis. About everything.

★

Jacinta took Marie to the town centre to change her compulsory money coupons: twenty-two days at the obligatory fifteen dollars a day. 'Is eleven thousand zlotys,' said Jacinta. 'But in dollars twice as much.'

In fact even with dollars the money was worth very little, as there was nothing to buy. The stock in the shops on the main street was sparse: a few apples and vegetables; some scrawny chickens, for which you needed coupons. The bread shop had no bread, the café offered only black tea – no coffee, no cakes, no cocoa, no milk, no soap, no toothpaste. One grocery shop was empty apart from some jars of cucumbers. Jacinta held up a bottle of shampoo. 'Two weeks for money for this,' she said cheerfully.

In the end she bought a chicken, some eggs and apples and a cauliflower, all of which Marie insisted on paying for in dollars. They walked home arm in arm, Jacinta carrying one bag and Marie the other.

When they got back, Jacinta's father-in-law Alon Piotr was sitting smoking at the table, a newspaper spread in front of him. Jacinta said something, obviously about little Piotr, and he nodded at Casia's bedroom door and said something in reply. Then he turned to Marie and spoke in very good English. 'The old one insisted that I take Piotr's cot and put it in her room. Is now *jam-packed*.' His eyes went back to his newspaper.

Marie glanced sharply at Jacinta, who shrugged. 'Casia is boss,' she said. She looked at the clock on the wall. 'At three o'clock David home,' she said. 'I make dinner.' She went into the kitchen, leaving the door wide open.

Marie looked round the room. Something was very different. 'It's warm!' she said at last. 'The heating's on!'

Alon Piotr looked up again. 'The authorities have turned on the boilers.' He shrugged. 'They will turn them off again.'

Marie looked at him sitting there, composed and entirely self-contained. She remembered Theresa's stories. 'Theresa told me you were a flyer in the war. That you dropped bombs on Germany.'

He smiled. 'Theresa would say *bloody* Germany.'

She nodded. 'So she did.'

Jacinta came in with an ironed cloth over her arm and Alon Piotr moved himself, his paper and his pipe to the couch while she opened another leaf of the table and spread the cloth on it. She glanced across at Marie still standing there. 'You tired. You go rest.'

Marie blinked at her. It was true. She *was* tired. It had been exhausting, making sense of this place with its streets and buildings, its rationing and its empty shops, and these people with their intense, stoical lives, their eager, stumbling communication. She drifted into the bedroom, shut the door, put the chair against it, got undressed and jumped into bed, relishing the warmth. There was a space where young Piotr's bed had been. 'Oh Casia,' she muttered to herself. 'Squirrelling the child away so I don't get my dangerous hands on him. Shame on you!'

Marie was just drifting off to sleep when it occurred to her that it must be a relief for Jacinta to have her guest out of the way for a while. This situation would be a strain on her as well: spending the day with a stranger who only spoke two languages, one of which she did not know, the other of which she could barely stumble through. 'I'll have to do this every afternoon,' Marie muttered into her pillow. 'Come in here and give Jacinta a break.'

A Riding Game

A violent rattling on the bedroom door forced Marie awake. She sat bolt upright, not knowing where she was. England? Poland? Oh, Poland of course. Her face was freezing again; it felt as though it were made of petrified wood. The old man had been right. He said they would turn off the boilers again. They certainly had!

The door handle rattled harder, so she got into her dressing gown and pulled away the chair. The door was flung open and Casia charged past her, nearly knocking her over. She went to the chest of drawers, pulled out a pile of children's clothes and barged out again.

'Well thank you, Casia!' Marie said, replacing the chair.

She could hear the clink of dishes and the rumble of men's voices in the room next door, raised above the sound of the radio. David must be home from work. Even with the door closed, the atmosphere in the flat was entirely different. He made a difference. Marie pulled on her clothes again, selected a different scarf from her case, redid her French pleat, put on some lipstick and opened the door.

David was sitting on a chair, his leg straight out in front of him, with little Alon Piotr sitting astride his ankle, clinging to his father's hands as the leg went up and down. David sang in English:

> *Horsey horsey don't you stop!*
> *Just let your heels go clippety clop*
> *Tail go swish and wheels go round*
> *Giddyap we're homeward bound.*

David smiled across at Marie. '*Bonan tagan*, Marie.'

'*Bonan tagan*, David.' She glanced at old Alon Piotr and Jacinta and switched from Esperanto to English. 'That's an English game,' she said.

'My father played game with me,' David said. 'They were first words in English for me.'

Alon Piotr nodded. 'In the war I take holiday in Scotland. I stay with a very nice family with little children.'

'Horsey, Papa! Horsey!' demanded little Piotr. David obeyed and they all, except Casia, who was sulking in a chair by the window, joined in the song.

'Now sit!' commanded Jacinta. 'All sit at table!'

They sat round the table, now set with fine china and silver: another surprise for Marie in a day of surprises. Jacinta brought in a spicy red soup, then pancakes filled with bits of chicken with cauliflower on the side, then some kind of apple crumble. The portions were small. As she ate her way through the courses, Marie watched David, whose presence seemed to bind the rest together. He was like a beam of sunlight. Casia became less dark, old Alon Piotr became less silent and Jacinta was full of smiles. Marie herself felt better, admiring his strong face and easy grace with an artist's eye.

David asked her about having cake with Theresa and going to the town centre. 'So, you like your day today?' he said.

'Well, I liked being at Theresa's. She is funny. She made me laugh.'

They all laughed at this, except Casia, who muttered something. David spoke sharply to her and his father laughed.

'What did she say?' demanded Marie, made bold by the laughter.

Alon Piotr broke the silence that followed. 'The old madwoman says Theresa is prostitute, but what do madwomen know?'

David turned again to Marie. 'And what was there about Chorzow that surprised you?'

'There are some fine buildings.' She paused. 'Some powerful modern buildings. But I was surprised at just how empty the shops were. I can't see how anyone manages here. Harder even than the wartime in England.'

'It is hard,' said Alon Piotr. 'We can get cigarettes and

alcohol if we make long queues. But nothing else now. There are no goods. Russians still bleeding off our harvests. It cannot go on. Is crisis.'

'Things will change,' said David quietly. 'One day the Russians will get off our backs and their Communist friends will tumble away. Then things will change.'

Little Piotr suddenly pushed away Casia's hand with its spoonful of crumble and shouted, 'Horsey, Papa! Horsey!'

David stood up, held out his arms and the child leapt into them. Marie's heart missed a beat at the power of feeling between these two: the beautiful child and the loving father. Her fingers ached for her pencil so she could draw this moment, hold on to it for ever.

Then the noisy game started again and Casia went to her room to sulk. Alon Piotr got back to his paper and Marie helped Jacinta to clear the table and wash up. When everything was neat, Jacinta said. 'Come, Marie. Is news.'

David was sitting with a sleepy Piotr on his knee. Jacinta turned on the small television to scenes of lorries delivering coal to power stations, and factories busy producing washing powder, soap and sugar. David glanced at Marie. 'Is a new deal between Solidarity who organise workers and government. They say try to produce Polish goods from Polish raw materials. And . . .' He paused. 'Less imports from Russia. So our masters will not be pleased.'

'Bloody Russians!' said Marie.

'Just so.' He grinned. 'You learn much from our dear friend Theresa!'

'But is no good,' said Alon Piotr. 'No food now. People very worried.'

'I say things change. There will be a strike about food,' said David. 'Solidarity is a great worry to the government. Change will happen. Be certain of that.'

'Walesa is heading for jail,' growled his father. 'A hero, that man. You see, Marie?'

Marie knew from the English papers about Walesa, the leader of the Solidarity union. She tried to think of something to say, but just then the electricity went off and they were plunged into darkness. Little Piotr started to wail. Casia lurched out of her bedroom with a lighted candle, the very image of a hunched medieval ghost. She rescued the child from David and vanished with him into the tiny bedroom, taking the light with her.

Jacinta lit candles in the kitchen and brought them in. Alon Piotr took one and disappeared into his own bedroom. Sitting there in the cold with David and Jacinta, with just candles for light, Marie had a feeling of desolation, isolation. Then she realised that the other two could only go to bed when the sitting room was clear. She stood up. 'Thank you for a wonderful dinner, Jacinta. I am really tired now. I must go to bed.'

Jacinta gave her one of the candles and they murmured their good nights but did not urge her to stay.

Later, in the freezing bedroom, hunched in bed, Marie closed her eyes and once again saw David Zielinski with Piotr in his arms. She moved the candle a bit nearer, took her drawing pad and sketched the two of them, just as she saw them behind her eyes. She held the drawing nearer the candle. It was rough but it was true. Then she blew out the candle, threshed her legs around in the bed for a good time to warm the sheets by friction and snuggled down. Oddly enough, despite the fact that it was colder than the night before, she was not miserable. If Jacinta and David could endure it, so could she. They were fine, stoical people. She had a lot to learn from them. She closed her eyes, and just as she slipped into sleep she had a vision of the horsey game, with father and son making a great noise and mirroring each other's delight. Perhaps she would draw that.

The Passion of a Few Old Men

Alon Piotr Zielinski was something of a shadow in the Chorzow apartment, politely accommodated around the impenetrable routines of work, survival and the acquisition of food and cigarettes. The only times he emerged from the shadows were when he listened to music on his old record player, played poetry games with the child or fought strident battles with Casia. When these two old people were together, the rhythms of long-rehearsed argument beat clearly through their voices, even in a language that Marie did not understand.

Watching these encounters, Marie tried to imagine the old man in former times; when he was a child and Casia was the nursemaid who made his breakfasts and pushed his perambulator through the park area surrounding the city that they called the green ring in Krakow. Then, from the surface of Casia's wrinkled, enclosed mask, she tried to excavate the face of the middle-aged woman, then the younger woman, then the little girl in clogs from the country, trying to make a good impression in her first job. But the eyes that looked back at her were flinty, opaque, giving no clue to the history or personality walled behind them. The only time that face came to life was when Casia crooned wordless songs into little Piotr's ear because she wanted him to sleep. She could pull this off even when the little boy was lively and unwilling, when he fought hard against dropping off. The hypnotic voice held sway and the child was poleaxed into sleep. Marie observed that the old woman had great power.

On her third day in Chorzow, Alon Piotr invited Marie to go with him on his daily promenade to the café. 'I go for coffee. You come.' It was not a question; she could not refuse. She went into her bedroom and pulled on her red quilted jacket and fluffy red angora beret. When she came out, Alon Piotr was wearing a long air-force overcoat with shining buttons and a long scarf wound twice around his neck. He was pulling on a cap with ear flaps. She was already at the door when he held up a woollen scarf. 'Look very nice but too cold for the English,' he ordered. 'You need scarf.' He wrapped it around her neck. She could smell bread and cabbages and a faint background of flowery scent that told her it belonged to Jacinta.

They went down in the lift. After they had walked for a while, Alon Piotr took her arm and pulled her to sit down on a seat on the edge of the green area between the soaring blocks. He offered her a cigarette, which she refused. She did smoke from time to time but she knew how precious and rare cigarettes were in this country – always relished by the inch before being smoked to extinction. He stared at her for a moment, then delved into his deep pockets and brought out a boiled sweet. 'Something,' he said. 'Something for you. While I smoke.'

It dawned on Marie now that Alon Piotr had few problems with English. His voice was rough from the smoking and his accent was marked but he could certainly speak the language; better than David and probably better than Felix Wosniak, who flourished his virtuosity like a totem. 'Thank you, Alon Piotr,' she said. 'You're very kind.'

He waved a hand to dismiss the gratitude and lit his cigarette, drawing on it deeply. He coughed, then said, 'I see you many times looking at my old Casia.'

She could feel the colour staining her cheeks. 'I'm sorry, Alon Piotr. It's rude to stare like that.'

He laughed hoarsely. 'My Casia a tyrant. She is like Russia in one body. Always the same desire to be top. Like Russia she would control the air we breathe.'

Marie laughed at this. 'So Casia was your nanny? Jacinta told me.'

He drew again on his cigarette and looked down at the glowing tip. 'Casia was the daughter of the sister of our cook. She was beautiful when she was young, but a tyrant then also. Very bad temper. Her auntie feared her and so also did we.'

Marie pursued one thought. 'She was beautiful?'

He nodded. 'Also Casia had no fear. Fearless, you say. I feared my father but *she* did not fear him. When little I thought she was brave and beautiful, like a princess in a fairy tale.' The air shimmered between them, his cigarette smoke lingering before them in silken wreaths. He sighed. 'That was a different age, Marie. Those years between the first and the second wars, another world. At this great time Poland was a free nation. Only this time. A great democratic time.'

'And it will come again?' she ventured. 'The wireless . . .'

He smiled slightly. 'The people rise, eh? Make order in their own lives! The party men shake in their shoes in these days!'

'There is much talk of Solidarity . . .'

He shrugged. '*Solidarnosc?* The men in the café say for certain this is the time for Solidarity and the people's unions. Brides hang their flowers on factory gates. The unions sell food, build flats. It is a thing of the people, not of clever men. A thing of the heart, and strong men shiver before it. Communist Party men shake before the Solidarity bosses and Walesa. But it is not over yet. It could be prison for them. But prison no new thing here, you know? The Germans put us in prison, the Russians put us in prison. They put in prison my best friend Pavel, who fought the Nazis from the forests. Pavel was a hero. And betrayed by his own. But they do not change our hearts.' He drew hard on his cigarette, now halfway down its length. 'Like in Warsaw, at the steelworks here in Chorzow, most workers in Solidarity. They carry badges. Jacinta, David. Both have badges. Solidarity rises like the tide from the sea. It will happen. But . . .' He sighed. 'The Soviets are here, lodged in the minds of their little puppets in the government, and at our borders now, playing war games with their tanks.'

'So you think the Russians will put a stop to all this?'

He smiled again. 'Perhaps is more like I say. Real change in hearts and minds. Solidarity tide is force of nature. Like my old Casia.' He lit a second cigarette from the stump of the old one. 'It will prevail, even here in this city.'

Casia surged into Marie's mind again. She looked around at the towering blocks. 'But you didn't always live here, you and Casia and your family?'

He looked around and gestured with his cigarette. 'We live much different then, my family. We lived in fine apartment in the city of Krakow. An elegant life, you might say.' He paused, anger seeping into his voice. 'Spoiled first by the Germans, then those bloody Russians. But I tell you. That time in those years between the wars we were free. We knew freedom. With Solidarity it could again happen . . .' She had a glimpse of him now as a younger man, smooth faced, full of fierce energy, radiant with hope.

He fell into a brooding silence, which she broke with a question. 'And did you work there in Krakow when you were young?'

He shrugged. 'My father wanted me to be like him, a

worker in silver. Or like my grandfather, a maker of violins. My father had very fine hands. An artist. But I was still in school, at my studies, when the Germans rolled in and set up their evil game, hunting families like mine to their deaths, stealing their houses, their fine objects. So at my father's urging I walked out of one side of the city as the Germans rolled in the other.'

'Walked?'

'On foot, by train, in farmer's cart. Eventually England. Many Poles there. Like them I learned to fight, how to fly, to rid Europe of that vermin.'

'And your father, mother?' she ventured humbly.

'Well, Casia and her aunt, who were not of our faith, sheltered both of them for a while. But too dangerous for them, so my father surrendered himself and was put on a transport. My mother stayed with Casia and her aunt, pretending to be another aunt. She wore the clothes of the cook.' He chuckled. 'Casia fierce against the bloody Germans. My Casia.'

For a while they sat there on the bench watching two boys, well wrapped up against the cold, riding a single bicycle. The boys stopped the bicycle and stared at Marie. One said something to the other, and they both laughed and went on their way.

'What did they say?' she asked.

'They say you are foreigner like splash of fire.' He pointed to her red jacket. 'Only foreigners wear such colours.'

'I am sorry.'

He laughed. 'Wearing red not forbidden.'

'No. But your family . . .'

He shrugged. 'Is all history. We win by surviving.' He threw away the butt of his cigarette. 'And now we die of cold if we sit still too long. Come on.'

'So,' she said as they walked along, 'you were a flyer? In England? This is why you speak English so well.'

He smiled and tucked his arm through hers. 'Very young then. A boy. Many English friends. Sweet years. Vengeance on enemies can be very sweet. Then you and the Americans give Poland to the Russians and it all starts again. They make us educate our children and take care of us when we are sick, and in return we give them our minds, our souls and all natural wealth of our land. A devil's bargain, but it will be broken soon. Like I say. Soon we take it back.'

In the café, three old men sitting at a table got to their feet and, in turn, bowed over Marie's hand. They urged her to join them in drinking small cups of bitter coffee and eating grey bread. When she smiled and sat down, they settled down again and a gale of talk exploded around her, excluding her. She picked up *Walesa* and *Solidarnosc* several times but that was all. She sat back, sipped her second, privileged coffee and watched these old men. All of them, like Alon Piotr, had lived through deportations, savage war and two occupations. They had lived through the betrayal of friends by friends. And still – virtually starving in these times – they cared enough to argue the toss on this dreary October morning.

In the 1960s she herself had walked in protest against the atom bomb and the Vietnam War. She'd been proud of her involvement then, but all that now seemed effete, mannered, beside the passion and involvement of these few old men.

Good For Trade

The next day after breakfast the telephone rang. Jacinta took the call and turned round, smiling. 'Friend Felix get petrol. I not work. He come today and we visit him house.' She checked in her dictionary. 'A real *treat*. A *treat*!' She referred again to the dictionary. 'He fifteen kilometres away.'

Jacinta bustled Marie across to Theresa's flat to tell her the good news that they were to visit Felix in his car. When she heard his name, Theresa told Marie to watch the bloody old goat. Jacinta, not understanding the words but interpreting the tone, shook an admonishing finger at her friend.

Felix drew up in his small car at two o'clock precisely. Marie, peering out of the window high above the square, could see the cluster of children around the car. David had told her that the few people here who owned cars rarely had them on the road nowadays. Obtaining petrol was like coming upon hen's teeth. It was a privilege. 'Of course people like Felix . . .' David had shaken his head. 'They have contacts, influence . . .'

Even from eight floors up Felix looked dapper in a long wool coat and his fedora. He swept off his hat to reveal slicked-back hair, like Gregory Peck in a post-war movie. This dated him of course. This was the eighties, after all. These days in England men only wore such formal clothes for the office. For a jaunt like this even older men would wear corduroys and a sweater. Or even jeans.

When Felix entered the flat he reinforced the old-fashioned effect by clicking his heels and bowing over the hands of Marie and the flustered, blushing Jacinta. Then he shook hands with Alon Piotr, who, Marie thought, was rather stiff in his greeting. Like Theresa he did not seem to have much time for Felix.

Among the words the two men exchanged she picked out the name *Walesa*. Like the old men in the café, they were talking about the situation with Solidarity. At least she got this. How much one could communicate and understand with very few words.

Now Felix was bowing deeply to Casia, who wrested her hand from his and glared at him. Then he ruffled little Piotr's hair and turned back to Marie. 'And now, dear Miss Marie, I wish to extend the hospitality of my home to you.'

'And Jacinta,' she said. 'Jacinta too.'

'And the beautiful Jacinta, but is a new experience for Marie. Is not so, Jacinta? My dear wife Agnieska has made

Jacinta's favourite cake, and I have potatoes and *burak* – beetroot for you from my garden.'

Felix's car was an old East German model, clean and shining in the crisp October air. It had no heater, so Marie was very glad of the extra jumper under her padded coat and Jacinta's scarf that smelled of cabbages and bread.

Despite her padding, as the car made its stately way out of Chorzow, Marie slowly began to freeze. Around them the wide, unfenced countryside looked sad and deserted. To take her mind off the cold she thought of her conversation with Alon Piotr on the way back from the café, about how many farmers had given up working the land because the bloody Russians cheated them by not allowing them to make a profit.

In the front of the car, ignoring the cold, Felix and Jacinta were deep in conversation, their breath visible in the cold air. Jacinta was more animated than usual, clutching to her breast the rose in cellophane that she'd bought for Agnieska, Felix's wife.

Marie was comfortable with her own thoughts. Living in the small flat had its difficulties, the worst of which was trying not to get in other people's way every single hour of the day. Usually when she was travelling it was much easier than this. She was always put up in small hotels or inns where there were separate tables and one could keep oneself to oneself.

Now, as the car bumped along on the virtually empty road, she pushed her cold hands further up her sleeves and deliberately turned her thoughts to her mission here: 'to see buildings, and to find out about the Polish people.' Well, she was certainly finding out about some of the people. She'd seen and drawn buildings in Warsaw. Her sketchbook was nearly full. Here in Chorzow she had already drawn some of the apartment blocks and the kiosks, and was getting on with her job of getting to know this family. On the surface the Zielinskis were a simple working family, but – as she was finding out – there was no such thing as an ordinary family here. David Zielinski in particular, with his gaiety and his charm, was different from anyone she had ever met. And Casia, half witch now, had once been so beautiful. Alon Piotr, who had had such a complex life, stuck here in that tiny room, still passionate about politics. And Jacinta, pretty and kind and so innocent. To Marie now the Zielinski family seemed to be as complicated as the country's own history.

The car made its grinding way through a small hamlet of low farm buildings edging the road. A man, ploughing a field with furrows raised like corduroy etched with frost, stopped his horses and stood still to stare at them.

They drove on into a more urban setting. 'Here we are!' said Felix in English. It was a small town with two low-rise blocks at the centre, set beside a medieval church and, Marie noted, some eighteenth-century municipal build-ings. Felix drove around the centre, and told Marie about these buildings, before pulling into a parking space under-neath one of the apartment blocks. The car park was empty apart from a single other car in one of the neatly marked rectangles.

Inside the building the lift went up only two storeys and Felix led the way into a flat where the doors were wider, the rooms larger and taller than at the Zielinskis'. It was obvious to Marie that Felix's house was a good step up from that of David and Jacinta.

A middle-aged woman, tightly corseted into a kind of mother-of-the-bride frock, came to greet them. Her black hair, piled up on top of her head, was kept firm with shining lacquer. Her cheeks were a warm pink. But her eyes, when she turned to Marie with a smile, were coldly curious. Jacinta presented her with the rose and kissed her on both cheeks, and the other woman put her arm round her, murmuring to her in Polish. Jacinta looked like a rather bedraggled sparrow being mothered by a peacock.

'Here is my wife, Agnieska,' said Felix. 'And here is Miss Marie Mathéve.'

Agnieska barely touched Marie's hand.

'To sit!' Felix pushed Marie towards a table crossed by two runners embroidered like altar cloths. At their centre was a chocolate cake decorated with whirling butter icing. On each bare corner of the table was a saucer of chocolate buttons covered with sparkling hundreds and thousands. Marie wondered if the Polish name for this colourful dust was a direct translation.

Jacinta sat down and clapped her hands at the chocolate

cake and the sweets. She touched the edge of one of the saucers. There were no such luxuries in the Zielinksi flat. At Agnieska's bidding, Jacinta took a chocolate button, popped it into her mouth and sucked very thoughtfully before she said something to her hostess. Agnieska answered her and vanished into the kitchen.

Felix glanced at Marie. 'Jacinta says we must have a secret hoard of these things. But we are very careful.' He paused. 'And we have some good friends.'

Agnieska returned with a jug of coffee and some beakers sporting an abstract American design. Marie thought how crude they looked compared to Jacinta's old Polish china; surely Jacinta would not envy these too! But she did. She stroked their surface and made loud exclamations. As they ate, drank and talked, Marie's head started to buzz with the strong coffee and the rich chocolate cake that hit her palate like fireworks after the spare diet of this last week. She thought Felix must have a very special job. Or very good connections.

'You say you are a professor, Felix?' She was curious. Were teachers and professors so different compared with managers like David, or bookkeepers like Jacinta?

Felix laughed. 'So! I work with two jobs. I am professor at engineering college near here. And sometimes I work at garage repairing engines. This is old skill that I have from a young boy. Car engines. Motorbikes. Aeroplane engines. I always love these things.' He watched Marie finish her cake, then stood up. 'Well, Miss Marie, you and I will leave

Jacinta and Agnieska to eat their cake and talk of their children and I conduct you to my wonderful most special place. And show you a most special thing.'

'Another car?' Marie rose obediently, thinking of his garage work.

He laughed. 'No second car. What I have, Miss Marie, is much better than a car.' He pulled on his big overcoat, his scarf and his broad fedora. Marie threaded herself into her outdoor clothes. He spoke to Jacinta, who was now on her second piece of cake, and she nodded happily, her mouth full. 'We have Jacinta's permission,' he said. 'I tell her we go get her some potatoes for her cellar.'

They went down to the car park and Felix opened the car door for Marie and helped her inside. She was very conscious of his physical presence, sitting there beside her in the close space. She felt stifled by the drifting scent of pomade from his hair. She had a close-up view of his long fingers on the steering wheel, more those of a pianist than a mechanic.

As they drove through the small town he carefully enunciated its history and its re-emergence under the strict development plans of the current Communist regime. He pointed out his college, a smart squat building near the centre, saying, 'Is very fine place.' In five minutes they were on the outskirts of the town, alongside a grey canal edged on both sides by a patchwork of small gardens, each with its own neat fence and hut. He parked the car at the far edge of the patchwork and led the way along paths, raising his hat to various individuals working here, who all returned his greetings with great politeness. Every garden was neatly turned over except where crops – mostly potatoes and cabbages now – were still growing. It reminded Marie of allotments near her home – though those were rather less neat, making an untidy foreground to a glorious distant view of her city's cathedral.

Felix opened the gate to his own plot, which was larger than the others and even neater. In the middle of the patch were two beehives, like twin turrets rising from the dug-over soil. There were raised beds to one side, with the tops of some kind of broccoli showing and the frothy leaves of beetroot. Beside these were row upon row of potatoes still to dig up. In the far corner was a hut in layered birch with a wooden tiled roof and a porch that had been extended to accommodate a deck with a seat. On each side of the arched door were identical windows with flowered curtains. It could have been the witch's house from 'Hansel and Gretel'. Marie's fingers itched anew for her drawing pad. Felix took out a large key and opened the door wide. 'Come! We will warm ourselves before we labour over the potatoes.'

One of the walls inside was neatly hung with tools. Below them was a work bench with two different sizes of vice. Beside a basket of logs in the corner was an iron stove, its steel chimney climbing up through the roof. Beside that was an unlikely mahogany wardrobe and a kind of chaise longue with tartan rugs thrown over it. Marie wondered in passing how they got hold of Scottish tartan rugs here in Poland.

Felix knelt, set light to the wood chips and paper in the stove and sat back on his heels as it flared and crackled. Once it was away he pressed two chunky logs into the heart of it and put a metal jug on the top.

'There,' he said. 'We have a nice fire, and coffee after our labours.'

Labours? What was he on about?

'Now we harvest potatoes,' he said.

We? Marie looked at her neat Clarks shoes; her thick Aristoc tights.

'Here!' He rooted in the bottom of the wardrobe and produced two pairs of wellingtons, one large and black, one smaller and green. 'We must not spoil our beautiful shoes!'

He took off his own shoes and pulled on the black boots, and, feeling helpless, Marie did the same with the green. She noted the care with which Felix folded his trousers on the crease to tuck them into his wellingtons. She noticed again the long fingers that did not look like the fingers of an engineer.

'Now!' He handed her two smallish sacks and kept two for himself. Then he picked up a large, well-used spade and led the way down through his garden to the potato patch. There he set about digging up the potatoes, brushing off the soil and filling the sacks that Marie held out for him. It was only when all four sacks were full that he stood up.

'There! Is a job done. One sack for Jacinta, one for

Agnieska and two for . . . who knows? Potatoes are always welcome in these days. Good for trade.' He lifted two sacks by the corners, as though they were rabbits' ears. He held them clear of his neat overcoat. 'We carry them like this.'

She tried to do the same, but could only carry one. And even then she had to clutch it to her rather than hold it out. 'No matter,' he said kindly. 'I will return for the other one.'

She trundled hers awkwardly back to the hut, conscious of the damp muddy canvas brushing her chest and thighs, suppressing her anger at this man for somehow forcing her to do something she would never have done at home. She felt wretched and filthy and even colder now than when she had been in the car.

After the chill of the garden, the hut – now hot from the blazing stove – was a welcome relief. They put the bags by the door and Felix took off his gloves and put them on a rack above the stove. He came to Marie and peeled hers off her frozen hands.

'Dry in no time!' He beamed. 'Now take off coat and we will brush off mud. You are very messy girl. First dry, then brush!'

She obeyed. She felt like a child, reprimanded.

Felix hung their coats on hooks beside the stove. 'Now sit!' he said. He poured coffee into two mugs. Marie wrapped her hands round hers and sat on the edge of the couch beside the healing warmth of the hot iron stove. He reached into the wardrobe and brought out a bottle and glasses. 'First coffee, now vodka!' he said. 'Very warm. Not the rotting-gut kind you get in Chorzow; this pure Russian.' He held the two glasses in one hand and half filled them with the gleaming translucent liquid. 'Nectar in garden!' he declared, then handed Marie a glass. She put down her mug and took it. It was no use protesting in this place that she didn't drink. In fact at that point she would have taken anything to banish the chill that had seeped into her bones on the potato patch.

Felix held his glass high. 'To Poland!' he said and drank. He held up his glass again. 'To Great Britain!' he said. And again. 'Polska!'

Marie held up her own glass. 'To Poland!' She gulped the vodka, allowing it to run around her mouth like velvet and down her throat like fire. Then she said, 'Great Britain!' and thought it odd how she'd never toasted her own country in this way, and how even now, even here, in this Polish garden hut, it felt ridiculous. What the hell! She gulped the rest of the glass and relished the glow that was spreading through her.

He refilled their glasses. 'Now! I will show you photographs.'

Her mind, quite fuddled, wondered passively whether they would be photographs of naked ladies. She would not be surprised. She wondered what she could do about that, but could not think of a single thing. Her insides were in turmoil. If he tried it on with her she'd just have to slap him. Or kick him. Something.

He reached into the cupboard, drew out a big papier maché box and came to sit beside her. He proceeded to show her photographs of his garden through the seasons: lupins up to your shoulder; sunflowers as high as the hut; small pink roses growing against the front fence; grapes with a velvet bloom clustering the fence between his garden and his neighbour's. Some of the photographs had been touched up with colour, but most, of course, were in black and white. Even these, though, blazed in colour in Marie's imagination. They were quite beautiful.

Up to now she'd been treading on eggshells with Felix, wondering what on earth he was really about. In the last year she'd enjoyed the correspondence between them, but since they'd met in the flesh his vaguely predatory manner had unsettled her. Now she found herself softening to him. He might be a spy, a black marketeer, a Communist government toady. Maybe that was what he'd chosen to do to survive. But a man who loved his flowers and plants like this could not be all bad, surely. She began to relax.

When they got back to Felix's flat with their bags of potatoes, the cake had been demolished and the chocolate buttons had gone, except for a few crackling in cellophane, rescued by Jacinta for little Piotr. In minutes they were all saying their goodbyes. Marie could feel no warmth or fellow feeling from Agnieska, who made her goodbyes quite formally, her eyes as cold as ever.

They bundled themselves into the car, with Marie in

the back with the potatoes. She was pleased again that Jacinta was in the front, chattering away to Felix. Her head was still woozy and she rested it gently on the high back of the seat. She remembered how churned up she'd felt in the garden hut. Then she realised that it was not just Felix that was churning her up. It was this whole thing: Poland; the cold; the strange perpetual hunger; and David Zielinski. Then, as they bumped along in the fading light, she dreamed of little Piotr eating his bright sweets, his face smeared with chocolate, his white hair gleaming.

Marie in Krakow

On my second Friday in Chorzow, David Zielinski as well as Jacinta had a free day from his work – as a consequence of some political thing I didn't quite understand. A strike over canteen changes, I think. To be honest I found David's presence so close in the flat a little disturbing, so it was something of a relief when he was out at work. When Jacinta was also at work, I could wander round the town with my camera and sketchbook, have coffee with Alon Piotr and his buddies and – when Casia was asleep – play games with Piotr and teach him some English words.

But still I was pleased and touched when David suggested we make a visit to Krakow. 'Is wonderful to visit,' he said. 'Many fine buildings. Old and even older! You draw in your book.' He turned and spoke to Jacinta, but she shook her head, throwing her hands up into the air, talking earnestly all the time.

He turned to me. 'Jacinta, she stay at home and clean for

tomorrow. Boy Piotr's birthday comes and for him we have party. Jacinta cleans flat and makes food.' He smiled knowingly. 'And she must fight Casia because old lady does not want party for Piotr.'

I could see Casia through the door of the kitchen, where she was washing Piotr, who was standing naked before her on a stool. Alon Piotr was hunched over yesterday's newspaper. He looked up. 'There is to be a general strike on the twenty-fourth. And Walesa is still in Paris, stuck there by a strike of French workers.' He smiled thinly. 'Ironic, perhaps?' Again I noticed that his English was smoother, better, than David's, although David's had a softer timbre. He had a wonderful singing voice. I knew this from the singing games he played with little Piotr.

'So, Alon Piotr, will you not come to Krakow with us?' I asked David's father. At that moment I wished he would.

The old man shook his head. 'Me, I have *seen* Krakow! I was *born* in Krakow. I *lived* in Krakow. Is a very old, holy city. Once the capital of all Poland. Many churches. The world even has Krakovian Pope in these days. A great man at the present time. But in the days when I lived there as a boy, Krakow had many Synagogues. It was a great city when I was small. Beautiful! Civilised. A city of merchants and scholars, artists and musicians. But the bloody Germans put paid to that.' His voice faded a little. He seemed about to say something but then shrugged. 'There is little to see in Krakow these days. It is a shell. The soul of Krakow has gone up in smoke, thanks to the bloody Germans. No! Me,

I stay here in dirty old Chorzow and discuss today's important news with my friends in the café.' His head went back down over his paper.

So it was just David and I who made the journey, first on the grinding tram to Katowice, then by train to Krakow. The adventure began as soon as we set off: the tram ahead of us broke down and our tram, creaking and squealing, had to push it slowly as far as a branch line. Even so, we arrived at the bustling rail station in time for the nine o'clock train to Krakow. Standing there, looking around, I felt conspicuous and aggressively jolly in my red anorak among so many greys and browns, like a robin among house sparrows. Like a shriek among murmurs. The only bright things around me were shining pale faces and the occasional thatch of golden hair.

When we got to our train I thought at first it was too full, but David led the way to an empty carriage. This, he told me, was a special carriage for invalids and mothers, but as no invalids or mothers had turned up, we might as well take the seats. I looked around, worried that one of the military-looking policemen with guns would interpret our actions as suspicious. But the two nearest took no notice of us, being more interested in a young man sprawled on the floor who looked dead drunk. They stood around looking at him as though he were a new species of human being.

The train was stately rather than speedy, and our journey took two and a half hours. Much of the time David and I sat in companionable silence while I watched the Polish countryside race by and scribbled a drawing in my notebook of Piotr sitting on Casia's knee.

David smiled and nodded, touching my book with his finger. 'To the life,' he said. 'To the life.'

The landscape streaming by was so different from the jumble of small fields that I was used to at home. Here the fields were feudal, long and narrow, the neatest of them ploughed for winter, laid out like a parquet floor. Some land, though, was grown over, unworked. I remembered what Alon Piotr had said about the farmers being disheartened by the eastern export of their crops and being forced to work for nothing. As he said, 'Is more profitable to work in the steelworks or the mines for a wage.'

Finally the train drew towards Krakow and we could see the grey sky weighed down on the landscape, welded to the earth by the layers of lead-laden air above steelworks and factories.

David nodded towards these sprawling sites as we passed through them. 'Our Russian masters and their Communist puppets encouraged these great industries to turn us all to worker ants. But they create . . .' He scrabbled in his dictionary. '*Incubus. Trojan horse.* We worker ants now join together and turn against our masters. We become Solidarity and change things. The Communist puppets are in retreat.'

As we walked from the station into the centre of Krakow, David took my arm. Of course it was only good manners, but the gesture made me feel exultant, welded into this place, this family. And the buildings, oh the buildings! Compared with its own industrial outskirts and with the functional architecture of Chorzow, this beautiful city was intoxicating – from the fairy-tale castle we could see on a great mound above the city to the broad central square surrounded by graceful old houses that told a thousand years of architectural history.

On the edge of the square, an old woman in a blue homespun skirt and a bright kerchief was selling paper flowers. Her stall was set out by the statue of Adama Mickiewicz – who was some sort of Casanova figure, according to David. 'And my namesake! Adama David is my birth name,' he said, rolling his eyes. I laughed with him, relishing the clasp of his hand on my upper arm.

As we walked, David related the city's seven-hundred-year history as an eastern bastion of trade and commerce. I made him stop so I could draw one of the baroque mansions with its magnificent carriage-size doorway that edged the dusty pavements of the enormous square – called Adolf Hitler Platz during the war, according to David.

'And here,' he said, turning me round like a magician revealing a miracle, 'is Sukiennice, the Drapers' Hall!'

You could not miss it. The elaborate Renaissance building with its colonnades and its decorations delicate as icing on a cake dominated even this enormous square. We could have been in Venice. David played the schoolmaster, talking as I drew the Drapers' Hall. 'In fifteenth century Krakow a great capital. In those times came merchants from the east and from the west. They make business here at the Sukiennice. They barter for spices, silk, leather, wax and many other things.'

Lecture and drawing finished, we walked on. As I turned each corner I kept catching my breath with pleasure, my fingers reaching all the time for my notebook.

'It is all so beautiful!' I said that too many times, I think.

David was amused. 'It is not beautiful,' he finally protested. 'It is a thing of fading beauty.'

To defuse the embarrassment of my enthusiasm I asked David about the possibility of a proper cup of coffee. Living at the Zielinskis' flat, real coffee was a rare luxury: we mostly drank sour substitutes that resembled dishwater more than anything else. The coffee at Felix's house had been an exception.

'Coffee? Your wish is my command!' David led the way to an elegant coffee house under the Drapers' Hall. It might have been elegant, and it smelled of coffee, but like every other place in those days they were short of the stuff and each customer was confined to half a glass. Seeing our crestfallen faces, the waiter vanished and brought us a silver plate of small cakes like golden discs. He bowed. 'Good old England!' he declared. We laughed and, I have to admit, wolfed down every one of the cakes.

After that we explored the booths of the hand-workers in the arcade underneath the Drapers' Hall. I'd hoped to find some woven or embroidered goods, which I'd often sought on my travels elsewhere. But many of the booths were closed and dark, and the only things for sale were a few quite fine wooden plates and carvings, and a bit of leather and metal work. The leather was very expensive but I did find a wooden carving of an aeroplane that, despite David's protests, I bought with dollars as a birthday present for little Piotr. It was a wonderful thing, intricately carved from a single piece of wood and immaculately painted in dark red and green. Loose inside the cockpit was a pilot, who must have been carved *in situ*. It was a very clever piece of work.

As we continued our walk around the town, the shortages even in Krakow became clearer. One smart shoeshop displayed a single elegant shoe in a perfectly dressed window. We peeped inside, but there was nothing there except the other shoe. We came back out on to the pavement and began to laugh hysterically until we had to clutch each other to stay upright. I have never acted so childishly, not even when I was a child. People walked round us, staring in amazement. One or two of them even smiled.

It took us some minutes to recover our dignity and walk on, David's arm round my shoulder. He wanted to buy the local Krakow newspaper, which was famous for its political perspective, to take back to Alon Piotr, but these were only available if you could prove you lived in the city. We tried to buy candles, but they too were only for Krakow residents. The city was so beautiful and ancient, but in matters of political fact Krakow presented the same picture as Chorzow – empty shops and long queues for anything that was off the ration. David shook his head at all this. 'Is like stories of wartime in Britain, you will think.'

Still, the great square was gay now with the stalls of the flowersellers. David explained that these were especially fine because November the first was All Saints' Day, when everyone put flowers and candles on the family graves. 'There are always flowers here in the square. Is tradition.'

I bought a great bunch of carnations, freesias and orchids for Jacinta, who, David said, always kept the All Saints' custom and would put flowers on her parents' graves this as every year.

He answered my unasked question with a shake of the head. 'My family have graves here no more. Destroyed like everything else by the bloody Germans.' His face darkened. 'Some of our people, you know, were made to walk on the gravestones of their ancestors to their deaths.' Then he hugged me closer and smiled. 'But we do not come here to weep! Paintings you like?'

He led the way back to the art gallery in the Drapers' Hall. Lined with marble, it showed off nineteenth-century Polish paintings – huge, with lots of writhing figures and horses. I enjoyed more some smaller landscapes from the turn of the century, which reminded me of French paintings I'd seen in the Louvre. David shook his head. 'Many of our fine paintings were lost to Krakow because of the Nazi looting.'

Then, with me carrying the bouquet like a bride, we

walked up through the town to visit the castle on Wawel Hill but only got as far as the courtyard because the castle was closed for repairs. I stood there, flooded suddenly with sadness. That said it all for me: Poland was indeed 'closed for repairs'. But now I was struck by the thought that Walesa and his bold comrades, with this new wave of quiet people like David and Jacinta at their backs, were beginning to force open the doors to that castle. This outrageously sentimental thought brought tears to my eyes.

David put a hand on my cheek. 'What is it, Marie? Tears after so much laughter? Is only an old castle, dear lady! Come! You cry because you are hungry. We find food.' He grabbed my flower-free arm and said, 'You have dollars, so we go finest restaurant. Finest!' He pulled me along and we started to run.

Once inside the restaurant, with its ornate marble-lined lobby and its sweeping staircase, we were met by a scar-faced, gold-braided commissionaire, who told us that the place was full but we might wait. For twenty minutes we sat submissively on a plush sofa and watched resentfully as the commissionaire fended off some people and let others march straight inside.

Finally David stood up. 'We will go another place!' He took my arm and marched me out, and with my arm closely through his, he led the way down a side street to a cramped little Hungarian restaurant. The interior was very dark and each table had a small guttering candle to supplement dim side lights that clung desperately to the deep red walls. Someone, somewhere, was sawing away at a violin, and every table was occupied by murmuring customers, some still in their work clothes.

When he saw my dollars, the manager found us a table and produced a very decent bottle of Hungarian red wine. He brought me a special chair for my flowers and smiled at us benevolently. He obviously thought us a very romantic couple. I could see why this was, as we sat at the table with the bouquet as the third guest.

We were not so lucky, however, on the meat front. All we were offered was the single choice of very peppery thick pancakes with mushrooms, accompanied by a side salad. We had drunk just one glass of wine and were still waiting for our pancakes when David did something very odd. He leaned over and took my hand and said, 'Is good you are here at this time, Marie. These are better times. But I watch you, Marie, and now I know you. You are the face of freedom, the epitome of elegance and civilisation.' His face broke into a smile that had the sun in it. '*Epitome!* I look that up in my dictionary. Today. Before breakfast!'

I let my hand stay where it was, feeling warm and happy but not quite knowing what to say. I was rescued by the waiter, who brought the steaming pancakes and a carafe of water, all of which he placed with a flourish and then bowed. '*Bon appetit, monsieur et madame!*' he beamed.

'French!' I picked up my knife and fork, pleased to have something neutral to say. 'I thought this was a Hungarian restaurant.'

David grinned. 'Is it not always very chic to be French with matters regarding food?' Then he tucked into his pancake with relish and I relaxed. Perhaps I had imagined that strange remark about me being the *epitome* of elegance!

As we ate, I asked David about his friend Felix with his grand apartment and fruitful garden. 'Felix seems very well placed. Those things must be a privilege here. He seems to have a . . . could I say *luckier* life,' I said.

David shot me a cautious glance. 'Old Felix is very clever man. Works hard,' he said.

'*You* work hard! Jacinta works hard!' I protested.

'But Felix good with party men. He fix their cars. Finds goods for people with . . .' He dug in his pocket for his dictionary. '*Influence*. Felix is cunning. He will change his hat when the changes come.'

'I noticed that your father is . . . well, not so warm with Felix.' Even as I said the words I wondered whether I was crossing a line, being more curious than polite.

'Ah, yes.' He demolished the last of his pancake. 'My father and Felix Wosniak are old comrades. They were flyers together in England.'

I was surprised. 'Together? Felix is younger than Alon Piotr . . .'

'Aha! Felix *older*!' David poured out the last of the wine. 'I say to you Felix clever. Good food, no smoking, dyes hair, digs garden. Very fit. Looks young. My father has much harder life.'

I thought of Felix dispensing vodka in his garden shed.

I remembered his unctuous manner. 'So they are friends? Your father and Felix?'

He gulped his wine. 'Not so much friends. My father admired Felix. Young hero when they fly together. Then these two heroes come back to Poland's shame of the camps and this affair of our Jewish people, a disgrace pushed on the Polish people by the bloody Germans. Polish are great heroes in war. Also many, many Polish dead. Then something happens – I do not know what thing happens – and Alon Piotr does not like Felix. Something about the partisans after the war. But still Felix comes to our house, he flatters Jacinta, he brings cakes, potatoes as though they are a . . .'

'A penance?'

'What it is I am not sure. But it feels like reparation. My father is cynical about it.'

Suddenly there was a hollow space in the conversation where nothing could be said. I gave David notes to pay the bill. He came back flourishing a parcel. 'Manager give candles and coffee!' he said. 'For dollar he sell us candles and coffee. Jacinta pleased.' United in our pleasure for his wife, my friend, we went out of the café, blinking in the sudden sunlight.

We stood there a second and David turned to me. 'Give me two dollars, Marie!' I obeyed and he vanished round a corner. He was back in a minute, walking alongside a car: some unfamiliar Russian make in petrol blue. 'We take taxi!' he said, and opened the door to help me in.

We sat in the back of the taxi, hand in hand, as it drove back up through the centre of Krakow, past Wawel Castle again and through the green ring that surrounded the old city, to a graceful street in what must have once been a superior district. It was now rather down at heel and dusty but its fine brickwork and elegant pediments located it in the late eighteenth century, when money and craft, here as in England, combined to make cities elegant environments for the new entrepreneurs.

David was peering through the taxi window, obviously looking for a certain building. He made the driver slow down. Then he told him to stop beside a four-storey house with a broad central doorway that had a pediment of sunflowers carved in stone. The peeling blue paint on the door could not disguise its fine carving and good proportions.

We got out of the car and David looked up at the building. I knew just what he was going to say. 'My many times great-grandfather built this whole block, Marie. One time a single house. And they lived here, you know. As far as my grandparents and my father. And Casia and her aunt the cook. I come here with my father to visit when I was small boy. He wish that I see where he was born.' He pointed to some tall windows on the second floor. 'They lived in that apartment.' Then he pointed to a narrow window at the far end. 'And that was where he was born; he slept there with Casia. He tells me this.'

Just as I was thinking of something to say, the door of

the house opened and a man in military uniform charged out, obviously in a hurry. His cap was too large, his tunic buttons were not done up and he carried a bulging briefcase. He rapped out a question at David, who gestured towards his grandparents' apartment, then held his hand out to me and smiled. The soldier stared at us, one to the other. Then he grinned, said something, rooted in his pocket, produced a single key and threw it to David, who caught it neatly.

The soldier strode away down the street, the last vestige of a military swagger in his untidy demeanour.

'What did you say?' I demanded.

'I say you are American and are visiting Krakow and wish to see the house of your grandparents.' He grinned. 'I also said I try to please you, so you will make love with me. So he gives me his key.'

I shivered, a ghost walking over my grave. 'What if he'd asked for our papers? We could have ended up in jail.'

He shrugged. 'I do not think so in these times. The military men are very careful now, in this time between masters. And this one, his mind is full of more big things today.' He called something across to the taxi driver, who turned off his engine and took out a packet of cigarettes. 'Now, Miss Marie Mathéve, I show you the house of my ancestors, who lived here for many hundreds of years, even before, when it was a single house.'

Through the door was a large courtyard with a sweeping stone staircase. Beneath the staircase were large bins and what seemed like acres of neatly stacked wood. We climbed the steps and made our way along to the second doorway. The key turned smoothly in the lock. The door opened into a large hallway decorated with a Greek frieze. There were many rooms in this apartment. You could have fitted the whole of David's Chorzow flat just in the salon that looked over the street. There were other rooms: one for dining, one for business, two rooms for sleeping and other bedrooms and salons half empty or piled with furniture. The floors were wide planks of very old wood, polished to the colour of honey. The furniture was a mixture of big old pieces and some smaller, modern American-style pieces that were dwarfed, out of place, here in these tall rooms. In the three main living rooms there were magnificent chandeliers of dusty Bohemian crystal. We gazed at them, entranced. 'Exquisite,' I said. 'They must have been here always. When your father was a small boy. And his father.'

'He cannot see them now,' he said sadly. 'He cannot tell us.'

'I know!' I scrabbled in my bag for my drawing book and quickly, quickly, drew the smallest of the chandeliers, that hung in the dining room. Then I drew the windows and the ornate doorway. From memory I drew the table in the Hungarian restaurant with the bunch of flowers sitting in its chair like a guest.

After a while David wandered away and as I drew I could hear him making his way through the empty rooms, opening doors, dragging furniture. By the time he came back I had finished, and he peered over my shoulder and exclaimed at what he saw. He kissed me on both cheeks. 'Is magic drawing, Marie. Magic! Everything to life.'

Then he grabbed my hand and dragged me once more through the apartment to a room at the far end of the wide corridor. 'Here is my grandfather's room. His nursery, I think you say.'

It was a long, thin room, as tall as the others but much narrower. There were bars on the window. Shoved in the corner was a kind of chaise longue covered with purple velvet. David picked up the edge of this. 'I find this cloth in a cupboard,' he said. 'Is curtains, I think. Very soft.' And he pulled me by the hand so that he and I were sitting side by side on the chaise. Then we were kissing and tearing at each other, seeking the silken feel of each other's skin. Soon we were lying together very snugly, wrapped around each other and I didn't have time to worry about not knowing the Polish word for virgin.

In the taxi on the way back to the railway station the two of us sat in sweet, stunned silence. In Alon Piotr's nursery I had not needed to blurt out my unbroken state to David, because by some alchemy he'd known, and joined with me in discovering a rather shocking, wonderful part of myself that I'd never recognised before. So what happened was a kind of tough epiphany. While we were making love I had no idea whether I loved David or not. But I knew this was right, right for me and perhaps even right for him.

For this one time. Just this time.

As we made our quiet way back through the apartment and down the stone staircase, I thought I should feel embarrassed or guilty, but I felt neither. It truly seemed that while I was here in this country, real life – normal life with its constraints, its intricate moral compulsions – had been suspended. I was no threat to Jacinta or even to David. My presence here was merely a passing incident in their more important lives. But now I knew that they were important to me, as was Poland itself. I had gone to Poland as one person and would return as another.

I knew that this epiphany happened to many people in their teens or twenties. I had had to wait until I was thirty-seven, but the change was complete. There was a before and there was an after. And nothing was ever the same.

Before we got on the train to Katowice, David put his arms round me and kissed me and for a second we clung together tightly in an embrace we knew would have to last us for the rest of our lives. 'Is a secret, Marie,' he said sadly. 'But I never forget.'

I pulled away. 'A special thing, David. A day in Krakow.' I tried to smile up at him, then turned away to climb up on to the train.

So our joyful adventure in Krakow was sealed off, separate. When we returned to the Chorzow flat it was as though nothing had happened. Not by a touch or a look during the rest of my stay did we betray our secret. Sometimes I would feel his gaze on me. And sometimes I would look at him when I thought he wasn't watching. I had to be content with that, and I knew that David was too. The cleverest part of the deception was that in the following days we were easy, not stiff or guilty together. That strange spark of passion lit in the nursery in Krakow could stay, glowing, in its secret place.

When we finally got back to the flat, Jacinta was excited by her flowers and candles and thrilled at the wooden aeroplane (shown secretly to her in the kitchen – little Piotr was asleep with Casia in her bedroom). David told her all about our day in Krakow and – including his father in this – of our visit to the house of his grandparents. He made a very funny imitation of the soldier who gave us the key, which made us all laugh. Then Jacinta went into the kitchen to make coffee from our precious new hoard and we all relaxed.

That was when David said, 'Show my father, Marie. Show him your drawings.' He turned to Alon Piotr. 'Marie make drawing for you.'

I handed the drawing book to Alon Piotr and he put on his glasses to examine it carefully. Then he smiled faintly. 'Yes. The same. The windows. The door. The chandelier. The same thing. In my house.'

Very carefully I tore out the page from the book and gave it to him.

That was when Alon Piotr looked at me, full in the face, and it was as though he knew; he knew everything that had happened to David and me in his grandparents' house. The corners of his mouth twitched. 'It is the same thing,' he repeated. 'A beautiful thing.' Then he repeated his son's word. 'Magic!' he said.

David put the television on, and after watching the latest stilted headlines about the political situation, we drank the superb coffee with much relish and watched endless speeches by ministers in response to written questions from journalists. Alon Piotr watched intently, occasionally nodding his head, sometimes shouting angrily at the screen. After that it was a relief to watch an old American film called *Our Town*, even though it was dubbed and therefore unintelligible to me.

Later, just before I fell asleep, I hugged myself and decided that I had just experienced a perfect day and that that was how it would stay: a sparkling bubble of experience – right out of time, with no past and no future. I had learned about David, about myself, and something about love. It had been the best day of my life, without any exception.

The Fledgling

I was not used to children's parties. The truth is that up till that day I'd never attended one, not even my own. My best experience of celebration up to then was a chorus of 'Happy Birthday' from my primary class and the right to sit beside my teacher at the dining table.

It's not that I had any regrets. At home my mother would make my favourite trifle, sing me nursery rhymes and, when I was older, songs from *The Sound of Music* or *The Jungle Book*. She had a very sweet voice. Of course there were presents – drawing books and crayons at first, paints and pastels later. There would always be a bound book – beautifully wrapped – about painters or artists or buildings of the world. I still own these books: they are the foundation of my present collection.

Life with my mother was a closed world: a convent of two, with Mum as the mother superior and me as the novice. In time, this life of secret grace set me apart – I was labelled as a quaint child, very reserved, the apple of her mother's eye. When I found myself among other children I felt out of place, irritated by their whining and bad manners. As I grew older I settled for the more congenial company of my mother, and my teachers and tutors.

The leap from such a convent to normal life with men was a big one. My first real romance was with my art tutor at college. He was a professional sculptor, married, with five children. He had plenty of functional sex in his life, but no romance. With me he enjoyed lots of lip-kissing, hand-holding, mildly urgent petting and that was all. The curfews imposed by his wife coincided with those apologetically set by my mother, who by then was not well and confined to the house.

This first experience with him set the pattern for my romances that survived even my mother's death, when I became top – and only – woman in our little convent. The fact that I didn't long for sex at any cost did not feel like a problem. My hours were filled with drawing and painting for my local university course. Even before I graduated I began to draw and catalogue little-known buildings in the county, a pastime that led eventually to my career as a buildings inspector. My neat reports became models of public accountability and eventually had national impact. I am not boasting: this is a fact.

I was not stupid enough to think I was normal. It was not normal for a reasonably attractive woman not to have a fiancé or husband. I realised that, despite a degree of worldly success, it was weird to reach thirty – then thirty-five – with such a limited sexual repertoire. In some ways this was hilarious if it hadn't been so limiting. So as I got older, I started to turn down long-term commitment from some very sweet and suitable men because, among other things, I was embarrassed at the thought of their faces when they discovered I was a virgin. A virgin at eighteen, lovely. A virgin at thirty-five. Yaargh!

But now, when I thought about it none of these men, sweet as they were, was David Zielinski. I suppose there has to be one special one, and my bad luck was to meet mine at the wrong time in the wrong place.

It's hardly surprising that these thoughts were still churning round in my brain on the day after my visit to Krakow, the morning of the birthday of Piotr Zielinski. But little Piotr himself also inspired these thoughts. Here was a child as confined by the old crone, the once beautiful Casia, as I was by my beautiful mother: unfledged quite beyond the age of flying. On Piotr's birthday I remember thinking that in the unlikely event of my having children of my own, I would never confine them in this way. They would be fledged very early.

On the morning of the party, after emerging for breakfast, Casia took Piotr back to her bedroom to play with the leather monkey, now his firm favourite. At first there was chuckling and sounds of play, then silence. Casia had obviously practised her sleep magic on him.

Alon Piotr and David went off together to the café.

They invited me to join them. David's urgent, encouraging smile was very sweet but I wanted to stay and help Jacinta. This was not from guilt at yesterday's events. That was a thing apart and always would be. I just wanted to help her, to be with her, to be part of this celebration, to learn how it was done, to enjoy a birthday party for the first time in my life.

But of course Jacinta didn't need my help. I just perched on the arm of the sofa, watching as she went about her birthday tasks with the stately grace of a temple maiden. She'd done Piotr proud. The flat was spotless and shining. She'd divided the flowers David and I brought back from Krakow between two crystal vases, saving a small garland to drape above the Mary icon. I imagined she would recycle all of these at the end of the month to put on the graves of her parents. Of course, I would be gone by then.

The table, with both wings raised, dominated the little sitting room. Jacinta spread it with an embroidered satin cloth and laid it with the old painted china and silver cutlery. At its centre was a chocolate cake, produced as if by magic from the depths of her freezer.

'Chocolate!' I exclaimed. 'Impossible!'

She beamed. 'Agnieska! She make it. Felix bring. I put in freezer.' She ran into the kitchen and brought out a calendar and pointed to the month of September. 'This time.' (Yet another gift of penance from Felix?) Jacinta had frozen it and saved it for this day.

On one side of the cake she placed a crystal dish

containing a simple dainty apple cake and on the other a painted platter with apple and potato cakes. (I had seen the boxes of apples – mostly wizened now – in Jacinta's ground-floor store, alongside the potatoes and beetroot supplied by Felix. Such things, at least, were not in short supply.) On the kitchen stove a pan of purplish-red borscht was simmering, a pile of china soup dishes warming beside it.

Jacinta was a true genius, making a feast of such simple fare.

She beckoned me into the kitchen and I watched as she tipped a bowl of shredded cabbage into the soup. When that had wilted down she dipped in a clean spoon, tasted it herself and gave it to me to taste. It had the sweetness of the beetroot and onion and a bite somewhere that I could not identify. 'Good!' I said. 'Tastes good!'

She shook her head. 'Not right. No meat. No carrot.'

'It's very good, I tell you!'

'Theresa bring *kwasna smietena* . . .' She frowned and grabbed David's battered dictionary. 'Is *sour cream*. Better.'

At that point the men came back, bringing the chill of the outside world with them. Side by side, it struck me how alike they were. Both faces ruddy with the autumn cold, eyes bright, their hair – one blond and one grey – pearled with rain. Both of them beamed lovingly across at me. I think they had drunk more than coffee.

Alon Piotr roared, 'Is there a party in this house?'

David looked under the table. 'Someone has a party here! Where is he?'

Alon Piotr banged on Casia's door and called something to her in a voice full of authority. The door opened
and Casia emerged with Piotr, rosy from sleep, on her hip.
The child's eyes widened when he saw the table and he
clapped his hands. David took him from Casia. 'Sleep?'
he said in English. 'No sleeping on a man's birthday, eh,
Marie?'

Casia closed the door behind her and stood before it
like a statue. Alon Piotr took her arm and led her quite
gently to a chair by the table, telling her to sit, sit! Then
suddenly the room was full of people. Theresa burst in, her
china jug of sour cream covered by a cloth; after her came
(I learned) her daughter and the daughter's little girl; then
an older woman I did not know who Alon Piotr said was
his cousin. A minute later Felix arrived, flourishing a bottle
of vodka, followed by Agnieska holding aloft a big glass jar
of chocolate buttons. The children squealed and the adults
clapped.

Theresa's daughter went out on to the landing
and brought in folding chairs and we all squeezed round
the table, Piotr sitting on his father's knee. Jacinta handed
round bowls of the borscht, now enhanced by a generous
dollop of sour cream, and everyone tucked in. It was
delicious: the sour cream cleared it of the taste of
earth.

When we had finished that, and Jacinta had cleared the
bowls and dishes, there was a silence. I wondered what
would happen now. Then everyone sang, the deep men's

tones blending with the lighter voices of the women and the piping tones of the children.

Sto lat, sto lat, niech zyje, zyje nam!
Jeszcze raz, jeszcze raz, niech zyje, zyje nam!

Everyone clapped and I joined in. David smiled and sang to me in English. '*For a hundred years may he live for us.*'

I nodded. 'That sounds very good.'

He kissed Piotr on the cheek and I touched my own cheek with my fingers, remembering David's kiss of yesterday. 'Now, my son!' he said in English. 'Marie has present for Piotr. Not so?'

I squeezed across to the bedroom and brought out the package and the card I'd made for him. It was a brightly coloured drawing of his block of flats with a banner across the top saying *Happy Birthday Piotr!* in English. The adults all murmured in appreciation but Piotr, more interested in the package, energetically ripped off the tissue paper. When the aeroplane emerged there were even louder shouts and applause from everyone except Casia. Alon Piotr was beaming from ear to ear.

Piotr held the plane high and made it fly in front of him, making buzzing noises. Then he brought it closer and when he saw the little pilot inside he squealed with delight. '*Dziadek! Dziadek!*' he said.

David glanced at me. 'Yes, Piotr,' he said. 'Is Grandpa!'

Alon Piotr was lighting a cigarette. 'Or is Felix?' His tone was ironic.

Felix looked across sharply at him at this.

Piotr shook his head. '*Dziadek! Dziadek!*'

Then Jacinta was handing around apple cakes and dumplings, and Felix was pouring vodka into glasses he'd brought with him. We were on to our third glass when Jacinta finally cut and shared the chocolate birthday cake and another cheer went up and everyone sang again, wishing that Piotr might indeed live for them for a hundred years.

After her fourth vodka Casia fell asleep with her head on the table and the children climbed down with the jar of chocolate buttons to play under the table with the aeroplane and the leather monkey.

And me? I sat on with these beloved strangers, as they murmured and laughed in a language I could not understand. Now and then my eyes met those of David Zielinski, who had changed my world. I felt comfortable and quite at home, pleased that my first ever experience of a birthday party had been here with these people, who, despite the troubled and scarred state of their lives, had welcomed me with passion and kindness.

The rest of the evening was a bit misty. The vodka of course . . . I remember Felix clutching my hand rather too tightly at one point. I remember begging David to sing a Polish love song. And I do remember singing 'A Spoonful of Sugar' and 'The Bare Necessities' to wild applause. Even the children mimicked the choruses. I remember David carrying Casia to her bedroom and coming back to stand with his arm round Jacinta to sing another rousing song. I remember someone murmuring as they tucked me into bed. I think it was Alon Piotr.

Then velvet, humming darkness.

Part Three

Sam 2004

The Big Lad

The label on the door said *Sam Rogers*. Adam knocked and it opened a crack. Round bright eyes stared at him from under a jet-black fringe. 'Yeah?'

He blushed. He hadn't expected a girl, not in a men's hall, not on this first day. He'd just put the phone down on his mother, making the lame excuse that someone was knocking on his door. Now he'd knocked on his neighbour's door to make the lie a half-truth. 'I was . . .' He hesitated. 'I just arrived. I thought I'd give you . . . him . . . a knock.'

'Rachel!' a voice bellowed from inside. 'Open the fucking door, will you? Two more heads and you'd be Cerberus.'

She opened the door wider. 'Come in, won't you? *Sam* has spoken.' She stood back to let him in. She was small, barely up to his breastbone, her head just a little large for her slight body. Her thick fringe covered a bulging brow above a kitten face – the eyes wide and round, the nose small. All she was wearing – as far as he could tell – was a man's oversize T-shirt. Her small feet were bare.

The boy, sitting Buddha-like on the bed, was massive: big boned and just the right side of fat, with ragged putty-coloured hair and a two-day growth of beard. He was off the bed in one leap and Adam's hand was engulfed in his larger one. He grinned, showing crooked, slightly yellow teeth. 'Ignore her, son. Gets a bit above herself, does our Rachel. Daddy owns half of Shropshire and the girl has a brain as big as an aeroplane and thinks that gives her the right to rule the world.' He was still grasping Adam's hand. 'Sam Rogers, me! Welcome to heaven.' He reached out to put a heavy arm round the girl's shoulders. 'And this is Rachel Miriam. Rachel, not Ray, if you don't mind. Otherwise Miss Hyper Active. Miss Hyper Bole. Sometimes Miss Take if you're not careful.'

The girl wrestled herself free and looked up at the boy called Sam with the tolerant affection of a mother for her child. 'That being so, you should take care, darling Sam.'

Adam broke in. 'I'm Adam Mathéve. I just got here.'

Sam Rogers laughed. 'Why, man, Mathéve! Now that's posh, isn't it, Rachel pet? Nearly as posh as *Miriam*.' He surveyed Adam head to toe. 'Funny surname, *Miriam*. Who'd 've thought of a first name for a second name? Like I told her when I first saw her on that Bali beach, it has to be posh, a first name for a second name, dunnit?'

His tones were very, very familiar. Adam put his head on one side. 'I think you might come from my neck of the woods.'

Sam put his head on one side too. 'I think you might come from my neck of the woods.' He was a very exact mimic. 'Mebbe the posher end?'

This made Adam laugh and Sam joined in, each laugh igniting another until they were both laughing hysterically. Rachel folded her arms and stared at them. 'Northern *oiks*!' she said glumly. 'Trust me to get mixed up with northern *oiks*.'

Adam felt included. She was putting him and this big lad in a pair and saying she was mixed up with them. He wasn't alone now.

'Take a pew,' said Sam, resuming his Buddha pose on the bed. Rachel sat on the floor with her back to the wall, facing him.

Adam looked around and then sat on the desk, with his feet on the desk chair. He glanced from one to the other. They both seemed old: years older than him. 'Are you second years, then? How d'you know each other?

They exchanged glances and laughed. 'No, first year. Long arm of coincidence,' said Rachel.

'Me having this year out, like,' said Sam. 'In downtown Hong Kong. Bar full of English and Aussies, half of them stoned. Boring, you know? Then I spot Miss Hyper Bole here sitting in a corner sucking her thumb, reading Jack Kerouac. Then she's standing on the table reading from it, them hanging on to her every word. Cool or what? Two nights and we were best friends for ever.'

'Kerouac was always a good gig,' said Rachel complacently. 'Two *days* and two nights, actually. Then Sam and I went our separate ways. I go places further east with packs on my back. End up in Bali and who do I bump into? Lover boy here!'

'It was fate, man! Never were souls so mated,' minced Sam, rolling his eyes. 'But then she went further south, I went north and our souls were torn apart.'

'Then yesterday? In reception?' drawled Rachel. 'It was like Bali all over again. I trip over a rucksack, prepare to send the dolt to Hades, and who is it. The Brobdingnagian!'

'Not that she's interested in me any more,' said Sam mournfully.

She jumped on the bed, sat in front of him in a mirror Buddha pose and said, 'Do you think, darling boy, northern lad, that I should saddle myself with a great galoot like you, with all these books to read and all these lovely boys and girls to pick through?'

He punched her shoulder. 'So, *Miss* Hyper Bole! What was last night about, then?'

'It was about the east and the light on the South China Sea. It was about reading Kerouac in Bali.'

'So . . . nothing?'

'So . . . friendship, dearest darling Brob. Better than anything, friendship. I'll be pushing you about in a wheelchair when you are old and grey. Or you me. That's what friendship is.'

He took her shoulders gently, then brought her towards him and kissed her nose. 'That's a relief! I thought I'd be stuck with you here – one of those endless dreary college twosomes, playing houses in hall. You know?'

She drew her small fist back and punched his shoulder. 'Oh you . . . northern peasant! You . . . imbecile!' She jumped off the bed, ripped off the T-shirt and started to pick up clothes off the floor and get dressed. It was the first time Adam had ever seen a girl naked, in real life rather than on a TV or video screen. Her head and body were more in balance without clothes. Apart from white bikini bands on her skin, she was the colour of toffee. She clipped on a tiny bra and pants that didn't quite cover the arc of her bottom. Then she lay flat on the ground to zip up her jeans, arching her back to fasten the button.

Adam crossed his legs to disguise his hard-on.

Sam laughed. 'Steady now, lad. You'll have to get used to old Rachel. No inhibitions, these posh lasses. I put it down to single-sex schools.'

Rachel pulled on a corduroy jacket that looked like an Oxfam find, picked up a battered leather bag and beamed at them both. 'Now you enjoy yourselves, children. I'm going off to St Ag's to see what female delights await me.'

The door banged behind her and Adam looked at Sam. 'Now that one's a firecracker.'

Sam grinned. 'Isn't she? Could buy and sell us ten times

over, son. And I don't just mean in money!' He leapt up off the bed. 'How about you and me going down the Union? Or into town? You gotta car?'

Adam laughed. 'Me? You must be joking!'

'No joke. Young Rachel's got one. And that's no joke either.'

'It's funny, that name. Rachel Miriam.'

'Rachel Miriam Wiener, full name. But she just uses the first two. Jewish, isn't she?' said Sam. 'She's in the Bible. "*And Miriam the prophetess, the sister of Aaron, took a timbrel in her hand; and all the women went out after her with timbrels and with dances. And Miriam sang unto them: Sing ye to the LORD, for He is highly exalted: the horse and his rider hath He thrown into the sea.*" That was when Moses parted the Red Sea.'

Adam blinked. 'Very erudite, that.'

Sam laughed. 'Gotcha! Thought you got a hippy heathen on your hands, dincha?'

'So what is it that I *have* got?'

Sam looped his scarf round his neck. 'You've got an ex-Christian, hippy, heathen, working-class archaeologist-stroke-theologist.'

'So you know the Bible, then?'

'Backwards. My mam's a big Methodist. I knew chunks of the Bible by heart before I was six. Was declaiming from the pulpit when I was seven. Converting people, even.'

'But not now?'

Sam shook his head. 'Not since I was seventeen.'

'And is she mad, your mam, 'cos you've given all that up?'

Sam's shrug seemed to ripple through the room. 'Me mam might be mad with religious mania, but she's not angry, if that's what you mean. She worries about me immortal soul but she loves the earthly body of me, so we get on. And I have to tell you, when I became a heretic my dad was relieved to have another sinner around.' He opened the door. 'No rampant Christians in your house then?'

Adam shook his head. 'There's just my mother, and she's a buildings inspector.'

'Buildings inspector! Christ!'

For some reason this made them both laugh. They walked through the campus towards the main building, a stately home that now housed all the administration. A building out the back, which had been the dairy and laundry, was home to the Union. They laughed a lot as they made their way there. Adam laughed when Sam told him he was going to do a theology degree. 'No point in wasting all that learning by heart, is there? Or maybe I'll do archaeology – theology in stone, after all.'

Sam laughed when Adam told him about the crap band he ran at school. 'So you didn't bring your guitar? Wise move. Too many talentless oiks around toting guitars.'

Adam laughed when Sam told him he'd tried to join the rowing club. 'There was this sniffy lad told me I was too heavy, I'd sink the boat. I told him they should get me a

Viking vessel. I joined the Archaeology Soc. instead. So I'm a digger. A big digger.'

Years afterwards, in his cell, when he was thinking about his time with Sam, Adam realised that by the time they got to the Union on that first day, the laughter between them had sealed their friendship and, indeed, sealed his own fate.

In the Union the smoky bar was heaving; voices shrill, excited, everyone 'on broadcast' in Freshers' Week. At this time new encounters could set the pattern of your term, or your year, or in some cases, like Adam's, your life.

Sam quickly colonised a piece of wall and leaned up against it. Adam pushed his way through the crowd to get some beer. When he returned (with four bottles – saving a trip – and two plastic tumblers), three people had connected with Sam, two girls and a boy. They made space for Adam and continued to talk about themselves: who they were, where they had come from, what courses they were about to do. Adam handed Sam his two bottles and tumbler and leaned on the wall beside him, not really listening to the chatter.

His eyes wandered towards the bar and in the steamed-up mirror behind the optics he caught sight of a tall girl with long fair hair in a loose pigtail down her back, standing looking lost between two groups of people in the crowd round the bar. She reminded him of Marie. Clutching his bottles he made his way towards her. 'Hello!' he shouted. 'On your own?'

She smiled faintly and moved to speak in his ear. 'Seems like. I can't even get a drink. Thought I should come down here. But . . .' She looked round at the throng.

He held up a bottle. 'I've got a spare one.'

'Lucky you!'

He thrust it into her hand. 'It's for you,' he shouted. Then he said in her ear, 'Oh Christ. Impossible to talk.' He took her hand and dragged her outside and they wandered across to the main building and found a deep windowsill, where they sat and sipped their beer. He told her a little about himself and she told him a lot about herself. She said she was at St Ag's and he wondered if she had met Rachel Miriam.

It was twelve when he let himself quietly back into his room. In a second there was a knock on the door and Sam danced in, singing a syncopated version of 'Tea For Two'. He sat on the desk chair. 'Score, then, son?'

Adam coloured. 'None of your business,' he said.

Sam laughed. 'You're right! Mind your own business, Sam.'

Adam said, 'Did you? Score?'

Sam shrugged his enormous shrug. 'Not the object of the evening, son. Just sussing the place out. Safety in numbers.'

Adam surrendered. 'Me and her just talked. And I walked her back to Ag's.'

'Looker!' said Sam. 'You go for blondes then? Bet your ma's a blonde.'

'Don't talk stupid,' said Adam. 'Anyway, haven't you a bed to go to?'

Sam reached inside his shirt and produced a quarter bottle of cheap Polish vodka. 'Thought we'd just top off the day, son. Gotta glass?'

It was a good way to end his first day here: drinking vodka out of his coffee mug with his friend Sam Rogers: in retrospect, a moment of perfect happiness.

Easter Dig

Adam retied his bandanna around his sweating brow and looked across at Sam, who was sitting in the shade of a piece of canvas hoisted like a sail above him. His wide-brimmed straw hat had slipped down over his nose. Adam called over, 'Don't know how you keep so cool, Sam. I'm losing water like a leaky kettle.'

Sam pushed up his hat a little and surveyed him. 'Inner chill, lad, inner chill. That, and the fact that I've got plenty of flesh to displace the water.'

'Fat people usually sweat more.'

Sam flicked a pebble at him. 'Not fat! When they bullied us at school my mam always told us to tell them I was just well made.' His hat slid down again, covering his eyes. 'Not that they bullied us for long.'

Adam looked down the site, wondering why he'd let Sam persuade him to come on this Cyprus dig. Of course his mother had been very enthusiastic when she heard about it, had taken out the notebook from her own expedition and showed him her drawings. She'd photocopied some of them and marked the copies up with things he should look for. Sam had whistled when he saw these and said that was cool, having a ma who knew about architraves and ashlars, bulwarks and brackets. 'All my mam is good for is Genesis, Leviticus and Deuteronomy!'

'My mother has her downsides,' said Adam. But he was pleased that Sam was impressed.

'Mams all have downsides, man. That's what mothers are for. Haven't you read your Freud?' His eyes closed again.

Now bored with Sam, who seemed only to want to sleep, Adam looked down at the three shelved trenches filled with crouching volunteers, wielding scrapers and brushes with the delicacy of surgeons.

In the ten days of the dig the volunteers had fallen into two groups: one comprised the graduate students from the same Cambridge college as the expedition leader, Joseph; the other consisted of everyone else – a mixed bag of students from other places, career volunteers and middle-aged hippy travellers who thought it might be a blast to handle something that was a thousand years old.

Rachel Miriam was ten feet away from him, under another sail, working at the 'finds' table with the tutor Joseph, making first labels for the artefacts that were emerging from the trenches. At this distance, in her enormous straw hat and in this white light that rendered her pure shadow, she looked a bit like a mushroom. She'd been getting on very well with this Joseph, a dry, erudite man in his forties. She frequently joined him in his tent after dark, returning to the tent she shared with Sam and Adam in the early hours, smelling of hash and euphoric with erudite knowledge and the last ripples of sexual feeling.

Sam grumbled that it was all too gross to think about and left her to it. Adam was not so complacent, revolted by the thought of Rachel's delicate body entwined with the dried-up husk of such an old man. Sam told him he should mind his own business. Rachel was a mate and Adam was gross even thinking like that.

Now, somehow drawn by his thoughts, Rachel put down her notebook and strolled across. Her arms and legs, burnt to a shade of light walnut, were veiled in a sheen of dust, and her small paw-like hands were ingrained with dirt. 'Well!' Her round kitten eyes moved from Adam to Sam and back again.

Sam shoved back his straw hat. 'Well what?' he said.

'Joseph says you lazy oiks should get up off your arses and get some work done.'

Sam lit a cigarette. 'Tell him to fuck off,' he growled. 'Adam and me started half an hour before the others. But then he wouldn't know that, would he? He was catching up on lost sleep, like you.'

She shrugged. 'Don't shoot the messenger, darling.'

Adam stared at her feet, bare except for the thong of her sandals. She had perfect feet. 'Don't know what you see in him!' The words exploded from him. 'He's an old man. Must be forty-five.'

'Adam, man!' Sam said.

Rachel drew herself to her full height and looked up at Adam. 'Adam, darling, I've known you for six months and I've loved you since we first met. I always thought we'd be mates for ever. But if ever, *ever*, you blast your mouth off about me and what I do, that's it! We're finished, I promise you.' She turned and stumped off, raising ancient Cypriot dust as she did so.

Sam stood up, fanned himself with his straw hat and then used it to dust off the soil still sticking to his knees. 'Told you, man! There are rules, and you just broke one. Now let's dig! Show these Cambridge boys what red-brick lads can do.'

That night Rachel didn't go to Joseph's tent. She came to the tent she shared with Sam and Adam, bringing joints she'd bought from the hippies. The three of them drank retsina and smoked till the early hours. They didn't say very much; just shared a few jokes. Rachel sang a Scottish folk song in her throaty voice. But mostly they laughed and let silence rule between them.

Adam woke in the early hours and crawled out of the tent for some fresh night air. He could see nothing. The whole campsite was buried in deep, unrelieved darkness. He thought it was worth coming halfway across the world to experience this enormous, undisturbed dark. It made you think about the beginning of the world and its very end. Then the thought struck him that his mother must have experienced this endless, powerful darkness many times. But she had never talked to him about it, about how it made her feel. Why had she not told him about this? He wishes she had told him, about this dark. Tears fell down his cheeks and he sniffed them away. He told himself they were not unhappy tears. It was the after-effect of the hash and the alcohol. They were just tears.

He crawled back into the tent and on to his mat. He was just drifting off to sleep when the thought occurred to him that he loved these two people who were snuffling and snoring in the tent on either side of him. He loved Sam and Rachel equally. He loved the body and the brains of both of them. He loved their very souls.

Then he decided that this slushy sentimentality was another after-effect of the hash and the alcohol, so he turned over and fell fast asleep.

An Easter Vigil

'Home sweet home!' Sam heaved his laden rucksack over the gate and looked up at his house: an east Durham council house with narrow windows painted pale green, its front garden down to shaved grass. 'Come on, son! Let's do the gig!'

They'd flown into Newcastle airport in the early hours and made their way here by a series of buses. Rachel had flown direct to London. 'Got to see the old dears, oh beloved,' she said to Sam. 'Otherwise they'll pine.' She had been brought up by loving and indulgent grandparents about whom she told extravagant tales, but it was clear she adored them and they her.

From his back pocket Sam fished out the bunch of keys that had been the cause of a full body search at the airport. In vain had he told the customs official that collecting keys was his lifetime hobby and having nineteen keys on a ring was not so odd. The officer told him that these days you could never tell what was odd or not. *He* knew that Sam wasn't a terrorist, '. . . but better safe than sorry, eh, son?' he had said.

Now Sam selected the house key and opened his door. Adam blinked. The hall and staircase were carpeted in a strident deep orange and the walls were vibrant lime green. His own mother would have shuddered at the sight of it.

A voice called from the back of the house. 'That you, Sam?'

'Yeah. It's me, Mam.' Sam pushed both their rucksacks into the under-stairs cupboard, leaving the hall pristine, and led the way through the hall to the kitchen.

Sam's mother was sitting at the square kitchen table, a cup in her hand and a leather-bound book propped up on a marmalade jar in front of her. She looked up and smiled. '*Then spake the Lord to Paul in the night by a vision, Be not afraid, but speak, and hold not thy peace. For I am with thee, and no man shall set on thee to hurt thee: for I have much people in this city.*' She smiled broadly. 'Hello, son. St Paul was in Greece, you know. I prayed for you while you were there.'

'We were in Cyprus, not Greece. Hi, Mam!' Sam leaned down and kissed her hair and she put a hand out and touched his arm.

'Blessings of Jesus on you, son,' she said. Then she stood up and held out a hand. 'And this must be Adam. Well, Adam, it was nice thinking that our Sam had a friend there working with him. Ecclesiastes says it all: *Two are better than one; because they have a good reward for their labour. For if they fall, the one will lift up his fellow: but woe to him that is alone when he falleth; for he hath not another to help him up.'*

The hand that gripped Adam's was smooth and firm. What surprised Adam was not the religious stuff, but just how young Sam's mother was. She was tall – nearly as tall as Sam – but slender. With her face scrubbed clean as rose marble and her hair looped back in a curly ponytail, she could have been twenty. She looked young enough to be Marie's daughter.

Her glance strayed longingly to her Bible then politely back to the boys.

'Dad down the shed?' said Sam.

She smiled at him, relieved. 'What do you think?'

The garden path was plain concrete; the garden just grass: no flowers or shrubs. No borders. The shed at the end was large, with a dusty window. Smoke trailed from its metal chimney and a TV aerial stuck out at an odd angle from the roof.

'Sam . . .?' said Adam.

'Don't ask!' said Sam.

Sam's dad was sitting beside an iron stove on a battered armchair reading the *Racing Post* with his feet up on a stool. The walls of the shed were a blaze of colour: one wall was covered with a collage of images cut from Sunday supplements – mountain scenes, seascapes, quaint villages and towns in eastern Europe. Another was devoted to famous faces, from Winston Churchill to Bono, from John Lennon to Tony Blair, from John F. Kennedy to Stan Laurel.

Half of the third wall was engulfed in cuttings of horses and riders with newspaper captions. One battered black-and-white image was captioned *Arkle to Sparkle Over the Hurdles*. The other half was devoted to the faces of beautiful, nameless women, all fully dressed.

Sam's father leapt up from his chair, grinning. 'This has gotta be Adam! How do, son! Our Sam wrote to us about you.' He grasped Adam's hand. 'Joe Rogers,' he said. 'Greece all right, was it?'

'Cyprus,' said Sam. 'It was Cyprus.'

Adam was gulping back another surprise. Mr Rogers was big and ungainly, and apart from his reddish hair he was Sam's double. And like his wife, he was shockingly young. He looked in his mid-thirties and could have been Sam's brother.

Mr Rogers looked round. 'I've got some Coke here if you want a drink?'

Sam shook his head. 'Thanks, Dad. Me and Adam are unpacking, then I'm showing him the sights. Dorcas Woods and the old bridge. Then mebbe the Smelter's Arms.'

Mr Rogers sat down again. 'Mebbe I'll see you down there. I'm going down the street to put a few bob on some dead certs and might look in the Smelter's for a couple. I'll get a bite to eat. You'd be well advised to do that too. Nothing in the fridge down home, like. Your mam's too busy. She's going down the meeting at teatime. Sorting themselves out for the Easter vigil.'

'Vigil?' said Adam.

Sam clapped him on the shoulder. 'All Greek to you, son, innit?' Then he chanted, '*The women saw how his body was laid; and they prepared spices and ointments; and rested the sabbath day according to the commandment.* Luke 23:55 to 56. Mam and her mates sit with their prayers and thoughts from dusk through the hours of darkness waiting for the day of resurrection. Magnificent, really.'

'Did you ever do that? Keep vigil at Easter?'

'Oh yeah, I did it till I was thirteen. Even then, Dad here came to collect me after two hours.'

Mr Rogers sat back in his chair. 'Enough's as good as a feast, like. I always say that.' He picked up his paper. 'His mam never minded. She's good like that.' He rustled his paper and his eye dropped to the back page.

Sam grinned down at him. 'Right! See you, Dad.'

Mr Rogers nodded. 'See you, son. You too, Adam. Nice to meet you.'

They made their way back to the house, skirted round Mrs Rogers, now on her knees praying in the kitchen, and climbed the narrow stairs to Sam's cell-like room. Adam finally spoke: a statement that was really a question. 'Interesting people, your mam and dad. Your mam looks so . . . young.'

Sam was half in and half out of a clean pair of jeans, his hairy, ham-like thighs filling half the space. 'Ha! I knew that would get you.'

'I mean,' said Adam, 'your Mam's so young I thought

you must be adopted. And then I saw your dad and knew I was wrong. You don't half look like him.'

With an effort Sam hauled together the waist of his jeans and zipped them up. 'Well I think Mam keeps young because Jesus blesses her every day. And Dad – it's gotta be that the horses keep him up to scratch.' He grinned, pleased at his own play on words.

'Sam . . .'

'Nah, just joking. They were married when they were sixteen, on Mam's sixteenth birthday. She hadn't found Jesus then. Bit of a naughty girl, I think. A month later she had me and I nearly died. The legend is I was a sickly, puling shrimp. And then, according to her, Jesus spoke in her ear and told her to fear not as he was with her. So she feared not and me, I got better, and He's been with her ever since. I don't think He said *Feed the brute!* But that's what she did, and I've been a big bugger ever since. Lucky for me she gave up cooking for Jesus when I was fifteen, or I'd be a mountain now.'

'And your dad?'

'Wisest man I know, mate. Built his life around her 'cos he loves her, but has never let her swallow him. He has his life. Horses and that. She doesn't try to convert him.' Sam pulled on a long corduroy coat. 'Come on, mate. First Dorcas Wood then the town. Have I got treats in store for you, son!' He looked around the room. 'You'll have to sleep on the floor in here. Spare bedroom is Mam's sanctuary. You know the score. Crucifix, picture of Christ with a bleeding heart in spite of her methodist stuff. Single chair. You don't want to go there. Last thing you want for a good night's sleep, mate, is a tortured man looking down on you.'

The two of them spent the afternoon exploring the woodland up above the town, yelling so that the echo of their voices pinged from tree to tree, swinging on an ancient rope swing that had survived from Sam's childhood. The swing broke when Sam had a try today, but luckily he was not over the water and just came down with a savage thump on to the grass. He took out his pen knife and carved SORRY! into the tree. After that they made their way through the town, picking up beefburgers on the way and passing Sam's primary and secondary schools, both of which were sunk in their Saturday silence.

They reached the Smelter's Arms at six o'clock to find Mr Rogers in a corner behind a pint of beer and a pile of sausage, mash and peas. He waved a hand. 'Sit down, lads!' He nodded towards the bar. 'I ordered you the same for when you came through the door. Now then! Tell us about digging history in Greece. Or was it Cyprus? Sounds good, that. Wouldn't mind a bash myself. I've got those two old books down the shed, Sam. Remember? A life of Sir Mortimer Wheeler and this little book of his called *Still Digging*. Now there *was* an archaeologist, son, never mind your ultrasound techniques on the telly!' He looked up over his fork at Adam. 'It's reading those books that turned our Sam away from Jesus and into Digging. Got his nose into them, and the rest is history.'

'Aw, Dad,' said Sam. 'Shurrup and eat your dinner.'

The three of them got home at ten to a silent, empty house and went straight to bed. Later, twisting and turning on the hard floor, Adam reflected on the relish with which his friend had watched him throughout the day, as all his patronising preconceptions of cosy Durham working-class lives came crashing down. He was a devil, that Sam Rogers.

He was woken by the smell of bacon. Sam's bed was empty. He followed the mouth-watering smell downstairs and found Sam in the kitchen setting the table and his mother standing at the stove. She turned to him, her face radiant. '*Jesus Christ is risen today*!' she said. 'Now, do you want fried bread with your breakfast, or just plain?'

Gathering Rosebuds

In the second year of his degree, Adam decided against a module subtitled 'Galleons and Caravans' and – with Sam and Rachel – opted for a sociology module taught by Janet Gallagher, a young tutor who was popular with the students and reminded him of his mother. Later when he'd had a drink with her, he had to admit she was not in the least like his mother. She was more short sighted, more thickset, more voluble and more fun.

She had a twinkle in her eye when, in her first seminar about the structures and functions of society, she asked her gathered students what they thought the functions of a university might be. She nodded encouragingly as individuals offered ideas about discipline, knowledge, skills, society's need for future doctors, lawyers and engineers. 'But what else?' she demanded. 'What else?'

They fell silent.

Sam said, 'To keep lecturers in work, maybe?'

She grinned. 'You've got something there. But . . . what else?'

Silence.

'It's an introduction agency!' she said, a note of victory in her voice. 'It's a whole raft of arranged marriages. Men and women, men and men, women and women, sorted by background, intelligence and achievement, presented to each other on a plate. There will be a good deal of trying on for size, but more life or long-term partnerships are fixed at university than by any other single means. You see? The structure of the university functions for society in making sure that like attracts like.'

There were jeers and cheers at this and it took quite a while for the room to settle down before she got down to her lecture proper.

In Adam's view, the idea was solid. He'd observed this relationship mart blossoming all around him – students pairing off, playing house, breaking off and starting again. He'd been tempted himself a couple of times, with girls he'd come close to. It was a small step from spending three nights a week over in your girlfriend's rooms, or cooking pasta for her, to moving in altogether. But when the adventure of the sex wore off, the alarm bells started to ring and he'd always cried off.

He was comfortable enough in the flat he now shared with Rachel and Sam. The fact that both he and Sam were half in love with Rachel brought them closer rather than driving them apart. It didn't really register with him that he himself might be half in love with Sam. The most difficult thing he had to handle in their shared life together was Rachel's casual habit of nudity. Sam would joke that he'd not mind going nude himself but he needed some kind of cover for the unexpected hard-on at the sight of Rachel's smooth brown skin and button-like breasts. 'Brothers and sisters?' he joked with Adam one day. 'Incest, more like.' But neither of them objected about her nudity to Rachel herself – far too uncool. One of the first lessons Adam learned.

Then, as his second year unfolded, Adam embarked on a three-month affair with Janet Gallagher. Both of them paid lip-service to the principle of discretion, but this situation was not unique on the campus. In the seminar room and the corridors Janet was cool, even offhand with him. Then, after lectures, they would drive in her car into the country and have drinks or a quick meal at a pub, before racing back to Janet's flat to spend the afternoon in bed. Her attitude to sex was expert and interesting, and she really saw the joke of it all, which was a big turn-on.

Afterwards, when he was desperate to go to sleep and she was on a post-orgasmic high, she would keep him awake by declaiming what she called self-evident truths about the nature of society, interspersed with comic pornographic poems. When he finally dropped off, she would run a manicured fingernail along his thigh and slide down under the sheet to help him get hard so that the whole thing could happen again.

Unusually for him, Sam disapproved of this relationship. 'Woman's like a fucking black widow spider, mate. Suck out all your juice and leave you for dead.' He raised a hand and intoned: '*Who so loveth wisdom rejoiceth his father: but he that keepeth company with harlots spendeth his substance.*' Then he winked.

Rachel, upside down by the window with her blouse round her chin (treating them to the sight of her naked upper body), said, her voice muffled, 'Leave the boy alone, Sammy Holy Joe Rogers. He's gathering rosebuds while he may. Old Janet'll move on, darling. Fresh flesh is what she's after.'

The ending of Adam's relationship with Janet was all very neat. The three of them finished Janet's module, had all their papers marked (Sam got a first for his, Adam and Rachel got seconds), and Janet moved on to a German exchange student she met in the library.

'*Deutschland über alles!*' said Sam, delighted. 'Back to the fold, lad. D'y'ever think you'd mebbe have got a first if you hadn't dallied with the iron maiden?'

'Maiden! Huh!' said Rachel. 'She wishes!'

Adam told Sam not to talk stupid, but privately he thought there might have been something in it. Janet had this discretion thing off to a fine art.

His longest-lasting girlfriend – and the only one who was not blonde – was Ermin, a Welsh girl studying fabric design, who was tall, with burnt-orange hair and long, capable hands. Adam was very comfortable with her. She was gentle and easy to be with, could take sex or leave it. Sam liked her, and she embroidered great waistcoats glittering with mirrors for him and Adam. Rachel had no time for her; called her a Flemish cow and refused to speak to her.

The relationship with Ermin faded away in their final year, when her already heavy workload tripled as she prepared for her final exhibition. She stopped calling Adam, Adam stopped calling her, and that was that. Rachel brought in two bottles of champagne to celebrate Adam's new-found freedom, and the three of them got very drunk and ended up sleeping together on the living-room rug. Rachel slept in the middle, holding both of their hands.

Mum!

Sorry I missed you yet again this Easter, you being in Germany and me being back in Cyprus with Sam and Rachel. Sam liked meeting you at half term and really went on about your drawings. On my way back home I met his mum and dad, who were great, although his mum is a bit religious. The weird thing was how young they both were. Married at sixteen, Sam says.

And no, there were not many buildings on the site in Cyprus – just earth and the odd pile of stones. Lots of clues about buildings that had been there, though. Since you ask, the course is going OK. Mostly good seconds in terms of marks, so I will be embarking on my third year hoping for a 2:1. You never know.

More digging in Cyprus before then, so we will be ships passing in the night over the summer vac.

Adam x

Last Days

Adam's last year at college seemed to whirl by in a maze of work, music, dancing and digging. He spent five weeks in the summer digging in Cyprus with Sam and Rachel before the autumn term began for real, with piles of work to do and good – sometimes bizarre – times with his two friends. Then at Easter the three of them spent two chilly weeks digging in a deserted village in Ireland. This was part of Sam and Rachel's course, but Adam just went along for the laughs and their special company.

He spent the last week of the holiday at home. Sam came across for a few days and they took day trips into the Dales to look at the residue of lead mines. Unusually, Marie was there, and she and Sam got on famously, laughing together and arguing into the night. Adam relished this in one way and suffered shaming bouts of jealousy in another.

In his last year at college Adam finally came out of his

shell. He didn't spend all his time with Sam and Rachel. He got involved with three girls – a fair-haired drama student, a fair-haired medic and a red-haired music student called Maura. The thing with Maura was quite important. He even took her home once to see his mother, but they just missed her as she was on a plane to Israel at the time. He even worked out that he liked Maura because like Ermin she was not like Marie. She did not look like his mother or act like her. Despite being an artist she was laid back, practical. He liked her down-to-earth charm and the fact that she made love with the same tough passion that consumed her when she played her violin.

In the spring term, before the Irish dig, Adam moved out of the house he shared with Sam and Rachel and moved in with Maura. The two of them had a merry time, like children playing house. He thought this was it, so he was very cast down when Maura fell hook, line and sinker for a flute player, a new recruit to the university orchestra. He did the only thing he could – moved back in with his friends: there was some comfort in the fact that his room had stayed just as he had left it.

He joined a band called Zebra but was expelled because when he had more than two spliffs or shots he lay down and went to sleep. Zebba, the leader of the band he had called after himself, told Adam that he really liked him, he was a cool guy, but he couldn't play his guitar when he was out cold half the time, so he was no use to Zebra. Or Zebba.

The house Adam shared with Sam and Rachel had its own routines. Sam did the washing, Rachel did the shopping; the two of them did most of the cooking. Adam did help now and then. More often than not he sat drinking Pepsi, watching them work and trying out chords on his newish guitar.

After Christmas, Sam swapped two custom-written essays for a bass guitar owned by another ex-Zebra player. (Zebba had high standards. He did not suffer fools gladly, so he threw most of the players out of his band sooner or later.)

Adam showed Sam some chords, but his friend's fingers were too big and clumsy to get the right effect so he threw the guitar into a corner, saying his hands were only good for digging, writing and bloody loading the dishwasher. Adam had to acknowledge that he was right about that. Especially the writing. Sam had just won a national essay prize for his academic paper evaluating the experience of the Cyprus digs, linking their finds to the ongoing documentation of that internationally important site. Also, facsimiles of his day books reflecting on his experience of the digs had been bought from him by the university, as exemplars for future courses.

As for Adam, he managed – just – to get work in on time and took ProPlus to stay awake for last-minute swotting for his exams. His 2:1 degree was rather sneered at by his tutor, who told him that he'd just scraped it. His 'Antifascism, Resistance and Liberation in Western Europe' essay had been mediocre, but his 'Legacy of Stalin' paper had been rather good.

Rachel was awarded a 2:1 and told by her tutor that she'd just missed a first; in fact she would have clinched it if she'd actually turned up to sit her last paper. Sam sailed through with a first and was told he was second in the whole country in his subject and would be awarded a national prize. His tutor persuaded him to do postgraduate studies at the university and told him that he had a great future in front of him. He turned down research offers from other enticing universities, including the greatest in the land: Joseph, the leader of the Cyprus digs, had been keen to land him for his Cambridge department.

Adam was close to Sam, knew him better than anyone else in his life, but he still couldn't work out why his laid-back friend was so successful. On his second glass of celebratory champagne (Rachel had given the first toast: 'Thank you, Grandfather, for two whole crates of Moët!'), he asked Sam what his great secret was. 'Clever bugger! How do you do it? How does he do it, Rachel? All he ever does is dance, drink and make love to passing women.'

Rachel said, 'Listen, darling. You know I have no visible panty line? Well, Sammy boy here has no visible study line!'

Sam raised a glass, 'Didn't you notice? Insomnia, mate. I'm awake twice as long as everyone else on this planet. After I've said my prayers there's nowt else to do at two o'clock in the morning, is there?'

Rachel — who now slept mostly in Sam's bed — vouched

for this. 'Trouble with insomniacs is they don't like other people having a good night's sleep.'

Sam winked at her. 'There's a bed in the other room, you know, pet.'

In recent months Sam had actually stopped bed-hopping and begun to focus on Rachel. At first this change of status had disturbed Adam, who told them up front it was incestuous. Rachel grinned. 'S'all right, darling. Incest is fun. It's an old tradition in my family.'

So most nights Adam was treated to gurgling squeals and deep laughter, quickly drowned out by heavy-metal music that made the walls thump. At least he thought it was the music making the walls thump. He usually ended up with a pillow over his head to stifle the noise, whatever its source.

The first official end-of-term bash was the Archaeological Society – known as ArchSoc – party. This was a comparatively sedate affair in the foyer of the city museum that had spawned the archaeology course when the university was built in the 1960s.

The three of them had attended this event every year. The hallway stretched through the ground floor of the museum, its floor a triumph of the Victorian tile-maker's art. On party night a thick silk rope barred access to the staircase that swept up to the mezzanine, where double doors led into the various galleries. Some of the collections on display here were quite mundane, but some showcased artefacts of considerable international significance. This year they knew that up there in the Cyprus gallery was a display of the prime finds from their own recent expeditions.

In the corner, under the mezzanine, a pianist would play jazz in the style of Oscar Peterson. In the opposite corner would be a linen-covered table laden with food that looked like a parody of 1960s catering, when this museum first pledged its troth to the university.

Tonight the three of them decided to have a pint in the Union before going across town to the museum. Rachel found a space at the edge of the Union car park in the shelter of a wall to park her zippy Escort. The two lines of cars were like a roll call of student types: neat Metros or Escorts to keep treasured daughters and sons, grand-daughters and grandsons safe; battered rebuilds for resourceful engineers; dingy vans for those with alternative occupations – bands or small removals, for instance. One rusty black van had words painted on the side in golden gothic lettering: *World depleted, man defeated*.

The Union was very quiet at this time of night, so they gulped down their beer and set out in Rachel's car across town for the ArchSoc bash. When they arrived, the sound of the piano was almost drowned out by the rasping buzz of talk from people very used to projecting their voices. Staff had their heads together in faculty clusters and students hung on to the edge of conversations. Adam noted his ex-girlfriend Maura in one crowd, her weedy flautist at her elbow.

All around them girls with shining hair were showing more gleaming tanned flesh than normal, and the boys were uneasy in shoes rather than trainers, practising the wearing of business suits bought for their forthcoming round of interviews. The invitation, after all, had said *dress marginally formal.*

Sam had laughed at this typically half-baked instruction and wore cream drill trousers and a generously cut corduroy jacket over a very white T-shirt. Rachel wore a long drooping lace skirt, and her hair was piled on top of her head in a teetering attempt at Restoration style.

Adam had copied Sam, wearing chinos and a T-shirt under a grey suit jacket. Earlier that evening, looking at himself in the mirror, he knew he cut a much better, more slender figure than Sam. But he also knew that it was Sam who had the real style. He would get all the attention. Wherever he was, Sam drew people to him like flies. Tonight, when they got into the room, he was instantly grabbed by his tutor, who hauled him across to meet some visiting academics. QED, thought Adam.

Rachel spotted someone she knew and vanished from Adam's side, so he made his way through the crowd around the drinks table and picked up two glasses of orange juice to save him going back again. He was on the wagon. After two days he had stopped drinking Rachel's Moët because his tendency to sleep made for a dull life. Sam and Rachel had continued to concoct champagne cocktails and drink them through the day as though it was their duty to empty both crates. Sam absorbed alcohol like a sponge, but Rachel had to pee perpetually and was goofily tipsy for a week. She had swerved the car twice on the way to the party.

Adam found a deep windowsill to sit on, so that he could melt into the wall and watch the crowd. A distinguished woman in an expensive black dress made her way towards him. 'Janet!' he said, smiling reluctantly at his amorous former tutor.

She waved her champagne at him. 'Adam! On the wagon, I see.'

'Champagned out. Too much of the stuff this week. All I do is go to sleep and that, I'm told, is boring.'

'Something to celebrate, I suppose: 2:1, I hear.' She smiled up at him. 'Bumbling old Sam must have rubbed off on you, darling.'

'I'm sure he'll be pleased to hear that you said that.' Adam thought of how much Sam disliked this woman.

Janet sipped her champagne. 'Even if he's been a help to you, Adam, we all know it's not such a good thing. What good has it been for you, traipsing about the world with him, grubbing in the earth like that? I'd have thought you'd have travelled more in eastern Europe now it's so open. Moscow, Warsaw! Everyone's going to Krakow these days. All that post-Communism! Stalin's statues rusting! That kind of travel would have backed up your own work, just like the digging in the sand backs up Sam's. Might even have got you a really good 2:1 rather than a scrape-home 2:1.'

She'd obviously been involved with the grading meeting.

Adam scowled at her. 'Hardly grubbing. Some good came out of it.'

'Good? For you?' She raised her fine eyebrows. 'Ah yes, Sam Rogers' famous paper. The faculty's so excited.' She didn't sound in the least bit excited. 'I hear the three of you are still inseparable. Are you a threesome?' She nodded towards Rachel, who was standing now with Sam's arm round her, talking to the Vice Chancellor, a tall, heavy, distinguished man with a bush of grey hair.

Adam exploded into bad manners. 'So, how is the new crop of freshers, Janet? Anyone take your eye at the interviews?'

She smiled, her eyes closing almost to slits. 'Funny you should mention that, Adam, but I think I may be rather too busy at the beginning of term.' She held her finger under his nose to give him a close view of her ring: a substantial diamond set in white gold.

He had to grin. 'Bingo, Janet! Who's the lucky boy, then?'

She laughed out loud at this. 'Well, Adam, you'll be interested to know that I decided it was time to play with the grown-ups. My fiancé's over there, talking to your friends.' She paused, then called in a low yet piercing voice, 'Alistair!' The object of their attention met her eye and lifted his glass towards her.

'The Vice Chancellor!' Adam's brain could not quite

take this in. That magisterial, distant figure, engaged to Janet, who was addicted to romantic romping with boys!

She put her finger to his lips. 'Shh! Don't spoil the surprise. Alistair will announce it in his speech tonight.'

'I hate to say this, Janet, or even seem interested, but why? Why on earth *him*?'

'Two things, darling. One, to be honest, I got rather tired of being the hunter and thought it might be relaxing to be the hunted. Two, lovely Alistair has this ability to turn me on by the sheer quality of his mind. To hear him discoursing on the theory of matter makes me weak at the knees. Beats dirty talk into fits, my dear. You will not believe how mundane are the thought processes of boys!' She put a hand over her mouth. 'Oops! I forgot. You are the expert in that!'

He forced a grin and treated her to a slow handclap. 'That's good, Janet. That's very good!' Then he gulped his second orange juice, turned his back on her and made his way to the great doors. He was gasping for fresh, clean air. The air around Janet seemed too thick with her familiar perfume. It was called Poison, if he remembered rightly.

Outside, on the wide, shallow steps, the air was warm and balmy, promising a much better summer this year. He hoped it would be good, because for the first time ever he'd decided to spend it at home. Sam and Rachel were going to America to visit her maternal grandfather, a professor at a Midwest university that was funding a dig on First American lands. The two of them were very keen for Adam to join them and he was tempted. But he found he couldn't do it. Sam and Rachel were very much a couple now, delighting in each other as though they'd just met. He had to leave them to it.

So he'd made the decision that he would spend time at home. He needed to look for a job, and he could do it as well from there as anywhere. And Marie, on sabbatical just now at a university in Boston, was due home in July and would actually be home for three months until the autumn. The thought occurred to him that he really should make an effort to see more of her. They should stop circling round each other like cats. He could work on getting to know her better – play the grown-up game, as Janet Gallagher would say. He was quite looking forward to that, spending time with Marie.

'What cheer, mate! All on our lonesome? Can't stand the clack of all these erudite minds?' It was Sam, his arm round Rachel. Her hair had lost its pins and now flowed down her back like a dark river. She could barely stand. She looked like some dark fallen angel. Sam grinned. 'A glass too far, innit, girl? Maybe they laced your ArchSoc champagne with blue bombers. Mine too. World swimming a bit.' He reached into Rachel's bag and found her car keys. 'Here, mate, you drive. Me and old Rachel here need our beddy-byes.' He threw them at Adam, who caught them neatly. 'Don't know what we'd do without our dear sober mate. Right, Rachel?'

Rachel fell against him and he picked her up in his arms

as though she were a puppy and grinned at Adam. 'Come on, mate. Where d'we leave the car?'

Adam was reluctant to drive them home. He'd often picked up the keys for short rides on and off the campus. He had no licence, but he was not a bad driver. He was careful not to drive during the day, when it might draw attention, but tonight he seemed to have no choice, with Sam sprawled in the back of the car with Rachel asleep across his knees.

As he drove out of town towards the university campus, he knew he'd be relieved when he reached the narrower, quieter roads that led to the campus. The traffic was lighter there and going slow didn't draw attention.

When they finally turned on to a quieter stretch of road he began to breathe more easily. Sam's voice came from the back. 'Saw you talking to the Black Widow in there, mate. Propositioning you, was she?' His speech was no longer slurred. Not for the first time, Adam thought admiringly about his friend's powers of recovery. He was amazing.

Adam glanced at him in the mirror and grinned. 'Not likely. You missed the best bit. She was telling me she's pledged her troth.'

Sam's deep laugh filled the little car. 'She's *what*?'

'Got engaged!'

'What? Who's the lucky little chicken, then?'

'No chicken. More an old rooster. The Vice Chancellor, no less!'

Sam roared. 'You bugger! The dirty old devil.' He paused. 'Him too,' he added.

'Doesn't bear imagining,' said Adam. 'Think of it!'

Then the two of them were both roaring with laughter, their voices blending together as they had so many times in the last three years. Adam was so filled with affection for Sam at that moment that he wanted to tell him just that: that he loved him, that he was the best thing in his life so far.

He turned round . . .

Police Press release:

Adam Mathéve (21) caused the death of one of his passengers and severe injury to another in a car accident. Sam Rogers (22), who was killed, and Rachel Miriam (22), who was badly injured, were his passengers when he hit a tree and lost control of the car he was driving on the A452 and collided with another vehicle, before skidding and turning over. The driver and passengers in the other car were not injured. The three students had been out celebrating the end of their university course. However, Mathéve's blood alcohol level was found to be below the limit. Experts found no defect in the car, which was owned and insured by one of the victims. Mr Mathéve had no licence. He was found guilty to causing death by dangerous driving and was given a sentence of 4 years with 6 years' disqualification.

★

Oh, oh! Here I am, back on the ceiling, looking down at my shell of a body and at the fair double-crowned head of my boy. My dear son Adam. Now, suddenly, charging into my mind is that time I got back late from the sabbatical in Boston. A shocking, shocking thing. On the doormat I find this letter from my son, my Adam, with a very strange franking mark. The letter is on lined paper with a printed prison address at the top and a space for a name and a number: 'Adam Mathéve. 47639'.

I remember that letter, every word of it. I could recite it in my sleep.

Dear Mum,

I'm sorry you have to hear this in this way. I did not want to disturb you in your work in America. You will see from the address that this is bad news. I was involved in a car crash where my friend Sam was killed and my friend Rachel badly injured, and have been charged with causing death by dangerous driving. At present I am on remand in custody. The committal proceedings are on the 19th. It's all very confusing at present. Please, please don't come charging down here. That will make things even harder.

Sorry again.

Adam

PS It seems irrelevant just now but I got a 2:1 degree, much to my and other people's surprise.

I remember thinking, 'That boy! What has he done now?' I remember thinking, 'Friends? Who were these friends?' Then I remembered Sam. Only met him a couple of times, but you could not forget Sam. And I met her once, that slip of a girl with no breasts. Now I realise, that those were the last days. The very last days of life as it was. For all of us.

I remember thinking, just as I thought all those years ago in Krakow, that things would never be the same after this.

Part Four

Trial

Lighting Tapers

The summer Adam went to prison on remand, Marie Mathéve's life changed for good. By the time he was sentenced, she had retired from her work for the Commission. She told herself that the two events were not connected. There had been a shake-up at the Commission and the parameters of her territory were arbitrarily changed. She had challenged such changes before, but increasingly she was met with a weary, patronising, jobs-worthian wall. This was exacerbated when she was unavailable for consultations and contributions because for the first time in her working life she had taken time off, to attend Adam's trial.

Marie had always ploughed her own furrow and avoided the domestic politics of the Commission. Her colleagues claimed they were patient with her because of her distinguished reputation, but now an undertone emerged implying that she was behaving like a prima donna. Her new boss – a bright young historian half her age – let her know briskly that she was valuable but not that valuable, and that things had changed since she first started drawing buildings.

So halfway through Adam's trial Marie retired, drew her lump sum and did her calculations. She would manage quite well with a couple of consultancies for building charities and the occasional lecture. One publisher was even interested in commissioning a book of her drawings. The brief was to illuminate three cities in a series of drawings. She chose Bruges, York and Krakow.

This was when – for the first time in decades – she saw her own home through different eyes: as immaculate but stagnating in the aesthetic aspic of custom. The day after Adam was sentenced, thinking of him more than ever before, she wandered into his dusty room and recognised that it too had not changed since he was a young teenager: the same science fiction posters, the same images of Mariah Carey, Madonna and Oasis. Hidden on the back of the door she discovered a picture of a singer called Bryan Adams, of whom she'd never heard. She looked closer at the picture, and realised that Adam must have modelled himself on this stranger: chiselled features, pale floppy hair. For her this was a new observation.

She didn't know her son. She hadn't known him. She stood there, her brain racing. She couldn't leave his room like this for four years. He would be twenty-five when he came out of prison. Or twenty-four. Her solicitor had explained that he might come out earlier if he behaved himself. Behaved himself! She told the solicitor that she couldn't imagine her boy not behaving himself. This awful event was a tragedy: completely out of character.

But now, looking around this obsolete room, she began to wonder what she really knew about Adam's character. Her aim, born in Krakow over twenty years ago, to let him fly free, unhindered in the world, had backfired. He had flown so far she had lost sight of him, and he of her. And now he was locked away, right out of her sight.

Since he'd been at university they'd only seen each other in passing. She'd been busy, absorbed in her work, at the same time happy that he was obviously enjoying his time there. They'd never discussed it, but she thought he must have liked his freedom at university. He'd always been independent, even as a little boy: quiet and happy in his own way. No trouble at all.

He'd been great with Jack, another quiet person, who had relished for ten short years this late shot at step-parenthood. Seeing them so happy together had made Marie happier in her own freedom.

Of course Adam, when he was ten, was devastated when Jack died so suddenly. She should have expected that. She too was bereft. This late love had rounded up her life, filling the edges with warmth and care. Oddly enough, Jack's death, which should have drawn Adam and herself closer, was the beginning of their going their really separate ways. Adam didn't seem to need her, except for the practical things like money. Her friends on the estate looked out for him and he seemed happy with that. He often spent time with them, even when she was home. This didn't distress her. She had been happy for him, pleased at his independence.

Now she sat down on his bed. What on earth had he been doing, driving that car? She'd offered once to buy him a car and pay for driving lessons. He'd taken the lessons but had turned down her offer of a car, muttering, 'Too complicated!'

At Adam's trial, hard as she tried, she did not succeed in catching his eye. She did catch the eye of Mrs Rogers, Sam's mother, a slender, pretty woman in an old-fashioned belted coat. Her curly hair was pulled back in a ponytail and her dark-ringed eyes shone more and more brightly out of her scrubbed face as the days of the trial unfolded. She looked much too young to have a boy of twenty-two. Marie remembered Adam saying that Sam's mother had been married at sixteen. Now she calculated that Mrs Rogers was the same age as she herself had been when she'd found out she was pregnant with Adam. Her glance moved to Mr Rogers, a big, bulky man who had to reach for his handkerchief several times as the details of the crash emerged.

In the row beside them were an elegant elderly couple, the woman in black with iron-grey upswept hair: the girl Rachel's grandparents. Neither of them glanced in Marie's direction; they barely moved during the proceedings. Marie admired their composure.

Finally, when it was all over, Sam's mother stopped Marie in the concourse outside the courts. Marie braced herself.

'How are you, Mrs Mathéve?' she said. 'This must be awful for you.'

The woman's kind tone shocked Marie into frankness. 'Sad. Bewildered. My son would not even look at me. And I am so very sad about Sam. So very sorry.' She bit her lip. 'He was an exceptional person.'

Mrs Rogers put a hand on her arm. 'Shame and remorse take many forms, Mrs Mathéve. You must bear with your son.' She paused. 'I thought he was a nice boy, your Adam. He was a good friend to our son, and our Sammy loved him like a brother. You must remember, Mrs Mathéve, that there are such things as accidents. There was no anger or forethought in what your boy did, that was clear. They made him drive them. It was an accident. We must see that. Just savage, savage fate.' Her voice had become blank, bleached of any feeling. Then she looked Marie in the eye. 'You would know the prophet Samuel, Mrs Mathéve? *How are the mighty fallen in the midst of battle? O Jonathan thou wast slain in high places.*'

Tears were running down Marie's face. This was the first time she had cried since Jack died. And Jack had lived a long life. 'How can you stand it, Mrs Rogers? How on earth can you stand all this?'

Sam's mother leaned forward and whispered in Marie's ear. '*The Lord gave, and the Lord hath taken away; blessed be the name of the Lord.*'

'Come on, will you, Jane!' Sam's mother was pulled away by her husband, who glared at Marie, offering no such Christian charity. Just then Rachel's grandparents stalked by, with not a glance in Marie's direction. Grateful for this, she turned and fled towards the railway station, relieved to be swallowed up by the Friday crowds.

In her professional life Marie had been inside hundreds of churches and chapels. She had drawn them, written about them, even saved some of these places from extinction. The fact was, though, that she had never entered a church with any spiritual intentions. But Mrs Rogers' profound kindness, her intense charity on the day of the trial stayed with her, the words drumming in her head: *The Lord gave. The Lord hath taken away.* The day after Adam's sentencing, she made her way up to the cathedral in her home city and sat there in the dim light, staring at the elegant screen behind the altar: substantial stone carved like lace. She closed her eyes and let the hum of bustling clergy and discreet tourists fade into the background.

Suddenly she was there again with David Zielinski in the Drapers' Hall in Krakow, walking down the fine marble gallery, looking at nineteenth-century Polish paintings and staring in distaste at figures of warriors and horses writhing in battle, some of them in their death throes. And then she was in the fine room in the old Zielinski apartment, staring down at the chaise longue covered with old velvet, his hand in hers.

The Lord gave. The Lord hath taken away.

That day in Krakow had been a time of passion and love, and she'd had the gift of a son to commemorate that time. And yesterday, standing in the dock with his sturdy frame and sculptured face, Adam had been his father personified. And now he had been taken away from her.

This so soon after David himself – her own secret relish of the idea of him living and breathing, laughing with Jacinta, singing to Piotr, talking to old Alon Piotr – had been taken away from her.

He had been taken from her in the spring, when Adam had been in Ireland, digging with Sam.

Felix Wosniak had turned up on her doorstep. At first Marie didn't recognise the fragile old man standing there. Still dapper in dress, Felix looked shrunken and bony. But he stood upright, and the thready elderly voice still had a purring quality. She had welcomed him in and made him tea. He looked around her sitting room and explained his visit. It seemed he was in England as an adviser at a symposium on Anglo-Polish relations in the light of the free movement of labour in Europe. 'The symposium is in York, and I see that I have only two more stops on the train to be in your city. I dig in my file and find the address from your old letters.'

She found herself blushing. 'Very kind of you, Felix.' She paused. 'How is everyone?'

He waited for a second, examining her closely. 'Is very sad, because friend David is no longer here with us. Struck dead by the toxic pollution, our damned legacy from the Communist times. The curse of Silesia. We have so many priorities moving forward for Poland in the new Europe. We make great efforts – but that damage has been done.' The old thread of confidence and authority was still in his voice. 'And now this same plague invades Alon Piotr, my comrade. The old man hangs on by a thread, as you say.'

'I am so sorry.' Marie felt bereft. Helpless. 'So sorry.' Her hand trembled as she poured his tea. At last she said, 'And Jacinta? Little Piotr?'

'Jacinta is well enough. Retired now from the steelworks. Piotr is very clever, like his father. He teaches now at the conservatory in Warsaw. For David, I watch over Piotr. And I bring medicine for Alon Piotr.' He sipped his tea, his eyes staring at her, deep socketed in a network of wrinkles. 'Jacinta, David, all of us were very sad you did not return.'

In one detached part of her mind Marie noted how good Felix's English was now. Very heavily accented but very efficient. Felix Wosniak was the great learner, the great adapter! She saw that by now he must have worked his way into the good graces of the new capitalist set-up, obliterating his connection with the old regime. His ability to thrive was a distinct life skill.

She gripped her hands together hard to stop them trembling. She'd ignored David's letters, just as Adam was to ignore the letters she would write to him in prison. To keep Jacinta safe. To keep herself safe. To keep Adam safe.

She was not sure exactly why. 'Life became so busy,' she said to Felix. 'I am so sorry.'

Words, just words.

'They spoke of being able to visit you with these new open borders. But alas it did not happen and will not happen. David was sick and they did not wish to intervene . . . no . . . *intrude.*' It was the first time a word had evaded him. This was a clever man.

Suddenly she felt angry with Felix for being so clever, for being the survivor, the deliverer of bad news. Then she remembered his garden, and the photos of lupins and sunflowers.

'And Jacinta? How is she really?'

'Dear Jacinta is heartbroken at losing David. Old Alon Piotr says nothing, but he fades by the day of this same cancer plague. He is my old comrade, the last to call me Saba, the name of my childhood.'

Marie remembered the hints of conflicted story of him and Alon Piotr: betrayer and betrayed, the penitent and the innocent playing out their roles. 'And Casia?' she said.

'Ah! Casia died in the sanatorium, the most ancient person there, old as the century. Once David became ill she just gave up the ghost, as you English say. Jacinta could not take care of them both.' Felix coughed. 'I telephone Jacinta that I call here and she say for you should come to visit her again.'

That was when he glanced around the room, and his eye fell on the three photos of Adam: one when he was five, sitting on Jack's knee; the second when he was eleven, in his big school uniform; the other when he was fourteen, at school camp, long-legged in shorts, his blond hair all over the place. Felix picked up this one. He put on his glasses and peered at it.

The room pulsed with a silence in which everything was suddenly clear. He was seeing what Marie had always seen: how much like the young Piotr Adam had been as a baby. How much like David he was as he grew.

Felix carefully replaced the photograph. 'Ah, I see,' he said, smiling faintly. 'Now I see.'

'Not this year, Felix,' said Marie slowly. 'I cannot go to see Jacinta this year. I have so much work to do. Perhaps another year.' But even as she said it, she knew that would never happen. She could never go there again. Never. Later in church, after Adam's trial, she thought of David, now not in this world. And then she thought of their son Adam in his prison cell. She shivered.

'Are you all right, honey?' Back in the cathedral an American voice purred in Marie's ear and she was dragged back to the present, from her thoughts of Felix and his awful news about David. The scented warmth of the cathedral surged through her again and she felt better. She blinked away the tears that had been welling up, unasked, all day and looked into the eyes of a woman in cotton slacks and a thick pullover. 'Are you all right, honey?' the woman repeated.

Marie stood up. 'I am fine. Thank you for asking. I am fine.' Knowing that the woman's eyes were on her, she walked slowly across to the bank of candles, put coins in the box, lit three tapers and whispered the precious name of David Zielinski and that of Alon Piotr, both gone from her now. A taper for each of them. And another for Casia, faithful unto death.

Marie knew this was a primitive thing to do, to expect to bring the magic of light where there had been darkness. She'd acted instinctively to escape the eagle eye of the American tourist. But as she took a fourth candle and lit it, she knew this one was for Adam, alive but locked away somewhere in his own darkness. And then a fifth for Sam, whose mother was sure he was in heaven with Jesus. Such faith!

Walking out through the great Norman arch on to the cathedral green she made a decision: she would sell the house where she'd brought Adam up and find somewhere smaller and start again. A flat, perhaps. (She thought of Theresa's elegant apartment in Chorzow.) That would generate some resources for Adam when he got out of prison. He'd need some support then, and she wanted to be there for him. She would write to him and tell him what she had decided.

So Marie Mathéve decided to move on, away from her work with the Commission, away from the house where she had lived with her mother, and later with Adam and

Jack, to 15a Merrick Court, nearer the centre of the city. Here she made a precious new friend called Sharina Mary Osgood, who was an unusual person, unlike anyone she'd ever met before.

The Last Child Remaining

The first big event in Sharina Mary Osgood's last year at school was the closure of the convent house on the coast that had been her home since she had stopped being a cute little doll and cultivated a feisty attitude that meant that her foster parents were relieved to get rid of her. Born to a South Shields mother and an African father, she was one of five children to be left in the care of the three old nuns at Rosemount, a small religious house that had operated in this seaside community for sixty years, and had been originally set up to accommodate twenty nuns who took in and cared for female orphans.

Gradually, four of the children moved on, leaving only Sharina, the last child remaining, to be cared for by just three nuns. The nuns loved Sharina. But eventually they had to acknowledge that their time with her was running out. For four years the diocese had been informing them that it could not afford to keep Rosemount open for a single child. The old nuns would have to find refuge with their sisters in another part of the diocese. This last female child, Sharina Mary Osgood, now fifteen, would have to go elsewhere.

The news was broken to her by Sister Mary Cornelia McAteer, who was Sharina's mentor and had known her since she was a baby. It was she who had forced the decision that Sharina should stay permanently with the community when she kept being returned by disappointed foster parents.

Even though Sharina was the only child in the narrow seaside house, she was happy in the company of these devout women. She liked her life in this quiet setting, where the television was only on for an hour a day, and radio only allowed with earphones. Here she learned the virtues of quiet study, how to knit, how to embroider and how to sing the offices and cheerful holy songs. She loved to sit in the small fragrant room the sisters called the chapel, where they chanted their prayers. She would look at the cross and the holy pictures and wonder at the magic that the nuns found in that space. She invented new child-sins to please the priest who came every other day to hear confessions. She was too young to realise that this in itself was a sin of pride. For a time, Sister Mary Cornelia thought that she might have here a rare new candidate for the religious life.

But then the energy and challenge of secondary school hit Sharina like a bomb. She had a good time there. She worked hard enough, but she relished the sheer noise and aggression of life at school after the quiet of the convent house. She bought Mariah Carey and Oasis tapes and played them through earphones. At first being the child of an African drew too much attention at school, but she rode out the prejudice and ignorance around her and made more friends than enemies. And at school she learned to dance and to sing chants more worldly than those that had echoed in her enclosed situation at home with the sisters.

Then one day, at rehearsals for an interschool debating competition on the theme of 'The Best Strategy for Safe Streets is Prison', she met Kevin Brownsey. Very good looking and unburdened by puppy fat or spots, he was a quiet, reserved boy two years ahead of her in school, whose life, if anything, was more enclosed than hers. He lived in a big house on the edge of town with his father, a kind of church bureaucrat, and his mother, a member of some grand northern family with pots of money. Kevin already had a place at his father's old college at Cambridge but was working just as hard at his studies in this, his last year at school.

The debating society travelled to London for the finals of the debating competition. Sharina and Kevin sat together on the bus and talked first about the competition and then about everything, from politics to poetry to Mariah Carey. Later, in London, they made fumblingly embarrassing, inexpert love in the grounds of the boarding school that was putting them up for the weekend. On the

223

bus all the way back north, the rest of the debaters were subdued, disappointed that they had not achieved their expected win. But Sharina and Kevin sat shyly together, hand in hand, bemused at the step they'd taken but quite pleased with themselves: they were smug as two sparrows on a line.

Over the next week she and Kevin met on the corridors and in the school grounds. They skipped lunch and went walking hand in hand on the beach. There was no opportunity to repeat their debating-trip sexual explosion. In any case, they were both unsure about the next step, which made them cautious rather than keen. As it happened, there was little time to worry about it, as they were both deep in their respective GCSE and A level mock exams and had little time together. Even so, Kevin left copies of poems and his favourite battered editions of *Slaughterhouse-Five* and *Catch-22* in her locker, and she read them in her convent bedroom at night.

On the morning of her last exam – her English oral – Sharina had to get up earlier than usual to be violently sick. Sister Mary Cornelia came upon her in the bathroom, held her head and went to get her a glass of water and some Setlers. She read the label. *Setlers bring express relief.* 'Don't worry, dear,' said Sister Mary Cornelia. 'Nerves, just nerves. Now take a little breakfast and get yourself into school. Remember, this is the last exam!' They both knew it was the last in more ways than one. They'd known the news for a while now. Rosemount was to be closed.

Sharina was sick the next day as well, and the next. Despite an anxious note from Kevin, she opted out of the post-exam bash at a local hall. When she was sick on the fifth day, Sister Mary Cornelia took her to the nuns' parlour and sat beside her on the stiff couch. She took her face in her hands and turned it towards her. 'Now then, my dear. What have you been up to?'

Sharina frowned, not really understanding what she had been asked.

'I'm no expert, but being sick like that every day means a certain thing.'

'I have a bad stomach, Sister.'

Sister Mary Cornelia shook her head. 'It is something else,' she said, biting her lip. 'I know in my heart that it is something else, dear. You must know that too.'

Then it came on Sharina in a crash. 'What? Oh sugar! Oh dear!' she wailed. 'It's not supposed . . . they say you can't . . . not the first time . . .'

'You talk about these things?'

'Yeah. Some girls talk about it all the time.'

'You?'

'No, not me, Sister. But I hear.'

Sister Mary Cornelia took her hand. 'Now then, dear. Tell me what you've done.'

So Sharina told her. How nice Kevin was. How shy. How he copied poems for her. How in the grounds of the school in London they had . . .

Sister Mary Cornelia closed her eyes tight for a

moment, then opened them again. She took a breath. 'And now you are expecting a baby. Conceived in sin, it is true. But a child in the image of God.'

Thoughts were tumbling through Sharina's head. 'It happened last year to Felicity O'Hare. And—'

'I know that case. We prayed for her, but to no avail.' She drew Sharina to her feet. 'We will go to the small chapel, dear, and thank God for this gift and pray for guidance.'

She summoned the other two nuns to the tiny chapel to pray for Sharina's child and for Sharina herself. Then all three of them went back to the parlour and sat looking at Sharina curiously, as though she were a different species. She felt numb, unable to say anything. Then Sister Mary Cornelia turned to Sister Mary Rose Maloney, the oldest and most respected of the remaining trio at Rosemount. 'I think we must speak with the family of this boy, Sister.'

Sister Mary Josephine O'Neill, the other sister, nodded. 'We must speak with the family of the boy.'

Sister Mary Rose Maloney nodded, then bent her head to look at her hands, which were clasped tightly in her lap.

The authority of the Church meant that Kevin's mother and father – however grand – were summoned that night to Rosemount and spoken to by the sisters in the parlour. From her fourth-floor bedroom window Sharina watched the big Volvo pull up outside the house. She sat like stone and listened to the voices down below, muffled by the thick walls of the parlour.

After twenty minutes the dinner gong – now a universal gathering call, since none of the sisters walked well – summoned her to the parlour. She opened the door and took a single step inside. Kevin's parents were a surprise: his father was small and neat, with a well-modelled head and highly polished shoes; his mother, who was glaring now at Sharina, was big and square, with rather full permed hair and bright lipstick. Sharina frowned. Somehow she'd thought they would both be good looking, like Kevin.

Sister Mary Cornelia rescued her. She held out her hand. 'Come here, dear, and sit by me.' She pulled her in close.

The woman burst out, 'I don't know what you've been up to, lady.' She had an old-fashioned voice, nasal, clipped. Like in black-and-white films.

Sister Mary Josephine O'Neill turned to glare at her. 'Mrs Brownsey! This is a child! I understand your son is nearer to manhood than this girl here.' There was clear reproof in her reedy voice.

'Well, you can see she's a—'

'Shut up, Shirley!' Mr Brownsey's voice was surprisingly deep for such a small man. He turned to Sister Mary Cornelia. 'Sister . . . '

Sister Mary Cornelia held Sharina's hand very tight. 'As we have discussed here, Sharina, this could be a matter for the police. What Kevin did was breaking the law.'

'Nonsense,' said Mrs Brownsey. 'Anyone can see who led who. Look at her . . .'

'Shirley,' growled Mr Brownsey. 'For the last time, shut up!'

'So,' went on Sister Mary Cornelia, 'that would be the simplest thing, to take the boy to court.' She paused. 'But in the opinion of my sisters and myself, it would be very hurtful to the boy and to you, Sharina. It would not be a wise path.' She put a hand over Sharina's. 'Unless you yourself wish us to go to the police, dear?'

Sharina shook her head.

'I told you. Only one way out!' burst out Mrs Brownsey.

'One more time, Shirley,' said Mr Brownsey, 'and you're in the car.'

'Mr and Mrs Brownsey here have a proposal that you undergo a procedure that they think will be the end of what they call *the problem*.'

A procedure. Sharina knew the words from school. *Abortion. Termination.*

'Do you have an opinion on this, Sharina?' persisted Sister Mary Cornelia, hiding her revulsion at the thought.

'I want to see Kevin,' burst out Sharina.

That was when Mrs Brownsey laughed out loud and Mr Brownsey took her arm and bundled her out of the door. He closed it behind her and turned to look directly at Sharina for the first time. 'We've had to take Kevin out of school altogether . . . er . . . Sharina. He'll do the last of his exams privately and then go on and visit his uncle in America for the summer. He'll only return for the beginning of his university term.' He paused. 'And he'll never come back north.'

Sharina put her chin up and glared at him. 'Well, wherever Kevin is, I'm having no *abortion*, if that's what you're wanting.'

'Thank God!' Sister Mary Josephine crossed herself and clicked her false teeth.

Mr Brownsey glanced at Sister Mary Cornelia. 'Sharina here seems like a determined young lady.'

'She is,' said Sister Mary Cornelia. 'Believe me, she is!'

'And she will definitely have this child?'

'I will!' said Sharina. 'I'm having no ab—'

'Sharina!' Sister Mary Josephine's voice was a whip on the air. 'Don't say that word!'

'Sharina has to go somewhere else in the summer,' said Sister Mary Cornelia quietly. 'The diocese is closing this house. My sisters and I are to go to a convent on the Tyne.'

Mr Brownsey frowned. 'Well. It would be a bit awkward if she were in this town—'

'I'm here! I'm here!' said Sharina. 'I am not *she*.'

He turned to her and sighed. 'I have sympathy with the sisters on this point. They have great affection for you. And I'm sorry my son has been so immature as to get you into this mess. So I have a proposal.' He glanced at the sisters, then back at Sharina. 'I have talked at length to Kevin, who is enormously chagrined by this news and very apologetic to you, Sharina. He wanted to come here, but I wouldn't permit it.' He removed a speck of dust from his jacket. 'My proposal is this. I have an interest in a small development in a city twenty miles from here. Apartments. To make poor compensation for my son's . . . er . . . indiscretion, I will gift one of those to you, Sharina, and guarantee a small income for you until this child is eighteen.'

The sisters murmured and nodded.

'However, this is conditional on the fact that you must *not* contact or pursue Kevin. You must leave him to be sorry – and so he should be – and to get on with his life.'

The silence that followed was broken by Sister Mary Cornelia. 'What do you think, Sharina dear? My sisters and I have to be out of this house by summer, but the order has a place where you could go until—'

'No!' burst in Sharina. 'I will not go to no *place*!'

Sister Mary Cornelia frowned. 'It is a very fair offer, Sharina. Not ideal, but under the circumstances, Mr Brownsey is trying his best.'

'I'm saying *no* to going to another sisters' house. I'm not saying no to Mr Brownsey. I'd rather go to this place he talks about and deal with this baby thing myself.'

'But Sharina! You're not yet sixteen,' said Mary Cornelia.

'I will be sixteen in five weeks. I can do this. I know it.'

'Bravo!' said Mr Brownsey unexpectedly. 'That's the spirit, young woman. That's the spirit.'

So it was that by the time she was sixteen, Sharina Mary Osgood had the keys to a new apartment. To her own dismay and distaste she also had a social worker, brought in by Sister Mary Cornelia in a kind of belt-and-braces move.

In the end, once the social worker saw how competent her new client was, she was very helpful over hospital appointments and financial affairs, which, although Sharina was good at maths and a quick learner, she found a bit baffling.

Sharina never heard from the Brownseys again. And though she thought of Kevin sometimes and could remember his shapely hands, in time she could hardly remember his face. Ever optimistic, she considered herself lucky. She had a place of her own and the promise of a baby who she felt certain would be good and who would thrive in her care. Her ability to tackle this was engendered by a combination of her own intelligence and *joie de vivre*, and the stringent, kindly discipline learned from the sisters. Sister Mary Cornelia, ensconced in her new house on the Tyne, promised always to be there for Sharina at the end of the phone. She had a dispensation from the diocese to do so.

So by her sixteenth birthday, Sharina Mary Osgood was pregnant, happy, optimistic and just a bit scared. And enjoying living in a neat apartment at Merrick Court.

A Place of One's Own

The day her new neighbour moved into Merrick Court, Sharina Mary Osgood had just come home from shopping. Noticing that the girl was pregnant, one of the removal men had lifted her shopping bags up the stone steps. She lingered on her doorstep, watching the men as they carried things into the neighbouring flat, noting the elegant bookcases and the modern furniture. She was just wondering whether the new owner was a young bloke or a young woman when a big, rather battered Mitsubishi swept into the courtyard. The woman who got out of the car was smart but she was by no means young. In fact she was quite old. She was trim and elegant, but that swept-up hair was silver-grey, not silver-blond.

The woman surveyed the building and her glance stayed for a second on Sharina's face. She smiled, and Sharina smiled back. Then, as the woman mounted the stone steps with a box in her hands, Sharina went inside. It might be very interesting, but after all, she realised, it wasn't a show.

Two hours later there was a knock on the door. It was the Mitsubishi woman. She held out her hand. 'I'm Marie Mathéve. I imagine I'm your new neighbour.'

Sharina shook the hand firmly. 'I'm Sharina Osgood. Well, Sharina Mary Osgood but I never use the Mary.'

Marie peered behind her. 'Is your mother in, or your father? I need some advice about setting the central heating system. The guidebook's pure bafflement.'

Sharina grinned. 'No mother, no father. There's just me.' She stood up straighter. 'This is my flat.'

The woman's glance now dropped to Sharina's considerable bulge. She blushed. 'I'm sorry. I . . . You're very . . .'

'Young? Pregnant?' Sharina grinned. 'It's been said before, Mrs Mathéve.' She was enjoying the tease.

'It's not Mrs . . . Oh, just call me Marie!' The woman blinked and paused a moment.

Sharina let her off the hook. 'I might be young and pregnant, Marie, but being also a genius I do know how to set the central heating. Wait! I'll just get my keys.'

It took her two minutes to set the central heating, crouching down before the cupboard by the door. She stood up. 'Ouch!' she said, holding her back.

Marie looked at her in alarm. 'Are you all right?' She took her by the arm and led her to the one clear chair. 'Sit down. Are you all right?' she repeated.

Sharina eased herself into the chair. 'Don't worry, I'm not in labour. Not for a month anyway.'

'A drink of water? A coffee?'

Sharina accepted a glass of water and looked around her at the boxes and bags. There was a stack of packing cases by the wall. 'You got a lot of stuff,' she said.

'The cases there are all books. I've just been wondering why I have so many.' Marie Mathéve pushed a lock of hair back off her glowing forehead. Sharina thought with some satisfaction that she was not as neat as when she'd arrived.

'Are you a teacher, then?' she said.

'No. I'm . . . I'm retired now.'

'Were you a teacher before? You kind of have that look but you're too smart looking for a teacher, like. Just my view, that is. I had some nice teachers, but none of them was smart looking.'

Marie blushed for the second time. Sharina thought it was funny to see an older person blush. You wouldn't think an older person would have anything to blush about, would you?

'No. I'm not – I wasn't a teacher.'

'What did you do, then?'

'I . . . well, I drew buildings and photographed them. I wrote reports and tried to stop people pulling them down.'

'Conservation? Great, that. We do . . . no did . . . a module on it at school.'

Marie blinked again. 'You go to school?'

'Nah. Not no more. Just till up to this last summer term. I did my exams. Then I left.'

'You did exams? Sorry. That's stupid. Of course you did exams.'

'Nah. S'all right. Yeah. Did my exams.' She paused. 'I got ten. Four A stars. Five A's. One C. French, that. I could learn it off all right. But speak it? Nah.'

'Ten? That's good. Congratulations.'

'Yeah. You're the first person I've told, apart from my social worker and a nun on Tyneside who's my friend. It *is* good, isn't it? I had to show 'em, didn't I?'

'It surely is.' Marie paused. 'Your . . . partner, is he here?'

Sharina stood up, rubbing the small of her back. 'Nah. No partner. No such luck.' She looked round. 'Look, Marie, when you're sorted here, you can come round mine for a break. I make mint beans on toast.'

Marie smiled uncertainly. 'That is so kind of you. But I think—'

'S'OK. You've stacks to do. Don't want to mess with me. I see that.'

'No. No. Sharina, is it? I'll be pleased to come. Thank you. Say seven o'clock? By then I'll be absolutely paggered!'

This was a new word to Sharina but she got the woman's drift. 'Right. I'll be all ready.'

Marie watched her front door close behind her new neighbour and sat down on the chair Sharina had just vacated. Well, the girl was a surprise. Marie had thought Merrick Court would be full of downsizers something like her. And here was a child no more than sixteen, living independently. Pregnant. Something interesting there.

She glanced at the clock. Five thirty. She would work like the clappers for a couple of hours, then go along and join the girl for beans on toast. It would be nice to eat in company. Decamping from the old house, getting rid of a lifetime of stuff had been a wretched process. Thinking about Adam. Wondering about Adam. Wondering . . . Her eyes dropped to a stack of smaller boxes with *Krakow* scrawled on the side. When she was packing she'd not felt able to sort through them, to decide what should stay, what should go. A lot of stuff had to go into storage but these boxes stayed. They would always stay.

She picked up the Krakow boxes, climbed on a chair and pushed them into the far corner of the top of the wardrobe. As she did so, one slid off and its contents scattered on the floor. One photo fell face up and a young Alon Piotr Zielinski looked up at her: a young man with a beret standing in front of a World War Two bomber. His thin face and the fair lock dropping over his forehead made her want to weep. So like Adam. Adam. She had to avert her gaze, stuff the photos and notebooks back into the box and almost throw it up on to the wardrobe.

With the Krakow boxes disposed of, she relaxed a little. She began to survey the piles, looking for the boxes marked *Bedding* and *Clothes*. She started to unpack in earnest. At last her concern about whether she was doing the right thing in moving here was beginning to evaporate. The deed was done. She would make a big effort to get as much as possible done before seven, and then she would relax in the company of that strange girl.

Sharina rushed around her apartment making the neat rooms even neater than they already were. She set the table – cloth, knives and forks, salt, HP sauce – then turned on the television with the sound down, and waited. She'd been here at Merrick Court for quite a while and no one, apart from her social worker, had ever crossed the threshold. Today, having her own personal visitor, was a first. She looked around at this place – paid for and furnished by strangers – that was now *hers*. The Brownseys had been generous in their own way. First the flat, fully signed over to her. Then the job lot of IKEA furniture – the packs they provided for diplomats and soldiers – to furnish it, right down to the last teaspoon. Mrs Brownsey had been the daughter of a general and knew about these things.

In the earliest days at Merrick Court, the boxes of stuff from her convent life had seemed out of place amongst all this Swedish kitsch. But within a few weeks she'd spread them around, and managed to tone all that chilly style down with her posters – Mariah Carey and Missy Elliott on one wall, Katy Melua and Norah Jones on another. And, of course, the full-length Morrissey tacked to the back of the kitchen door. A small white image of the Virgin Mary – a gift from the sisters – sat in the corner window in her bedroom. When she'd done that last thing she knew the apartment was properly hers.

At five to seven she opened a tin of beans, tipped them into a bowl and covered it with clingfilm ready for the microwave. She went into the bedroom and brushed her hair, making it crackle with electricity and stand out even more from her head. She had plans to put a streak in it but couldn't decide whether to make it pink or white. She peered hard at her reflection but decided not to put lipstick on. That would have been strange, wouldn't it? Putting on lipstick to entertain an old woman.

The doorbell rang and she put the bread in the toaster, the beans in the microwave, and went to answer it, a smile on her face.

Sister Mary Cornelia rang, as usual, at teatime on Monday. She had special dispensation for the call, as even in her new religious house her pastoral care for Sharina was seen as part of her vocation. She'd told Sharina that her new place was much more modern than Rosemount. They had colour television and a ping-pong table and some of the younger sisters there even worked in the city as accountants and entrepreneurs. 'Obviously entrepreneurs for the Lord,' she added hastily, 'raising money for a new school in the slums of Santiago. It's the modern thing.'

Tonight she asked after Sharina's health and thanked her for the copy of the recent scan of the baby. 'Sure it's a miracle, dear. Those little legs and arms. That button nose.

A miracle.' She paused. 'And what have you been up to, dear?'

'I made a friend,' said Sharina. 'A neighbour has just moved in. I like her.'

'Now that's nice. So what does she do, this neighbour?'

'Well, she doesn't do anything now 'cos she's retired. But she used to draw buildings. You should see her drawings, Sister. They're mint!'

Sister Mary Cornelia's laughter boomed into her ear. 'Oh Sharina, my darling. An old woman! You made friends with an old woman? You should look for people your own age.'

'I tried that, and look where it got me, Sister.'

The laughter was more subdued now. 'Oh Sharina. How I miss you, my darling girl.'

'Come and see me, then.'

'Not permitted yet, not until we settle properly in the new house.'

'But you'll come to see me when the baby's here?'

'You can be sure of that, dear.'

'Say a prayer for me, Sister.'

'I always do, dear. Four times a day. And our dear sisters. They send you their love. Even those who don't know you pray for you.' She paused. 'Sister Mary Josephine is not so well these days. I think she misses the sea air.' She paused again. 'I think she misses you. We all do. God bless you, dear girl.'

The telephone went dead and Sharina put it carefully

back in its cradle. She was alone in her room but she could still feel the tidal warmth of the love of those three old women who had managed the small miracle of bringing her up unscathed in a world where – as she saw on her new television – so much cruelty stalked the homes of children and the streets where they played.

Catch-22

Marie on the ceiling again.

My young friend Sharina has visited me here in hospital quite a few times now, sometimes with Adam, sometimes without. And she has brought little Arian. So nice to see them both, even though I'm frustrated that I can only see the tops of their heads from up here. I never see their faces. And when I'm down there in the husk I can hear them but I can't see them. It's frustrating. I keep wondering if Adam's face has changed while he's been in prison. I imagine it has. His voice is certainly different.

The child Arian is very good, as always. You'd think there was little reward, Sharina, coming here to see this husk of a body. But you're full of surprises, aren't you? My first mistake with you was thinking you were just another young woman in trouble. The papers are full of them. But you're not one of them, not by a stretch. Your little one is immaculate. Your apartment has flair. You know how to set a table. You read books. You have quite distinct opinions and you're formidably self-sufficient for one so young.

Quaint. I suppose. Strange in this world.

Why are you so good, Sharina? How can such a thing come from an orphan state and a patchwork childhood? Your saving grace, I suppose, was taking sanctuary with those old girls, who mothered rather than converted you. That's clear. You don't seem in the least bit religious, even though your manners are immaculate and you lay a very dainty table.

Seeing those magenta streaks in your hair and your short frocks, any outsider would think you were one of those ordinary girls you see on the bus or in the street. You talk like them at least: that telegraphese you use, with sentences circling back for confirmation, ending with 'inn't?' or 'don't it?' or 'you know?'. But still, there's something quaint and old-fashioned about you. And there's no denying your charm.

You certainly charmed me from the first day we met. And in all this time that charm has not faded. I always felt myself with you. A rare thing. Apart from Jack, you are the only one who makes me feel easy. I love Adam, but he doesn't do that. Make me feel easy. He has always been so watchful and quiet around me. It's not that he's not a lively person. I used to see him laughing and joking with his friends as they came down the drive in the old house. Especially Sam. But once inside the house he'd go silent and they'd do the talking.

The most talkative of all of them was this Sam Rogers. Sam laughed a lot in my house and made Adam smile even when I was there. I only met him a few times but I remember his deep laughter and his fine mind. He had a charming soul. Just like you, Sharina.

The first time he came to my house he poked around and asked bold questions that demanded direct answers. He quoted the Bible to me at the drop of a hat. Of course, he told me he was not a believer, but — as he said — the words are magic, aren't they? Meeting his mother that time at the court, I see where he got that from.

Sam sat there one day, shuffling through my drawings of Venice and Pezenas, and asked me about scale and proportion. We talked about his finds in Cyprus and he admired my Greek drawings of the Erechtheion and the Athena Nike and the wrecked temple of Pythian Apollo.

When you were with Sam you could sense him filing away all the information in that great brain of his. Like you, Sharina, a person could be deceived with Sam. Superficially he could be any 'canny lad' from round here. But he wasn't. He had a kind of universal genius.

After that time Sam visited he sent me a hand-made thank-you card. On the front was a stiff, cartoonish drawing of his own east Durham council house. He had addressed the envelope: To the Woman Who Draws Buildings, Miss M.M. *Inside he had written:* Thank you for having me. This drawing lark is not as easy as it looks but I hope you like my drawing of Venice on the Tyne. Like I say, thank you for having me, Sam.

Such nice manners. Like you, Sharina.

Even now, up here on the ceiling, halfway lost myself, on a journey I don't know where, I could weep with sorrow for Sam's mother, who lost her amazing boy. And I feel guilty for my gratitude that the crash took her son, not mine.

Whoosh! Thump! Down inside the husk again. Now I can't see anything, just hear their murmuring voices.

Marie did have this deep, guilty gratitude that – however dire the circumstances – Adam was the one who had survived rather than Sam. She felt that her punishment for that gratitude was losing him to the prison system. He did not allow her to visit him there and he made sure her letters were returned unopened. He even moved prisons in the second year and left Marie with no idea where he was. From time to time she would come across worrying pieces in the newspaper describing in disturbing depth the evil things that went on in prison. In the end, when she saw such a headline, she didn't read the article. She could only keep going by not thinking too closely about it all. Adam was always somewhere there in her head, and most particularly in her heart. Always. But she stopped writing letters. He had rejected her and she – for the time being – stopped trying to reconnect with him.

Her therapy was action. She got out of the house that had first been her mother's, then hers, then hers and Jack's. She'd loved that house, but it was good to leave it. And Adam? He could find her if he really wanted to. After all, he was a very bright boy. She put a brave face on it all, but gradually her heart was turning to stone.

That is, until Sharina Osgood came into her life.

From the beginning Marie enjoyed the freshness and difference of Merrick Court. On that first day she met

Sharina, and after a month or so she met Arian, Sharina's son: a brand-new life. She could feel the gears changing and her own life moving on.

Sharina put Arian in her arms the day she came out of hospital. Slim and fit now, she kept asking Marie questions about caring for a little baby. It reminded Marie of the early days with Adam when she didn't know what to do herself. How much she had loved him and marvelled at him, tracing his face with her fingers to make sure he was real, thinking how she and David had made him in that narrow room in Krakow. Those days were a bit of a struggle, as she was working freelance, and no work meant no fee.

But then Jack came into their lives, and as he and Adam drew close, it became possible for her to continue to travel and write and earn money to keep them.

Everything in those days, with Jack around, seemed so well ordered. But she had not anticipated the downside. Jack and Adam became so close that when she came home from her travels she began to feel like a beloved outsider. Afterwards, she felt that she had never managed to get the balance right. The fact was, when Jack died, she and Adam were both unhappy for their own reasons, left circling around each other and barely touching. Just circling around each other and not touching.

Her new friendship with Sharina meant that she got to go to young Arian's christening in the chapel of the convent on the Tyne. Sharina insisted that she should join the three ageing sisters as godmothers to the little boy.

Marie enjoyed talking with the youngest sister, Sister Mary Cornelia, who glowed with love and admiration for the girl. It was easy to see where Sharina's confidence had come from.

In the car on the way back from the christening she glanced into the rear-view mirror and asked about Arian's name. Sharina was sitting strapped in the back of the car, the baby on her knee. She smiled. 'Oh that's easy. You know *Catch-22*?'

Marie nodded. 'Famous American novel. I'm afraid I haven't read it.'

'Well Kevin – you know, the boy who's Arian's dad – he loved that book! Nearly read the words off the page, even though it was really old. Used to read bits to me when we were – well, close, like. It made us laugh. Anyway, the last time I saw him he'd left a copy of it in my locker. Then he went to America and then went off to his university and that was that. So then I read the whole book right through. Again and again. I was missing him a lot then, like, and very worried about things.'

'I can see it would be hard.' Hard to know what to say. Marie wanted to ask Sharina more about Arian's father and how she got to be pregnant. But that would not be polite. Sharina was very good at drawing boundaries: quite a subtle skill.

Sharina went on. 'Well, that book's about this lad Yossarian who was a pilot in the war. He flew planes. The story's kind of serious and funny at the same time. You know?'

Arian started to squeak and she put a knuckle in his mouth so he could suck it and be soothed. Marie knew that without even turning to look, because the girl did it when he was restless and it always worked.

'Anyway, it's a funny old book. You keep getting to know about the same thing that happens from different people, kind of circling. And you have to keep reading and reading if you want to get to know the point of the whole thing. It's, like, you know about things but you don't, and then you find out things you didn't realise and it makes sense of what went on before. It's like some great round puzzle with no edges. Well, in this book they go on about this Catch-22. Kind of damned if you do and damned if you don't – that was what it was like when you were at war. And that Yossarian, he's some man! Funny, you know? He says, "That's some catch, Catch-22!" It tickled him. I loved that Yossarian when I read that book. I wanted to call the baby Yossarian, but Sister Mary Cornelia said it would be a bit of a burden for any baby. So we decided on Arian.'

Marie could hear the baby gurgling. And Sharina's voice as she spoke in his ear. 'You like your name, don't you, pet? Suits you, Arian, don't it?'

Catch-22! Marie thought that was a bit like her and Adam. She'd been damned by rejection when she did pursue him. And now she felt damned by her own conscience because she hadn't kept on trying.

She changed gear and her thoughts went back to Jack.

He would have known what to do. He would have bridged the gap that yawned now between her and Adam. He'd had a gift for it.

Jack

When Jack Longland met Marie Mathéve he'd been a widower for a year and the thing that sustained his life was routine. Every Monday he did his washing – whites separate from darks – went to Gloria's café to read the *Guardian* and then went bowling with an ex-army friend. Every Tuesday he ironed, had his lunch and went to read the *Guardian* in Gloria's café. Then – rain or shine – he went for a long walk through ancient woodland to the east of the city. He particularly enjoyed May, when the bluebells were out. Later on he would take Marie and Adam on those same walks.

Each Wednesday and Friday Jack did essential cleaning in his council bungalow, changed his library books – he liked World War Two fiction – then went on to St Thibery's Hospice, where he had his lunch with the residents then chatted with people in the day room until teatime. And every night he played his records, mostly romantic string quartets, a taste he'd caught from his own father.

But Thursdays were Jack's personal treat. On Thursdays he would walk right through the city to the cathedral, where he paid his respects to his Lord and to his late parents who, like him, were intelligent people of simple faith. He sometimes thought of his wife, Beatrice, whom he'd met in the south of England on demob leave in 1946. Fair, plump and pretty, she was a sight for very sore eyes after his last mission, as part of the liberation force in the Far East. Beatrice thought all that faith stuff was baloney, which was a pity as when she was dying she told Jack she wished she'd listened more. Still, her carer at St Thibery's, who was a Quaker, found ways to comfort her.

After his Thursday cathedral visit Jack always visited the rather plush lounge of the Imperial Hotel to read his *Guardian*. He had a cappuccino, then proceeded to the indoor market to buy his week's supply of fresh produce. He liked the Imperial lounge. These days there was a sprinkling of coffee shops across the city – very chi-chi places – but they fell down on one thing for Jack: there was nowhere to stretch his long legs and no table big enough to spread his broadsheet newspaper. The Imperial, as well as deep sofas and large tables, had a stunning view of the river and the cathedral. And that, he would say, was very refreshing for the spirit.

Then, one March Thursday in 1982, just as he was settling down with his paper, he caught sight of a youngish woman, mid-thirties perhaps, sitting on the next couch. She was fine-featured, and wore a long fair pigtail down her back that reminded him of a girl he went to school with before the war. And this girl looked, thought Jack, as though she had a baby on the way. No cause to cry, surely? He'd never been blessed himself, but he was certain babies *were* a blessing. But this girl was silently crying. Tears were falling down her cheeks and dripping off her chin. She was trying to swab them off with the back of her hand but they kept coming.

He looked longingly at the headline before him — something about new amendments in the Polish constitution re-establishing the traditional Polish principle of government by rule of law. This — according to the article — represented yet another major step in the evolution of the democratic concept of government by the consent of the governed.

Jack closed his newspaper and went across to offer the girl his freshly ironed handkerchief. She took it and mopped up part of the flood. Her pale eyes, still swimming, looked into his. 'I never cry,' she said. 'Really. I never cry.'

He sat down opposite her. 'Well you are now, love,' he said. 'You're crying buckets.'

She mopped and mopped her face and dabbed her eyes until finally the tears were reduced to the occasional damp hiccough. The eyes that finally emerged from the swamp were a startling slatey green. Jack swallowed and felt himself flush with feeling — shy, yearning, certain, uncertain. The last time he'd felt like this was in Singapore in 1946 when a dance-hall girl of pale eggshell beauty and witty demeanour caught his eye and came to live with him in his billet for three months before going back to her parents in China. His heart had ached when she left and the bruise that girl left behind was always there. He still had a tiny square black-and-white photo of her tucked away.

Now this girl was offering him his sodden hankie. He shook his head. 'You keep it,' he said.

She surveyed the hankie. 'I don't blame you,' she said.

He looked at her more closely. She was older than he'd thought. Late thirties perhaps. He looked down at her fine, slender hands on the table then glanced round and nodded at a young waitress who was hovering. 'Maybe we could have tea? A cup of tea will surely help. Or so they say.'

Her sudden smile was like a rainbow after rain. 'Do they really say that?'

'Well I just did! Now. Tea or coffee? I think I'll have another cappuccino.'

That first day they spent the next hour talking about everything except the reason why she'd been crying. He told her about being retired now from the factory, where he'd been a line leader and a foreman, and about Beatrice, his wife, who had been what she called a *modiste* – working in mature women's lingerie all her life. He even told her about Beatrice turning down the option of children, as it would ruin her figure.

'She died in harness, you know. Maybe you could say *in*

corset.' He smiled briefly. 'Anyway, she got ill while she was working, and by the time her sick leave was up . . . well . . . That's how I got to volunteering at the hospice when I retired. I spent months there with her. They're nice people there. Lots of Quakers. Nice people, Quakers.' He became aware that the young woman was staring at him, her eyes quite dry now and her face flushed. 'I'm sorry. I'm talking too much.' He was flustered. He cleared his throat. 'I never talk about those things. Not to anybody.'

'It must have been very sad for you.' Marie felt that, truly. 'Losing Beatrice like that.'

Then the girl came with a tray and took her time arranging the heavy silver coffee pot and china cups and saucers on the table. Jack watched her depart and cleared his throat again. 'That's plenty about me. What about you? Do you work here in the city?'

'Not just now.' Marie shook my head, and told him about what she did for a living.

'Sounds interesting,' he said. In truth he was never quite sure exactly what Marie did. *Something about documenting buildings and taking and making pictures of them* was how he always described it.

She shrugged. 'Suits me. Suited me, I should say. I've just been told I'm expendable. That after . . .' She looked down at her bump, very visible at five months. 'I think after this my work'll be cut because I need to travel to do the job properly.'

'Not that secure at the moment, then?'

'You're telling me!'

He laughed at her truculent, childish tone.

She frowned at him. 'Not funny, you know.'

He toned down his laugh to a smile. 'I'm sorry. I think I'm just laughing because I'm enjoying sitting here talking to you. And I'm smiling because I can't imagine anyone letting you go.'

She stared at him.

'Look,' he said, 'I haven't talked normally like this, not since Beatrice . . . well, not for months before that.'

She stared at him for a second, then relaxed, settling back on the plush couch. 'Well then. No offence taken! It probably was just a bit funny.' She looked around at the Imperial Lounge, which was now filling up with mothers and children from the nearby private school, putting off the moment when they had to go home. 'Do you come here often?' she said.

They both laughed at this. Marie put her hand to her mouth. 'Did I really say that?'

'Well,' he said, 'to answer your naff question. I come here after I've done my shopping on Thursdays to read my paper and have a think, maybe do my crossword. Beatrice and I used to come here on a Saturday morning. She'd have a coffee, then go up the road to Marks and Spencer, and I would stay here with my paper. I like the place. You see different kinds of people here. And the staff don't bother you.'

'First time I've been.' Marie nodded at her plastic

shopping bag. 'Like Beatrice, I've been raiding Marks and Spencer.'

He wanted to ask her then whether she'd come here specially to cry, but thought better of it. He sipped his coffee.

'Will you be here next Thursday?' she said suddenly.

'Very likely,' he said. 'It's my habit.'

She stood up and he did too. She looked him in the eye. He was barely her height. 'I'll come next Thursday and bring back your hankie,' she said.

'Thank you,' he said. 'Good of you. It'll be nice to see you.' He watched her stride across the thick carpet, admiring her confident, swinging gait. He thought she carried herself very well, despite her condition.

Then Jack shook out his newspaper, spread it before him, and finished reading about Solidarity being dissolved by the Polish government. He took in all the information, but one part of him was buzzing with excitement. This excitement wasn't gratitude because someone much younger and infinitely more attractive than himself had paid him attention. It was sheer exuberance: a feeling he'd last enjoyed in Singapore when Jan Lee turned up on his doorstep with a kind of silken sack that contained all her worldly goods, announcing that he was a naughty person running away from the dance hall so fast but that luckily his sergeant had told her where to find him.

It had only been by chance that he'd been there in Singapore. He'd been called up as part of a communications unit ahead of the Normandy landings. He thought that, the European war being over, he'd get his demob. But instead of home leave, he'd been shipped out to Singapore with his unit to support the relief of that island. It was a standing joke in the unit that he'd been such a busy boy, moving as a very young soldier from the chapel virtue of his Durham home to the exotic streets of Singapore, that he'd not managed to lose his virginity. It was no accident that his sergeant had made sure Jan Lee found her way to his billet.

Jack finally stopped daydreaming about Jan Lee. He was driving home in his red Cortina when it occurred to him that although he had every intention of going to the Imperial next Thursday to retrieve his handkerchief, he'd not even introduced himself to the young woman in the corner seat. He had no idea what she was called. Not Beatrice and not Jan, he thought. But maybe something in between.

He felt that there would be plenty of time for that. But really there was not enough time. Ten years was not enough for either of them. In that ten years they loved each other and he got to know a good deal about the girl in the Imperial lounge. But not everything. Marie was always good at keeping her secrets.

Close Call

In the third week, on her return from lunch, the consultant Jessica Stanley stopped by the smokers' shed, where Sharina was waiting for her turn to visit Marie. 'Bring the baby in,' she said. 'It might be a treat for Marie to hear her grandson's chatter.'

'But he's not her grandson, is he? He's her friend.'

Jessica smiled slightly. 'Well, let's say he's her grandson. Makes it less complicated. His chatter might just strike a chord in Miss Mathéve. There's no saying what might bring her back to life.'

This was convenient for Adam and Sharina, as it saved them taking turns minding Arian in the shed. By now Adam was taking it for granted that Sharina would come each day. He liked her and found her presence a comfort. More than that, it seemed to him that Sharina knew his mother better than he did, and that could be vital.

Now Sharina sat Arian on the bed by Marie's elbow and talked to him about herself and Marie, telling him how Sister Mary Cornelia had taken him from Sister Mary Josephine and placed him in Marie's arms, saying, 'Sure, here's your other godmother, Arian! Be sure to take notice of her, as she's a very clever woman.' Sister Mary Cornelia had noticed Marie watching them with Arian, and knew she wanted her turn.

'Mary Cornelia knew that, Arian, didn't she? Mary Cornelia knows everything. She'd take one look at you and know the secrets of your heart. Did that time and again with me when I was living with her.'

Adam, on the other side of the bed, thought that wouldn't happen to him. He prided himself on being hard to read. He emerged from behind his *Private Eye* and stared at Arian, trying to imagine himself falling into his mother's eager arms. His imagination failed him.

Sharina caught a fragment of his thought. 'She's very good at the baby thing, you know, your mam.'

He shrugged. 'I wouldn't know, can't recall any of that. It was mostly Jack who did that kind of thing.'

'Jack?'

'My stepfather. Well, they were together but I don't think they were married. Well, if they did, they didn't tell me. They got together after I was born and he died when I was ten. He took care of me a lot. He was old but I liked him.'

Sharina stared at him over Arian's head. 'So you didn't

know your real dad? That's like me. I know he came from Gabon in Africa and then went back, and that's that.'

'Like I say, he was all right, Jack. A lot older than her. Already retired then, so he took care of the house and Marie as well as me. Helped me choose my clothes. Sewed on my name tapes for school. All that.'

Sharina frowned. 'Couldn't imagine Marie not being on her own . . . funny him being quite old . . .'

'Neither of them acted like he was old. They clicked together like two halves of a puzzle when she was at home.' He paused. 'He was good, was Jack. That was the saddest day, his funeral. That is, until . . .'

'Until . . . ?'

He shrugged away the question. 'There've been worse things.' He wondered if Marie had told Sharina that her son was a murderer. Probably not.

Sharina's attention was turning back again to Arian, who was starting to grizzle. Adam went on thinking about her. In these weeks they'd become close. Their day-by-day lives had become entwined. He'd got into the habit of going to the shop for milk and taking it along to her apartment so they could all breakfast together, she in a long T-shirt, mussed hair and bright morning eyes. She was more open with him than he was with her. As the days went on, he pieced together her life, with its battles at school, her pride in her cleverness and her confidence that was partly innate and partly instilled in her by her nuns. He was curious about Arian's father but could not voice the question. So many missing fathers. He did discover that Sharina felt no bitterness against the boy, whoever he was. She did volunteer, 'Things were left very well for me, considering. Hard even to think of his face now. And me and Arian manage, don't we?'

Watching the fair young man and the black girl with that stripe of pink hair, Jessica Stanley wondered what this story was. She knew the boy had been in prison. One of the nurses who lived locally said he'd killed someone, but he didn't seem to be the type. If there was a type! She'd read somewhere that murder came in various guises. There were killers who were psychopaths, for whom murdering was a pastime. There were people who took life as part of a criminal business routine involving greed and envy, and sometimes recruited psychopaths to do the work for them. There were those who killed almost by savage domestic accident. There was that woman whom the police brought here with old breaks, burn marks and bruises, who had finally exploded and killed her husband with a heavy pan as he lay there drunk. It must have taken some force.

But what about Adam Mathéve? On that first day he'd looked as scared as a rabbit in a foxhole. He had to be persuaded even to touch his mother. Still, he'd taken Jessica's advice and stayed close to Marie, reading those interesting notebooks to her. Sometimes she left the door to Marie's room ajar and listened to him. She liked to listen to those clear young tones, even when he stumbled over the Polish names. She got the impression that this was new to him, that he hadn't read the words before. He'd even begun to ask the unresponsive Marie questions. The adventure outlined in the books clearly belonged only to his mother.

Marie and these two youngsters were a source of refreshment for Jessica Stanley. People came in and out of her ward all the time, only individualised into 'the elbow in bed seven', or 'the stroke in bed two'. The shovelling-out of patients as soon as they were reasonably ambulant meant that the cases rarely evolved into personalities with their own life stories and histories. These days a life saved was a personal victory, an institutional success, only occasionally related to a real live human being.

But Marie Mathéve had been different. She'd turned up with blood seeping through that awkwardly long hair. She had looked shrunken then, old as the hills. When they'd swabbed off all the blood she still looked old, even though, unlike other older patients, she had no dentures to remove. All her own teeth. That was something.

With her still face and passive body, she was unrewarding to attend to. But there must be something about her. Something. Why else would the handsome son with grief in his face keep coming and coming? Why else would the black girl with her soft northern voice struggle here to be with her, buggy and all? She seemed very fond of the old girl.

Jessica had become so interested in this patient that one night after a late shift she'd returned home and Googled the name *Marie Mathéve*. It was distinctive enough. She found then that her patient was a woman with a small but substantial reputation to do with saving buildings. There was one short article by her in an archive, recounting a visit to look at buildings in Poland in the eighties, a trip sponsored by the Soroptimist movement. Extraordinary. That would account for those Polish names the boy stumbled over.

So in the end Jessica Stanley could no longer think of her patient merely as an old woman who had knocked herself senseless, as another body to shuffle through the system. Now Marie Mathéve was beginning to be rounded out. Jessica had even worked out that she was only in her sixties. Not so old at all, these days.

This afternoon she watched from the doorway as Adam took a red ring-bound notebook out of his pocket and began to read. The girl called Sharina had pulled the grizzling child on to her knee and started to play a child's game to soothe him. She slid him off her knee on to her ankle and started to waggle it up and down.

Horsey, horsey don't you stop!
Just let your heels go clippety clop
Your tail go swish and your Wheels go round
Giddyap we're homeward bound.

Suddenly Marie's hand flipped up in the air. Adam stared, the notebook dropping from his hand. The boy stopped crying.

Adam grabbed her hand. 'Marie!' he said. 'Marie!'

The baby chuckled.

Jessica glided across, took Marie's hand from him and laid it back on the woven counterpane. 'Let me see.' She took a small torch from her pocket and peered into Marie's eyes. Then she leaned across and hit a button. A nurse came running in and got between Adam and the bed, shouldering him out of the way. She looked across at Sharina. 'Perhaps you could take the little boy outside?' She exchanged glances with the consultant.

Sharina left but Adam stayed, his back to the door. The consultant and the nurse spoke urgently to their patient and more apparatus was brought in. Then after what seemed like hours of thumping, organised chaos, Jessica Stanley breathed out and stood back, nodding to the nurses now gathered round the bed.

She turned to Adam. 'Stable now. Just a flutter. I think she was straining to come back. She tried to touch the wall, then came back. We'll keep a close eye on her and I'll book her a brain scan to check on any change. But she's OK now. Truly.'

He stood hesitating by the door.

'You go home, Adam. Leave her to rest. Any change and I'll tell you. Believe me.' She came and pushed him on the shoulder. 'Go!'

He picked up the notebook from the floor and thrust it back in his backpack, intensely angry without really knowing why. He stalked away without looking at the consultant. Jessica wondered who the boy was angry at. Her, for not bringing his mother back to life? Himself, because he couldn't do it either? Now she was bemused. He'd been a model son so far. That anger. It seemed way out of character. As far as she could tell.

Whoosh! It was the song! That blessed nursery rhyme. For a minute I thought I was back in the flat in Chorzow, singing it to Piotr, old Alon Piotr looking on approvingly, smoking a precious cigarette. Then I thought it was Adam, here in this side ward, being jiggled on my ankle while Jack put together our evening meal. Crikey! What's this? Who are this crowd? What are David and my mother doing here, Jack with them? Alon Piotr too! Arms out, beckoning me into this aureole of light, begging to join them. Smiling. My mother looks young, like she did when I was at school. Alon Piotr too is young, in his flyer get-up, fair hair flopping to one side. They're smiling. All of them. I can't hear their voices but they're reaching for me, hauling me as though I'm at the opposite end of a tug of war. At my end of the rope I can feel the strong young spirits of Sharina and Arian. But most of all I can feel Adam. He's saying no, no, he's not finished with me yet. Stay here! Stay with me! I feel like a Native American tied to two trees that are being hauled apart by horses. Oww! Ooh! It hurts.

Whoosh! Back inside the husk, covered with stretch marks. I can see nothing, but I can hear the voices of the doctor and the nurse.

★

'Close call, that, Miss Stanley.'

'You're not wrong there, Sister. That was a really close call.'

Beloved of the Lord

Adam trudged up the steps to his mother's apartment to find a person at the door. For a split second he didn't recognise her, then his heart sank as he realised who it was. She was wearing the belted raincoat she had worn in court and seemed smaller, paler and even younger than she had then.

'Mrs Rogers,' he said.

She smiled at him. 'Now, son!' she said. 'How are you? I hear your mam's been in the wars. It was in the paper. Coma, it said.'

Ice chipped its way through his veins. He could hear the rough tones of Sam's voice in hers, as though Sam had fused himself into his mother's slight body. 'Mrs Rogers, I . . .' he began.

Her eyes stayed steadily on his. 'Aren't you gunna invite us in, then? Nice if you did, son.'

'Yes. Yes. Come in.' His fingers felt cold and numb as he

fumbled with the lock. When he finally got it open, he led the way inside. She followed him in and sat down on a dining chair, her knees together and her small leather handbag clasped in her lap. Her hair was pulled back in its curly ponytail, her face was scrubbed clean and shining. She was as neat and wholesome as a heroine in a 1950s film.

Adam did not sit down. 'Can I get you a cup of tea?' he said miserably. Then he burst out, 'How are you here? Why are you here? What brought you? Look, I can't tell you how . . . I'm sorry . . .'

'Hush!' She held up a hand to silence him. 'Your mam's in the papers, isn't she, Adam? She was famous once, it said. Then I saw the name. You have an unusual name, don't you? I used to comment on that to our Sam. An unusual name.'

'But how did you find us . . . here?'

'Easy, son. Your old address is on Sam's letters. My Joseph has them all, date order, in boxes he made. He likes order, does my Joseph. It's order that keeps him going. Then I enquired with the woman who lived there at your old address. And she gave me this one.'

Adam lifted his shoulders. 'Sam's dad looked so angry at me, that day in court. Don't blame him, of course.' He bit his lip. Behind his eyes flashed an image of Mr Rogers, with his easy-going smile, in the pub with his pint, his newspaper and his sausage and mash. It had happened before. The prison shrink had called these things flashbacks. The one with Sam's dad was an easy one. Not like the flashbacks he had of the crash, all the splintered images and visceral fear.

'He was really nice to me that time I came to see you,' he said miserably now. 'Sam's dad.'

'He's a good man, my Joseph.' Mrs Rogers stood up. 'Tell you what, son, I'll get us a cup of tea. Now,' she looked round, 'where's the makings?'

He led the way to the kitchen and stood by helplessly as she handled his mother's teapot and china beakers. Then he followed her back through to the living room, sat down and let her pour him tea.

'Now!' she said briskly. 'Was it awful in there, in prison?'

He didn't know what to say. If he said prison was OK then that would be rotten for her. Given what he'd done, he should have suffered hell. He agreed with that. Then at least justice would have been served. After all, he'd killed her son and injured their friend. But prison hadn't been hell. It had been dull, grinding and occasionally dangerous, but it had never been hell. Finally he said, 'Whatever it was like, I'm sure it wasn't as bad as it's been for you. Christ! That sounds pious.'

She regarded him steadily. 'Don't you dare take the Lord's name in vain, son.'

He flushed. 'Sorry. I'm sorry.' He couldn't think of anything to say so he put his cup to his lips to avoid putting his foot further into his mouth.

Then she said, 'I did pray for you, you know, when you

were in there. In fact I prayed for you last night, thinking you were still in prison. I prayed for the Lord's indulgence in your immortal soul and I prayed for the reparation of your heart. I always knew very well that you'd be beside yourself with grief, just like we are.' She paused. 'I knew you loved our Sam, like he loved you with the love that Jonathan had for David, *beloved of the Lord.*'

She paused again.

'But I have to tell you about something that happened to me. I was sitting in the quiet time once in chapel, and suddenly the Lord let me know I was a hypocrite, that what I was doing – forgiving you and praying for you – was all empty *piety*. I'd been telling myself what I *thought* I should be thinking. You know? But really, deep down, I was full – spilling over – with *hate* for you, Adam, for taking away my own ewe lamb.'

Adam shivered.

She went on. 'I was grudging that your own mam should still have you here on earth, even though you were in prison. Not like me.' She paused again, this time to take a thoughtful sip of tea. She looked at him over the rim of her cup. Suddenly her eyes were bright and jewel blue, lit from inside, just like Sam's.

He just managed to stop himself from groaning.

She went on. 'Then the next day, I saw this thing in the paper about the woman in a coma. And the name! It struck me then that this deep inner cursing I'd been doing against you, and grudging your mother your presence on earth, could – by some strange alchemy – have landed her there in that bed, comatose. I realised that there and then. I was frightened, Adam, Frightened.'

Me too, he thought.

'Anyway, I talked to my minister and she said I was flattering myself if I thought I had such powers. That the best thing to do was to remember my Sam and the gift he was to me for all those years. All that knowledge in his head. All those smiles. All those people who loved him. You should have seen the letters, Adam!

'Anyway my minister said I should treasure that memory, keep it bright and not sully it with all this hatred or this thinking I could cast spells, succumbing to Satan. And she said I was to remember that the Lord says vengeance in His, that He will repay. That it's not our business to second-guess the Lord.'

Suddenly Adam felt again that rare, pure streak of anger. Only in prison had he felt like this. 'Are you telling me that you think Marie is lying there in hospital because your Lord is taking revenge on her for what I did?' The words were like chips of dull black iron clunking from his lips.

Now, mate! Steady on! Steady on! Sam's voice was whispering in his ear. Now Adam truly was mad. He shook his head to get rid of that voice, like you would shake it to get rid of a fly on your face.

Mrs Rogers was frowning. 'Now! No, son! Not that. I was thinking that my bitterness at losing Sam was somehow seeping out of me and wreaking havoc in the world outside my head. That's why I came here to see if I could help. That's what Sam would've wanted – for me to see what I could do for her, your mam. It was about her. I have to admit I was surprised when I saw you walking up them steps.' Her eyes examined him from head to toe. 'I thought you were still inside prison, see? No one told me. Doesn't seem long . . .' Her voice trailed away.

'Two years and two months,' he said. 'It seemed a long time to me.'

'I tell you what! It just seems like yesterday when our Sam . . .' She saw his face change and stopped herself. 'Your mam was at the court every single day, you know? Her face was still as a carving on a tomb. I saw you didn't look at her. I was sorry for her. We talked a bit. And I thought she was a nice woman. Gracious, like.'

'She *is* a nice woman,' he said. He was desperate now for Sam's mother to go, willing her to put down his mother's china beaker, get out of his mother's chair and move. Go away. Get lost.

Mrs Rogers went on. 'I was wondering, like, if I might go and see her. Which ward did you say she was in?'

'I didn't,' he said.

She looked straight at him, her eyes gleaming, just like Sam's used to when he was on his high horse. Then she said carefully, 'Look, Adam. Me, I'll do your mam no harm. I promise you that. Our Sam'd want me to give her my kind of comfort and *he* was an atheist, the scamp.' Her tone was full of affection. 'I know it. He'd want me to give her comfort. You know it.'

'Ward Eleven,' he said. 'She's in Ward Eleven.'

'Mebbe,' she persisted, 'you could just give them a ring and tell them I'm going along there. They might not let me in otherwise.' Her eyes rested on the telephone. 'You could ring them now and tell them. It'd only take a tick. Save you remembering after.' Her blue eyes were soft now, appealing.

Adam could feel Sam there in the room, somewhere behind him. He picked up the phone, talked to the ward sister and did the deed. Then he turned back to Mrs Rogers. 'She said it'd be all right. My mother had a bit of a turn today but she's settled down again. Sister said it would be all right for you to go,' he repeated. 'Tomorrow. In the morning.'

She put down her beaker, stood up and picked up her bag. 'It'll all be better son, afterwards. Believe me.'

He looked at her and was still full of fear.

At the door she turned to smile at him. 'Don't worry about this, son. My God is a gentle God. And His Son is a gentle man. Do you remember the prayer? *Gentle Jesus, meek and mild . . .* For Him you are as a child, Adam. Believe me.'

And she was gone.

Adam locked the door behind her and leaned on it. Then he cried – first a splashing waterfall of tears, then great racking sobs exploding so deep from within his diaphragm that his ribs ached. His body became drenched, overflowing, ringing with feeling; his skin prickled and became tense and erect in every sense. He could not bear the fact that Sam wasn't there, that he was not in this world. For a very long time, apart from obligatory discussions with the prison psychiatrist, he'd avoided thinking directly about Sam. Now it was as though Mrs Rogers had left him here, present in every corner of the room, grinning his easy-going smile. *Come on, mate, chill!* His voice seemed to sit in the air.

Blindly Adam felt his way to the bathroom and, fully clothed, turned on the shower. He stood there under the gush of water and banged his head on the tiles until the tension left him and he was numb, with no feeling left in any part of him. Finally he turned off the shower, slid down the cubicle wall and sat in the shower tray in sopping clothes until he was frozen and stiff.

Much later he dragged himself out of the shower, peeled off his clothes and left them in a sodden heap on the floor. He crept into Marie's bed, curled up in her blankets and stared at the wall. There was a hammering on the door and he knew it was Sharina. He ignored her and made his mind go perfectly blank, as he'd done many times in prison. It was the only way.

From somewhere then, for the first time in a long time, his father was on his mind. He'd tried once to ask Jack who his real father was, but Jack had just said, 'Your mum's a very private person, you know. She keeps her own counsel.' Then Jack had died and Marie had still kept her own counsel. And Adam could never ask her about the man who was his father.

But now suddenly he was suffused with curiosity about the man whose genes he carried. Why had his mother never mentioned this person? Was he the kind of man who would kill his best friend?

'Oh Jack.' He thumped his mother's pillow very hard. 'What about him? What about me?'

The Truth About Caring

At the Imperial the following Thursday Jack Longland was pleased to find the young woman sitting there on the same seat. She passed him a package wrapped in tissue. 'All washed and starched,' she said. 'And I'm sorry I cried all over you. It's not like me. My name is Marie Mathéve.'

They shook hands quite formally.

His grip was firm. 'Jack Longland,' he said.

She signalled the waitress. 'Let me get the coffee.'

Over two cups of coffee he found himself telling her more about his life; about his working day in the factory where they made fridges and cookers. He found himself expressing the excitement of being part of an urgent machine where every day, every week your input was important. 'I have this cousin who was a probation officer,' he said. 'He looked down on us factory workers. Called us cannon fodder. But I couldn't see it. His life was all forms and knocking on doors at midnight.'

She was interested. 'I've never been in a factory,' she said. 'I've always seen them as working places of the past, built at a time when they were the new cathedrals.'

He laughed. 'Dark satanic mills, you mean?'

'Well. Well-built dark satanic mills,' she said. 'I work for a commission that gets some of them listed. Preserved.'

'And turned into museums?' he said.

'Something like that,' she said.

'Well, the place where I worked was no museum, and no classy building. It was built ad hoc. Wartime munitions factory with 1960s extensions. Big blocks. But it worked. Lots of people employed there.'

Marie looked at Jack, whose face was sparkling with enthusiasm, and had a passing thought about age. He must be more than twenty years older than she was, but he had the sparkle, the life of a much younger man. The hands that held the Imperial teacup were strong and unblemished. But deeper inside she could see that Jack Longland had the gift of happiness. He was happy in his skin. It radiated from him.

'So what do you do now you're retired?' she asked.

He shrugged. 'I have plenty to do,' he said. 'House to run. I grow vegetables on my allotment. I read my papers. Like to know what's going on.' He paused. 'Then I spend an afternoon most weeks at St Thibery's.'

'St Thibery's?'

'He was a saint who cured the insane. This is a kind of hostel for people who come out of psychiatric hospitals and can't cope on their own. They also have a hospice attached to the place. It's where Beatrice was in the end.'

'Are they mad?' she said.

He looked at her quite severely. 'We're all mad, one way or another,' he said. 'It's a mad world, you know.'

She felt properly rebuked. 'Have I stopped you reading your paper?' she said.

He smiled then, and she felt herself being let off some kind of hook. 'No. I got it read before I came. I hoped you'd be here.' He finished his coffee. 'Look, I thought I'd walk up to the cathedral. P'raps you'd come? It's a very nice walk.'

She knew the walk. She'd done it many times as a child with her mother. In fact she'd first got her love of buildings from that quarter of the city with its graceful ancient cathedral, its looming adjacent castle and its gorgeous curving Georgian terraces. She said now, 'I haven't been up there for years. I sometimes think that these days I only know my way to the station.' She stood up, leaning back a bit to balance her bulge.

She stumbled as they walked up the steep hill to the cathedral and he took her arm, an old-fashioned protective gesture. She felt comfortable and safe, and calmer than she'd felt in the months since she'd returned from Krakow.

In the fudgy calm of the cathedral they sat side by side for a while, their shoulders touching. Then they moved out to the cloisters and her fingers itched for her drawing book to note the columns and the open windows of the cloister.

She made up her mind to return here on her own to draw, to feel her way with her fingers around these old stones, to share with the ancient masons the quiet elegance of this building.

The two of them continued out to the cathedral close and sat on a seat in the war memorial garden. Again they sat easily, shoulder to shoulder.

She said suddenly, 'Do you believe in God, Jack?'

He heaved a deep sigh. 'Well, I do believe – in the Lord my God – but if you ask me what He, She or It is, I'm stumped. I do believe in something. My wife didn't. She liked to argue about it, to be honest. But in the end there was a yearning about her. The people in the hospice were Quakers. They were very good. She took to them and you could sense all that determined atheism kind of unravelling.' He sighed again. 'I have since supposed that the world kind of alters in shape when you're dying.'

That was when she took his hand. 'Don't think like that, Jack; don't think about leaving me like that.' She hesitated. 'I've only just found you, haven't I?'

So they became friends. At first they met in the city, then, when her work slowed down and he wasn't at St Thibery's, he would pick her up at home and they would ride up into the hill country for tea. He would stop the car so she could draw dry-stone walls and collapsing cottages. In the final week of her pregnancy he moved into her spare bedroom, and when her time came he went with her to the hospital. It was only when the nurses called him Mr

Mathéve that he realised they thought he was her father, so he went along with it. And then, when he held her son in his arms and looked into that small face, he fell in love for the third time. First in Singapore, then in the Imperial Hotel, and now in the County Hospital.

In all the time they were together Jack never pursued the point about Adam's father. Marie told him of her wandering life, her fascination with buildings, her vocational obsession with their survival. He shared with her the disappointment at being eased out of the Commission and her worry that she would lose her foothold in that world. He was as outraged as she was at the hubris of her usurper.

So it seemed natural, when the usurper was sacked for inefficiency and bad communication, that Jack should urge her to grasp the opportunity with both hands and get back to her proper work. That was when she asked him to move in, to stay with her permanently. So he arrived with three suitcases and rented out his neat, spare bungalow to a theology lecturer. The rent provided them with an income while Marie got back up on her professional feet.

Jack took care of Adam with a strange, unique combination of motherliness and fatherliness. He changed nappies and made feeds, sewed on labels and organised the domestic routines with a kind of military efficiency. He took Adam to nursery and playgroup and school, making an odd grandfatherly figure among all the young mothers at the gate. He wiped Adam's tears and tended to coughs and sneezes with motherly care. He took the boy to local football, showed him how to swim, and taught him that even gentle souls could face bullies down. Adam ran to his mother when she returned from her journeys, but he still ran to Jack if he fell down and scraped his knee.

In their early months together Jack's relationship with Marie, although full of mutual appreciation and affection, was platonic. But one day she returned from a journey that involved meetings in Liverpool closely followed by meetings in London, and arrived home dog tired. She was, unusually, relieved that Adam was fast asleep. She kicked off her shoes, threw herself on the sofa and lay there, eyes closed.

Jack looked down at her. 'Can I get you something? Wine? Coffee? Food?'

She shook her head. 'Ate on the train,' she mumbled.

Then, as he watched, tears forced themselves from under her eyelids. He knelt beside her where she lay. 'Can't I do anything?' he said. 'Anything to help?'

She put an arm out and pulled his face close to hers. 'Just hold me, Jack, will you?'

That was when he kissed her properly. It was not their usual custom of a kiss on the cheek. He turned her face towards him and kissed her. Her eyes flew open and her hold tightened and she kissed him back. The connection between them was bright silver. They made love there, and then again later in her bed. When Adam cried, she got up and brought him in between them and they both played and talked to him until he went to sleep, when Jack took him back to his cot. When he came back he stood beside the bed, watching her watching him.

'Do you really want me with you?' he said, his voice tentative, slightly rough.

She pulled back the duvet. 'Always, Jack. Just always.'

But despite their intimacy and the accepted fact that the three of them were now a family, Marie never told him the truth about David Zielinski. He hinted now and then that some day Adam should know this truth, but she blandly overrode his enquiry and moved on to something else.

Still, there was never one night in the ten years of his life with Marie that Jack didn't thank his Lord for the good luck that had come to him at this time in his life after a chance meeting at the Imperial Hotel.

And Marie was heartbroken when, after ten years, Jack fell ill with some kind of pleurisy and faded quickly. In his last week, in a shaky hand, he wrote a note for Adam, which he left in a kitchen drawer. *Be a good lad, Adam. You will be the man of the house. Your job now is to take care of your mam and be very brave. God bless and keep you. Love Jack.*

Sources of Power

Jessica Stanley surveyed the neat figure before her, a woman in a belted coat clutching a small bunch of chrysanthemums.

'I've come to see Marie Mathéve,' the woman said. 'Her son rang the ward and the sister said it would be all right.'

The sister had told Jessica of the call. 'Well,' said Jessica, taking the flowers, 'I'm afraid she's not responsive. She had a bad turn yesterday. But perhaps if you sit with her . . .' Her tone was tentative. This pale woman with her belted raincoat was hardly charismatic. She would hardly sparkle Marie back to life. But then, Jessica supposed, she could do no harm.

Jane Rogers pulled her chair very close to the bed, inhaling the warm, unfamiliar, antiseptic air of the hospital. Neither she nor Joseph had ever been ill enough to be in hospital. Never. She'd even given birth to Sam at home. The very first time she'd been in hospital was to identify Sam's remains, in the cold place reserved for those beyond help. Nice really, she'd thought then, for them to make the place so quiet and peaceful. Joseph couldn't bear to come, but Marian, her minister, had accompanied her and they had said a long prayer together for the safe journey of Sam's soul. At the entrance to the hospital they'd met Mr Wiener, who was visiting his granddaughter Rachel, who, it seemed, was still in a bad way. Marian had offered him some comfort too, but he had turned it down, with cool, old-fashioned courtesy.

Now Jane Rogers looked down at Adam's mother: the smooth face with its polished marble look that she recognised from the courtroom. Marie's hands, well manicured, were folded on top of the hospital coverlet. Someone had tied her long plait with a bright red ribbon.

Jane reached out and put a hand on that of Marie Mathéve. She felt the familiar shock running through her, like filaments of gold loaded with the power of the sun. 'The Lord bless you and keep you, my dear. The Lord let His light shine on you, for ever and ever. Amen.'

Then, keeping Marie's hand in hers she started to talk to her. 'We met at the court, remember? And in spite of being so still and quiet, I could tell you were very upset.' She squeezed the woman's hand. 'Our sons were a bond between us, pet. Even then, in my world crashed about with my Joseph's anger, I knew that.' Her gaze went to the window on the other side of the room. It was raining outside. The raindrops were falling down the window, making glittering pathways, each drop of rain its own moving universe of light.

She went on. 'He liked you, our Sam, you know. He came home and told me about you. About your drawings and all your books. About your journeys and how famous you were for saving buildings. He said you were cool. He quoted Kings to me, where Solomon builds his house. *And the house, when it was in building, was built of stone made ready before it was brought thither: so that there was neither hammer nor axe nor any tool of iron heard in the house, while it was in building.*

'I could never be that kind of mother, Marie, clever like you. I admired you even though I didn't know you.

'Strange, the way they use that word cool, Marie! Sam used it to mean the opposite. Hot! Exciting. More exciting than his poor old mam, who lived so close to her God. When he was a child, Sam was witness to grace, you know. He had true faith.' She sighed. 'Of course later on he talked in that sweet, cynical way of his, about *faith and culture and traditions*. The whole boat of belief, he concluded, was a comfort. An imagined thing! Well, I told him it might be a comfort, but in the middle of that imagined thing was my Lord, and He spoke to me. When I said things like that he would give me these great bear hugs and kiss me. Cool, he would say.

'Joseph loved our Sam, you know. Sam used to go down the allotment with him in the autumn and they would dig for England and come back laughing and clapping each other on the back. Men's stuff. You know, Marie?'

She paused, squeezing Marie hand tight. 'So that's what I lost, Marie, when Sam went. That's when I learned that my God was a jealous God. *Thou should have no god but me. This saith the Lord.* That's what my Sam did for me. I worshipped my son. I loved his bear hugs. I worshipped him and he was taken away.'

She sat quietly for a moment, listening to the sounds of the ward outside: the clatter of a bed being wheeled, the twitter and hum of voices, the clash of a door. Then she said, 'Do you know, I liked your Adam from the first time he came to my house. Course, he was a wisp of a thing beside my Sam. He was quiet, watchful, but he and Sam fitted together like a key in a lock or a lid on a tin. I used to watch them and think they'd be friends all their lives. Grow old together. David and Jonathan. Now I admit to you, Marie, the sin of envy. I was not left alone, like you. I know that. I had Joseph, of course.

'Our Sam'll be having to rethink his clever thoughts now, won't he? There in Paradise with his grandma and grandad, and his little brother the Lord took when he was three. I bet that he still has them all hooked there, just like he did in his primary school. But he'll still have to rethink his clever theories, won't he? Don't you think that, Marie?'

She stood up, leaned over and put both her hands just above Marie's head. She felt the familiar heat coursing through her. 'Dear Lord,' she said in a low voice, 'consider thy servant here, Marie Mathéve. She is a good woman. A woman who has used her talents well. But she is lost to her son and her son is lost to her. I met the boy, dear Lord, and he is truly a lost soul, burdened with the consequences of his acts and more than ever needing his mother. Consider this, Lord! If You take Marie to Your bosom, as is Your right to do, then this boy will tread further from the Way called Straight. Dear Lord, you took my son to sit at your side and now at last I don't begrudge you! He was my blessing for twenty-two years. But I pray to You, sweet Lord, and to Your own Son Jesus, that for now you will spare your servant Marie, so she can get on with mothering her son properly and heal him from the hurt he endures. I beg of You, Sweet Lord, do this for me, who has now willingly sacrificed her own son to You. Amen.'

She felt her hands drawn like a magnet to Marie's brow, where the heat, instead of flowing through her, seemed to catch fire. Her body shook and her hands shook, nearly lifting Marie from the bed.

Then strange hands were hauling her away. The sister grasped one arm and the doctor the other. 'What were you doing?' asked Jessica Stanley. 'What in grief do you think you were doing?'

Mrs Rogers wriggled free. 'I was helping her. She needed my help and I was helping her.'

The consultant bent over her patient.

'What did you say your name was?' said the sister.

'Mrs Rogers,' she said. 'My son was her son's friend.'

'She seems all right,' said the doctor. 'No change.'

The sister walked Mrs Rogers out of the ward on to the

corridor and left her there. She appeared quite calm now, and it seemed she had done no harm.

Well, to be honest, I didn't feel a thing. Except the heat of her hands that finally heaved me out of my bed and whammed me here on to the ceiling. So much about the Lord. I've never thought too much about it. Haven't I been in hundreds, best part of a thousand churches built by gifted men, and perhaps invisible women, in His name? Don't I know the poetry of the King James Version because of going to church every Sunday with my mother? But then, I have to admit that when she stopped obliging me to go, I didn't go. She herself went every Sunday until she died. She was carried up the same aisle in the same church where she walked on her wedding day and where I was christened.

I have to admit that through the years I've sought solace in our cathedral from time to time. There's something about those great columns, I suppose, and the whisper of boys' voices in the afternoons. And didn't I light candles in there for Adam and David, Alon Piotr and Jack?

That place – so primitive, with all its flames and fine carvings, its smooth plainsong and its thundering organ. Quite primitive. But when you think of it in that way it's real. A light to lighten the darkness.

So what is it about Sam's mother: this virtuous woman, this crazy woman, who thinks that she can lay her hands on me and whoop! Her God will cure me? Cure that lumpish head laid now like marble on that neck, unmoving as any cathedral column? Could her God make this brain send messages to my heart to make it beat faster, so it can send messages to my arms and legs to move, to my lips so I can speak to my son, who comes here day after day, day after day?

Sam's mother believes that her God is a phenomenal engine at the very core of things, who somehow has a many-mansioned house with rooms for the souls of everyone who has ever been, who ever will be. Ridiculous! But then haven't I just seen in the eerie light the souls of the departed in their prime, so vivid with life? There in the light I saw them as real.

Even down there my dumb mind still races. Races. It may not be able to move my stubborn arms and legs, but it really races with these inner speculations. Look! I know they are delusions – those fountains of light, those figures in the light up here were figments of my imagination. But down there in the husk I knew that this was a thing of dying, a trick of the brain dismantling itself.

That God inside Sam's mother's head is a much more powerful God than anything in my weak imagination. He might be of her own making but He has great power. I could feel it in the heat of her hand, even before it touched my body. It seemed to me to make a great searing mark on my head. I swear I could smell the acrid sourness of burning hair.

And now the woman has gone, there is a vacuum in the air: a cold space where she has been. Although I don't see any reason for God on this earth, I do think He was there, somewhere in the room with her, inhabiting her. He was sitting within her, mocking my disbelief.

Oh, well. There you go.

Flashback

Rachel is struggling to sit upright, protesting that she's all right, all right! Sam is laughing, struggling with her, his deep chuckles resonating through the car. Adam is turning round to tell Sam how much he loves him, and just at that point the car bumps something; there is a juddering thud and it veers in a swerve, brakes squealing, towards the verge and a big oak tree, as wide as a house. All around them is the crackling energy of breaking glass as the world turns, splinters and booms in slow motion. Then everything is still; only the shudder and creaking of metal, the wheeze of the car settling on its roof and the despairing churn of the engine break the silence.

Adam's shoulders are heaving, his head splitting. A black serpent of fear turns swiftly in his heart. Everything is slow, slow. His thinking is slow. This, this is his life in slow motion – the whole of his life . . . Marie . . . Jack . . . Sam . . . Rachel . . . Marie . . . Jack . . .

The car's engine is still turning, rasping like a jackdaw chorus. Adam can't move his left arm or hand. So much pain. With his right hand he unclips his seat belt and tumbles out of the open door.

'Sam! Sam!' he sobs, scrabbling awkwardly at the back door. Sam and Rachel are in a weird tangle on the back seat, their safety belts unclipped. One part of his mind is clear, full of accusations. How many times have I told you two about the belts? How many times has he said to them, 'Think you're bloody immortal, you two!' And how many times has Sam said, 'S'right, mate. I *am* immortal.'

Adam reaches in and turns Sam's face. His friend is looking at him, eyes wide and wise; eyes that once sparkled like a combination of the sun and the moon are now blank as marbles. And Adam feels his heart break: a deep, searing pain in his chest. His eyes move across to Rachel. Her leg is twisted and there is a great gash on her forehead but her eyes are closed.

'Rachel!' he says. Her eyelids flutter.

Now hands are grabbing him from behind and pulling him away. He is shrieking, 'My friends! Get my friends! They are hurt.' Then he is in the ambulance, and a large man in green with gentle hands is easing his arm into some kind of support. 'Easy does it, son.'

Another voice is saying, 'Nasty bruise, that.'

Adam woke up with a very bad headache. Gingerly he felt the bruise on his forehead. Fool! Banging it on the tiles. He pressed the bruise hard so that it hurt more. That was a relief, how much it hurt. In the air was that lingering last-night-pizza smell. Pillows! His head was on the big square pillows of his mother's bed. He wasn't in his cell. Funny, that. All this had happened the other way round in prison: the flashing back to the horrors of the crash, then banging his head till it hurt and making it hurt more to get rid of the images.

The crash flashbacks hadn't happened for a while now. He thought all that had stopped. He groaned. His head was ringing like a struck bell, the pain made worse now by a banging on the door. 'Adam! Adam! Open this door or I'll get the police to come and do it for you! Adam! I promise you!'

He could hear Arian crying.

'Wait!' He jumped off the bed, wincing at the pain. Then he glanced down to see he was naked. He kicked his wet jeans into the corner, looked in the mirror and pulled his long hair across the bruise, then pulled on the wet T-shirt and some dry jeans. He padded across to open the door.

Sharina was standing there, Arian on her arm. 'Bloody hell,' she said. 'You look like you've had your own personal earthquake!'

He took a step back and she walked past him. 'And this place smells like a pigsty. Marie wouldn't like it.' She went across and pushed two windows open, letting in the cold October air.

He shivered. She felt his top. 'This is damp!' She looked at him more closely. 'What the freakin' hell have you done? Were you mugged?'

He stood there in silence, staring at her. She was wearing thick tights and wedges under a flounced skirt. Her wavy hair was slicked back, making her eyes look enormous.

'That bruise!' She shook her head. 'You did it to yourself. Idiot!' She sat Arian on the floor and put a dummy in his mouth. Then she came and put a hand on Adam's forearm and looked him in the eye. 'I seen that before. A lass at school used to do it. No, two! The other one cut herself. Sad pair. What is it? What's the matter? *You idiot.*' She stared at him and then pushed him hard. 'Look, you go and get out of those stinking wet clothes and have a shower. Then you can tell me just what really happened.'

He went and stood under the shower, squeezing Marie's lily of the valley shower gel into his hair and all over his body. He worked it up into a lather and let the water run, watching the suds slide off his shoulders, down his chest and on to his thighs. He stood there until the water ran cold and at last remembered the hospital yesterday and the deathly bustle of the crash team busy around Marie's bed. He could hear Jessica Stanley's firm tones. He turned off the shower and reached for the towel. Crash team. Crash. Dreams. That was it!

He pulled a towel round his waist and went into the kitchen to get a clean shirt and pants out of the dryer. Sharina looked up from the frying pan. 'That's better. Full

English breakfast, good for shock,' she said. Then she groaned. 'You look so canny with your hair plastered down like that. It's hard on a girl, seein' such beauty.'

'I have to get to the hospital, Sharina.'

She nodded. 'Not before you've had this, you don't.' She paused. 'I rang before. The sister said your mam had had a good night. They think I'm her daughter.'

Adam ate his breakfast, and afterwards Sharina blow-dried his hair for him, playing games, making it float into the air like spun silk. Then she said, 'What you gunna do about the bruise? They'll know you for a self-harmer the minute they see you at the hospital.'

He peered into the mirror and pulled a bit of his hair further forward. 'Not their business,' he said.

She vanished into Marie's bedroom and came out with a tube of foundation. 'We'll rub some of this in. It'll be less purple.'

He sat while she did this, savouring the rare touch of gentle fingers. 'Mebbe one time you'll tell me why,' she said.

'Why what?' he said.

'Why you do this and why you're so – well – murky underneath your winsome ways.'

He caught her hand in his, squeezing it tight. 'You're a very nice person, you, Sharina.'

She shook him off. 'Don't you go soft on me, Adam. You just get along there and see your mam. Me and Arian have to go to the clinic, don't we love? They like to keep their eye on us, don't they?'

★

As he jogged towards the hospital in the light drizzle, Adam thought about himself and Sharina. She was really young but they'd certainly hit it off straight away. Her obvious easy affection for Marie drew him to her. In the short time he'd known her they'd gone through the stages of friendship, arguing and quarrelling and making up just like real friends. He'd enjoyed playing with Arian and marvelling at his child magic. And now, as he padded along to see his mother, he wondered where all that was going.

He'd never been sure of it, this thing about women. If they thought Sharina was Marie's daughter, that made him her brother. Maybe that was it. Brother and sister. Safer that way.

When he first came out of prison, it was as though he'd crash-landed on a very strange planet inhabited by highly potent females. Everywhere he turned there seemed to be breasts and bare brown legs, light fluttery clothes and made-up eyes. The attention of any woman, even the voice of the lady in the post office, was like wine.

On that holiday in Cornwall, his post-prison neediness had been like honey, making girls and boys flutter around him, bringing offers he only just managed to refuse. He thought it might be safe to get closer to Sharina but he couldn't take that step with her. Wouldn't it spoil everything? He shook his head to clear it, and raced on. What was he doing, thinking like this with his mother in hospital at death's door?

The sister greeted him at the nurses' station. 'Being Jesus Christ, are we today, Adam?' She nodded at his tumbling hair. Then she frowned. 'Been in the wars, have we?'

He lifted his hand to touch his bruise. 'I walked into a door.'

'That's what we all say,' she said drily. She paused. 'Anyway, your Mam's none the worse for her little upset yesterday. Scan shows no different.' She led the way to the side ward. 'This woman you sent to visit her today, Adam. An unusual woman.'

'Yeah,' he said vaguely. 'Mother of a friend of mine. Keen to help. She means no harm.'

It was only when he got to the side ward that Adam realised he hadn't brought anything to read to Marie. So, after wandering round the room, peering through the window and shutting the door tight, he sat down beside her and told her what had happened last night. How she had flapped her hand when she heard the nursery rhyme. 'That really got to me, you moving like that. They seemed to think you were a goner. And I was frightened you were leaving me. And look, I didn't want you to go. Not now, when I'm finding out so much about you. All the Polish stuff, and how you are with Sharina and Arian. New to me.'

He told her how he'd gone home and battered his head on the wall with frustration. 'Look! See this bruise? But you don't have to blame yourself, Marie. It's not the first time. It happened in jail from time to time. Flashbacks. Had to see the shrink about it. I told the sister here that I'd walked into a door and she said she'd heard it all before. Sharina too. She knows about these things, people hurting themselves.'

Out on the ward, he could hear the clatter of the trolley, the confiding laughter of the nurses.

'But I promise you, Marie, I promise you here and now, I'll never do it again. If only you'll wake up. Just wake up, will you? And we'll talk and we'll get to know each other all over again.'

But his mother just lay there on the pillow, hooked up to her tubes, very white and still.

He told her about his recurring dream of the crash, and the whole tale of how it happened, right from the point at the party where he'd discovered that promiscuous Janet had hooked the Vice Chancellor. He actually laughed when he told her about this, about Janet flashing her diamond ring. Then he told her about having to drive back because the others were too far gone. 'Then the car crashed, see? And Sam was lying there, Marie, with eyes like marbles, and Rachel had all this blood on her face and her leg was twisted!' As the words tumbled from his mouth he could feel a block of ice breaking up inside him, creaking and sheering off, bit by bit. 'Marie! Marie! Listen to me, will you? Listen! Please. I'm sorry I didn't write to you, sorry I didn't look at you in the court. I just . . . I just didn't want . . . Listen to me! Listen to me, will you?'

Fancying

'The thing is,' said Sharina, 'I just don't fancy you.'

They were sitting on Sharina's floor, drinking coffee. Arian had grabbed the opportunity to crawl all over Adam, poking into his ears and mouth. He smelled of apple purée and milk. Adam glanced across at Sharina, who had obviously been busy the night before, changing her magenta streak to silver and straightening her hair, now moulded to her scalp like a Greek helmet. He'd mimed shock horror at the sight of it when he called in to see her on his way back from the hospital. 'What's that?' he'd said.

Lovingly she had touched the hair above her ear. 'This? This is me being Helen of Troy.'

'No,' she repeated now, 'I just don't fancy you.'

He revisited the thoughts he'd had jogging to the hospital. For one thing Sharina seemed very young, even with a baby on her hip. His friendship with her had been a rest, a retreat from the difficulty of his worries about his mother. Sister and brother worked for him.

'It's not as if you fancy me, is it?' she persisted.

'Sharina, I don't think—'

'Wrong answer! All I'm saying is that it's a good job I don't fancy you.' Again she left a very deliberate pause.

He snagged on the hook. 'Why is it a good thing?'

'Right question! It's a good thing because we can be mates. No passionate clinches, no poached-egg eyes in the morning. No vicious falling-out just to make up. Just good friends.'

He swallowed a sigh of relief. 'What made you an expert in relationships? I thought the only relationship you'd had was with Arian's father.'

'I watch television, don't I? That's the one great thing now about not having Mary Cornelia and her sisters around. I can watch television. All human life is there, you know. Dramas about people. Documentaries about people. So it's best that we can be just good friends. You know?'

He took Arian's fingers out of his mouth and folded the little paw inside his. Friends! He'd had friends, hadn't he? And killed and maimed them. He had no right to friends. He shook his head violently. 'No!' he said.

She placed the cup in her hand carefully on the floor. 'You don't even want to be my friend? Is that what you're saying?' Arian started to grizzle and she pulled him on to her knee.

'It's not that,' Adam said. 'It's just . . . I'm a lousy friend, if you want to know. Lousy. You don't want to be my friend.'

She laughed, and Arian giggled too. 'I don't believe it,' she said. 'You've been banging yourself on the head and lost your marbles.'

'You'd better believe it,' he said glumly.

'I don't. Haven't I seen you being a good friend already?'

'You've been a very OK friend. But I'm telling you, if your Sister Mary Cornelia had met me she'd've known. She'd've smelled it on me in a second. All this badness. I've smelled it myself on other people, when I was . . . well, in a certain place.'

'Don't talk crap!' She leapt to her feet, suddenly looming over Adam, very angry. Arian, clutching her leg now, started to cry. 'You'd better tell us what it is you're freaking on about, Adam Mathéve. No lies, or I'll give you such a kick, where it really hurts. You just watch me!'

He looked up at her. 'Right.' He paused. 'I had this friend once, Sharina. My best friend. And I killed him. Well, no. I had these two friends. I killed him and maimed her.'

'I told you!' Her voice was hoarse now, with genuine menace. She glared down at him. 'I told you I'd kick you if you told any freakin' lies.'

He laughed uneasily. 'I bet you were a power to behold in the playground!'

'You'd better believe it!' she growled.

'Sit down, will you? You're making my neck ache.'

She stayed where she was. 'The truth!'

'Well. OK. It was an accident. Car. I was driving.'

'Idiot! Were you drunk? Or stoned? You cretin!'

'No. I was neither. The two of them were. That's how come I was driving.'

'So how come there was an accident if you were OK?'

'I turned round to talk to Sam, then wallop! Car swerved, whammed sideways into a tree and turned over two, three times. They told me that was what happened but I can't remember. I dreamed it last night, though. I often used to dream about it. And last night I dreamed it again. But how can I dream about it if I can't remember it? I think all I remember is the dream.' He closed his eyes, not believing he was saying this to this girl.

Sharina slid down and sat beside him on the floor. Arian waddled to his toy box in the corner and started throwing toys about. 'So what happened then?' Her voice was bleak.

'Then, they charged me with death by dangerous driving. It didn't help that I had no licence and no insurance.'

'Christ!' she said. 'You're seven kinds of idiot. And then what?'

'I pleaded guilty and went to prison. For two years. I'd not been long out of there when I found Marie at the bottom of the steps. I came to look for her and I found her half dead.'

She stared at him. 'Why d'you always call her Marie?' she said abruptly.

He shrugged. 'I copied my stepdad when I was little. He called her that so I did. He talked about her to me and called her Marie. About how clever she was and how beautiful and all that. She wasn't there so often and when she turned up she was Marie to me. Just Marie.'

Arian toddled back to Sharina and lay across her knee.

She sighed. 'Funny, innit? I'd've loved to have someone I could call Mam. Really! Even if she was only round now and then. I dreamed so many times about calling somebody Mam. I still do. An' I love it when Arian calls me *mamma*. And now he's calling Marie by her name. I love that!'

He sighed. 'Well, I was never really aware of the privilege.'

'Lucky you.'

'I didn't feel lucky. Not at all.'

Arian squirmed about as Sharina put her knuckle in his mouth, then he blinked and turned his face into her shoulder. Adam watched as his body stretched out and his legs sagged sideways, his chubby hand creeping inside Sharina's cardigan.

Sharina looked at Adam over Arian's head. 'Tell me about your friend. What was his name? Sam?'

So he tried to tell Sharina about Sam. But words were too thin really for the purpose. He told her how clever and funny Sam had been. How cool. All those Bible quotations, even though he didn't believe in God. 'But his mother did. He was brought up with it. She was a believer. Born again and all that.' He hesitated. 'She came here the other day.' He couldn't quite remember now when it was. 'She went to see Marie. The sister said she'd been.'

'Did she scream vengeance at you?'

'Nah. It was worse than that. All forgiveness and understanding.' He put a hand over his face and his index finger connected painfully with the bruise.

'That's very clever of her, like. Knowing that would drive the knife in even more.'

'No. I don't think she meant to do that. She's just this little woman from Consett, see? But she has this big soul. Just like Sam did. She's like him.' It was painful getting the words out. 'He had this big soul, Sam.'

For a few minutes the only sound in the room was Arian's snuffling, sleeping breath.

'You know what, Adam?' Sharina said finally.

'What?'

'I think you really loved him, that Sam.'

He leaned across and stroked the soft hair at the back of Arian's head, smoothing it into the nape of his neck. Sharina had hit on the problem, he thought, though she didn't realise it. Turning round to tell Sam just that, that he loved him, was what had caused the crash. He said slowly, 'Neither of us would have *said* that. Ever.'

'Men don't, I suppose. But you loved him?'

'I suppose so. Some people might say that.'

'But you didn't fancy him?'

'Definitely not. No! Fancy? What's going through that crackpot head of yours?'

'Like we said in science, QED. Me, I love you, but I don't fancy you. I've just worked that out. Like you loved your Sam but didn't fancy him.'

'He wasn't my Sam. He was nobody's Sam. He was everybody's Sam. That was the best thing about him.'

'You know what I mean.'

'So where does that leave us, you and me? If you don't fancy me and I don't fancy you?'

She frowned at him. 'Mebbe you're like my brother. If I had one, that is.'

He shuffled so they were sitting very close, shoulder to shoulder. 'Sounds good to me. I've been thinking that myself. I could have had a worse sister.'

She leaned across and put on some music. They listened in silence for a while, then she said, 'Will you tell me what it was like in prison?'

'No. I won't.'

She tried again. 'Do you believe in dreams?'

'I don't know.'

'Well, you said you see the crash in a dream.'

'Everybody dreams. But that was like some kind of warped memory, not a dream. Something to make me remember, maybe. Like pressing this bruise.'

'Do you think dreams come true?'

He took a breath. 'Dreams are just a funny reconstruction of things that have happened to you, all jumbled up and reshaped.'

'Tell me the last dream you had.'

He tried honesty. She was worth that. 'The crash, like I said. I dreamed about the crash. Not jumbled up, to be honest, so I'm contradicting myself. Correct in every detail. Like a slow-motion film. But I can't remember it. The detail came from what I was told about it. And from what I've dreamed before.'

She frowned, still puzzled.

'Tell me about yours,' he said, letting her off the hook. 'Your last dream.'

She relaxed. 'Well, I did keep having this one dream. Variations of it, anyway. In it Sister Mary Cornelia comes to see me with this man in a very black suit. Black shirt, even. Sometimes a black T-shirt. She says he's my father and he's come to take me home. I'm saying no, no! This is my home, here with her and her sisters. She's my mother now and my place is there with her. Then suddenly he has Arian in his long hands with their pink nails and he's stuffing him into this black leather briefcase. Sometimes it's a black rucksack. I'm screaming, wringing my hands, shouting at Mary Cornelia to get Arian back. Get him back!' She paused. 'Then I wake up because Arian is crying his heart out beside me. Then I cry too because I'm so relieved that it's just a dream.' She paused again. 'It doesn't bother me because I know it's just a dream. Something about my father from Africa and me wondering about him, I should think.'

Adam took her free hand, the one not still being chomped on by Arian. 'Such a wise girl. Anyway, no such thing could happen now, could it? *Now* you've got this big brother and Arian has all those formidable godmothers, hasn't he?'

She wrestled her hand free. 'I don't need no one, me. I can manage.'

He laughed. 'We all know you can manage. The world knows you can manage, Sharina. The thing is, maybe we need you to help *us* manage.' He stood up. 'Now I'm going along to Marie's to have a shower and get changed, and then I'm going back up to the hospital. You coming?'

Arian was stirring. Sharina held him up and shook him awake, her face close to his, 'Not this time. Me and Arian have to go somewhere.'

'Where?'

'Don't ask! It's a secret quest.' She grinned up at him and he hesitated, then left it at that.

As he walked along the landing, Adam found himself thanking a God he didn't believe in for Sharina and Arian. He thanked this unbelieved-in being that his mother was still hanging on in there at the hospital. And most of all he thanked him that he'd been able to talk about Sam, just for a few minutes, without pain.

On the Ceiling Again

Back bobbing on the ceiling. I can't hear Adam but I can see him from up here, looking like Leonardo with that hair flowing over his shoulders. Not his face. How I wish I could see his face. He's such a tender boy. So tender. That was something I had never realised. I wonder where all that gentleness came from. Me, I'm a very still person but not a quiet one, nor a gentle one. Adam must have got his gentleness from David. Or perhaps Jack, who dealt with him as kindly as any woman, while teaching him the ways of men.

Strange to think now how much I loved Jack in those ten years. If ever there was a relationship of convenience ours was it. For me Jack was at the end of a life half lived. I was experiencing a late beginning, but not just with Adam coming into the world. That beginning started with David so briefly in that narrow room in Krakow. It was as though the passion awoke my true spirit, the real me; it broke me away from the reserved, self-sufficient, enclosed self that was the product of my mother's careful upbringing.

David symbolised for me forever the physical entrancement of making love, the sheer delight of surrender so oddly combined with a sense of power. The confusion I felt on my return here alone was only half about being pregnant. The other half was about the change that was just beginning. Thank God that I was not to be denied this unique experience. Funny how God keeps cropping up in my thoughts. Jack was a simple believer, of course, like my mother. And they were both rewarded with deaths that had the silver lining of optimism and belief.

Maybe that's why I saw Jack and my mother here in the eerie light, because in life they had been believers. But if that's so, what on earth was that great galoot Sam Rogers doing there in the light with them, this last time, enticing me on? That joyously arrogant atheist called God a 'deliciously human construct'. I remember him saying that.

Whatever! Without making such brilliant love to David Zielinski in Krakow I'd have returned home and confirmed my spinsterly ways. I'd have continued to draw my buildings and write my reports and live on in my hermit fashion. In the end I'd have solidified into a prim intellectual virgin who never pierced the curtain of real experience.

As it was, I made love to David, conceived Adam, and that morning in the Imperial Hotel I was so overwhelmed with the power of these changes that I – who had never wanted or needed to speak to strangers – made this strange connection with Jack Longland.

How that man smoothed my life and made it whole! How he cared for Adam like mother and father rolled into one! With him there I could still be myself, could still do my drawings and reports

*and come home with tales to tell. Safe with Jack, I blossomed out
of my spinsterly ways and men I met casually were interested in
talking to me about more than buildings. And in those ten years
with Jack I experienced more love and passion than I'd any right
to expect. Jack was a tender lover, resourceful and full of surprises.
To put it crudely, his long experience with his corset lady more than
compensated for my inexperience in bed – except of course for that
all-defining, glorious, child-producing moment with David
Zielinski.*

*But now, even up here, I can see that all this has a sting in the
tail. Of course at the time it seemed to work brilliantly. What a
fool I was to think that Adam was content with our lives together.
Now, so late, I'm learning something different. I'm stuck here,
bumping on the ceiling, but I can hear Adam's tone. I can hear the
sadness, the anger in his voice. But I can't hear the words from up
here. I need to be down there in the blind husk to <u>hear</u> his words.*

*I want to hear him. I've never managed to will myself down
there. But now I must. I'm no use to him up here, no use at all.
Never mind going into the cosy light. He needs something from
me. Try, Marie! Try!*

After Adam had gone, Jessica Stanley went into the side
ward and stood by Marie's bed. She looked at her patient's
bleached–white face. The pale hair was brushed off her
bandaged brow, her hand curled slightly on the
counterpane. Then as Jessica looked down, the hairs stood
up on the back of her neck. Something peculiar had
happened here. She no longer felt an absence in Marie, but

a presence. The figure was still, the eyes were closed, the face was blank. But there was something present in that still body. She put out her hand and stroked the side of her patient's face. 'Come on, Marie! Come on!' she said. 'We're nearly there! One last pull, one last effort!' She laughed. 'Come on! *And with one bound she was free*! You remember those adventure stories. Come on, Marie!'

Returning

The next day as they made their way to the hospital, Adam asked Sharina about her secret quest. 'You went to the clinic? With Arian?'

She shook her head. 'I can tell you now. I went to see somebody about doing this course. I went to the college.' She manoeuvred the buggy around an overhanging bush in the path. The pavement was dry but the trees and bushes were still unloading the overnight rain. Behind the transparent plastic cover on his buggy, Arian looked like a spaceman in a bubble.

'You went yesterday?' he said. 'To the college?'

'Not that I have to ask your permission. Like I told you, it was a quest.'

He let that settle before he prompted again, 'So, you went to the college?'

'And I asked about courses, but they said it was too late 'cos the term's already started.'

'So you couldn't start? Well, not this term anyway.'

'Wrong!' she said triumphantly. 'The lad on reception sent me to this woman. She teaches sociology and he said she only has a little class. Needs bums on seats. She took one look at me and almost salivated.'

Adam frowned. 'Funny thing to do, that, salivate.'

'Not literally, you dumb duke! Metaphorically. Think of it! *Single mother* – big gold star. *Different*. Another gold star. I tick all the boxes.'

'*Different?*' he said.

'African dad my trump card. The woman even mentioned ethnic diversity modules. I told her it was the others needed ethnic diversity lectures, not me. She laughed then, and I knew I was in.' She paused. 'I've signed on for two courses really. Sociology and English. They gave me reading lists and a library ticket. So we went along to the library and got this pile of the books. You couldn't see Arian for books! Covered with them, weren't you, love, in your buggy?' She went on. 'And they have this crèche. Would you believe it? And free to me, so that ticks all *my* boxes!'

Adam thought about Arian. 'What if he doesn't like the crèche? What if he's ill?'

'Well. You'll be here, won't you? He likes you, doesn't he?'

Adam thought about that. Since he'd got off the train – it seemed like weeks ago – he'd lived entirely in the present, in an eternal round of hospital, Spar shop, Marie's flat, Sharina's flat. The future was another country. Things were different there. Now here was Sharina making him think not just in terms of a week or two, but a whole year. These courses took a year, didn't they? Then there was Marie. What about Marie in all of this? Where would she be in a year's time? And where would he himself be? According to Sharina, he would still be here at Merrick Court.

Sharina noted the silence. 'I told Sister Mary Cornelia last night on the phone. She was worried about Arian, like you are. Then I told her you'd be my backstop. And you being Marie's son, it made sense to her. Well, her being reassured about that let her be pleased about me getting on with things. She was glad I wouldn't just be settling for what I've got. We had this joke about Arian being my "year out". She can be funny, Sister Cornelia.'

He sighed. 'Course I'll be here,' he said soberly. 'That's what friends are for, isn't it?'

In the hospital entrance he unbuckled Arian from his buggy, handed him to Sharina and pushed the buggy behind the wheelchairs. Their theory was that people visiting the hospital would have more on their minds than pinching buggies. 'Well,' he said, as they walked down the dry, warm corridors, 'you can talk to Marie about your course and all those things. I'm running out of things to say.' He'd been through the Polish notebooks twice. In fact he felt he knew them by heart. These days he could see and smell Krakow. He kept imagining Marie carrying mucky potato sacks. He could smell Jacinta's borscht. And just now any news on television about Poland's role in the new Europe was beginning to snag on his consciousness.

Of course the notebooks had left him with questions. And he was gnawingly aware that he'd have to wait for Marie to wake up so he could ask her those questions. *If* she woke up. He corrected himself. *When* she woke up.

Jessica Stanley and the ward sister met them outside Marie's side room. 'We told you about your mother's visitor,' said the sister. 'There was a bit of a kerfuffle, to be honest.'

'I know her,' said Adam. 'Like I said to Jessica. She's all right. She means no harm. Honestly, Sister. I know her. She's kind of religious. A good person.'

When he got to the side room, Marie was there in the bed, her cover immaculate, her hospital corners in place. Her face was as pale as ever, her plait over her shoulder in its usual place. One part of him really wanted to see some signs of turmoil: her hair scruffed up, some ruffling of that eternal statuesque stillness.

He glanced up at Jessica Stanley. 'She looks just the same.'

'Well, she's as she was, if that's what you mean.'

They all stood round the bed, staring down at Marie. Even Arian, in Sharina's arms, was gazing down at her with his gleaming eyes. Adam suddenly realised that they were all doing the same thing, maybe what Mrs Rogers had tried to do: trying to heal Marie with their willpower, urging her awake; wishing that they could work some magic on her that might or might not involve the hand of God; wishing that pure human love and care would bring her back into the land of the living, return her from the shadow world in which she now dwelt. They certainly needed help. Then Sam's voice was purring in his ear: *Even though I travel through the valley of the shadow of death Thou art with me.'*

Arian started to whimper. 'Mama! Mama!' And inside his head, Adam could hear himself crying out to Marie in the same way. Then, like an electric charge, he could feel Jack's hand on his shoulder. *You can but hope, son . . .*

There they are, standing down there round the bed like people at a graveside. Even Sam and Jack have joined the throng. Christ, and now David . . . Just look at them, standing there. Hopeless. Helpless. Stop it! Stop it all of you! It's enough to push anyone over the edge, make them give up the ghost. Stop it! I'd rather have Sam's mother in here with her burning hands. But all they can do is stare at the husk. That not-me. Pathetic! Wake up, you silly woman! Wake up! What am I saying? Now I'm one of the gawpers at my own graveside. Crazy! That's what it is. Crazy. Stop it! All of you.

Oh Christ, oh Christ! Here I come!

It was Arian who saw it first. His tears dried. 'Maa-wy,' he said. 'Maa-wy wake now!'

Then they all saw it. Her eyelashes stirred, then fluttered

on her cheeks. Adam moved closer, grabbed her hand and squeezed it hard. 'Marie! Come *on*, Marie!'

Sharina stuck Arian on the bed and took Marie's other hand. 'Come *on*, Marie,' she said, echoing Adam's emphasis. Arian patted Marie's leg, chuckling and chattering.

Marie's eyes snapped open and for a second they were clouded, unseeing. They all held their breath. Then Adam felt her hand grasping his. 'Marie,' he said. 'You're here. Come on!'

Her gaze moved behind him. 'David?' she whispered. Then she blinked, and her eyes, now brighter and sharper, were on her son. 'Adam!' she said.

Arian clapped his hands and laughed even more.

'Well now, Miss Mathéve, Marie!' said Jessica Stanley, her normally brusque voice brimming with pleasure. 'Welcome back!'

The ward sister coughed, as though to remind everyone that she was there, that this was her territory.

'You've come back, Marie,' said Sharina softly. 'Good, that. You've come right back here to us.'

A frisson of a smile passed over Marie's face. 'You all looked so blinking gloomy standing there,' she whispered hoarsely. 'I had to put a stop to that.'

Adam was struck dumb, his tongue thick in his mouth. Feelings cascaded through him – relief, joy, fear, regret streaming together with a surge that make his skin prickle. Somewhere deep inside himself he'd thought that losing Marie was a well-deserved punishment for taking Sam's life. Such a thing would hurt him more than if he himself had been struck down. Well, now he knew that feeling had been wrong. Marie was neither dying nor dead. Her quizzical eyes were on him, as though she were somehow drinking him in.

'Well, Adam, Sharina,' said Jessica, her voice now gruffer than ever, 'I think you should go off and take ten minutes to have a cup of coffee or something. Sister and I will check Miss Mathéve, see just how she is. Then we can make her comfortable and you can come and have a proper visit.'

Adam didn't want to go, but Marie squeezed his hand and whispered, 'Go.' Then she smiled, and he felt a streak of pure, unadulterated happiness. Filtering through to him now were the feelings he'd had when he was small, standing on the doorstep as she returned from a trip, or waiting in the corner of the room for her to look up from her drawing board. *To see him.*

Sharina picked up Arian from the bed. 'Come on, Adam. Let the professionals get their oar in. Your mam'll be here when we get back.'

At the door he looked back, but he couldn't see Marie for the broad backs of Jessica and Sister as they bent over their patient.

Sharina tugged his sleeve. 'Come on, Adam! Leave them to it!'

He let her go ahead of him along the hospital corridor so she wouldn't see his tears.

★

The hospital café overlooked an enclosed green space with two spreading trees and a single flower bed. It was empty, and the tinny musak – the Everly Brothers, Adam thought, old stuff – echoed around the empty tables, the faux-marble floor.

Sharina went to the counter, and Adam found a table beside one of the trees and gave Arian one of his special biscuits from the carry-bag on the buggy. Sharina brought the drinks – Coke for her, juice for Arian and coffee for Adam – and sat down beside the buggy. She frowned. 'You look like thunder, Adam. Aren't you pleased, like? I'd've thought you'd be jumping up and down, your mam being back with us. Busting with joy.'

That was a feeling he had to learn, he thought, to be bursting with joy. 'It's a shock, I think. When I got out of prison, I had to brace myself to come back here to see her at all. Then I went to Merrick Court and found her dead to the world at the bottom of the steps. Now I've got used to her being silent there on the bed. That was easy, in a way. Kind of being with her without having to . . . without her knowing . . . without having to try . . .' He hesitated. 'I felt safe. Now I'm back at square one.'

'What do you mean, square one?'

'Now I have to think how I should be . . . how I can be with her now.' One part of him wished Sharina wasn't here, so he didn't have to explain.

She frowned again, sucking Coke noisily through a straw. 'She's your mam, isn't she? S'easy.'

He sighed. 'Look, I haven't seen or spoken to her for more than two years. Even before that I only saw her now and then. I never learned properly how to be with her, even when I was young.'

She shook her head. 'I don't get it.' She paused. 'Well, me, I think you should be pleased she's here, come alive again. Not dead in the grave.'

'I am! I am!' He stared down into his coffee cup and sighed. 'But now all I want to do is go away and leave her. Leave her to it.'

'Freakin' selfish, you are.' She leaned over and forced his head up and stared into his eyes. 'It's not about you, Adam. It's about her. You don't go away and leave her! You do that and I'll kill you. What will Marie do without you?'

He stared at her and freed himself from her touch. Then he looked at his watch. 'Ten minutes! They said we should go back in ten minutes.'

They had raised Marie's pillows, so she was sitting partly upright. There seemed to be fewer tubes going in and out of her. Someone had combed the hair round her face and tied her plait with a fresh ribbon. She smiled faintly as they came in. Sharina went straight across to her and kissed her cheek, and held Arian's soft cheek against hers. 'Pleased you're feeling better, Marie. Me and Arian are really, really pleased, aren't we, pet? We've all been worried about you, like. Sister Mary Cornelia and all them up at Tynemouth have been praying for you. Lighting candles and everything.'

Marie lifted her hand very slowly and touched Sharina's arm. 'You are a good friend, Sharina,' she whispered hoarsely.

Sharina stood back. 'Takes one to know one, Marie. Now me and Arian, we'll make our way back home. I thought you and Adam here . . . well . . .' Her voice trailed off, then she backed away, grinning, and shut the door behind her.

Marie raised her eyes to Adam. 'Well then. Here we are, Adam,' she whispered.

Feeling hot, flushed and awkward, he moved across and sat by the bed. 'Seems like that,' he said. 'Here we are.'

She held out her hand. 'Let's not bother saying anything just yet. Let's just be pleased we're both here.'

He took her hand. It felt dry and warm in his. 'Your hand felt like this when we went for walks with Jack,' he said suddenly. 'His hand one side and yours the other. I've missed him.'

Marie sighed. 'I miss Jack. Even now. I . . . thought I saw him when . . . before . . . in this room..' She glanced at the ceiling. 'I think it was a dream.' She squeezed his hand tighter. 'But now you're here and I don't have to miss you any more. Do I?'

He thought that the danger was that things might go back to how they'd been before. And what good was that?

She read his mind. 'It's different now, Adam. Believe me,' she whispered. 'Not the same at all.'

He let out a very big sigh and awkwardly took her other hand. 'No, Mum, you don't have to miss me. I'm here, aren't I? Aren't I?'

Part Five

Awake

The Butterfly

His mother's awakening set in train changes that amazed
Adam in terms of their sheer speed. One minute Marie was
dead to the world; the next she was free of the tubes that
had shackled her for weeks, eating soft food with a shaking
hand. In a couple of days, she was being helped by physiotherapists to take the short walk out of the side ward to
the bathroom. Then they helped her to walk by herself
with the aid of a three-pronged stick. The day after this,
Jessica Stanley said Marie should take a look at the world,
so Adam pushed her in a wheelchair around the hospital
corridors to sit in the café to watch the customers and view
the new garden in the glassed-in courtyard. Sitting there,
by unspoken agreement they talked of immediate things.
The hospital. How good Jessica Stanley was. How
Arian had grown while Marie took her long sleep. How
cheering were these brighter autumn days. As they talked,
Marie's voice became less breathy and rusty and the clear,

certain tones of her old self began to emerge.

After a week, having administered final tests and consulted her colleagues, Jessica announced that it was time for Marie to go home. 'The swelling in there is right down, Miss Mathéve, and as far as we can see there's no lasting damage.'

Marie was unsure. 'But I'm so wobbly.'

'You're wobbly because you've been in bed so long. You'll have your stick and the wheelchair at first. And you have your son. Just take it day by day, Miss Mathéve, and you'll get on your feet. Honestly! We'll have you back here every week to check. But the signs are good.' She touched Marie on the shoulder. 'In here we have lots of bad outcomes to handle. Recoveries like yours brighten our days.'

Marie glanced around the room, then briefly up at the ceiling in the corner by the window. 'I've had good care in here,' she said. 'I'll certainly tell people about it.'

Jessica nodded. 'That'll be a change. People usually rush out to say what crap we are. Excuse my language.'

Marie looked up at the woman whose care she'd experienced in these weeks, either from the ceiling or from down there on the bed in the blind husk. She noted a chunky, solid woman, white-faced, red-haired. The hair was untidy and there were shadows of chronic tiredness under her eyes. 'You like this job of yours, don't you?'

Jessica shrugged. 'I wouldn't do anything else.' She paused. Then she thought about how silent the mother and son had been, more so since Marie's awakening. 'Your Adam came every day, you know, while you were asleep,' she said. 'Every single day. Like clockwork.'

'Did he? That's nice.' Marie coloured slightly. 'I hadn't seen him for some time, you know. Before all this.'

'Well I have to tell you, he's been very concerned. Upset, quite naturally. I found him sitting here in tears more than once. He read to you, you know. There were notebooks, little old notebooks. He spent days reading them to you,' said Jessica. 'And talking. He seemed never to stop talking.'

A thread of memory shot through Marie's mind, of the top of a blond head and a thin young voice reading something. 'Notebooks?'

'Yeah. He told me they were all about your travels. Poland, I think.'

Marie frowned.

'Anyway, I imagine the two of you have a lot of time to make up,' Jessica persisted. She now knew Adam's side of the story; at least the public aspect of it. She had Googled his case. No secrets of that kind these days.

Marie looked at her again, carefully. 'A lifetime,' she said simply. 'We have a lifetime to make up. I was never a good mother to him. Never.'

'I can't believe—'

That was when Adam crashed through the door, all arms, legs and hair. 'Marie! The sister just told me you were coming out today! I didn't realise.'

Jessica looked at her watch. 'You nearly missed her. The ambulance is booked for two thirty. Sister's been trying to ring you.'

'I went to get my hair cut.'

Jessica surveyed him. 'Not that you could tell . . .' she said.

Adam looked down at Marie sitting on a hospital chair, wearing clothes Sharina had brought in for her. Her hair was swept up and back into a ponytail held by a scarf. 'Are you sure? Are you ready to come out?'

She smiled. 'Jessica here says it's OK. Really, I'm dying to get home.' She paused. 'Can't wait.'

He watched as the ward sister got her settled in a wheelchair and placed her three-pronged stick carefully across the arms.

Marie looked up at him and smiled. 'Well, Adam?' she said.

He coughed. 'Right. Good.' He took hold of the handles.

Jessica handed him a carrier bag. 'Here's Miss Mathéve's things. And a leaflet of do's and don'ts. She's been brilliant, but you should both read them closely. Better safe than sorry. Now then, I'll take the stick and you push.'

They waited a few minutes for the ambulance, and Adam watched as the men lifted Marie in her chair inside.

He looked at Jessica Stanley. Then, to his own surprise, he ignored her proffered hand and hugged her tight. 'Thank you. Thank you.' All the emotion he'd felt on seeing his mother in day clothes, ready to go, he packed into this hug for her doctor.

Jessica held him at arm's length. 'It's my job, Adam!' But she knew that he knew that caring for Marie Mathéve had been more than that.

'I'll miss you,' he said, looking for something to say. 'You've been—'

'I've just been *here*, Adam, where I'm supposed to be.' She gave him a little push. 'Now go! You take care of Marie. Get to know her. She's precious cargo, your mother.'

Marie looked white and small as they bumped along in the ambulance. Adam sat beside her, dumb and embarrassed, thinking of the mess he'd left behind him in the flat. 'I didn't realise it was today,' he blurted out. 'I haven't cleared up.'

She grinned broadly. 'Do you think I'm worried about *that*? After all *this*?'

'Just wait till you see it!' he said gloomily. But he was warmed by her smile.

Only minutes later, still sitting in the hospital wheelchair, Marie surveyed her elegant sitting room: the remains of a pizza perched on the small side table with cake crumbs beside it; towels and tea towels draped over the back of her fawn-linen-covered sofa; lurking trainers; books heaped on the coffee tables. Among them she spied her spiral-bound notebooks.

'I see what you mean,' she said. 'You've certainly made your mark.'

'Sorry!' he said helplessly.

'Don't say that,' she said firmly. 'I don't want you to think like that. To be sorry for anything. Such as it is, this is your home as well as mine. I'm glad you made yourself comfortable.'

'Why didn't you let me know?' he burst out. 'That you were moving from Three Hills?'

'I did,' she said wryly. 'But the letter came winging back. Just like the others.'

There was an awkward pause. Then, 'Look!' she said. 'Will you get me a drink of something? An orange juice?'

'There isn't any,' he said miserably. 'No milk either.'

'Well go to the Spar and get some.' She reached out and gave him a push, just as Jessica had done earlier.

Half an hour later, when he got back, the sitting room was more or less clear of detritus, and looked a little more as it had done when he'd first arrived. 'You did this?' he said. 'You shouldn't. The leaflet says you shouldn't tire yourself.' He poured her some orange juice and gave it to her. 'You really shouldn't.'

He looked at the coffee table. The Poland notebooks had gone.

'I did it mostly from this chair. Now I intend to abandon it and manage with the stick. Could you fold the chair and put it in the hall?' She stood up and used the stick to make her way to the sofa. Then she said, 'And I did take a peek at my bedroom. But I just left that.'

He groaned. 'No. I'll clean it. Now! I should clear out.'

'Put your things in the spare room,' she said. 'Perhaps change the bedding. But there's no question of clearing out.' She smiled tentatively at him. 'You're staying put, Adam. Please say you will. We've so many things to sort out, you and I.'

Suddenly he was energised. He disposed of the wheelchair, stuffed dirty sheets and clothes into the washer, found clean linen in an ottoman, remade the bed, made up the spare bed, put his shoes in a line under the tiny spare-room window, his rucksack on a chair, his iPod on the bedside table. Then he got out her stubby electric cleaner and hoovered the whole apartment. He'd just got out the spray polish when, from her place on the sofa, she put up a hand. 'Stop! Enough! No polish! You're making my head swim.'

He looked at her. They'd been together two hours and had barely said a word. He wondered if this sorting out would ever happen; if even in the same space they would be as separate as ever.

She handed him a sheet of paper. 'Would you do this for me, Adam? There's this art shop on the way up to the cathedral. You can't miss it.' She gave him her credit card and pin number. 'Will you manage to get this lot back here? It'll be bulky.'

He looked at the list: acrylic paints in specified colours; paintbrushes of various types; four stretched canvases of particular measurements. 'No problem,' he said.

She smiled. 'Get a taxi if it's too bulky. Do!'

'Right!' he said uncertainly.

She tapped him on the forearm. 'Don't worry, Adam,' she said quietly. 'There's nothing to worry about. Nothing even to think about. You're here at home, that's what counts. And at last there's time. We have time.'

'Right.' He tied his hair back in a rubber band and picked up his rucksack. 'Right,' he repeated.

With Adam safely out of the way, Marie pulled out a clean notebook from the bottom cupboard of the dresser and awkwardly transferred herself to a dining chair beside the table. Then, elbows down, brow furrowed, she began to sketch in the verticals and horizontals of the hospital entrance, an image fixed like a snapshot on her brain in the minutes she'd sat outside in her wheelchair waiting for the ambulance. She scribbled in the shady interior and drew a few lines to suggest the bulk of the back of the ambulance, then alongside it the tall, slight figure of Adam and the more solid one of Jessica Stanley, and a wheelchair in which she sketched the small figure of a woman with a ponytail.

Then, swiftly, she turned to a new page and started drawing the side ward where she'd lain for the last weeks: the verticals and horizontals of the bed with the still husk of a figure, mummy-like, lying on it; lines suggesting the wide, shallow window with its horizontal glazing bars, and above that the horizontal line of the fluorescent light. Beside the bed, the vertical lounging figure of Adam, all long legs and streaming hair.

Marie's hand paused in the top right-hand quadrant of the page. She wanted to draw something there. She had to. She glanced back at the figure on the bed, striated like a chrysalis. And Adam sitting beside it. Then, in the top right-hand corner of the room she drew a butterfly, its wings half open, its body holding them in tension. She held the drawing up, away from herself. That was it. That would be the first one, she thought.

Cadmium Yellow

Adam called on Sharina on his way back from town. 'She's home! Marie's back.'

Sharina was tying a woolly hat under Arian's chin. 'Marie? Home? Me and Arian were just getting ready to go to see her, weren't we, Arian?'

'Well she's just along the landing. So you won't have far to go, will you?'

She untied Arian's hat. 'That'll save us, won't it, pet?'

'Well, are you coming along to see her? I'm sure she'll want to see you.' He could hear the pleading in his voice. Anything, anything rather than be on his own with his mother. Sharina should see that. He knew she would see that.

She looked at him carefully. 'Nah . . . Mebbe I'll come along later. You and her'll be settling in. You'll need time.' She met his gaze.

'Time for what?'

'Just time. For the two of you.' Her eyes moved to his bulky packages. 'What's all that then? You been shopping?'

'For Marie. She gave me a list for the art shop.'

'Oh yeah. She's a very good drawer, your mam. I seen those drawings in her books.'

'This is different. There are thick gooey paints here, Sharina. And these boards are five times the size of her usual drawings. It's not her usual style, big, splashy painting. Her stuff is neat. Precise. That's Marie Mathéve.'

Sharina poked at the packages. 'Mebbe she's planning something really big. Mebbe lying there all that time in the hospital, like, it's changed her.'

'Don't know about that.' He shrugged. 'I've got no idea what she's planning.'

She picked up Arian and lodged him on her hip. 'Well,' she said, 'hadn't you better get along there? Find out what she's planning?' She paused. 'What's wrong, Adam? Like I said, you'd've thought you'd be jumping for joy: your mam back to life like the Count of Monte Cristo. "Called Back to Life": one chapter was called that.'

He stared at her. 'I told you what happened before. I told you I cut her off, didn't want to know. I've not seen her since those events. Since Sam. Since the crash. And before that, her and me, well, we were always kind of semi-detached.'

'All that means, lover, is that you've a lot of ground to make up. Together. The two of you.'

'You might say that, but—'

She pushed his packages back towards him. 'Well, start making up, you divvy! Now!'

As he let himself into his mother's flat he was met by the plangent sounds of a string quartet. The precise notes filled the flat with life. He found himself smiling at his mother, who was crouching at the table over a fat drawing pad. 'That's nice,' he said. 'Makes me think of Jack.'

She smiled back at him. 'You remember! Jack loved chamber music! He used to say it reminded him of gypsies. And me. Always on the move. We used to try and dance to his records but it didn't always work. Even with him gone, his music has always made me feel right somehow.'

Adam shook his head. 'I didn't know that. I remember that he liked music.' He searched his memory for something that linked his mother to this music. He really didn't remember. Nothing. He heaved a big sigh.

'Adam?' She was looking at him with a slight frown. 'What's the matter?'

He put his packages on the coffee table. 'They had everything on the list except the cadmium yellow and scarlet crimson. But I've ordered those for you.'

They unpacked the packages together. She exclaimed at the fat tubes, smelling them, and fingered the soft brushes, running her hand over the coarse cream surfaces of the boards.

'What's all this about then?' Adam ventured. 'I thought you liked your pencils and pastels.'

She shrugged and he realised how narrow and fleshless

her shoulders were. 'It's just an idea,' she said. 'It came to me in the ambulance. I've always shied off anything bolder than watercolour. Sort of cowardly in a way. Then in the ambulance I realised there was something more I had to do.' She looked at him. 'Do you know what I really fancy, Adam?'

'What's that?'

'I fancy a soft-boiled egg. I see you've bought eggs.'

It was a relief to do something. He made her two soft-boiled eggs and soldiers. She smiled when she saw the soldiers. 'Jack used to make these for you,' she said.

'I didn't think you'd remember,' he said.

She ate them with relish. When she'd finished, she wiped her mouth with a napkin, then she looked at him very carefully. He held his breath. Here it comes, he thought. The whys and wherefores. The whens and hows. Poland.

'Could you do something for me?' she said finally.

Breath out. 'Yes. Anything.'

'Well, there are some old draw-sheets in the bottom of the ottoman in the bedroom. Can you take one out and spread it on the floor over there inside the bay?'

The bay window stretched across the broad wall of the sitting room and looked outwards from Merrick Court over the rooftops and across to the rising northern hills. She had a reading chair there with a small table beside it. He'd noticed that end of the room was always filled with light.

He cleared the area, then laid the draw-sheet carefully over the fitted carpet. It looked dingy and old against the pristine beige.

'Now,' Marie said, 'could you pull the dining table across and open the leaves? I need a big surface. Then get the other draw-sheet and cover the table.'

When that was done she stood up, swaying a little, then she was still. 'Yes. That's it,' she said.

He moved across to take her arm and he felt good as she let him help her as she made her way to the table. 'Right!' she said victoriously. 'Let's set it up.' He helped her lay out the paints and brushes and went to get two white plates from the kitchen for palettes. 'Now then!' She picked out one of the canvases and he put it at the centre of the table.

'Ok,' she said. 'Reach me my drawing pad. It's there on the coffee table.' She laid it on the dining table and propped it open. Adam recognised the scene outside the hospital. He stood and watched as she used charcoal to block in the hospital entrance and the back of the ambulance. And himself and Jessica Stanley. Last of all, herself in the wheelchair. She worked very quickly.

'This is not like your usual thing, is it?' he ventured.

Lost in her drawing she didn't answer him. Annoyed, he said, 'Why are you doing this? You should be in bed. Resting or something.'

She looked up as though she had forgotten he was there. 'What? Oh. Sorry. Listen, Adam. This was the first thing on my mind when I came in here. I kept seeing myself sitting here painting. Big canvases and nice squashy paint. I don't know where that came from but I know this is what I want to do.' She squeezed out some yellow ochre and some ivory black.

'And you wanted to paint the hospital? You wanted to paint that?'

She looked down at the figure she was blocking in. He realised it was himself. A second version of him. 'I had these dreams while I was in there, Adam. I thought I might try to get them down. But first I wanted to do this one about me getting out of there. Me surviving and you, my dear boy, being there!'

She leaned over and sketched in a tumble of plants by the smoking hut, survivors from the summer planting. Then he watched as she drew a small creature sitting on a leaf: a mere speck, but it was clearly a butterfly.

'I didn't see any butterfly,' he said.

'I did,' she said. 'She was just out of her chrysalis. See? There's the husk.' She put down her charcoal and surveyed her blackened fingers. 'And suddenly I am very tired. If you just pass me that stick, Adam, I think I'll go and sleep off all this excitement.'

He helped her through to the bedroom and stood there helplessly. She looked up at him, smiling faintly. 'You can leave me. Honestly. I can manage very well now. It might take me longer, but I can manage.'

He turned to go, but the touch of her hand made him turn back.

'I'm pleased – really pleased – you're here, Adam. I thought I'd lost you,' she said sadly. 'I truly did.'

It was only later, when he was going to bed himself, that he suddenly realised something about his mother for the first time – perhaps, he thought, now that her fragility had made him feel her equal: he knew now that like him Marie was shy, really shy. She knew there was something between them, something to sort out. She had said as much. But then she had generated that flurry with the paints and canvases as a way of avoiding the fact. How many times had he done the same thing? Going off digging to avoid her in the holidays? Burying himself in prison life and not facing her letters. It was like a Mexican stand-off about who was the most shy, who had the least emotional courage.

But she'd shown courage – hadn't she? – in the face of his cowardice when she'd come to the court and by writing the letters. Well, maybe now it was down to him to step up to the plate. Tomorrow he'd get out the notebooks and make her talk about Poland. Then this change that seemed to be happening to them might have the chance of becoming real and true.

Real Life

Despite Adam's good intentions, he had no opportunity to talk to his mother about Poland. In the days after she arrived home, Marie started painting like a woman possessed. Adam made meals, he did the washing, he did the shopping. He looked after Arian while Sharina was at college. He collected more paints and admired the striking images that Marie created sitting in the bay window. But slowly their day-to-day life created a new ease between them and the tension he still felt in her presence began to fade away.

So he postponed his intention to challenge Marie about Poland and what it really meant in their lives, and settled for the new ease on the surface of their lives together. Time enough, he thought, to sort that out. There were other realities, after all. One of them was to look for work. As he said more than once to the approving Sharina, he couldn't live for ever on his mother's charity.

Then one morning a week later, reality solved his

problem. That morning he woke up with a start, sitting bolt upright, thinking for a split second he was still in his cell. Then relief flooded through him. This narrow room was Marie's spare bedroom, not his prison pad: too much light, for one thing. The sound of the bell had been his phone. It rang for a second time. He scrambled across the room for it in his rucksack.

'Adam Mathéve?'

'Yes. That's me.'

'My name's Bridget White.'

The name sounded vaguely familiar but he couldn't place it. 'Bridget White?' he scrabbled again in the bottom of his rucksack and found a creased brown envelope. 'You're my—'

'Probation officer. You're assigned to me.'

Yes. They'd written down her name for him when he signed on. And the date of his first interview. They'd written him quite a threatening letter when he missed it. 'I'm sorry, but you see—'

'Well I *do* see, Mr Mathéve! I see you missed your first appointment, so we were unable to make a second.' The voice was clipped, severe. 'You should know this means trouble.'

His heart sank. He knew the conditions of his licence well enough. You keep contact with your officer. You attend. You accept that your freedom is conditional on the discipline of this contact. 'I'm really sorry, Miss White. You see, my mother—'

'Stop!' Her voice was very sharp now. 'There are always the most miraculous explanations, or, as we would say in our office, *excuses*!' It was clear she was used to hustling people on. 'Just get down here at eleven o'clock this morning and deliver your explanations in person. Right? I'm going to take you to see the Briar Rose.'

'What's the Briar Rose?' he said.

'You'll see.'

The phone went dead.

He smoothed out the letter and peered at it. His appointment with this Miss White had been last week, the day Marie came back to life.

By eleven o'clock he was sitting opposite Bridget White, listening to her now quite amiable voice explaining to him again the conditions of his licence. 'At least you have a proper address. Your mother's, you say?'

That was when he told her about the events of the last weeks. She listened carefully and checked entries on her computer. Marie's full address. The house phone number. 'So you're still there? Good. And she was ill. I can see there's a degree of mitigation there. No black mark this time.'

He was suddenly angry at her moderate, even tone. As though he were ten years old. Like some of the counsellors and psychiatrists in prison: she wore her savage neutrality like a protective cloak. Feeling so angry, he knew it best to say nothing: another prison lesson.

She scrolled down his file. 'Good education. Nose clean

in prison. A few things to offer here.' She sniffed. 'Me, I'm always that bit suspicious of the virtuous ones. Give me a bad lad any day.'

He had to leave that too, but really he could have thrown his chair at her.

'So,' she said, 'what are you doing about money?'

'I'm OK, I think,' he said. 'My mother . . . She sold her house, put money by for me.'

She smirked. 'Oh, Mummy's little . . .' She paused, and scrolled up her screen again. 'Lucky you've not got a habit, then. You'd've gone through Mummy's nest egg in a month.'

That was enough. 'That's not fair. It's not like that,' he snapped. 'I think you . . .' He stopped.

She was smiling, her slightly heavy face transformed. 'Attaboy! I was waiting for a spark of life.' She shuffled some papers on her desk, 'Now then, Adam, I'm aware that you're keeping an eye on your ma, but what about a job? It says here that you should be actively seeking work. What do you think?' Her tone was quite amiable now.

He shrugged. 'I'm not against it.'

'Well, hallelujah! Get the flags out.'

He was conscious of her staring at him. 'What am I supposed to do?' he said. 'There's all that stuff that happened with my mother. And now I'd like to be paying my way. I should be paying her . . .'

She looked blank for a second. 'That's a new one. Well, well! All I can say is that you gotta move forward. Never look back. Live in the present, it's the only way to go.' She sniffed. 'The shrinks'd say otherwise, of course. Always looking backwards, that lot!' She shoved a piece of paper across the desk. 'Now you have your first test. Be here at nine o'clock tomorrow morning. I'll drive you over there.'

He got back to a house that smelt of paint, thinner, garlic, tomatoes, baby milk and lemons. He followed the sound of laughter to the kitchen. Marie, Sharina and Arian were jammed around the kitchen table, which had an empty place set for him. Arian was eating lemon curd and bread; the other two were eating shop-bought pizza.

The women looked up. Sharina grinned. 'Look at me. Back here to collect Arian, and Marie's feeding me again!'

Adam smiled down at her. 'Course all right?'

'Brilliant. They love me 'cos they know no better. A plus for my first essay.'

'Great. Well done.'

'So how was it, Adam?' said Marie. 'The probation officer? Was she an ogre?'

He squeezed on to the spare seat. Sharina leaned over and took his pizza from the oven and put it on the table in one economical movement. 'We got quattro stagioni. Is that OK?'

'She wasn't an ogre, Mum. Funny woman, though.'

'At least she's not going to throw you back in the clink.' Sharina put a hand over her mouth. 'Sorry. Stupid thing to say.'

Adam laughed, and tore off some pizza and nibbled it. 'No, she's not gunna throw me back inside. Seems she could have found me a job. Well, not a job really. Just some work experience.'

'What at?' said Marie. 'I hope she finds you something that . . . well . . . you have your education, you know.'

He burst out laughing. 'You have to be realistic about this kind of thing, Mum. Any job is a job.'

'Well then, what is this wonderful work experience she's getting you?'

'I don't know. She says it's a surprise.'

Sharina scowled. 'That's no way to go on.'

He shrugged. 'It doesn't bother me. I'm just marking time till . . .' He glanced across at Marie.

She smiled. 'Till I'm better? Look. I'm fine. Jessica Stanley called today to look me over. Didn't have to. I told her that. She's just a nice woman. But she says I'm wonderful. Says I have the constitution of an ox. Just that I shouldn't think of doing the Great North Run again.' She paused. 'And she asked about you.'

'In fact I asked her if I could drive. But it'll be six months and another scan before they let me do that. So . . .' She glanced at Sharina. 'As the Mitsubishi's there in the garage, and you can't drive, Adam, I thought Sharina should have lessons and she can use it.'

Sharina's head shot up. 'Me? I can't drive.'

'You can learn. You're a quick learner,' said Adam. 'It's a great idea.'

Sharina was eager and disappointed at the same time. 'It costs a lot, doesn't it? To learn how to drive.'

'I'll pay,' said Marie.

'But that's not fair . . .'

'Look,' said Adam, 'think how good it would be for Mum. You can take her around a bit. It'll be company for her even when she's driving herself.'

'Put like that,' Sharina said, 'I suppose—'

Then Arian started to wail and she extricated herself and him from the narrow kitchen table. 'Needs his nap, doesn't he? Busy morning at the crèche, eh, Arian?'

As they walked to the door Sharina said, 'I noticed!'

'What did you notice?'

'You've stopped calling her Marie.'

When he came back from locking the door behind Sharina, Marie was back in the sitting room. This space was transformed from the neat, elegant room that Adam had found on his first day. Now it was dominated by the painting table in the bay window, with its rows of paints and its jars of brushes and charcoal. Leaning up against the furniture and the bookcases were Marie's new large, splashy paintings. Some of these were surreal but fundamentally realistic scenes in and outside the hospital. Others were more abstract – dark lines and globes of light and shadowy faces emerging out of nothingness. None of them bore any relationship to Marie's meticulous drawings and watercolours carefully mounted and hanging on the walls.

She was already at her table, blocking in a painting that

was just a big, heavily carved door in a wall. She was working on something above the door. Some kind of carving that was as yet just a series of charcoal lines that made no sense.

He stood behind her. 'So, Mum. What's this one?' He was even risking direct questions these days.

'I saw a door like this once,' she said. 'It was a wonderful door in a wonderful house.' She seemed about to say something else, but at that moment their own doorbell rang.

It was Sharina. 'I forgot. A girl rang,' she said. 'This girl rang for you when Marie was in the kitchen.'

'The probation woman? She rang?'

'No, not that kind of woman. You can tell. More a girl. She had this very posh voice. Young. Throaty. She asked if you lived here and I said yes but you were out. I asked her name but she wouldn't give it. Said she'd ring again. It felt important, Adam.' She looked up at him. 'Anyway, I'm off. Arian's asleep and I've got reading to do. I gave her your mobile number. I thought it would be OK.' She paused. 'You all right, Adam?'

He nodded. 'Course I am.' He shut the door and leaned his forehead against it.

Marie called from the sitting room, 'Everything all right, Adam?'

'Yeah, fine,' he said. 'I think I'll go out for a run.'

Later, pounding his way along the river bank, past the rowers in their skiffs and the tourists taking in the most famous view of the cathedral, Adam tried to stop his head spinning and to slow the thudding of his heart. Back-to-square-one. Back-to-square-one. His feet beat the rhythm into the dirt path. *Back-to-square-one*.

The fragile house of cards he'd built in the last few weeks was tumbling around him. His friendship with Sharina, the tentative remaking of his sense of Marie, even today's common-sense meeting with Bridget White about his future – it was as though none of that had happened. The voice on the phone could only be one person, and that was Rachel Miriam Wiener. The nightmare was back.

Rachel

Adam was just about to turn and jog back up through the town towards home when his mobile rang. 'Yeah?' he gasped, jogging on the spot.

'Adam, is that you?'

'Yeah.' He stood very still.

'It's Rachel.'

'I know. I knew it was you. The message you left.'

'Who was it? Who answered at the house?'

'It was my sister.'

'I didn't know you had a sister.'

'I don't, but . . . It's a long story.'

'Where are you?'

'Just up from the river bank. I've been running.'

'Me too. Not running, though. I'm on the river bank too. Parked by Priest's Bridge. Come and talk to me, Adam.'

He paused, still breathing heavily. 'You don't have a gun or a knife, do you?'

'Don't be stupid. Just come.'

It took him ten minutes to get there, half walking, half jogging, half frightened, half exultant. Rachel was in a bright blue Jeep parked by the river wall. She leaned over and clicked the door open. He jumped in and sat beside her.

She turned and surveyed him.

He flinched. 'Don't look too hard,' he said. 'I've been running.'

She looked just the same, except for slight shadows under her round eyes. Big hair, colourful clown's clothes, long boots. He leaned forward and lifted her straggly fringe to reveal the neat white scar. 'That must have been bad,' he said. 'Really sorry about that. I've been so sorry.'

She shrugged. 'Nothing to be sorry about it. I deserved it and worse. Me drunk, my car. Do the maths. Cause and effect. Fact is, you look better than I thought. I thought you'd be a pasty grey, have a number one haircut and tattoos.'

He grinned. 'Watching too many movies, you are. Inside is both better and worse than you see. Anyway. How d'you find me?'

She lit a cigarette and drew on it. 'I did try and failed. Then I got my grandfather on the job. He *knows people*. Had your address and phone number in an hour.'

'He didn't mind?'

'No option. I said I *had* to do this, and in the end he agreed. He usually does.'

'Had to do what?'

'Come and see you. And Sam's parents. That's why I caught up with you today. I want you to come with me and go and see them.'

He looked down at his clothes. 'I'm scruffy. Covered with sweat.'

'Doesn't matter. How scruffy was Sam?' Rachel let off the handbrake. 'There's a map in the glove compartment. You can make sure that I don't lose my way.'

'Do they know that you . . . we're coming?'

'Mrs Rogers does. She said come and welcome. She said she didn't know about Mr Rogers.' She steered the car back up into the city. 'We're going east. Keep your eye on the map, will you? I hate losing my way.'

As they drove along the winding road into the higher land in the east of the county, Adam told Rachel about Mrs Rogers coming to the house and then to the hospital to try to cure his mother with her healing touch.

'She said your mother was in hospital. Did it work?' said Rachel. 'Did she cure your mother?'

'Well, somebody did. She's out of hospital now.' Then he found himself telling her everything about Marie. 'Being in there like that changed her,' he finished.

'So you've sorted things out with her?'

'What things?'

'Things! Sam used to say that your mother was a wonderful woman but you two had things to sort out because you were both alike, closed as clams.'

Adam paused a second to absorb the echo of Sam's words in Rachel's mouth. 'Well, as you are asking, things are *not* sorted. Not yet. But maybe you could say they're moving on.'

They drove on in silence for a while, then Rachel said, 'Do you think of Sam? That old bear?'

'Yes. Every day.'

'Me too.' She peered at a road sign. 'Nearly there. That's the place, isn't it?'

Mrs Rogers opened the door wide and welcomed them both. She sat them down and clapped her hands when Adam told her of his mother's recovery. 'I knew it! She was on the brink when I went to visit her. She has a very strong spirit and was not ready to go.' She beamed at him. 'I knew she had things to do here, on this side.'

She turned to Rachel. 'And you, Rachel. How are you now? I had two very nice letters from your grandfather on your progress. I prayed for you.'

Rachel smiled. 'Head's fine and my limp's just about gone. How have you been, Mrs Rogers?'

Sam's mother hesitated. 'Well, I miss our Sam all the time, you know, even though I know he's in a better place. I had these bad, hypocritical feelings about him going the way he did. But they got sorted, really, when I went to see Adam's mam. Now I've stopped thinking about myself and can mourn him properly. Seeing Adam and his mam helped with that. And now seeing you will help me too.'

'And Mr Rogers?'

'Oh, Joseph is another kettle of fish, isn't he?' Jane Rogers shook her head sadly. 'Refused to stop in to see you. He has a way to go has Joseph, poor lad. He's got his television in his shed now. Never in the house more than five minutes. He's inconsolable.' She paused. 'I've put an application in at the council to move house. Thought mebbe that'll do the trick for him. Get rid of the unfinished business. Mebbe.' Her voice faded away. Then she looked around the kitchen where they were sitting. 'Now!' she said more briskly. 'Can I get you a cup of tea?'

'No thank you.' Rachel stood up and Adam followed suit. 'We should go now. It was so very kind of you to see us.'

Mrs Rogers did not urge them to stay and they hurried out of the house, down the path and into the Jeep. Rachel gunned the engine, drove off the estate into the woodland at the edge of the town and stopped.

Adam looked around at the trees, losing their leaves now with the onset of winter. 'Sam and me walked here,' he said. 'Playing like kids. He broke this old swing.'

She was already out of the Jeep. 'Show me!' she shouted. 'Show me where you played, on that old swing.'

It took them twenty minutes to find the big tree. The broken rope had been replaced by a brand-new one, thick and yellow and barely used. Adam took hold of it and threw it with all its strength, making it swing right out over the cut. He turned round to see Rachel standing there, staring at the broad tree trunk. He went to stand beside her, then pulled her to the other side of the tree. 'Sam carved something on the bark. He apologised to the tree for breaking the swing. Look!'

He traced the word with his forefinger. *SORRY*. Rachel's fingers followed his, then trailed further down the trunk. 'Look! What's this?' Underneath the word someone had carved the initials *AM + RMW + SR*.

'That's us, isn't it?' said Rachel.

Adam shook his head. 'He didn't carve that when I was here with him.'

Rachel traced the letters with her fingers. 'He must have come back another time and done it.'

That was when Adam and Rachel clung together, clutching each other. Rachel was sobbing and shuddering, but Adam, holding her very tightly, was dry eyed. He enjoyed the feeling of her slight body against his. He wanted to kiss her, make love to her. He could feel Sam's presence as surely as he could feel the bark of the ancient tree. And he knew with equal certainy that Sam didn't blame him for what had happened. More, he was telling him to get on with things. *Go for it, mate! Life's too short! Don't I keep telling you?*

So he went for it. Kissing Rachel was a good start.

Later, from Rachel's room at the Imperial Hotel, he rang Marie. 'I met a mate, Mum, and we're staying down in town for a drink and maybe something to eat.'

There was a slight pause. 'That's nice for you.' Marie paused again. 'But don't be late, will you? You've got that meeting with the probation woman in the morning. Oh dear! What am I saying? You do exactly what you want, Adam. I'm getting very possessive in my old age.'

'That's all right, Mum.' He grinned down the phone. 'I don't mind possessive. It'll make a nice change.'

In the end, it was two o'clock when he got back to the apartment, having spent the evening with Rachel. Mostly they talked of the good times they'd had with Sam, alternating the lovemaking, the eating and the drinking with talking: 'Remember that time when you and Sam . . .'

Part Six

New Beginnings

The Bike Shop

'So what's this place?' Adam lifted his bike from the boot of Bridget White's car and surveyed the gaggle of buildings scattered around what looked like an old school yard. He tucked his bike under a van by the gate

'I told you. The Briar Rose Bike Centre.' Bridget White was watching his face. They had driven through the estate with its rigid lines of houses and its ragged gardens. Some of the houses were boarded up. Others were clean and bright with neat curtains.

Adam peered through the mesh railings. The big tarmac yard was broken down like bruises connected by veins. Inside an open-sided workshop some boys in overalls were dismantling wrecked motorbikes and rebuilding them.

'They build them up, and if they're good they get to ride them,' said Bridget. 'You should see'm doing it, whooping like bloody cowboys.'

'Is it a charity or something?' he said.

Bridget nodded. 'Police, magistrates, probation officers all in on it. You know? Bit by bit. Blagging money left, right and centre. Then we got hold of this lad called Vince, who's a wonder with these tearaways, and he found this old school. All that was left was the yard, that prefab classroom and the big open shed. Right here in the middle of the Briar Rose estate.'

'Vince?' said Adam, just for something to say.

'You'll see. He's quite something, is Vince.'

'So you think *I'm* a tearaway, like those lads there?'

Bridget White laughed. Her laugh was prettier than her looks. 'Hardly! Anyway, you're ten years older than these kids. No. I thought you could give Vince a hand. He's got this one volunteer but he's only part time. Some musician from the university. Never met him, although Vince rates him.'

'It's an interesting idea,' said Adam cautiously.

'It works,' said Bridget. 'Vince has his rules and they like it here so they obey them. Compulsory attendance. No smoking – dope or anything else. No fighting. No knives. No mobile phones. The boys all sign a contract. Three strikes on any of the rules and they're out. Never lost one. They all keep coming back.' She opened the gate. 'Well then, Adam! Onward and upward!'

Adam followed her in. Just inside the gate was a big red Honda motorbike trussed up like a chicken in chains. The boys working in the open shed looked up. One of them whistled. Bridget grinned and gave him a wave,

The prefab classroom was half workshop, half office. Some boys were sorting bike parts on sheets of Visquine on the floor. By the desk, a tall, fair man was peeling himself out of battered bike leathers. Beside him was an enormous man in a flowing tweed jacket and white linen shirt. His face creased into smiles when he saw Bridget. 'Why, if it isn't Bridget White come to grace us with her presence,' he said. He reached out and grabbed her hand in his bear paw. Then he turned to the man beside him. 'This is Bridget White, Peter, the probation lass,' he said. 'I told you about her. She gets me lumps of money now and then, and she brings me my little troubles. No offence, son.' He nodded to Adam, who was taking all this in.

'I'm Peter,' the blond man said, grasping Bridget's hand.

She smiled up at him, and for a second her double chin became single. 'I've heard of you, Peter, coming out of your eastern mists, driving your red chariot around the Briar Rose. Vince says you're working miracles here.'

Peter laughed. 'Is nothing,' he said, shaking his head. 'Vince is miracle-worker. I am here in the city for my music and I am bored. So I come here to Briar Rose.'

'Fascinating. *Have music, will travel.*'

'Is nothing,' he repeated. 'I come to England for six months to see the cathedrals and play music. For six months I am here to teach at your university and soon perform in your cathedral.'

'You like our city?' she said.

He shrugged again. 'Is beautiful,' he replied. 'But many

beautiful churches in my country also.' Then he grinned widely. 'I like best Vince's workshop. A cathedral of motor-bikes!'

'Gerraway with you,' said Vince. 'Full of crap, you for-eigners.' His eye moved across to Adam. 'And who've we got here?' His meaty paw now engulfed Adam's smaller hand.

'I'm Adam—'

Bridget butted in. 'I thought Adam might give you a bit of a hand, like Peter does,' she said. 'He's due to be job-hunting but his mam's been bad and he needs some breath-ing space. A bit of slack, you know? I thought maybe he could come and . . . well . . . chat to your lads.' She paused and then said carefully, 'For instance, he could advise them that prison's not a cool option, not an easy ride. Things like that.'

Adam was worried. 'Look, Bridget, I don't know anything about motorbikes . . .'

'Didn't you say you'd played in a band at university?' she said. 'The lads'll like that.'

He'd said no such thing. She'd read it in his file.

'Yeah, but I was rubbish at it,' he said. 'Just fiddling with a guitar.' He was miserable and wanted to escape.

Peter glanced from Bridget to Adam and back again. 'I bring here my old guitar,' he said suddenly. 'And you and me, Adam, we play for the boys in tea break.'

Vince pulled down his creased linen shirt and stroked a hand down his great belly. 'Might work. Lads might like it.' He turned to Adam. 'You gotta bike licence?'

Bridget shook her head and scowled at Vince. 'Adam's got no licence of any kind, Vince. I thought maybe he'd just tinker on with the lads and get round to some useful talk with them. OK?'

Vince stood up straight. 'You got the funding for that, Bridge?'

She nodded.

'Then Adam here's very welcome. He can try us and we can try him and he's very welcome. Now!' He reached out and took her arm. 'D'you park outside? You should know better. I'll walk you out.'

Adam watched the two of them walk away, their heads together, and he knew that Bridget was filling Vince in as to just why her client had no licence of any kind.

Peter followed his gaze. 'That Vince is a great guy,' he said. 'You will have a good time here.'

Adam took a closer look at the other man. He was tall but quite thickset, not much like some fragile musician. His short fair hair had been pushed up into a kind of cockscomb. The eyes that were boring into his were glittering and somewhere between brown and black.

Adam shook his head. 'I know nothing about motorbikes,' he repeated.

The other man grinned. 'But me, I know about motorbikes very well. I worked in my uncle's workshop since I was eight. My uncle was professor of engineering with head and engineer with his hands.' Peter splayed his hands before Adam. 'My music teachers were always so angry. *Piotr,* they say, *your hands! You will ruin your hands!*' He lounged against the wooden filing cabinet. 'Still, I wear gloves here to work because I must keep the nails on one hand long. Makes boys laugh. They ask if I am gay.'

Adam made an effort. 'So you play the guitar?' he said.

'Yeah. I play guitar,' said Peter.

'And that's what you're doing at the university?'

'Well. No. There I play other things that are plucked. The harpsichord, the harp and the theorbo.'

'You're kidding. What's that, then?'

'Is a strange thing. My special thing. Is like a long, long lute. Or mandolin. You hear of these?'

'Yeah. I think so.'

'Well, the theorbo is like lute but very, very long neck. And many, many strings. This most wonderful sound it makes.' He paused. 'It is the music of history.'

Adam couldn't think of a thing to say to that. He was tired as well as exultant after his late night with Rachel. And on top of that, all this new stuff was suddenly very baffling. He'd woken up wanting to talk to Rachel, to make plans, but it was too early in the morning. And now his mobile was turned off on Bridget White's instructions.

The man called Peter was grinning at him. 'But really, here at the Briar Rose, Adam, we know the roar of the motorbike is the music of these times. Is that not so?'

Adam looked down the dusty workshop, absorbing the echoing chatter of boys and the smell of engine oil and dust. He repeated, 'I know absolutely nothing about bikes, you know. And I don't know whether I've anything at all for *them*. These lads. Can't think of a thing to say.'

Peter stepped away from the filing cabinet, burly in a thick black T-shirt and jeans. He was adjusting his thin black cotton gloves. 'We all have things to say to each other, Adam. We just have to open our mouths. I would give them a try, Vince's lads. Why not? You lose nothing.'

Vince had returned from escorting Bridget off the premises. Adam watched him make his way across the workshop, stopping by his lads one by one, having a word here, a word there, for all the world like a shepherd checking his sheep.

Adam took a breath. 'If Vince still wants me here after he's heard what Bridget has to say, I'll stay.'

Peter looked at him sharply then, but didn't pursue the point.

Vince joined them. 'Well, son, what about it? Do we pass muster?' he said.

Adam looked him in the eye. 'Well, it's up to you. Do *I* pass muster?'

Vince grinned, showing a line of crooked teeth. 'Bridget says you're OK, so you're welcome here, son. Adam, is it? Adam was the first man, wasn't he? Well, here you're our third man, after me and Peter.' He paused. 'So what are we gunna do with you?'

Peter butted in. 'Adam and me, we will talk about the guitars to the lads. And he will help the lads with the WD40 and the unscrewing. Easy stuff! Then tomorrow when we stop for dinner, he and I get our guitars and teach each other all we know. And soon, your lads they bring guitars.' He laughed. 'Everyone play guitars.'

'Whoa! Whoa!' Vince scowled at him. 'Listen Pete! You two are not gunna turn my workshop into a bliddy talent contest, charm or no bloody foreign charm.'

Peter was already shaking his head. 'No, no, Vince! Just dinnertimes. Bridget says Adam must tell them that prison is no good. So dinnertime, we have sandwiches, coffee, guitar. Easy to talk then, about anything. Even prison, maybe?'

Vince laughed so much that his belly jiggled. 'Clever bugger, you, telling me how to do my own job.'

One of the boys came across. 'You gunna gas all morning, Pete? We got the chassis balanced now, but—'

'OK! OK! I come!' Peter walked back down the workshop with him, talking quickly about the next stage in their rebuild.

Adam, watching them, waited for Vince to say something – maybe even mention the crash.

Vince said, 'Bridget tells us your mam's been ill in hospital. That it was in the papers.'

'She's out now. Wobbly, but—'

'Fragile, aye, I know about fragile. I've had it myself with my lad.' Vince left it at that. 'Now then, Adam, mebbe like Pete says you can join the demolishers. That's the first thing any lad does when he comes in here, anyway. They take the wrecks to pieces. Have to do it with great care, of course.

Like they were surgeons. No waste. That's what I tell them.'
He paused. 'I look at it this way, Adam. They've been taking
things to pieces all their lives, one way or another. So it's
nothing new to them, is it?'

He walked over to the demolishers. 'Here, lads, show
Adam the job. He knows bugger all about bikes, so it's your
job to show him. OK?' Then he strode off and left Adam
to it.

One boy, crouching down loosening a nut, looked
across at Adam, his eyes sharp, bolder and wiser than any
fourteen year old's should be. 'So, what naughty have *you*
been up to then?'

Adam fended that off. 'What naughty have *you* been up
to?'

'Well, me,' said the boy, 'I got an ASBO for nicking
off school, letting down tyres and shouting at people.
Beejay here got his for lighting fires in council bins and
carrying gear for older lads.' He grinned. 'Among other
stuff, like.'

He finally managed to loosen the nut and whooped. He
threw it up to the boy called Beejay, who caught it and
chucked it in a tin with the same size bolt stuck on the
side. 'Go on, mister,' he said. 'Tell us. What naughty d'you
do, then?'

'I'm just out of prison,' said Adam. 'On licence. No job
yet.'

Beejay whistled. 'Get you then!'

'What for?' said the other. 'Whatfor d'you do time?'

'Mind your own fucking business,' said Adam, hardening back into his prison self.

That was when Vince growled across the workshop, 'You on strike, Beejay? I want that stripped down before dinner. Stat! Stat, man!' He had a very penetrating growl.

They worked on steadily till dinnertime, when Vince produced a stack of thick, slab-like sandwiches from a big cardboard box ('Made by my own fair hand, lads!'), and a crate of Asda own-brand cola.

Adam, sitting exhausted against the wall, did not catch Peter slipping away until he heard the roar of the motorbike and saw the flash of the red machine through the big double doors. He listened blankly as some of the lads chatted away to Vince, saying, 'That Pete this . . .' and 'That Pete that . . .'

One of them complained, 'He should'a come all day, not just the morning. We gotta come all day, so he should.'

'Ah, bonny lad,' said Vince. 'But he's not the naughty one, is he?'

'Anyway, where's he gone, then? Lazy f—'

'Stop that,' said Vince. 'That word and you're out!'

'Anyway,' said another boy, asking the question for Adam. 'Where's he gone?'

'He's gone up to this posh college in town, to teach posh lads their posh music.'

Beejay sniffed. 'Well, he'll hafter go through plenty Swarfega to get the grease off his hands first. Gets everywhere, even under those fancy black gloves.'

'Dead right there, son,' said Vince calmly.

Adam, looking down at his own blackened fingers, thought the lad must be right.

Much later, at the end of the day, the boys waited restlessly for Vince to inspect their work. When they had all been noted and signed off, they melted away. Adam stood with Vince in front of his desk and looked down the grey, dusty but now entirely orderly workshop. He wanted to melt away himself, but didn't know just how to do that. He wanted to tell Vince how impressed he was, how wonderful this set-up was.

Vince saved him. 'You did all right, son, sticking with those two all day. Did a good job of taking your cue from them. Clever, that. You gotta bit of savvy there.'

'I didn't really know what to do.'

'Good instincts,' said Vince. 'Good instincts. Useful, that.'

Adam tried to say something. 'All this is marvellous . . .'

Vince waved a dismissive hand. 'Some good lads here, underneath. Lives in chaos. All they need, like, is some shape to things.' He was pulling on his big old overcoat.

Then they were shoulder to shoulder, locking the door of the workshop, walking across the pockmarked, crumbly yard and through the big mesh gates. Vince padlocked it once, then hauled another padlock out of his big coat pocket and padlocked it again.

Adam retrieved his bicycle from under the battered white van that looked as though it had been parked there for ever. Vince grinned. 'Good thing, using a pushbike.

Savvy! Like I said, you got instinct. Whether it came from inside or out, it'll prove useful.' He climbed into the white van, settled in and leaned out of the window. 'See you tomorrow, then?'

Adam smiled broadly. 'I'll be here.'

It was only when he was weaving his way through the four o'clock traffic streaming in and out of the city that Adam thought again of Rachel. The thought hit him so hard that he had to pull up and stand a moment in the gutter, the cars around him pipping their horns. He turned on his mobile and saw three missed calls from her. Good. He'd ring her when he got home.

And then he would have to sleep. The adrenaline of the day was leaking through his heels and he was very tired. He was sure of one thing. Whatever else happened tonight, he would sleep. And maybe not even dream.

Truth

When Adam got home, Sharina was just leaving Marie's flat, her book bag on one shoulder and a sleepy Arian clinging to the other. She nodded at Adam. 'So, how's the world of work, then?'

'It was all right. Gotta say that. Bit strange. Bit long. But it was all right.'

'Will they pay you?' asked Sharina, ever businesslike.

He nodded. 'You get a kind of allowance.'

She looked at him, her head on one side, her face serious. 'And how was your date? Last night? Marie told me.'

'It wasn't a *date*. Rachel's an old friend. It was a bit strange but it was all right.'

'Rachel?' She nodded. 'The girl on the phone?'

'Yeah.'

She smiled slightly. 'Good for you,' she said. ''Bout time you stirred yourself in that direction. I was just saying that

369

to Arian.' She stood to one side. 'Marie's OK today. Pretty on the ball. She's been teaching Arian how to make paper aeroplanes.'

Adam touched Arian on his fat cheek, and as he watched the two of them going down the landing to their own apartment he suddenly thought of the story in Marie's notebook, how she'd bought the carved aeroplane in the Drapers' Hall in Krakow for the Zielinski boy.

As he came through the door, Marie looked up from her painting. He peered over her shoulder. At the centre of her canvas was some kind of mountain carved out of thick acrylic. Great streams of light – almost roadways of white and yellow – charged forward towards the front of the painting. On these roadways were tiny dim figures of men, women and children moving towards the front, arms out, palms upward.

'Wow!' he said.

She smiled ruefully. 'Strange, isn't it? Even I think it's strange.'

'What is it?'

She frowned. 'I don't know. I think it's something from when I was asleep. Something I saw or felt.' She frowned. Then she smiled. 'I think I'll give Mrs Rogers a call. Ask her what she thinks of my visions. She's a bit of a visionary herself.'

He peeled off his jacket and redid the elastic band on his hair. 'Any calls for me?'

'Yes. I was working so I didn't answer. Then the message machine clicked.' She wiped her hands on kitchen roll, hauled herself up to her feet and reached for her stick. 'I suppose this is where I ask if you want anything to eat after a hard day's work.'

'Nah.' He shook his head. 'I could ask you the same. What d'*you* want to eat? After all, you've been sweating all day over a hot paintbox, haven't you?' One part of him marvelled at the jauntiness of his tone, and the ease that was growing between them now. Another part of him was already wondering about the message on the machine. Rachel?

Marie stood there looking at him. 'I had some sandwiches at three. You make something for yourself and I'll come and watch you. Stretch my legs. Jessica says I must keep moving. I'm taking a walk along the landing at six to see Sharina and Arian. Oh! I've fixed up driving lessons for her. Found someone in the telephone book.'

He led the way into the kitchen. 'Good idea, that, about the car.'

'You only need to see that girl charging around the city with that buggy of hers to know it'll make a difference. She got me some shopping today, so there's bacon and eggs and things. I minded Arian for half an hour while she was out. We made paper aeroplanes.'

'She told me. Were you all right with him on your own?'

'Fine. We played singing games too.' She paused. 'Sharina

371

has been a godsend, you know, Adam. I liked her before, but now . . .'

He peered in the fridge. 'I like her. She's very fond of you.'

Marie sat down at the table. 'She makes me laugh. Brings sunshine into the room with her.' She paused. 'She's very fond of you, too.'

'Yes.' He set bacon and eggs on the bench. 'But not like that. We've worked out that we're like sister and brother. She doesn't fancy me. She told me that. So we can be proper friends.'

She looked at him narrowly. 'And that's all right with you?'

'Something like that. Yes, it is. At the beginning there was something, but then that kind of . . .' He concentrated on making a meal of eggs, bacon and tomatoes under her gaze.

'So,' she said. 'Tell me what happened today. Where did that woman take you?'

'This bike shop where school refusers and a few bad lads work on bikes. It's run by this amazing man who reminded me of . . .' He stopped, just realising who Vince reminded him of: Sam.

'Who?'

'No one really. He's big in every way. An original.'

'So what are you supposed to do there? You're not a school refuser or a bad lad.'

He explained about the breaking and the making good.

'I kept telling them I knew nothing about bikes. Bridget's idea is that eventually I'll be able to give them dire warnings about prison. But that didn't happen today. All I did was unscrew bolts and screws and count them.'

'This man runs this place on his own?'

'There was this foreign bloke there; rides this big red beast of a Honda. He seems to know bikes inside out, upside down. But he knows nothing about prison, so I suppose that there I have the advantage over him.'

Marie raised her eyebrows and smiled slightly, acknowledging his irony.

He went on, 'One boy I worked with said the bloke was Hungarian.'

'Exotic!'

'He plays music. He's gunna teach me the guitar. Zebba would be pleased.'

'Zebba?'

'A lad who had a band at uni. He chucked me out of his band because I wasn't good enough.'

Marie looked at him thoughtfully. 'Yet another thing I didn't know about you.' A ripple of distaste crossed her face. 'I *was* a rotten mother, wasn't I?'

He wouldn't let her off the hook. 'You *were*, weren't you?' As he stared at her, to his horror he saw tears in her eyes. He hurried on. 'Not really. I was OK, wasn't I? You took care of that. And there was Jack. He mothered the pair of us, didn't he?' He grinned.

'Jack!' She smiled through her tears. 'Yes, we both had

Jack, didn't we?' She stood up and reached for her stick.

He finished his meal and followed her. She was sitting in the high-backed easy chair. On the table beside her in a neat pile were the Polish notebooks. Adam stared at them, then back at Marie. 'I've been thinking, Mum. It's gotta be time you told me about Poland,' he said. 'That's overdue.'

She touched the pile with an outstretched finger. 'You know all about Poland. You read all these to me in hospital. More than once, I think.'

He blinked. 'You heard? I thought you were dead to the world.'

'I was. Well, I think I was wandering somewhere between this world and the next. But somehow through the mists I *did* hear you reading about Chorzow and Krakow and the grey, grey buildings.' Marie thought she wouldn't tell him just yet about bouncing around on the ceiling. Perhaps another day.

He drew closer to her. 'You've got paint on your cheek.' He leaned down and tried to brush it off with his finger, but smeared it even further. Her skin felt soft under his hand. 'Whoops!' he said.

She laughed. 'Put some liquid soap on kitchen towel. That should do the trick.' She sat and let him clean the paint off, the barriers between them melting away. Then she caught his hand. 'Sit down, Adam. I want to talk to you.'

He sat by her, shoulder to shoulder, and put a hand on the books. 'I found them here at the apartment when I arrived, when you were first in the hospital. I thought it was really odd. The one thing you always did to perfection was tell me all about your travels, but you never told me about any of this. I thought it was amazing, you being in Poland at that time. History. Solidarity and all that. But you never told me.'

She sighed. 'Those events were very private.'

'*Private!* Of course, I'm only your son, aren't I? Too private for me?'

'No. Of course not. I always thought there'd be a proper time.' She leaned over and extracted a sketchbook he'd never seen. 'You won't have looked at this one. I've always kept it in my bedroom drawer.'

Tucked in front were photographs of David and Jacinta and Felix. 'That one. He's the one with the allotment, isn't he? I read about him,' Adam said.

'That's right.' Then she started to turn the pages of the drawing book, moving through quick, fluid sketches of Jacinta, David, Alon Piotr, Felix in his garden shed wearing gumboots over his city trousers. There was a heavily scribbled sketch of Casia, and lighter ones of little Piotr playing with the monkey or the aeroplane or just sitting, reading, laughing.

'I read about the monkey,' Adam said. 'The old woman didn't like it, did she?'

As she turned the pages Marie told Adam about them all, and about the time she spent with the Zielinskis: stories that echoed but did not replicate what he had read in her notebooks. This book was unusual, in that she had drawn only one building; this was on the last page. 'I drew it from memory, on the plane home,' she said. 'It was the very last drawing.'

Adam took the book from her and peered more closely at the drawing of David Zielinski standing in front of the carved door of a fine, tall building with long windows. Marie put her fingers on David's face. 'Do you know, David Zielinski was very special, Adam. It seemed impossible, then, that we could love each other for that brief time. It seemed impossible afterwards. But I did love him. This building is where old Alon Piotr was born and where *his* father and grandfather were born.' She paused. 'And this is the building where you, if you'll forgive the expression, were *made*.' Her shoulder, next to his, felt very tense.

Then so many truths were crashing in on him, rippling through him, taking possession of him. He nodded slowly. 'One part of me had started to work that out. You went there in 1981. I was born in 1982. I knew that something . . .' He was realising the solid truth as he spoke the words. 'Is David Zielinski still there? In Chorzow?'

She shook her head. 'He . . . *was* there. With Jacinta. Till three years ago.' She told him then how Felix had brought her the news.

'And you told no one about me? Not David? Not Felix? Not Jack? Not me?' His voice hardened with the familiar strain of anger at her gift for obdurate silence, her distance.

She sighed. 'It seemed necessary, Adam. Felix guessed about you when he came. He saw your photo. He was a strange old man. But very astute.' She took Adam's hand in hers and squeezed it very tight. 'I don't know if I can make you understand. What happened was ridiculous, unthinkable and utterly marvellous at the same time. Those events were the very best times of my life. They made me the person I became. I was more alive then than . . . well . . . any time until now, here with you, woken up to life. In those early days I felt I had to close off my time in Poland, seal it into the past, just so that I could go on with my life. I felt I had to do this, just to take care of you and make our lives work. But even so, as you grew up you were always a beautiful, wonderful and terrifying reminder of those days. My reward. How could David know about you? How could my sweet friend Jacinta? How could *you* know about them? It seemed tidier . . .' Her voice tailed off. 'But in these recent weeks I've begun to understand that my need to seal all that away made me keep *you* at a distance as well. It was easy to let Jack take the reins with you. He loved you so much. Then, when we lost him, my old habits meant we two were somehow lost to each other. However much I wanted to, it seemed it was too late for me to open up and tell you all the things I'm telling you now.' She paused again. 'You'll laugh at this, Adam, but now I think I was brought back to life to tell you all this. *Is* it too late, do you think?' She sounded nervous, tentative.

'Late?' Adam's anger fell off him like a cloak thrust away when the sun comes out. He picked up the photograph of David and Jacinta and propped it up beside Marie's drawing of David in front of the old Zielinski house. 'Late?' he said. 'Just think, Mum, at least we have years in front of us, you and me.' He put his arm around her and kissed her on both cheeks. She laughed and kissed him back. He could feel her tears on his cheek.

'The future starts here!' he said, grinning. 'The past is in its place.'

Just then his phone rang. It was Rachel. He withdrew to his bedroom and shut the door. 'Where've you been? I've been ringing you all day!' she said. 'I'd thought you'd call. I almost gave up on you.'

He told her about the Briar Rose and the 'no mobile' rule. 'And I've just got in and had this big chat with my mother. The past revealed. That kind of thing. Then you rang.' He could not tell her all that had happened since he had come through the door. There was time enough for that.

'Oh well, you're forgiven, I suppose,' she said. 'Me, I went to Edinburgh on the train. I have cousins there. I'm just back and, to be honest, a bit knackered. I've got this bath running and am desperate to jump into bed. If you remember, we didn't get much sleep last night! But I just wanted to tell you that last night was special for me. And to say, could we meet again?'

He was smiling. 'I'd like that.'

'Tomorrow night then? Ring me at six!'

'Right!'

'Oops. Gotta go. My bath, like my cup, runneth over.'

When Adam got back into the living room, Marie looked up enquiringly.

'It was Rachel Miriam. You remember her? I saw her last night.'

'Ah. I see. Rachel! I remember her. Is she well?'

'She's great. Full of beans.'

'Yes. She always seemed a very lively girl.' Marie paused. 'And things are all right between you now?'

He reached out and hugged her. 'Yes. Seems like it's all right between us. Things are very all right. Like I said before, the future starts here.'

Eating the Breeze

The two weeks since he had joined the Briar Rose project had raced by for Adam. He knew the boys very well now, coming to appreciate their earnestness and laconic style. He was absurdly pleased with himself to graduate from breaking down bikes to building them up.

Most days he'd ended up exhausted, not used to a full day's activity at anything, even before prison, even before then, at university. He revived most evenings when he saw Rachel, still in residence at the Imperial. Twice she'd been home with him and talked to his mother about her paintings, her travels and sometimes about herself. Sharina, when she'd met Rachel, had asked her directly if she were loaded, staying at the Imperial like that. Rachel explained that she was up for interviews at two museums and if she got a job she'd look for a flat.

'So you're staying round here?' said Sharina.

Rachel had glanced at Adam. 'I think so.'

Despite the exhaustion, Adam started to enjoy the Briar Rose days. They worked from eight thirty through till four with forty-five minutes for lunch. No one was allowed out of the workshop at lunchtimes except Peter, who on three days had afternoon seminars in college. On the other days he stayed, helping to build up bikes and tinkering around at dinnertime with the guitars that Vince had scrounged from a bankrupt shop. Adam retrieved his old instrument from the top of the spare-room wardrobe. He was surprised that it was still there, but Marie had packed it in a suitcase full of blankets and stowed it away. There was a note of triumph in her voice when she told him. 'So I'm not such a useless mother after all!' she said.

Their lives together had been evolving since their big conversation. One day Adam came home from the workshop to find the picture of David, Jacinta and Felix on his bedside table, alongside a picture of the young Alon Piotr in his RAF flying suit. 'I found frames to fit them,' Marie said, leaning on her stick, watching him from the doorway.

As the days went by, their faces became as familiar as his own face in his shaving mirror. Of course he knew he would never see them in the flesh. He knew his father and grandfather were dead now, slain by pollution according to the strange Felix Wosniak. He examined the sweet face of Jacinta, who knew nothing about him, her husband's son. Jacinta, Marie had assured him, was still alive, as was Felix. 'He's quite a big businessman in the new Poland. He lives in Katowice now, the large city between Krakow and Chorzow, where David and I caught the train that day.'

He relished the easy way she said the words. He relished the new harmony between them. Their mutual wariness had entirely melted away. It was as though their skins had become permeable and he was at last becoming part of her, and she part of him. Sharina noticed it. 'Marie's really kind of different now with you here, Adam. Or maybe it was dicing with death there in the hospital. But I'm telling you, she's different than she was before, before you came here.'

One day he was finally able to say to his mother, 'Were you really in love with him? With David Zielinski?'

She hesitated. 'They were outside reality, those weeks in Poland. Surreal. I felt both very invisible and hyper-visible in my red jacket. But David made me feel so very real that day in Krakow – making me for the first time in my life a participant not a watcher. I am sure I loved him then, in those hours.' She paused. 'And then there was *you*. Eternal proof of that reality.'

'Didn't she realise? Jacinta? Really?'

She shook her head. 'No. Jacinta was my friend. His beloved wife. That wouldn't have been kind or right to hint at it or show it at all.' She paused. 'Sometimes I wondered, even wished it had been different. That I had met him when he had no ties. That was why I was crying the day I met Jack. He knew I was heartbroken but never knew why.'

That night in bed Adam got out the notebooks again. He found the 1939 edition of *Buildings of Krakow* and read, with new insight, the inscription. *To Marie Mathéve from David Adama Zielinski. With love*. He traced the words with his forefinger, imagining David's hand writing the words. His father's hand. Then he turned again to the pages that described in Marie's chaste fashion the memorable day that she'd spent with David in Krakow in 1981. Now, he thought, I've read my way at last into that capsule of time in Krakow that made me. And I know that my mother loves me in her own strange way. And that she loved my father in her own strange way. I've survived the guilt and pain of losing Sam. And Rachel is back in my life.

The boys in the workshop had loved the idea of the guitars, but the reality was a different thing. Stripped of the romantic notion, the actual practice of tuning the instruments and the challenge of proper fingering proved too much for most of the boys, who abandoned that corner of the workshop and, rain or shine, went out to kick a ball around the yard.

Some of them did stick with it and played along with Peter and Adam in the tea break, particularly Beejay, who wore frayed jeans, his greasy locks of dark hair poking through a hole in his baseball cap. ('Less than no money at home. His mam's got a habit and it's not called *mothering*,' Vince told Adam.) Beejay loved the guitar practice. He drank it all in, his sharp eyes glued to Peter's hands.

One day Peter – saying he was really not too good with the guitar – brought in his second-best mandolin, slung on his back in an elongated padded rucksack. That day he played properly for them at dinnertime; even the boys outside left their football to come and listen. It was a long and complicated piece and when he was finished they all whooped and hollered and begged for more, more!

Peter glanced at Vince.

'I heard sommat like that once on telly,' Vince said drily. '*Deliverance*. Cracking film. They had these duelling banjos.'

Adam grinned. 'One more? Let him play one more, Vince,' he said.

Vince nodded. 'One more. Don't bring that thing in again, though,' he said to Pete. 'Proper stop-work, that is.' But at the end of the encore he was clapping as much as the lads, even though, unlike them, he didn't shout and whistle.

At the end of his second week, Peter asked Adam if he fancied joining him on his regular long Saturday ride on the Honda. 'We will go right up coast to Northumberland and then cross the country and come back through the high land. I look at map,' he said. He slapped Adam on the shoulder. 'You will be my guide.'

'You'll need a bliddy interpreter up there,' growled Vince. 'They talk a different language up there, you know. All grunts and growls.'

'Not like us, like?' said Beejay.

Adam told Peter he had no helmet.

Peter shrugged. 'I have helmet and old leathers in my trunk. You borrow them. No problem.'

'What about us, then?' said Beejay. 'Why cannot us go? Teacher's pet, you, Blondie.' (Adam, like the others, now had a nick name. Vince had laughed when he first heard it. 'Blondie, eh? Can you sing too?')

'I give you a ride home tonight, Beejay, if you want,' said Peter calmly.

Beejay's eyes gleamed. 'An' yeh'll give us a ride round the block as well?'

Peter nodded. 'Two times round the block.'

'You're on!'

Adam's hidden excitement more than matched Beejay's glee at getting a ride twice round the block. In the weeks they'd worked together he'd got on well with Peter. But the getting on well had been to do with the mechanics of the bikes and the guitars, with Vince's unique magic with the boys. They had rarely spoken about themselves. Of course this was nothing new to Adam. He'd spent two years in jail with men who spoke about anything but their real selves, and that had suited him very well.

Adam felt as though he were flying. His borrowed leathers sat snugly against his skin and he had a peepshow view of the world streaming by his visor. It had been quite a performance pulling on the leathers at the bus station where he'd met Peter. He'd had to hang on to the rail to keep his balance while he changed. The leathers were old but very serviceable. They were a bit loose on the thighs, but apart from that they were a great fit.

Once they were north of the Tyne and into the wild country, Peter opened the throttle and let the red monster have its head. They rode on and on, through villages, sometimes following the sea, sometimes powering down empty lanes, sometimes slowing down to make their way through villages and hamlets built of grey stone.

Peter finally pulled the bike to a stop in a village on a promontory with the brewing turmoil of the North Sea surging all around them, lapping steel-grey rocks and smashing into the redundant staithes just along from a low pub: a building barely distinguishable from the squat stone houses. The air was full of rain that was not quite falling and they were both chilled, so it was a relief to get into the warm pub with its roaring fire and smell of last night's beer. Apart from a man sitting right up to the bar, and the young landlady, the place was empty.

They ordered cheese toasties and took two bottles of beer and packets of crisps to sit on the settle by the fire. Adam's creaking leathers, comforting and secure on the bike, now felt bulky and choking. He unzipped the jacket and eased his shoulders.

'So,' said Peter, slipping his jacket off altogether, 'not on a bike before?'

Adam shook his head.

'So,' repeated Peter, 'what do you think?'

'Amazing.' Adam searched his mind. 'Like flying.'

Pete laughed. 'I met this bike guy in London, he tell me it's *eating the breeze*. I like that.'

The landlady brought the toasties and smiled at them, one to the other. 'Off the beaten track, then?'

'Just riding around,' Adam said.

'Good day for it.' The landlady nodded at the window, where the rain was lashing down and the line between the sky and the sea had been obliterated.

Adam laughed. 'A bit mad, maybe.'

'Always good to be a bit mad,' said Peter.

She laughed with them. 'Well, enjoy the fire and your toasties. Look, don't worry, lads. It'll be better inland. Always bad out here. Good for business, like.' She had a very nice smile. 'People need to get warm and dry.'

Peter turned back to Adam. 'Would you like a try? On the bike?'

Adam spoke with his mouth full of toastie. 'Can't. Banned from driving anything. Didn't Vince tell you?'

'No. Vince said nothing about you.'

Adam reflected on Vince's discretion, then launched into the truth. 'Like I say, I'm banned. I had this crash three years ago. My friend was killed and I got sent to jail. I'm banned for six years.'

'Is hard,' said Peter.

'Hard on who?'

'Is hard on you. And on the other person.'

'The other person was my best friend.'

'So! Is extra hard on you.'

They finished their toasties and beer in silence, watching as the rain softened and the horizon re-emerged.

Peter stood up. 'So we are here by the sea. So we walk by the sea!'

They passed a woman perched on a bit of the sea wall in a big Barbour coat and woolly hat. She was watching a bundled-up toddler dig in the wet sand.

By some miracle the rain stopped and they made their way to the edge of the water, where the sand was hard and their big boots didn't dig in too far. They followed the tide's edge until the reach of the waves barred their way. Then they stood still and looked across the surging grey expanse of the North Sea.

Peter said, 'North Sea is very big. Right from here to the Netherlands then on to Germany. And beyond that to my country.'

'Hungary?'

Peter laughed. 'Who tell you this? Hungary?'

'Beejay told me. He said you came from Hungary.'

Peter shook his head. 'No. No. Is Poland! My country is Poland.'

Adam's heart leapt. 'Poland?'

'I come from a city called Katowice. You would not know it. Not so far from Krakow, which all Englishmen know for their stag nights. Cheap flights, cheap beer.' There was sorrow in his voice. 'Good business but like the plague. You know?'

'Krakow?' Adam's head whirled with images from the notebooks, the delicate tracery of buildings in the book that David Zielinski had given to Marie. 'Well,' he said carefully, 'Krakow is full of Englishmen getting drunk and England is full of Poles getting rich before everything falls apart. Kind of parable of the times, that.'

'Parable?'

'A story that has more meaning than the words that tell it. Like in the Bible.'

'I see that. Is good.' Peter paused. 'Now! We go up into the hills and make very fast speed home. We will eat the breeze. I will take you home. Not bus station like before. You show the way and I take you home. To your house.'

Adam decided this would be a good idea to take Peter home. There would be things to talk about, after all. They had something in common.

At Merrick Court they parked in the courtyard, and when Adam opened the door to the flat and heard the familiar laughter and chatter, he knew Sharina was visiting. She brightened when she caught sight of Peter. 'You're the one with the bike!' she said. 'I heard of you.'

He clicked his heels and bowed. 'I must be that man,' he said.

She eyed him closely. 'I've done a lot of things but I've never been on a bike.'

'It will be my pleasure to give you a ride.' He grinned back at her.

'This is Sharina, a good friend of mine,' said Adam, zipping off his leather jacket. 'Sharina, this is Peter.'

'Hello, Sharina.' Peter took Sharina's hand lightly in his.

'And that young man, looking at you from behind the sofa, is Arian, my little boy.' Sharina watched Peter's gaze flicker behind her.

'And this is my mother,' said Adam. 'Marie Mathéve. Marie, this is my friend Peter.'

Peter looked at Marie, then glanced around the room, taking in the big paintings of hospital scenes, mixed up with rangy paintings of buildings, some of which he knew well. His eye settled on a surreal depiction of Sukiennice, the Drapers' Hall in Krakow.

Marie glanced up, looked him full in the face and held out her hand. 'I'm Marie,' she said, frowning slightly.

'Your paintings are wonderful, Madame Mathéve.' He bent over her hand and kissed it and looked back up into her face.

She turned to Adam. 'Sit down, both of you, and tell us about your journey. Weren't you freezing on that bike?'

They both laughed at that, and talked about their trip. Adam told them about eating the breeze, which made Sharina laugh. Peter told them about the pub and the sky vanishing beneath the rain. Sharina looked at him with close interest. Arian clambered along the edge of the couch and leaned against Peter's leather-clad legs.

Peter surveyed Marie's pictures again. 'I see you know Krakow, Marie. Is a city I know well.'

She eyed him carefully. 'I only knew it for a very short while, a long time ago.'

'But it stays in your memory?' He flourished his hand to

take in all the paintings. 'Krakow is a beautiful city but a sad city. Is glorious heritage but has weeping at its heart. Me, I like Warsaw. Very modern. Like New York. About the future, not the past.'

At that point Arian climbed right on to his knee and started gently poking his fingers into Peter's mouth and eyes. Sharina said crossly, 'Arian! Stop that!'

Peter shrugged. 'Don't stop him!' He winked at Arian. 'Hey, Arian, we play a game, no?' He crossed his legs and lifted Arian down on to his ankle, and began to move it up and down. Then his sweet baritone voice filled the room.

> *Horsey horsey don't you stop*
> *Just let your heels go clippety clop*
> *Tail go swish and wheels go round*
> *Giddyap we're homeward bound.*

Arian laughed and giggled and clapped his hands. Sharina clapped too.

Adam felt the hair on the back of his neck prickle.

Marie sat up abruptly, then stood up – very straight, without even reaching for her stick. 'How did you know that? Where did you learn it?' Her tone was sharp. 'Where did you learn that song?'

'The song? Is English nursery rhyme. I learn it at my grandfather's knee. And the knee of my father also.' He laughed. 'We only played it when my nurse not there. She did not like the English game.'

Marie took a breath. 'Just what did you say your name was?'

'My name Peter. Well, Piotr, in my country. Piotr Zielinski.'

Adam blinked. 'Peter Zed. They call him Peter Zed at the Briar Rose,' he said desperately.

'*Piotr!*' Marie frowned and looked closely at him. 'I think I know you, Piotr. I think I know you very well,' she said slowly. 'I knew your father and your mother and the old nurse who did not like the English song.'

They stared at each other. Sharina took Arian on to her knee and shushed his chatter.

'So this is Piotr, Marie?' said Adam. 'Piotr Zielinski?'

The three of them stared at each other for a very long time. Sharina muttered something about Arian's tea and slipped away.

'It can't be a coincidence, you being here,' said Marie eventually, standing straight as an arrow, staring down at him.

Piotr shook his head. 'I could choose many cathedrals, many universities, but this one I choose because I know *you* live here. I know from the old letters of my mother. And I know from my godfather Felix where you live. He tell me about you and about Adam just after my father died.'

'But the Briar Rose!' burst in Adam. 'We met at the Briar Rose. You couldn't have known that I would be there!'

Marie nodded. 'You couldn't have known that.'

'Ah. *That* is the coincidence. That was joy getting to know Adam without . . . Still, I would always have come here to find you. And I knew you as my . . . brother. Adam, when I see you coming through the door at the Briar Rose . . .' He paused. 'It was like looking at my father.' He glanced up at Marie. 'I would have come here to see you anyway. I was building up the courage. So Adam and I go for long ride and end up here.'

Marie sat down, closed her eyes, then opened them again, looking stricken, lost.

Adam leapt to her rescue. 'We've been looking at some drawings my mother did in Chorzow, Peter. You're in them. Well, little Piotr's in them. Would you like to see them?' He picked up the sketchbook from the side table.

Piotr looked across at Marie. 'Would you sit here beside me, Marie, and show me your drawings?'

Then Adam put his arm round her and kept it round her as she sat on the couch beside Piotr. Side by side the three of them went through the notebooks. As they turned the pages Piotr started to exclaim out loud as he recognised places and people. 'That's my Auntie Theresa! You have her exact face, her exact figure.'

'Is she still complaining about the bloody Russians?'

He shook his head. 'These days it is the bloody Americans.' He laughed. 'But it is the same Theresa!'

He closed the book on the figure of David before the house in Krakow and said quietly, 'Now I have it, the whole story.'

'What will you do now?' said Marie anxiously. 'Will you tell Jacinta?'

'No. I will not tell her.' Piotr shook his head slowly. 'It was always clear to me that they loved each other very much, my mother and father. And now it is clear to me that he loved you, for those days. And you loved him.' He shrugged. 'It is a private thing.'

'So . . .' said Adam.

'So, now I understand my father better. And now I have friends here in this city. Perhaps I have a friend who is a brother. It cannot be a bad thing. Is a very good thing.'

Marie sniffed and blinked. 'Adam,' she said, 'I think I have some very good rosé in the fridge. Perhaps we should drink to Piotr's wise thought. And to David and Jacinta and Alon Piotr. Even to old Casia. And to ourselves, to all three of us.'

In Concert

The battered white van looked out of place beside the neat Rovers and Fords parked outside the music school. On the side of the van, scrawled in thick motor paint, was the legend *Briar Rose Project*. Beside it, heavily padlocked, was Peter's red motorbike. Adam slid his own bicycle underneath the van and sat on the low cathedral wall to wait for Marie and Sharina to arrive in their taxi. Sharina was frustrated that they could not come in the Mitsubishi. She was having her driving lessons but she wasn't good enough yet to drive on the road.

Now Adam surveyed the magnificent cathedral square with its early-afternoon trickle of tourists. There were no signs of Vince or any of the Briar Rose crew. They must be on the wander. Adam wondered if Vince was as surprised as he was that all nine of the lads had opted to come to Peter's concert in the cathedral. But as Beejay had said, 'Anything beats a day in this bloody sweatshop.' He had asked in a worried tone if you had to wear anything special.

'Well, Adam!' Piotr's voice came from behind him. 'You came.'

Adam leapt to his feet.

Piotr's toe touched the bicycle handles where they jutted out from under Vince's van. He looked around. 'They are here somewhere, the boys?'

'Casing the joint, I think!' said Adam.

'And the others?'

'Sharina is still learning to drive and is mad that she and Marie'll have to come in a taxi. And Arian, of course.'

Peter nodded. 'Is good. I like your Sharina and Arian. Now I must go. I have reserved seats on the third and fourth rows left-hand side for all of you. They are marked by the papers with *Zielinski* on them. You are my honoured guests.' He reached out, put his hands on Adam's shoulders and hugged him. 'I am pleased that you come, brother.' He winked, then swung his way down the broad path to the great cathedral door.

Adam sat down again and breathed in deeply. He thought of Tom, the chiropractor who had helped him in the early days in prison. And old Henry Masterson, a bad person who had been his sanctuary in a bad place. Then he saw Rachel's blue Jeep turning the corner and his heart leapt. She drove past him once, Sharina and Arian waving madly out of the back window. She came round again and parked the Jeep in front of Vince's van, deposited her passengers, and hauled Marie's wheelchair from the back. Marie climbed out of the car and looked around the square. She smiled faintly at Adam. 'Your Rachel came with her Jeep so we sent the taxi away.' She looked up at the building. 'Last time I was here was nearly three years ago. I lit candles for you and Sam, and for David and Alon Piotr, and for Casia. It seems a long time ago now.'

'You lit candles?' Adam was surprised.

'Yes. Strange, that, isn't it?'

Rachael hauled the wheelchair upright and Marie sat down in it with a fragile grace. 'I told Sharina I didn't need this thing, but . . .' She looked at the long pathway to the cathedral. 'Perhaps she's right.'

Arian toddled across to Adam and held up his hands to be lifted. Sharina looked around. 'Peter here yet?'

'Been and gone,' Adam said. 'He's in there setting up.'

She nodded. 'Right!'

'Look,' Rachel said, 'I'll go off and try and park this thing. You'll wait here for me?'

'Oh yes,' he said. 'We'll wait.'

She looked up at him. 'Sam's mother's coming, you know.'

He knew she'd been to see Mrs Rogers several times since that time they'd gone together.

'What? Why?' he said.

'I told her about the concert, and Peter, and your funny tale about just who Peter is, being a kind of brother. She said Sam would have liked to have come, to be here with you and to meet your brother. And she says she's always liked the cathedral, although it shouldn't be her kind of place. The overdecorated Jesus and all that. She's coming with her minister friend. I got her two tickets.'

After Rachel sped off, the pavement suddenly filled with boys in trainers and fatigues, number-one haircuts and glittering earrings – all except for Beejay, who had washed his hair so it streamed down his shoulders like black satin, and was wearing new combats, bought for him by the lads, who had all pitched in.

Vince emerged from the crowd. 'Now, Adam,' he said, his head twitching to one side in greeting. The lads shouted and said hello, and Jonno sidled up to Sharina and asked her name.

Adam grinned. 'Now, Vince!'

'I've had these lads walking round the river bank to blow off steam before they have to sit down for a whole hour.' Vince surveyed his boys. 'Full house here. Not one cried off. Now there's a surprise!' He raised his eye to the long windows of the cathedral. 'This place'll not know what's hit it.'

Then Rachel rushed up, breathless, and Jonno asked her what her name was. Then Tikka joined in and asked Marie what *her* name was. After that the boys all made their way in a cluster down the long path towards the door of the cathedral. Their energy went before them and the trickle of concert types stood back to let them pass.

Inside the cathedral Adam had to suppress a grin as he

led his party down to the front. Wheelchair! Baby! Beautiful girls! Shaven-headed youths. Long-haired types! Beejay looked around and upwards at the great columns and whistled. Vince thumped him on the arm and said, 'Shh!'

In the crosspiece of the nave, Peter was setting up and tuning his instruments with the help of a girl and a boy from the music school. The centrepiece of the concert was a harpsichord with its lid up, displaying a painted pastoral scene with a man on horseback at the centre. Beside that was a harp. Against a chair was a lute. Across a bench was the theorbo they all knew from the workshop.

Beejay called, 'Hey, Pete! Nice gear!'

Vince said, 'Shh!' again but Peter looked up, winked and went on with his tinkering.

Marie, at the end of the row in her wheelchair, picked up her programme. *Born in Chorzow in Poland, Piotr Adama Zielinski trained at leading European conservatories and has performed with prestigious baroque musical ensembles all over Europe. His virtuoso performances in the field of baroque music accompanying his own singing has made a unique contribution to the interpretation of baroque music in the present era. Zielinski has been musician in residence in our music school for six months, supporting students and staff working here in this field.*

Marie closed her eyes, sad that David and Jacinta weren't here to take pride in all this. Of course Piotr was not her son, but he was the son of the father of her son, and today she found herself tearful, sitting here full of pride on his behalf and on behalf of his mother. She thought again of the leather monkey, which Casia had hated and which the young Piotr had loved so. Feelings and memories washed through her, leaving her trembling. It was a relief when Arian put out his arms so she could pull him on to her knee and put her face close to his. Sharina let her son go, not wanting to take her eyes off Peter as he tuned his instruments.

Vince, sitting beside Adam, stood up and with a flourish took off his big coat, folded it and put it under his seat. This flamboyant gesture and the sheer bulk of the man brought Sam back into Adam's mind, now without pain and with less guilt.

Rachel, on Adam's left, took his hand and held it in both of hers. Often, it seemed to him now, she read his thoughts. 'Sam's mum's here!' she whispered. He turned round to see, four rows behind them, Mrs Rogers sitting beside a small plump woman in a pink clerical shirt. She smiled and nodded, and he returned her smile.

Vince's lads, in the row in front of him, were sitting in silence, finally subdued by the grandeur of the building and the magic of the occasion. All around them the prickle of talk had died down. The lights in the side chapel faded and Peter and his musicians were bathed in soft medieval light.

Then the performance began. Peter explained the songs and the composers briefly, but allowed the music and singing to do the real work. Adam let the warm voice and the plangent sounds of the instruments filter through him.

Times past. Times present. All time in one. All meaning through time. Sam's voice in his ear. *That's right, mate. You've got it.*

Rachel's hand gripped his even tighter. He wondered if she'd heard Sam's voice as well, but in truth he knew that it was the sweet music that had moved her.

'And now,' Peter took his theorbo and made a fractional adjustment to the strings. 'Now, ladies and gentlemen, we have the legend of Eurydice, whose lover Orpheus lost her and took his music into Hades to rescue her from the darkness of her life. Then he lost her once more. This song holds the tragedy of true love, found very briefly and then lost again.' He looked across at Marie and, very slightly, bowed his head. Then he sang the song, it seemed, just to her.

When the undulating notes of the song and the last resonant bass notes of the theorbo faded upwards into the high void of the church, there was a silence. Then wild applause broke out, echoing through the chancel and into the side chapel. Even Beejay's whoops were drowned in the applause of the true aficionados. Tourists wandering into the back of the nave strained their necks to see what all the fuss was about.

Arian, his ears bursting now, started to whimper. Marie stroked his face and, securing him on her knee, manoeuvred her wheelchair to the back, where one of the stewards helped her up the ramp, through the great door and down the long pathway.

The cathedral square was deserted and the edges of the buildings looked crisp and sharp in the white light of the winter afternoon. Marie's fingers were itching now for the blank notebook that she always carried in her bag. Arian was still squirming on her knee. She hummed to him to calm him, thinking of Casia, who could poleaxe little Piotr with a wordless song. Suddenly her evocation of the spirit of Casia seemed to work, and Arian fell fast asleep.

That was when Marie manoeuvred the chair so she could just catch the edge of the music school and the reducing perspective of the medieval buildings as they dropped down towards the river. Then she got out her book and began to draw.

Epilogue

From the *Northern Echo:*

Visionary Painting Exhibition for Woman Coma Survivor

Our Arts Correspondent

Marie Mathéve, in the news last year for surviving weeks in a coma and emerging unscathed, has carved a new career for herself in painting. Her work is thought to reflect some startling insights from her near-death experience during the coma. The artist refuses to comment on the inspiration for these pieces, but it is impossible not to speculate that her experience of coma has inspired this new work.

Already eminent in the field of building conservation, where her books are illustrated by her own fine architectural drawings, Mrs Mathéve has turned to a much more expressive style in this collection. Here we see exaggerated images of hospital life, surreal figures bathed in light, strange sunrises and ethereal faces layered on top of each other.

Mrs Mathéve (pictured below with her family) would only say that her recovery has been entirely due to the support and inspiration of her family. 'They are the reason I am here now,' she says. 'They brought me back to life.'

The proceeds from this exhibition will go to the ground-breaking Briar Rose Motorbike Project, of which her son Adam is co-director.

In photograph (left to right): Marie Mathéve's son Adam Mathéve; his wife, the archaeologist Rachel Miriam; Marie Mathéve; her nephew, musician Peter Zielinski; her adopted daughter Sharina Osgood, and her grandson Arian.

International news:

Pensioner Arrested

An 88-year-old pensioner has been arrested in Katowice, Poland, for alleged crimes during the Russian occupation. Felix Wosniak had a distinguished career in the wartime Polish air force in Britain and more recently as a business-man and an advocate for Poland's emerging role in Europe.

It is alleged that in 1947 Wosniak gave information to the occupying Soviet authorities that led to the arrest, imprisonment and deportation of several members of AK, the underground army that had fought to free Poland during the years of German occupation. The Russians slaughtered many of these partisans as they saw them as a source of unrest and opposition to their regime. It is alleged that one of those betrayed by Felix Wosniak had been a close schoolfriend.

A spokesman said that this arrest, among others, reflects the determination of the country to go forward into their new European future with a clear conscience.

Now you can buy any of these other bestselling books by **Wendy Robertson** from your bookshop or *direct from her publisher*.

FREE P&P AND UK DELIVERY
(Overseas and Ireland £3.50 per book)

Riches of the Earth	£6.99
Under a Brighter Sky	£6.99
Land of Your Possession	£6.99
A Dark Light Shining	£6.99
Kitty Rainbow	£5.99
Children of the Storm	£5.99
A Thirsting Land	£5.99
The Jagged Window	£5.99
My Dark-Eyed Girl	£5.99
Where Hope Lives	£5.99
The Long Journey Home	£6.99
Honesty's Daughter	£6.99
A Woman Scorned	£5.99
No Rest for the Wicked	£5.99
Family Ties	£6.99
The Lavender House	£6.99
Sandie Shaw and the Millionth Marvell Cooker	£6.99

TO ORDER SIMPLY CALL THIS NUMBER

01235 400 414

or visit our website: www.headline.co.uk

Prices and availability subject to change without notice.